PRIM & PROPER

BARBARA CUTRERA

Published by On My Way Up, LLC
P.O Box 1962
Bradenton, FL 34206

ISBN: 978-0-9913642-2-0
Second Edition

My readers' enthusiasm warms my heart. It consistently reminds me of the profound effect the written word has on the lives of others. This book is dedicated to you!

Chapter One

Sean Proper wondered how many other thirty-year-old men were stuck late at work that Friday night with stiff necks, sore backs, and no one waiting for them at home. He ran his fingers through his brown hair and then massaged his neck with one hand in order to ease a crick that he'd developed during days spent reviewing mounds of paperwork. He'd had too much coffee, too little food, and not enough sleep.

The principal who'd been his predecessor had left in a hurry with an eighteen-year-old graduate and a million dollars from the school's funds. The Kensington Board of Directors had hired Sean to collect the debris, provide damage control, and move forward as quickly as possible. The fate of the school, its employees, and the students rested in his capable hands.

As much as he'd prefer to work all day Saturday and Sunday in order to get more accomplished, Sean was well-aware that appearances were everything on the first day of school. He had to make the right impression with the staff and students if he was going to be an effective leader. Looking tired would not bode well for him, especially not during his first address on campus. He would have to take the weekend off and relax.

Sean left his office and went to his car. Before leaving Kensington for the night in order to head for his rented home in the nearby picturesque town of Aurora, he cruised around the expansive grounds of the school. The northern Georgia hills provided the perfect backdrop for the one-hundred-year-old residential campus. Sean loved the atmosphere and academic reputation of Kensington. As an eighth-grader, he'd applied to the high school and had been accepted. The problem had been that his parents' combined annual income didn't come close to the amount of a year's tuition. He'd known that when he'd submitted his application packet but had wanted to do it anyway. Simply being accepted was an honor, and he'd been proud of his accomplishment.

The following morning, Sean rose and then dressed in shorts, a Polo shirt, and tennis shoes. He soon set out on foot to the Town Square. By 8:45, he was sitting at the counter at LouAnn's Café. After ordering coffee and breakfast, he picked up what appeared to be some sort of bulletin from the end of the counter. It was labeled *The Aurora Town Talk*. Sean began to read and quickly realized that this was the local version of a newspaper. Sean had never seen anything quite like it in his life and considered it amusing but charming. He finished reading the few articles and advertisements before his food arrived.

"You're the new principal, aren't you?" asked the pudgy, middle-aged blonde woman in the flowery top and lavender knit pants behind the counter. "I'm LouAnn, and this is my place. You moved here last week."

Sean confirmed this and introduced himself. Glancing around the packed restaurant, he remarked, "This seems to be the hot spot for food in Aurora."

"Great food served with great smiles," LouAnn offered. "We don't get too many new people moving into town. What made you pick Aurora?"

"I've lived in big cities all my life and wanted to try small town living. When I was offered the job at Kensington, I happened to take a drive around the area and passed through Aurora. I liked it and decided it would be a nice place to live. I work long hours and don't want to waste time fighting traffic to and from Atlanta each day."

"We locals sure love it," LouAnn said enthusiastically. "Aurora's a little different from some other small towns. We're all friendly no matter what color or religion you happen to be, and we don't have anything against dancing or drinking in moderation. I wish every town could be like ours. We're old-fashioned but progressive, if that makes any sense. Plus, we can enjoy a slower pace here, but it's easy to drive to Atlanta if we want to spice things up a bit. I'm glad you decided to settle here for now. You'll love it as much as we do."

"If everyone is as nice as you, then I'm sure I will."

"Oh, you are such a flirt!" she said with a laugh, but it was obvious how flattered she was. "You're welcome here anytime, Honey!"

Once he'd finished his breakfast, Sean paid his bill at the old-fashioned cash register near the door and set out to explore his new hometown. LouAnn's sat on one corner of the Square. Sean skipped the dress shop next door, entered a store called The Book Nook, and was instantly in love. The shop was crammed with books of surprising variety. There was a reading area that included a fireplace for colder months. The store's owner, Remy Artigue, was a black-haired man who appeared slightly older, taller, and thinner than Sean, which meant he was too thin. He had wire-rimmed glasses and wore khaki pants and a white button-down shirt with the sleeves rolled up. The two men chatted for a half hour then Sean spent another hour perusing the shelves before purchasing several books and heading out to do more exploring.

He bypassed a men's clothing store and a pet shop and then entered Aurora Hardware. There were bins of screws and nails, tools of all kinds, mailboxes, plumbing supplies, squirrel feeders, bird baths, and much more. Sean, who had never lived in a house before, was intrigued. Even though he didn't need anything, he felt compelled to buy something. After wandering for forty minutes, Sean decided to purchase a set of chimes for the porch of his rented home. He paid the store manager, an older man named Buddy Brown, made conversation with some local men who happened to be standing near the register, and left the hardware store.

The final shop on that side of the street was named Prim's Corner. Looking at the displays in the windows, Sean couldn't quite discern what kind of store it was. There appeared to be furniture, framed photographs, art pieces, greeting cards, jewelry, blankets, and bric-a-brac. With a mental shrug, he decided he'd take a chance and go in. If it was a "girly" store, then he'd make a hasty exit.

The place was humming with activity. Sean reflected that all of the stores along the Square appeared to be busy and wondered if they always did that much business or if this was an unusually active Saturday. He scanned the shop and decided to brave the unknown. As he slowly made his way around the corner store, he observed that it held an interesting mixture of the types of articles he'd glimpsed in the window plus some vintage-looking toys, candles, and quirky knickknacks.

"May I help you?"

The woman was young and had pale blue eyes and strawberry blonde hair that fell past her shoulders but was pulled away from her face. About five foot seven, she wore a long dress that had a muted pink-and-white print. Little white sandals were on her feet. The bones in her face were delicate as was her frame. Sean couldn't tell if she was wearing make-up but quickly decided she didn't need any. She had that all-natural beauty he found most women lacked.

She asked again in her soft, melodic voice if he needed help.

"I'm not quite sure. I'm new in town and am exploring the Square. I came in not knowing what to expect."

"And that's how I hope all my customers feel when they come and go," the woman told him. "I like to change up my inventory as often as possible, although there are some standard favorites. I have quite the following in this region, which is great for me and my shop. I'm Prim, and this is my corner."

"Prim?"

Rolling her eyes, she said dramatically, "Primrose Anastasia Cassandra Aurora, but everyone's called me Prim for as long as I can remember."

"Nice to meet you, Primrose Anastasia Cassandra Aurora. I'm Sean Proper. Are you a descendant of the founder of this town?"

"Yes. There used to be a bunch of us here. Now, there's only me. Well, me and Uncle Buddy, although he married into the family and is a member of the Aurora clan by default."

"Buddy at the hardware store is your uncle?"

She grinned, and Sean thought he might stop breathing. He had never, ever reacted this way to any woman, and he wasn't sure if he liked it or not. He was used to being in charge and wasn't certain what to do with this unexpected response to Prim Aurora.

"The hardware store's been in my family for a century. It was passed down to my Aunt Myrtle. She died last year. That's when I moved back here from Atlanta. I missed my hometown, and I couldn't leave Uncle Buddy all alone."

"Your parents didn't want to stay in Aurora?"

Prim gave him a sad little smile that made his heart hurt and said, "My mama was eighteen when she got pregnant with me. She never would tell anyone who my daddy was. They found out she had leukemia when she was pregnant and wanted to treat her for it, but they told her that the treatment would probably kill me. She refused to have an abortion and wouldn't take any cancer-fighting drugs, radiation or chemo. She died when I was three months old. Uncle Buddy and Aunt Myrtle raised me." Smiling, she said, "Forgive me. You're my customer, and I'm talking your ears off. Is there something in particular you're looking for?"

"My sister's birthday is in two weeks, and I have no idea what to get her. Maybe you could give me some suggestions."

"What does she like?"

Emotionally abusive alcoholic men, Sean thought grimly.

"I don't even know anymore," he admitted. "She's a paralegal in Nashville. We've kind of grown apart."

She looked sympathetic and suggested, "Tell me about her, and maybe we can find something you think will be fitting. How old is she?"

"Twenty-four."

"I'm twenty-four, too. Being the same age as your sister might help me to help you find a present she'll like. Do you know if she likes fanciful or functional? Was there something in particular she was really into when you were close?"

"She liked Sock Monkeys and stories of magical creatures when she was small."

Prim smiled broadly and suggested Sean accompany her to the back of the store where there was an area devoted to Sock Monkeys.

"They've become very popular again over the last few years. I carry the actual toy and all sorts of things that display the traditional Sock Monkey image on them. Why don't you look around here while I help the elderly woman who just came in?"

Sean stared at the Sock Monkeys for a few minutes. They made him think of his little sister as she'd been as a young child and preteen – a cute kid with a happy-go-lucky attitude and lots of charisma. What had happened to that girl? Would buying her a Sock Monkey remind her of what she used to be and help her break away from the behavioral patterns she'd developed as an adult? If he knew it would work, Sean would gladly have bought every Sock Monkey article in the shop.

Deciding on a robe, slippers, and stuffed toy, Sean went to the register in the center of the store and placed the items on the counter. Prim was helping a man who was interested in buying what looked to be a refurbished medicine cabinet, but she nodded to Sean who nodded back that he understood she'd be there to help him when she could. He was in no hurry.

While he waited, he looked down at the display case in front of him and saw several figurines of realistic-looking people and animals. One of the statues caught his eye. The figures all had brown hair and brown eyes and were seated at a square table. There was a mother, a father, an adolescent boy, and a young girl. A nondescript board game rested on the table, and the family members were obviously enjoying playing the game and interacting.

Sean thought of the many times his family had played games like that, put puzzles together, or engaged in card games like Go Fish. When he visited his parents, he still had fun doing those things with them, and he knew his parents played with friends or by themselves when there was no one else around.

"Mr. Proper?"

Blinking rapidly to clear his vision, he looked up at Prim Aurora and said, "Call me Sean, please."

"Are you ready to check out, Sean?"

He nodded but pointed to the statue and said, "I'd like to buy that as well."

"Is that for your sister, too?"

"No. Why?"

"Because I gift wrap if you buy something as a present and was going to wrap your sister's gifts in birthday paper."

"Oh. That would be helpful. I'm not the best at wrapping things."

"Is the statue a gift? I could wrap it, too."

"It's a Christmas present for my parents."

"Christmas paper it is."

After he'd paid for the presents, Prim showed him different kinds of paper. For his sister's gifts, he asked her to pick whichever one she thought would be best. She wrapped the robe, slippers, and toy separately and put a different type of bow on each. He complimented her on her wrapping skills, and she thanked him as she withdrew the Christmas paper and showed him the selections available. He chose one that had cartoon-like reindeer, snowmen, Santa Clauses, and stars on it. Once the box had been wrapped, Prim asked if this gift was also going to be shipped.

"I'm hoping to have them come here from Tallahassee for Christmas. Why?"

"Because I have a special topper for it that would get squished if you mailed it."

Turning away from him, she attached whatever the topper was. He watched her from behind as she bent over the package and studied the rounding of her shoulders as she secured the topper. Turning back towards him, Prim announced, "Ta-da!"

Sean laughed. The topper she'd selected looked like a Christmas tree that was curved in the center and seemed as if it would topple over at any moment. His parents would be fascinated by the thing, and that warmed his heart. However, he was worried about getting it home without knocking the topper off, despite the fact that he knew it was surely well-fastened. He voiced his concerns to Prim, who suggested he leave all of his purchases in her back room and then return to her store on his way home to pick them up.

"All the shops on the Square close at 5:00," she told him. "LouAnn's stays open until 9:00."

"Are you sure it's okay with you to leave my stuff here?"

She assured him it would be fine and said she'd see him later that afternoon. He thanked her and left the shop, returning to LouAnn's for lunch.

"Fancy meeting you here!" LouAnn greeted him, as he took a seat at the counter. "I guess your breakfast wasn't too bad, considering you're back for a late lunch."

"Late?"

"It's 2:00 p.m. That's late for most folks. Any time's fine with us."

Sean ate meatloaf and mashed potatoes with green beans and loved every bite. He had a piece of chocolate pie with whipped topping for dessert and told LouAnn before he paid his bill that he was going to be gaining a lot of weight eating at her café.

"You could stand to put on a few pounds," she said seriously. "You're not as thin as Remy, thank goodness. That boy always looks undernourished. Maybe you could get him to come in here once in a while so I can fatten him up a bit!"

Sean promised her that he would try to talk the man into sharing a meal with him sometime, paid for his food, and left. He wandered along the side of the Square that housed City Hall and the United States Post Office. Sean crossed the street and walked past a lawyer's office, a doctor's office, a veterinary clinic, a pharmacy, and the local bank. Crossing to the last block that edged the Square, Sean read the sign in front of the large church with its high steeple and was surprised.

Aurora Community Church
Services: Sunday 10 a.m. and Noon.
Everyone is welcome here.

Curious, Sean climbed the steps and went up to the front doors, which he expected to be locked. They weren't, and he stepped inside and looked around. He calculated there were enough pews to seat three hundred people. There were stained glass windows but no depictions of saints, only beautiful glass in interesting patterns.

Sean went up to the front pew and took a seat. He enjoyed the silence and tried to simply relax, but his thoughts kept returning to his little sister. He felt as if he'd failed her somehow, that her current predicament was his fault. He closed his eyes and said a prayer for her.

"Hello there, Friend."

Sean opened his eyes and twisted around in the pew. A very muscular, fit man who was perhaps fifty-five sat smiling at him. He was of average height, blonde, green-eyed, and evidently extremely strong. Something about the man instantly made Sean feel at ease, and he reached out a hand and introduced himself.

"Nice to meet you. I'm Caleb Geller. I'm the pastor here."

"What kind of church is this?"

"This is a non-denominational church. It's the only church in Aurora. We decided we should focus on bringing all those who believe in God together. So, we have people of all religious backgrounds here. It's actually worked out really well for our town. If you have a particular denomination in mind, you'll have to travel to another place."

"I'm Episcopalian but don't think I can only find God in an Episcopal church."

"Happy to hear it. We'd love to see you at one of our services tomorrow. We usually have a full house for both. The first service is kind of traditional, but the second one is more contemporary. Perhaps you could try the earlier one this week and the later one next week. See if our place of worship fulfills your spiritual needs."

"I'm really liking Aurora, so far. Have you lived here all your life?"

"Over twenty-three years. I love the place. I hope it retains its charm as times continue to change."

"I think I'm going to be really happy here once I adjust. This is certainly a different kind of lifestyle from the one I'm used to."

"Aurora's different in a good way," Caleb told him. Reaching into his pocket, he withdrew a business card and passed it to Sean with the words, "In case you have a spiritual emergency or just want some information on Aurora. If you can't reach me for some reason, then just drop by the feed store. I work there during the week."

"Thanks. I wish I had a card with me, but I'm taking the day off for once." Glancing at his watch, he said, "I'd better get moving if I want to get back to Prim's Corner before it closes."

"Prim Aurora is a lovely girl and a great businesswoman for someone so young. I'm glad she moved back after her aunt died. Her uncle's a wonderful salesman and a nice man, but he's not really good with the books. I think the family hardware store would have folded if his niece hadn't returned and taken over his accounts. Her aunt used to handle all that as well as the rest of the business affairs."

"Rest of what business affairs?"

"The Auroras own that whole block and the main structure that rests on it. They've sold the free-standing places that don't face the Square, but the one long building that's two-stories high and runs along the Square is still theirs. They collect rent from everyone who has a business there as well as from the tenants who live in the apartments above some of the businesses."

"And Prim handles all of that business and runs her own store?"

"She does. She's a very intelligent, determined young woman."

"Does she attend church here?"

"She alternates services each week. She'll be at the early service tomorrow. I'll see you then."

Sean returned to Prim's Corner at ten minutes to 5:00. She welcomed him, asking if he minded waiting while she shut down her computerized register, counted her drawer, and locked up the money for the night.

"It doesn't take long. If you can wait, then I'll walk with you and carry the Christmas present. Your place is on my way home."

"You know where I live?"

"Everyone knows where you live. It's the white house with the red door, big porch, and the wooden swing. This is a small town. Newcomers are an oddity."

"I don't want to put you out."

"It's no trouble."

As she flipped the sign that hung in the window from Open to Closed, a little girl knocked and Prim opened the door for her. Sean estimated that the child was six. She wore denim shorts, a faded Sock Monkey t-shirt, and white tennis shoes. Her dark hair was in pigtails.

"May I help you?" Prim asked the child in the same tone of voice she'd used with him and other adults when he'd been in the store earlier that afternoon.

"I need a birthday present for my grandma," the little girl said seriously. "I brought all the money I had in my piggy bank. I don't know if it's enough for a present."

"Well, let's find out," Prim told her. "Why don't you put your money on the counter so we can count it?"

The child walked over to the register area and proceeded to withdraw many coins and a dollar bill from her pockets. Sean stood nearby and watched as Prim counted the money, which he saw totaled four dollars and fifty-seven cents.

"Is it enough?" the child asked expectantly. "She's a really nice grandma. I live with her."

"Tell me what you'd like to buy for your grandmother and then we'll see if you have enough money," Prim instructed. "You take your time and look around."

Sean watched as the girl walked carefully through the store. When she got to an area that had nice costume jewelry displayed, she stopped and pointed to a small silver filigree heart necklace and asked, "Do I have enough for this?"

Sean knew that the necklace was definitely more than four dollars and fifty-seven cents. He stuck his hand into his pocket so he could retrieve his wallet, but Prim motioned for him to stop. She gave him a miniscule shake of the head and went over to lift the necklace from where it hung on a hook.

"Let's see," she said, as she looked at the price tag. "Well, this necklace was twenty dollars, but it's on clearance today. That means it's on sale for four dollars plus tax. I think you've got a little more than enough money. Would you like me to gift wrap it for you?" When the girl said she'd like that very much, Prim asked, "Do you want me to write out a birthday message to put in the box?"

"I love you with ALL my heart!"

Prim wrote the note on a small ivory-colored card and asked the little girl for her name, which turned out to be Lindsay. Prim added this under the message. She placed the necklace and card in a box and then wrapped it in birthday paper that had balloons printed on it. She topped it with a bow made of red squiggly ribbon. Then she rang up the necklace, typed something on the screen, and printed a receipt, which she directed Lindsay to keep until after she'd given her grandmother the gift. She handed the girl some change. Then she put the wrapped box and receipt in a plastic grocery bag and told the child to go straight home and not to show anyone what she had on the way so the grandmother would be completely surprised. Lindsay thanked her, leaving the shop with a huge smile on her little face.

"You didn't know her," Sean stated.

"No, but I know *of* her. She moved here not long ago when her parents were killed in a drunk driving accident. Her grandmother, who's not in the best of health, is raising her alone."

"That was a wonderful thing you did. I could pay you the difference. Why didn't you let me?"

"Because I didn't want you to, but I really appreciate that you were so willing to do it."

"Why did you insist on giving her the receipt?"

"Because I figured her grandmother would know the necklace cost more than four dollars. I just manipulated the computer so that it read CLEARANCE and overrode the amount."

"And the plastic bag?"

"So no one would see she had a present and try to steal it as she walked home. She doesn't live in the best of neighborhoods."

"Should she be walking home by herself?"

"Probably not, but I saw one of our policemen on patrol through the window. He'll keep an eye on her until she gets home safely."

As she used the touch screen on the computer, Prim asked, "Do you mind coming in the back room with me while I count the money? I don't want anyone to see someone in the shop and think we're still open. I'm tired and hungry."

As he followed her into the small office, he asked, "What did you have for lunch?"

"I didn't. I was too busy to eat, which means I was doing a great business all day. That's a trade-off I'm willing to live with."

"How about if we stop by LouAnn's for dinner? I've already had breakfast and lunch there, so I might as well eat all three meals there today."

She paused, and he had a sinking feeling she was going to decline. However, she surprised him by accepting. Within twenty minutes they were seated in a booth at LouAnn's. Sean had his purchases stacked beside him, except for the Christmas present that rested on the seat beside Prim.

"So, how did you like your tour of the Town Square?" LouAnn asked after she'd taken their orders for Sean's chef salad and Prim's beef stew.

"I think I did everything except explore the grass and gazebo in the center."

"We can do that as we walk home," Prim told him. "It won't take long."

"I'd like that." After accepting a glass of iced tea from LouAnn, Sean asked Prim, "How long were you in Atlanta?"

Prim talked of attendance and graduation from college and of work at an art gallery both as a salesperson and an accounts manager. She'd returned permanently to Aurora the previous September. Prim's Corner had opened in early November and had been doing well ever since.

"What about you?" she prompted, as their food arrived. "I know you're the new principal at Kensington, but how did you end up here?"

As she ate her stew, Sean explained that he'd wanted to see what it was like not to live in a big city. He finished with the words, "It's so…different here from what I'm used to. I've never lived in anyplace this small."

Prim flashed him a quick smile and tucked a loose strand of strawberry blonde hair behind one ear. She warned him that small-town life had its ups and downs, just like every other place. However, she was quick to add that she truly did love her hometown and couldn't imagine leaving it again.

Sean insisted on paying for dinner. Then he and Prim collected his bags and the Christmas box, leaving the restaurant and walking across the street to the grassy area in the center of the Square. A large, wooden gazebo had been constructed on one end. Sean and Prim went inside, sitting on a bench for a few minutes. They then set out for Sean's house since she assured him it was truly on her way home.

When they reached his place, Sean asked, "Do you mind coming inside so that we can put down my purchases? That way, I can walk you to your house."

"You don't need to do that," she protested.

"I insist."

Prim lived in a large, two-story Victorian home one block down the street from Sean's rented house. An official sign was posted at the edge of the white picket fence that surrounded the place. The sign proclaimed that the dwelling was a historic landmark and was the oldest existing home in Aurora. It had been built in 1898 by a member of the Aurora family. The exterior was white with plum-colored shutters and trim. The front door was stained and looked original to the house.

"This is amazing," Sean said with appreciation, as they stood at the gate. "Did you grow up in this house?"

"I did."

"So, you live with your uncle?"

"No, he moved out when my aunt died. He said he couldn't stand to be in the place after she'd passed. He does come to see me here and does work on the house if it needs it."

"It must be nice to have someone who's handy to keep this place up. I never learned how to do any repair work because I've lived in apartments my entire life."

"Is there anything you need where you are now?"

"A shower attachment on the tub. I love baths but would appreciate being able to take a quick shower when I need to. The owners said I could do it and take the expense off one month's rent, but I've only been there for a week and figured I'd ask around for a referral to a good plumber."

"Uncle Buddy could do it. You should ask him about it."

"I will. Does he go to the Community Church? I was planning on attending the first service tomorrow to see if I like it."

"I'll be at that one, but Uncle Buddy doesn't go to church."

"I'll have to ask him next weekend then. This upcoming week's going to be pretty hectic for me."

"I can imagine. I know it's the first week of school. I hope you like it there. It seems nice, but that scandal at the end of last year really tarnished its image."

"That's why they hired me. I'm sort of the go-to principal for schools with problems."

Cocking her head, Prim said, "I get the impression you're sort of the go-to man for people with all sorts of problems."

"That's true." Looking towards the house, he muttered, "It can be hard sometimes, can't it?"

Prim didn't answer. Sean turned back to look at her and saw that she was staring at her feet. Being the "go-to" man he was, Sean wanted to take her in his arms and comfort her. He knew exactly how she felt – appreciated by everyone for her ingenuity and perseverance but isolated by choice and circumstance.

After telling her he'd see her at church the following morning, Sean thanked her again for her help and her company. He wished her a good night and then walked unhurriedly back to his rented home. He took his customary long, hot bath and tried to get the image of Prim out of his mind. He felt like a teenager, except he'd never reacted this way to any girl even when he'd been a teenager. He'd felt attraction, admiration, and lust, but he hadn't found the perfect combination until that day.

Sean went to bed, trying not to think of Prim undressing, bathing, and putting on her nightclothes. He reminded himself that he needed to retain his focus on work but to no avail. When he finally fell asleep, Sean was wondering what it would be like to run his fingers along Prim Aurora's skin and to kiss her soft lips.

Chapter Two

Prim sat on the mattress of her white cast-iron bed and thought of her time spent with Sean Proper. The moment she'd spotted him standing in her shop, she'd felt something akin to a rush of adrenaline and had experienced a sensation of being literally drawn towards him. That had never happened to her in her life, and she was terrified, yet oddly excited.

Standing, Prim removed her dress, slip, bra, and panties and took them to the white wicker clothes hamper in her bathroom. Then she walked naked through the house and down the stairs towards the huge full-length mirror that hung in the formal living room no one ever used anymore. As she entered the room, Prim flipped on the lights. Squaring her shoulders, Prim stepped in front of the mirror. She had never examined her reflection when she'd been nude and wasn't certain what she'd think. Was it a good idea to scrutinize her body? She wasn't sure but decided it was time. After all, she was twenty-four years old. It was past time.

Prim was thin and had small bones and fine facial features. Her lips were defined but not overly plump. Her skin was pale, and that seemed to go well with her strawberry blonde hair and blue eyes. Her breasts were firm, and her nipples were hard in the chill of the air-conditioned house. Her hips had soft curves. Turning sideways, she focused on her backside, which was slightly rounded. She figured the daily yoga she performed was helping to keep her in shape.

She'd never thought of herself as pretty. Sean Proper seemed to be attracted to her. She didn't understand it and wondered if the man would like her body if he saw it. What was his body like under his clothing? The fear gripped her then, and she hastily switched off the lights and went back upstairs to get ready for bed.

Trying not to think about Sean Proper proved fruitless. Prim didn't know what to do about this and was unnerved by her physical and emotional reactions to the man. She wanted to talk to someone about it, but there was no one. She was friends with just about everyone in town but had no close girl friends with whom she could confide and wouldn't dream of mentioning it to Remy, her uncle or someone like Pastor Caleb. She considered having a talk with LouAnn.

Stop it, Prim told herself. *You can't tell anyone.*

And yet she knew she needed to confide in someone. She knew there was something wrong with her, had known it since she'd been a small child. Although everyone seemed to genuinely like Prim, she'd never felt as though she could share her deepest fears with any of them.

When she was thirteen, she'd tried to talk to her aunt about her feelings regarding the terror she felt at the mere thought of having any male kiss or touch her in a romantic way. Aunt Myrtle had stiffened and told her that some women didn't like to have men touch them, that Prim was better off for it, and that it would spare her pain in the long run. She told Prim not to worry about how she felt and that everything would be fine. But it hadn't been fine. Prim had eventually accepted that she'd never marry or have a family. She was broken, and nothing could fix her.

However, now Sean Proper had appeared in her life, and she'd responded to him with her mind *and* body. He seemed to be drawn to her as well, and Prim didn't want to push him away. She wanted him.

Before she fell asleep, Prim decided she'd talk with Dr. Stanford the next week. After all, he was the town's most established M.D. and was bound by an oath to keep his patients' information private. He'd been her doctor since she'd been born.

The following morning as she stepped into the church wearing a mint-green dress that she hoped Sean Proper would find appealing, Prim's heart was pounding. She greeted people as usual but was scanning the crowd for Sean. She waved to LouAnn, who was sitting in the front pew before taking a seat next to Remy. As the time for the service drew near, she began to wonder whether or not Sean would come after all.

"Hello, Prim."

She turned, and there he stood, wearing a dark blue shirt and khaki pants. Prim felt elation and worked hard not to allow her overwhelming relief to show on her face. She smiled pleasantly at him and told him she was glad he'd made it to the service.

"Could I sit next to you?"

"Of course," she said graciously.

As Sean exchanged introductions with those sitting nearby, Prim studied him. He presented himself as a man who was relaxed but in charge. However, Prim had glimpsed a side of the man during each of their encounters the day before that led her to believe he was not quite as in charge as he'd like. The look he'd had on his face when they'd talked about his younger sister had been the most telling example of some deep sadness within him.

The church service started. It was evident Sean had no idea what to expect, and that was understandable. Prim whispered to him here and there when it was time to sit, stand, kneel, and sing. He appeared surprised but not displeased when those gathered began to file up to the front for Communion. After the final hymn, Prim turned towards Sean and asked him what he'd thought about his experience at the Aurora Community Church.

"That was one of the oddest services I've ever attended, but I liked it. It was interesting the way it seemed to combine a bunch of different traditions. I just felt a little lost at times. I'll figure it out."

Their departure from the church took quite some time, as it seemed everyone present wanted to meet the newcomer. When they finally made it to the door, Prim and Sean were two of the last people to leave the building. Sean talked with Caleb about the service, while Prim stood waiting, not knowing exactly what to do. After Sean had thanked the pastor, Prim told Caleb to have a beautiful afternoon before heading down the steps with Mr. Proper.

"Do you have any special plans for the afternoon?" Sean asked as they walked back in the direction of their respective homes.

"I usually go to Uncle Buddy's for lunch then do whatever for myself or work on the business accounts in the afternoon. You?"

"I'll make a sandwich, maybe read and play some video games, and then call my parents. They live in Florida. I always call them at least once a week to talk and to see how they're doing."

"That's sweet."

"They're sweet. I feel great after I talk to them. It's like getting a shot of happiness."

"Everyone should be so lucky. You want to come with me to Uncle Buddy's for lunch? He's a great cook but always makes too much."

"I wouldn't want to intrude on your family time."

"We'd both be thrilled."

Sean shrugged and said, "You know him better than I do. Whatever he's cooking is probably tastier than my turkey and Swiss sandwich."

Scared but pleased that he'd decided to accept her invitation, Prim said, "Whatever it is will be horrible for your arteries."

"How long were he and your aunt married before she died?"

"Thirty-eight years. My aunt was seventeen years older than my mom. She and Uncle Buddy were thirty-five when I was born and had been married since they were twenty. Uncle Buddy's sixty now."

"He seems like a great guy."

"He is. Hey, maybe he can come look at your bathtub later today."

"It's his day off."

"He likes to feel needed and important. He's an excellent carpenter and plumber. You'd probably make his day if you ask him."

Prim's uncle was very happy to have Sean join them for their lunch, which consisted of a sugar-glazed ham, black-eyed peas, sweet potato casserole with marshmallow topping, and macaroni and cheese. He'd made cupcakes for dessert.

"You're very multi-talented," Sean told him during the meal. "This is all delicious."

"Cooking is kind of like building," Buddy remarked. "You construct the meal like you construct anything else. If you don't take your time and do it right, then it doesn't work and everything falls apart."

Prim listened to her uncle regale Sean with stories of his long life in Aurora, of how the town had retained its character, and of his years spent with Myrtle and Prim. After they'd each eaten a cupcake for dessert, Buddy packed those that remained in a tinfoil pan and gave them to Sean to take home. Prim took this opportunity to explain Sean's desire for a shower attachment in the bathroom, and Buddy eagerly agreed to see what would be involved. The three of them walked the five blocks to Sean's house.

Prim took her time, surveying the living room more carefully than she had the previous day. The modern furnishings and décor were out of place in the older dwelling. The living room was well-kept, but Sean's purchases from the day before still rested on the coffee table. As her uncle went with Sean to the bathroom, she sat in a black leather recliner, half-listening to their conversation. Then the pictures caught her eye.

Prim went across the room to the entertainment center and looked at the three framed photos that rested on one shelf. The first was of a middle-aged couple who had brown hair and brown eyes and looked very relaxed, happy, and in love. There was a family portrait of the couple with a teenaged boy and a preteen girl. The final photo was of the children when they'd been younger, showing Sean dressed as Wolverine from the X-Men, while the little girl was a princess.

Prim suddenly felt eyes upon her and turned. Sean, who was looking rather melancholy, was staring at her. She felt like a snoop and was compelled to apologize.

"For what?" he asked. "I wouldn't put these pictures out if I didn't want to display them." Walking over to where she stood, he pointed to his parents and said, "That's Mom and Dad. Her name's Tiffany, and his is Kenny." Pointing to the next photo, he went on, "The whole family when I was seventeen and my sister was eleven." Lifting the final picture, he said, Of course, this is Wolverine and Princess Debra."

"They're all wonderful. You and your sister look so much like your parents."

He smiled and nodded as he stared down at the photo of himself and his sister in their Halloween finery. Then he said, "My mom made our costumes every year."

"You're kidding! They don't look homemade."

"She's good with cloth."

"Is she a seamstress?"

"For the family. Her actual job is working in a laundry. She likes the repetition."

Confused but not wanting to pry, Prim continued by asking, "And your dad?"

"Bags groceries and collects shopping carts. He likes repetition, too. Both of them like to work hard and do a good job." Replacing the picture on the bookshelf, Sean said, "My folks are beautiful people. They're also developmentally delayed."

Prim was at a total loss for words. She tried to think of what one should say in response to this admission.

Sean grinned and said, "It's okay. I'm not ashamed of my parents and their limitations. They gave me and Debra more love when we were growing up than most parents do with their kids."

"How did they take care of you? If they're delayed, then how could they be responsible parents?"

"I didn't say they were severely delayed. They just have lower IQs than the average person. They're great parents and always have been; they simply have their own special challenges."

"Like what?"

"Learning in general. It was a good thing Debra and I were both smart because our folks couldn't have helped us with homework after about the fourth grade. I started taking care of the bills when I was nine. Things were sort of a disaster business-wise before then. I still have to help them manage their money."

"That had to be hard for a nine-year-old boy," Prim said quietly.

"It taught me to like challenges."

"You didn't resent them?"

"For having lower-than-average intelligence levels? For falling in love and having me and Debra? For loving us unconditionally and doing whatever they could to make us happy? How could I resent them for that? They're amazing. You'll see when they come for Christmas."

"I'd like that very much. Will Debra come too?"

"I doubt it. We'll see."

They heard Prim's uncle walking down the hallway and greeted him as he came into the room. He announced that he could have the job done by that evening if Sean didn't mind his running to the hardware store to get a few supplies. Within minutes, the older man had left the house promising to return shortly.

Once Buddy had gone, Sean asked Prim if she wanted to have a seat on the couch. She nervously accepted. The two of them sat a couple of feet apart. There was an awkward pause.

21

"Aurora's having a strange effect on me," Sean admitted. "I'm used to being really private, but being in this place makes me want to share."

"Is that a bad thing?"

"No, just unusual." He was quiet for a minute then said, "I'm really attracted to you. I've been attracted to other women before but not like this. I guess I don't really know what to do with how I'm feeling, yet."

Prim looked across the couch at him and said, "I'm very attracted to you, too. I've never felt this way about any other man. I don't know what to do about it either."

"You mind if we take it slowly?"

She shook her head and said, "Slow would be preferable. I'm...I'm kind of scared."

His eyes narrowed, and she worried that she'd said too much. Perhaps he would think she was crazy. She considered the possibility but dismissed it. She wasn't crazy, but she wasn't normal either.

Her uncle's return to the house saved her from further discussion on the topic. As he worked in Sean's bathroom, Sean asked Prim if she wanted to play a video game with him. Her face flushed, and she admitted she'd never played any video games outside an arcade.

"I could teach you. Do you want to go on a quest or shoot something?"

"Questing sounds better to me."

He selected a game that involved a boy's looking for his sister in a magical land and spent the following hour instructing her on how to play. At first, she wasn't any good, but her skill level increased as she quested. By the time her uncle finished the work in Sean's bathroom, she was thoroughly enjoying herself and suggested to the older man that he try it.

"Another time," he told her. "It's getting late, and I need to get back to the house before the sun sets so I can fix those boards on the fence in the backyard." Turning to Sean, he asked, "Did you hang those chimes, yet?"

The chimes were soon hung. Buddy shook hands with Sean and told him he could come by anytime the next Saturday to pay his bill for the work in the bathroom and get his receipt for the house's owners. Sean thanked him for all of his help and the food. Her uncle said it was his pleasure. Then he told the two younger people to have a good evening and set off for his own home.

There was a breeze, and the chimes gently clanged against one another.

"Prim, do you want to sit on the porch swing with me for a while before you leave?"

She hesitated for a moment but then agreed. They sat and pushed the swing slightly back and forth. Sean seemed to be resisting the urge to kiss her, and she was thankful for that – even though she wanted him to try.

"Prim, am I doing something wrong?"

She stared at the chimes and shook her head.

"Are you afraid of me?"

She nodded, and tears filled her eyes.

"Will you tell me what I did to make you scared so I can undo it?"

Refusing to look at him, she said softly, "It's not you. I can't explain it, and I'm…I'm afraid you're not going to be attracted to me if you know that I…." She let her voice trail off and wiped at the corners of her eyes before saying, "I wouldn't blame you."

Sean stopped the swing and said, "I meant what I told you earlier. If there's some problem you have that you can't talk to me about yet, then that's okay. I only met you yesterday. I'm not going anywhere. Take your time."

"Thank you. I'm sorry."

Sean leaned towards her. She expected that he wanted to take her in his arms and instinctively drew back. He immediately stopped and asked, "Can I hold your hand?"

"I don't know."

"May I try?"

Feeling miserable and sick, she forced herself to nod. Sean held out a hand and waited for her to put hers into it. She did so with effort. She could feel herself trembling with anxiety, but she was relieved that she'd managed to place her palm in his.

Sean didn't say anything or ask her any questions. He did start the swing moving again, and they listened to the chimes. Prim realized she wasn't trembling so badly and relaxed. After about an hour, she told him that she needed to go home. She declined his invitation to walk her to her house.

Once she'd shut and locked her front door behind her, Prim burst into tears. What was wrong with her? Why was she like this? She wanted to be with Sean and to get to know him better. She wanted to be eager to hold his hand without trembling, to kiss him, to embrace him, and to make love to him.

She wondered what it would feel like to have Sean kiss her deeply, touch her body with his hands and mouth, and have sex with her. It wasn't as if she didn't know what men looked like naked, and she'd seen people have sex on television and in movies. She'd read fiction and non-fiction books that talked about sex. It seemed as if sex was all couples really wanted. So why did the thought of physical intimacy leave Prim petrified?

The following morning, Prim went directly to Dr. Philip Stanford's office. His and his partners' clinic faced the Square, and she had plenty of time to see him and open her store unless there was a long line of people waiting for appointments after the weekend break. As it turned out, she was the first person to arrive and was accepted as a walk-in patient. When asked what her problem was, she told the receptionist she had a sore throat.

Dr. Stanford was about her uncle's age and had silvery gray hair and a good bedside manner. When he inquired about her sore throat, she confessed she'd fabricated that illness in order to talk with him.

Frowning, the doctor said, "I need to check your vitals before we talk. I have to document them for your records." Once that had been accomplished, he asked, "What's really going on, Prim?"

She burst into tears as she had at home the previous evening and told him she wasn't sure. The M.D. offered her some tissues and encouraged her to tell him the cause of her problem.

"I don't know. I've never known. I'm afraid to have men touch me, and I don't know why. I've always been afraid, and I've *never* known why."

Dr. Stanford reminded her that he'd seen her since she'd been a newborn. He had touched her as part of his examinations, and he'd seen her shake hands with men and hug them in a friendly manner or to comfort them in times of sadness.

"You're my doctor, and those men didn't want to…to be romantic with me!" she clarified. "If a man touches me in an ordinary way, then it doesn't bother me. But I've never been able to…to even kiss a boy in high school or afterwards or to let them hold me or anything else." Her face burning with embarrassment, she admitted, "I had to force myself to take a man's hand yesterday, even though I really wanted to."

The doctor looked contemplative and asked, "Is there anything you remember from your childhood that might have led to your fear? Did someone ever try to touch you inappropriately when you were a young girl?" When Prim shook her head, he asked, "Are you afraid to read about intercourse or watch people having sex on television or in films?"

"No, not at all. It's only when it has to do with *me*," she said as she wiped at her eyes. "I'm so scared, and I know it's irrational. What can I do?"

"Well, I think the first step is to forgive yourself for feeling this way. Whatever triggered this response was not your fault. The next thing I'd recommend is that you see a licensed mental health counselor."

Prim quickly got to her feet and insisted. "No. I can't."

"Why not?"

"I just can't," she said, reaching for her purse.

She began to walk towards the door, but the doctor stopped her.

"Prim, listen to me. I've literally known you since the day you were born. I wish I'd known about this problem sooner because I would've recommended therapy a long time ago and it might have saved you years of suffering. Did your Aunt Myrtle know?"

Prim explained about the conversation she'd had with her aunt, and Dr. Stanford looked startled. Then he asked if her uncle knew.

"I never talked to him about not being able to let boys touch me. It's not the sort of thing you say to your uncle."

"I understand. I also understand that there must be someone you want to touch you. Otherwise, you wouldn't be here today."

"Sean Proper."

"Isn't he the new principal at Kensington?"

"Yes, we met Saturday and spent a lot of Saturday and Sunday together. He…we both…he said he wouldn't run off because I can't explain about…because I couldn't even hold his hand without struggling. But how long will he wait, and what if I never get over this?"

"Did he try to do anything with you over the weekend?"

"No, he was very respectful, but I know he wants to do *something* eventually. I want to be able to, but I'm so scared."

"Prim, you need a psychologist or a social worker to help you through this."

"My aunt always told me therapists were bad people."

"There are some who are bad, just like there are bad people in every profession. There are also some very good therapists out there. That would be the best way to assist you with your fear. I could recommend someone in Atlanta if you don't want to see anyone in the area. Please, consider it."

Feeling slightly calmer, she agreed to think about it.

"I'm your primary care doctor, which means I'm responsible for your overall medical care. Let me reflect on this for a bit and see if I can come up with an answer. In the meantime, call if you need help day or night."

Dr. Stanford escorted her out to the waiting room, which was now full. As she headed for the door, he reminded her to take some ibuprofen for her sore throat and asked that she come back to see him soon. She gave him a grateful smile and told him she would. Then, she headed for her shop and a world she knew she could handle.

At 1:00 p.m. she answered the phone at Prim's Corner and was surprised to hear Sean Proper's voice. She was glad that at that moment she had no customers in the store.

"Isn't today your first school day at Kensington?"

"It is, and it's going great, so far. I just thought I'd take a minute to phone you and see if you could meet me at LouAnn's tonight at 7:00 for dinner. I want to share what's happened today with someone and decided that someone was definitely *you*."

"Really?"

"Why do you sound so shocked?"

"What about your parents?"

She could hear the smile in his voice as he said, "I'll tell my parents that my new job is going great and a few details, but they'd get bored with the rest. They'd listen, but they wouldn't really make the connections."

"You could talk to Remy."

He paused then asked directly, "Are you blowing me off?"

"What? No! I just didn't know after last night if…if you were still interested. If you're not, then I'd understand."

"I'm very interested in you, Prim."

"Because you feel sorry for me?"

"No. I told you how I felt yesterday. That hasn't changed."

"Even though you know how I am?"

"I love a challenge and can be very patient if I have a goal in mind."

"And your goal is?"

"In the short term, I'd like to be able to hold your hand without upsetting you."

"And after that?"

"I don't know. Maybe put my arm around your shoulder. Can we shoot for that?"

"Yes, but –"

"Not today. Don't panic. We're going to take the whole thing slowly, remember?"

"I remember."

"So, see you at 7:00 at LouAnn's?"

She was waiting in a booth at five minutes to 7:00. Sean was ten minutes late and was full of apologies, telling her he'd gotten hung up with paperwork and hadn't been able to leave as early as he'd wanted.

"I think my administrative assistant, Maureen, was shocked that I left at 6:30 on the first day. I'd told her to remind me if we were still there at 6:00 unless it was an emergency, but she figured we'd stay a lot later today."

Prim was amused by how excited he was. She listened with interest as he told her about his successful address to the staff and students, his interactions with visiting Board members, and his productive first staff meeting after school. There had been problems, but he felt as if he'd promptly handled them all. The students seemed to respect him, but also seemed to think he was cool because of his youth and energy, which were a plus.

"I know every day won't go as smoothly as today did, but it was a great start."

"It sounds like it couldn't have gone any better."

They left LouAnn's at 9:00 when the restaurant closed. Sean insisted on walking Prim home and asked her if he could hold her hand.

"I'd like that."

"But you're afraid."

"Yes, but I'd still like it."

He extended his hand towards her. She bit her lip and took it after only a few moments of hesitation.

"You're not trembling as badly as you were yesterday."

She realized he was right and smiled before impulsively squeezing his hand. He grinned at her, and she experienced an ache within her. It made her want to tell him to kiss her, to hold her, to make love to her and –

"Prim?" Sean asked with a worried expression on his face. "What's wrong?"

"I want to be normal and don't know why I'm not," she confessed, as tears trickled down her cheeks. "I can't touch men who might be romantically interested in me."

"And you had no idea why? Have you seen a therapist about it?"

She immediately pulled her hand from his and said rather loudly, "I can't!"

"Okay," he said soothingly. "No therapist. Got it."

"I'm sorry. You should walk away from me now. All I'm going to do is make your life harder."

He laughed rather bitterly and said, "My life has always had its share of hardness. The struggles only make the successes more sweet." When they reached her house, Sean stopped at the gate and asked, "Can we meet for dinner every night this week?"

"People will talk."

"So? Let them. How about if I call you each day to set a time? I doubt if it will be exactly the same Monday through Friday."

She put a hand on the gate and confided, "I don't know if I can do this, Sean."

"I do, and you can."

"I wish I had your confidence."

"Someday you will."

Prim went into her big, empty house and wandered to what had once been her mother's room. Her aunt had kept it exactly as it was when her mother had been alive, but Prim had never gone in before. She felt responsible for the woman's death, and her guilt was magnified exponentially by the mere thought of entering her mother's bedroom.

Now, she opened the door and went in without pause. Aunt Myrtle had come in to dust every week. Myrtle had been dead for over a year, so there was visible dust on the exposed surfaces. It didn't detract from the room or its contents.

Prim looked at the peach-colored bedspread and white ruffled skirt on the bed. There were cheerleading trophies and yearbooks on the bookshelves. A framed photo of her mother's dark-haired, heavyset parents was on the desk. White curtains hung in the windows; posters were tacked to the walls; and her mother's clothing still hung in the closet.

It's time to move on, Prim thought. *I know Uncle Buddy will be upset, but it's time to do a little housecleaning and not just in this room.*

Prim suddenly got the idea that Sean could help her. Perhaps it would give them something to do that would keep them together but occupied. She would have to broach the subject with him the next time they talked.

Feeling encouraged, Prim left her mother's room. She wanted to be done with the past and wanted her future in the form of one Mr. Sean Proper.

Chapter Three

"Mr. Proper?"

Sean hit the intercom button on his office phone and said, "Yes, Maureen?"

"Dr. Philip Stanford of the Aurora Medical Group is on the line for you. Should I put him through or direct him to your voicemail?"

Confused, Sean requested that Maureen send the call straight to him and lifted the receiver when the line rang.

"Sean Proper here. How may I help you?"

"Philip Stanford, M.D. here. I was thinking maybe *I* could help *you*. You've been in our town for well over a month, and I doubt if you've gotten yourself established with a local physician. I was thinking that would probably be a good idea, especially since you work around such a large group of young people at Kensington. Having a doctor on hand might prove very useful to you." Pausing, he added, "I've been Prim Aurora's doctor since the day she was born, so I'm sure she'll vouch for me."

Sean immediately deduced that the man wanted to talk with him about Prim but was bound by confidentiality oaths and laws. He suspected the internist had formulated a plan to somehow circumvent this and was more than willing to do whatever the doctor suggested if he could get help for Prim. He'd fallen in love with her over the past six weeks and longed to have a normal relationship with her. So far, that had proved impossible because of her fear of being touched. She was suffering, and so was he.

"What do you propose?" Sean asked the doctor. "If I come to your office –"

"I was thinking more along the lines of my making a house call. I do still do that sometimes, although I am very busy this week. Maybe when I take my nightly walk I could drop by your house, get some basic information, and then we could chat."

"I'd really appreciate it. What time?"

"Is 9:00 too late?"

"9:00 would be perfect. Thank you. I'll see you tonight."

Sean hung up and immediately dialed Remy at the Book Nook.

"I have to cancel Game Night this week," he told his friend. "Sorry. I'm swamped with work and am going to have to bring some home this evening. No video games for me."

"No biggie. We'll just skip a Wednesday for once. Life happens."

"Thanks. I'll be dropping by the store Saturday as usual."

"Great. That thriller you ordered came in. It's waiting for you behind the counter. I was going to bring it tonight, but it'll have to wait."

"Thanks. Sorry again."

Sean disconnected the call and sat, staring blindly at the papers in front of him. He felt badly about canceling on Remy, who had quickly become his closest male friend. The man was three years older than Sean and was also still single. They liked the same books, games, music, and had similar thoughts on politics, religion, and women. Whereas Sean had taken responsibility at a young age for himself, his parents, and his sister because of his parents' challenges, Remy had become the *de facto* head of his family at age eight when his alcoholic parents began to spiral out of control. Remy had run their household and been in charge of his younger brother, who was Prim's age. Unfortunately, the boy had turned to alcohol himself when he'd graduated from high school and died when he'd driven drunk and crashed his car into a tree. Remy had never forgiven himself, even though he knew it wasn't his fault.

Just like I feel guilty about how Debra turned out, Sean thought. *It's almost like Prim feels about her fears. It doesn't make any sense, but I feel like I'm to blame.*

He'd received an e-mail the day before from his little sister that had made him cry. Her current boyfriend had demeaned her at a company function while he was drunk, and it had been a huge embarrassment to her and the firm. The man had gotten fired for his actions, but he'd blamed the entire incident on Debra. Instead of telling him to get lost, she'd accepted the blame and apologized to him. She had even tried to get the firm to rehire him.

Sean had e-mailed back what he always did when she sent messages like that. He reminded her how smart and pretty she

31

was, what a good job she had, and how proud he and her parents were of her accomplishments. He never mentioned whatever jerk she was currently dating. When he'd encouraged her to leave the early destructive relationships in which she'd engaged, she'd withdrawn from him completely for months. So, he'd written and promised her he wouldn't talk about them anymore. She'd re-established contact through e-mail, and he was hoping that someday he could try to approach her again about the topic of relationships.

He called Prim before he returned his attention to his paperwork and told her the same story about being overwhelmed with work and canceling his Game Night with Remy. Being a businesswoman, she understood and sympathized. When he wanted to know if she could meet him for dinner at Lou Ann's the following night, she declined.

"I promised Pastor Caleb I'd meet with him after work at LouAnn's tonight and tomorrow to finalize the details for the Aurora Christmas Festival. He's been in charge of it for the past decade and asked me to help with coordinating things this year. I knew you and Remy had Game Night on Wednesdays, so I told him tonight and tomorrow would be good. How about Friday?"

"Friday is great."

"Call me tomorrow anyway?"

"Of course."

"Good. Try not to stay up too late," she advised.

"I'll try. Have fun organizing the Christmas Festival."

"I will. You're going to love it."

Sean took a deep breath and said what he'd wanted to say since the day he'd met Primrose Anastasia Cassandra Aurora.

"I love *you*, Prim."

There was a sharp intake of breath on her end before she said very quietly, "I love you, too. I –"

He heard the jingling of the bell on the front door of Prim's Corner and knew she had a customer. She apologized for having to go and wished him a productive evening.

When Sean arrived at his house at 6:00, he went to his home office and lifted weights for a half hour. It was part of the routine he'd let slip during his early days at Kensington, and he had decided he shouldn't let it slip any longer or his muscles would pay the price. He used his weight bench to give his legs a workout; then he went to take a long, hot bath.

He'd used the shower Buddy had installed but still preferred his baths. Now that he was working out again, Sean's muscles appreciated the indulgence. He imagined Prim naked in the large, claw-foot tub with him, but he decided that he should redirect his thoughts or else he would have to take a cold shower before his guest arrived.

Dr. Stanford was right on time. Sean ushered him in, asking him to sit on the couch. He was surprised to see that the M.D. actually had what looked like an old-fashioned black doctor's kit with him.

"It was my father's," Stanford explained. "I really do want to get you established as a patient. It's good practice to have a doctor you know close by, especially when you live in a more rural area like ours."

"Makes sense. What do you want to do? Take my blood pressure or pulse?"

"In a while. I think you're probably a little nervous because of the circumstances. It would skew the results. I would like to listen to your heart and lungs and take your temperature. We'll go over the paperwork and review any questions either of us might have concerning your health. Then I'll take your pressure and pulse."

"Then we can talk," Sean prompted.

"Yes, then we can talk."

The doctor pulled out some forms and a clipboard and asked Sean for the information needed. When Sean questioned him about this practice, the internist said it helped him to retain the information about each patient when he filled in the blanks himself. Sean nodded and answered all of his questions. Most were easy. The only one that gave him pause was, "Are there any other abnormal conditions in your family's medical history?"

"I don't know how to answer that," Sean told the older man.

"How do you want to answer?"

"No."

"And what do you think the answer is?"

"Yes."

"What's the problem?"

"Both of my parents are developmentally delayed, but it's because they were preemies. They're in their fifties."

"Ah. Yes, the care for preemies was a lot more limited back then. Do they have other problems like cerebral palsy or blindness?"

"No, they were very lucky, if you can call being brain-damaged lucky." He smiled and said, "They're so giving and gentle. I'm planning on having them come for Christmas."

"I can't wait to meet them. How long have you played the role of caregiver in your family?"

"About twenty-one years."

"That's quite some time. Does your sister help with them?"

Sean shook his head and confided, "Debra's ashamed now. I've never been ashamed of our parents. I'm proud of how independent they are. I love them and would do anything for them, just like they would for me."

"I'm glad you shared that with me. Part of being a doctor is about treating the whole patient, and that includes the stresses and support one gets from family members."

The M.D. asked Sean to remove his shirt, refrained from commenting on the tattoo of outstretched wings that covered his chest, and then listened to his heart and lungs. Once he'd taken Sean's temperature with a digital thermometer, he instructed him to put his shirt back on and returned to his seat on the couch.

"I'll check your blood pressure and pulse now that we've had a chance to chat for a while. I'd like to run complete lab work on you so I have a baseline. Your health appears to be very good in general, but I want to check your cholesterol and other things. I'll give you the lab orders before I leave. It'll be a fasting test, so nothing but water after midnight. The lab's on Seventeenth Avenue and is open 7:00 to 5:00, so you can't use work as an excuse to put it off." As the doctor put away his forms, the stethoscope, and his pen, he said, "Now that we've taken care of that, we can have a neighborly chat."

"Sounds good," Sean said cautiously. "Why don't you start?"

"Certainly. Aurora is a wonderful place to live. My wife and I have raised our sons here, and both have stayed. They're very happy, which is the most important thing to me.

"However, Aurora isn't perfect. Our town has its own secrets and problems, and I'm not only talking about drugs and prostitution." Sighing, he said, "I know that you and Prim Aurora are seeing each other. Everyone in town has known that for some time. However, I also know there are some...issues. I can't talk about Prim's care with you because I'm her doctor. However, I'm not Buddy's doctor, nor was I Myrtle's, Sandra's, or Prim's grandparents' doctor."

"Sandra? Was that Prim's mother?"

"Yes. She was a very energetic girl. Very different from her parents and Myrtle."

"Different how?"

"In many ways. I grew up with Buddy and Myrtle and knew their families. Buddy's were all in construction and as healthy as could be, but they tended to work themselves too hard. Myrtle and her folks weren't very active and tended to be overweight. They all died of heart problems in their fifties or sixties."

"But Sandra wasn't like that?"

"Not at all. She was athletic, vivacious, a champion cheerleader and swimmer."

"Was Prim's aunt vivacious?"

"No, but she was a nice woman. She and Buddy were sweet on each other from the sixth grade on. Everyone knew they'd get married, and they did."

"But?"

"Well, they never had any children. Everyone thought that was a shame, since they were such nice people. Then when Sandra was a senior in high school, she turned up pregnant. However, she was feeling so poorly that my father, her doctor, ran some tests. That's when they found out about the leukemia. I'm sure you know the rest."

"So, Sandra dies a few months after giving birth and Buddy and Myrtle adopt Prim."

"No."

"No?"

"They were her legal guardians. They never adopted her."

"Why not?"

Dr. Stanford shrugged and said, "I never understood it either."

"But they raised her. Were they good parents?"

"Seemingly. Prim was sweet, smart, pretty, and easy-going."

"Seemingly," Sean repeated. "Do you think there was abuse?"

"If I'd ever thought that, then I would have turned them in to the authorities immediately, friends or no."

Sean struggled with what he should say. How much did this man know about Prim and her fears? Could he really trust the man with the knowledge if she hadn't shared it with him?

"Prim said her mother never told anyone who the father of her baby was. Is that true?"

"Yes."

"Do you think it was Buddy?"

"I…I truly don't know. Sandra was…well…let's just say she had a reputation."

"Did Myrtle have a reputation?"

"Not at all. Like I said before, she and Buddy were sweet on each other from the time they were about twelve."

"So, what am I missing here? I'm so…so…Prim is really…she's been hurt somehow. Whatever happened to her when she was younger is tearing her apart now. I don't know what to do. I love her, and it hurts me to see her in so much pain. I suggested therapy, but she flat-out refuses. What do I do?"

"Perhaps you and Buddy could have a talk. Maybe he can shed some light on several mysteries here." Cocking his head, he asked, "What are you thinking?"

"That maybe Prim was raped as a child and blocked it out of her head somehow."

Stanford stood, picked up his bag, and headed for the door. He paused with his hand on the knob and said, "I'm going to break a professional confidence here for the first time in my life, and I trust that you won't ever reveal what I'm about to say to anyone. I wouldn't say it at all, but you need to know because of Prim's concerns. As her doctor, I need to keep her best interest in mind."

"I would never say anything."

"I believe you." Stanford turned back to him and said, "You and I both know what Prim is afraid of. I only found out recently. I wish I'd known years ago so I could have gotten her some help." When Sean nodded, he continued, "I have access to all of her medical records. She may have been molested and doesn't remember, but she wasn't raped in the traditional sense. Am I being clear? If you do get her to overcome her fears...."

"I understand. I'll keep that in mind." Standing, Sean walked over to the M.D. and shook his hand before thanking him for everything. He accepted the papers for lab work and thanked him again before seeing him out.

When he returned to his living room, Sean sat on the couch and reviewed his conversation with Dr. Stanford. It had all been very informative and rather mystifying. There were obviously several major pieces of the puzzle missing, but Stanford evidently didn't know what they were. His advice was sound. Sean would have to approach Buddy.

The last thing the internist had told Sean was both relieving and disheartening. The doctor had intimated that Prim was still a virgin, which would mean that she'd at least been spared that violent attack as a young girl. It also meant that she'd never been with a man. He would have to hurt her the first time if they ever made love.

Sean had deflowered two virgins in his life, one in high school and one in college. He'd tried to be as gentle as possible, but both girls had complained of terrible pain during the encounter and for several days afterwards. How would Prim, who was afraid of sex, react? What if it damaged her psyche even more?

Sean rubbed at his temples and wondered if he should go to Buddy's at that moment. He glanced at the clock. It was after 11:00. Buddy would be in bed and not at his best. Sean wanted to handle his encounter with Prim's uncle very carefully. That night was not the night. The following evening would do nicely since Prim would be occupied with planning the Christmas Festival.

Sean fasted the following morning and stopped by the lab on his way to work. His day was hectic, and he had no time to think about helping Prim, hurting Prim, or talking to Buddy. He did make time to call Prim on her cellphone as he left work, but she said she was on her way to LouAnn's to meet with Caleb.

"Did you get everything accomplished last night?" she asked him as she walked.

"Not everything. I'll try to take care of more tonight."

"Well, then I'm glad we set our dinner date for tomorrow."

"I suppose that did work out for the best."

"Talk to you tomorrow," she said gaily. "I love you, Sean."

"I love you, Prim."

Sean arrived home, parked his car in the garage, and walked through the cool, late-September night air straight to Buddy's. It was 6:30 when he knocked on the wood frame of Prim's uncle's screen door. Buddy opened it and smiled at him.

"Sean! Come on in. Isn't it a lovely night? I've got the doors open in the front and back, and it feels so good in the house. I just finished eating some lasagna I made yesterday. You want a piece?"

"No, thanks."

Buddy sobered and asked, "What is it? You look mighty stressed."

"I am. I need to talk to you. It's important."

Nodding, Buddy gestured for Sean to sit at the kitchen table and got them each a soda before taking a seat himself. He asked Sean what was wrong.

"A lot, and I don't know how to fix things."

"Can I help?"

"I really hope so."

"What can I do?"

"Tell the truth."

Buddy frowned and asked, "What's that supposed to mean?"

"It means there's something wrong with Prim's past, and I need to understand it. More importantly, Prim needs to understand it. I really don't want her to know I came to see you, but I'm more concerned with her welfare than anything else. I love her."

Scratching his head, Buddy asked, "Did you come here to talk to me about proposing to Prim?"

"No. I came here to talk to you about why I can't propose to her."

"You're totally confusing me."

Sean took a sip of his soda then asked, "Are you Prim's father?"

All of the color drained from Buddy's face, and his jaw literally dropped. Sean had expected an immediate denial, but Buddy simply sat and stared at him. After a couple of minutes had passed, Sean repeated the question.

Buddy looked very sad and muttered, "I don't know."

"You don't know?"

"No."

Sean ran his fingers through his hair and asked, "Will you just tell me what the hell is going on? Something is so completely wrong with things in your family, but I don't know what it is. Neither does Prim, but it's hurting her."

"Hurting her how?"

Sean shook his head and said, "If she never talked to you about things, then she certainly didn't want you to know."

"Know what? Is she okay?"

"She's afraid of certain things but doesn't know why." Dropping his head, Sean said, "Please, just explain it to me but don't tell her I came here or that I ever told you anything. Or, better yet, don't tell me anything, pretend I never came, and just talk to her."

Buddy shook his head and said, "You asked. I should explain. If I talk to Prim without knowing what's bothering her, then it might hurt her worse."

"Good point."

"What do you want to know?"

"I want to know about Prim's grandparents, about you and Prim's aunt, about whether you slept with Prim's mother, and what happened in the old Aurora home."

Buddy took a swig from his soda bottle and said, "Myrtle and I knew each other forever. Our mothers were friends, and we went to the same school. My daddy owned a construction business, and Myrtle's daddy had money because of his family. He was a good businessman and ran the hardware store as well as managed his other holdings.

"From the time we were in what they now call middle school, Myrtle and I knew we were meant to be together. We shared our first kiss at the eighth-grade dance. When we were sixteen, I told her I wanted to marry her. That was about the time things went wrong."

"Wrong how?"

"Myrtle had always been a real nice girl. She was heavy, but I didn't care about that. I loved her and wanted to marry her when we got out of school. But during the first part of that school year, Myrtle started acting...different. She would cry for no reason, and nothing would make her stop. Finally, old Doc Stanford suggested that her parents take her to Atlanta to see a psychiatrist."

"And?"

Buddy shut his eyes and said, "They did, and the man recommended Myrtle stay at his hospital for some sort of observation. It would only be for a few days." Shifting in his chair, he said, "You have to remember that this was a long time ago when people didn't go see psychiatrists because there was shame attached to it a lot more than there is today. The only reason I knew was because my mama was such good friends with Myrtle's mama, and I overheard them talking. The Auroras told everyone else in town that they were taking a short holiday to Atlanta."

"So, Myrtle stays at the hospital for a few days. Then what?"

"Then she came home, but her folks didn't let her out of the house. Myrtle's daddy surprised everyone by announcing that he and Myrtle's mama were going to have a baby after all those years and that she'd seen a doctor in Atlanta about it while they were there. This other doctor had said she needed to rest a lot because of her age. She said Myrtle wasn't feeling well, so Myrtle was going to stay home with her and rest, too. Old Doc Stanford tried to see both of them, but Mr. Aurora said his wife and daughter would be fine. Nobody saw them until after Sandra was born. They made up the excuse that she'd come so quickly they hadn't had time to get to a hospital."

Sean and Buddy stared at one another for a long time before Sean asked, "And people bought that?" They didn't piece together that Myrtle was the one who was pregnant?"

"You've got to remember that no one knew where Myrtle had gone. They believed her folks' story about her taking a trip to Atlanta with them."

"When was Sandra born?"

"Late July. Myrtle returned to school in September and was back to her old self. Well, that's what everyone else thought. I could tell the difference. She'd kiss me, but it wasn't the same. It was like a quick kiss, kind of like a peck on the cheek but on the lips. Before, she'd really liked to kiss."

"So, what was the real story?"

"I didn't find out until after we were married. On our wedding night, Myrtle hadn't…she couldn't…she broke down and explained everything. The psychiatrist had told her he was going to help her overcome her obvious problem, which was that she was afraid to admit she wanted to have sex. She said when she'd told him that wasn't it, that she was unhappy with her looks and didn't agree with the way her parents viewed certain things, he told her she looked mighty fine to him. He forced himself on her multiple times during her stay. He was brutal." Starting to cry, Buddy said, "My poor Myrtle. She was sixteen years old, wanting to marry me, and was raped by a man in a position of authority over her who was at least twice her age. And then, she ended up pregnant by him…."

"What about the baby?"

"She wanted to give it up for adoption, but her mama and daddy wouldn't hear of it. They were sort of crazy about religion. They said God had allowed the baby to be conceived for a reason, so they'd keep it and raise it themselves. They hid her away until Sandra was born." Wiping at his eyes, he confided, "Myrtle said it took days for Sandra to come. She said it was like a never-ending torture and that she begged her parents to take her to a hospital. They told her they couldn't, and that once the baby came, all of the sadness Myrtle had felt before would come out of her, too. She said the odd thing was that they were right. She was so relieved to deliver the baby that she believed them and let go of the severe depression she'd had the year before. It was like she'd been freed from it. The only problem was that she was never able to let any man touch her like a husband should."

"Are you telling me you never had sex with your wife?"

"No, I never did. I suggested we talk to a counselor about it, but she was opposed to seeing a therapist of any kind. You can understand why. I loved her, so I just made up my mind that sex wasn't going to be part of our marriage."

Things were falling into place in Sean's head, but there were still missing pieces. He needed to know more.

"How did Myrtle feel about her daughter?"

"She loved her in a way, but it was difficult for her to have Sandra around. After her confession to me, Myrtle told me that Sandra took after her father with her looks and personality. She

41

was slim and athletically built and was what they'd call ADHD today. She was real pretty and knew it. She made sure boys knew it, too."

"How old was Sandra when you started sleeping with her?"

"We were only together one day. She'd turned eighteen the week before. I was doing some work on the Aurora house, and the rest of the family had gone to visit an older relative in a town four hours away. Sandra had said she didn't feel well and asked to stay home. They knew I'd be there with her, so they said it would be fine."

"Did she come on to you or did you come on to her?" Sean asked, trying unsuccessfully to keep the anger out of his voice.

"I was working on a piece of rotting trim in the master bedroom. She came in wrapped up in a robe. I found out soon enough there was nothing else underneath."

"So, you slept with your wife's daughter, the one your wife couldn't hardly look at because she'd been the product of a rape and looked and acted like her father?"

"Sean, I made a mistake. I was in my thirties, had been married for years, and had never had sex with my own wife, whom I loved dearly. Sandra was quite good at knowing what to do when it came to sex. Once we got started, I couldn't stop."

"Did you regret it?"

"I regret that it happened with Sandra. I didn't regret the sex."

"So, Sandra not-so-conveniently ends up pregnant. I bet her crazy religious parents were thrilled," Sean said sarcastically. "You didn't wonder if it was your baby?"

"Of course I wondered. I asked her if it was mine. She said she didn't know, that she'd slept with someone else on her birthday and that it could be his. She said it didn't matter, since she wasn't going to tell anyone who might be the father. She told me she'd had sex with lots of the boys in her junior class, so everyone would suspect all of them. They'd never consider me or the other man."

"Other man?"

Buddy nodded and said, "She was proud of the fact that she'd seduced me and another older man, although she'd told me that he wasn't as old as I was. When I pressed her for details, she insisted she'd never tell and that I'd always wonder if that day we'd spent together had led to the creation of the baby she was going to keep and love. That was when she told me she'd figured out that Myrtle was her mother, although she didn't know who her father was. I certainly didn't tell her. I couldn't say to the girl that her father had been a rapist."

"What happened when she found out about the leukemia?"

"She said no one was going to murder her baby. Of course, her very devout, supposed parents agreed. She refused all medical treatment until after Prim was born. By then it was too late. Myrtle's parents were in bad shape physically, and Myrtle told me she wanted to take care of her granddaughter the way she'd never been able to take care of her own child. We became her legal guardians, but Myrtle insisted she didn't want to adopt the baby. She said it was her daughter's child. What she didn't realize was that Prim was also possibly my child. I never told her."

"Did you ever consider genetic testing?"

"That wasn't readily available at that time."

"It is now. Don't you want to know?"

"It wouldn't change anything," Buddy said resignedly. "I love Prim like she's my own daughter, whether she really is or not. What good would it do to share all of this with her? It's a lot of old pain that's best left alone."

"Except somehow it hasn't left her alone. I don't know what happened, Buddy. Maybe Myrtle told her things that scared her or maybe she found some old letters or something." Sean drained his soda bottle and said, "I love your niece, your niece who has no idea who her father is or what's causing her such distress."

"Why won't you tell me what's wrong with my Prim?"

"Why won't you tell Prim the truth?" Sean stood and announced, "I have to go."

"It was real good to be able to tell someone," the older man admitted. "I've had a lot of years to keep all that tucked inside."

"Talk to Prim."

Buddy looked away and said, "I'll think on it."

"Don't think on it too long. Prim needs to know. She *deserves* to know."

"I said I'd think on it."

"Do right by Prim," Sean snapped. "I'll show myself out."

43

Chapter Four

Prim stood stunned in her uncle's backyard. Caleb had been forced to cancel their meeting because a church member had called him saying that she and her family were in crisis and needed spiritual guidance. Prim had decided to surprise her uncle by appearing at his house for dinner. She'd expected the usual reaction whenever she dropped by in the evenings– a warm welcome and an invitation to join him for dinner, conversation, or watching television.

That night, she'd stepped up to the screen door on his front porch and heard talking coming from the back of the house. She'd gone around to stand close to the screen door and arrived just in time to hear her uncle telling Sean the story of his life with her aunt, the secret of Prim's mother's paternity, and the possibility that Buddy was her father and not merely her uncle. She'd been horrified by all of it but found herself immobilized by curiosity and the need to know the truth.

Prim could tell by the way Sean was talking that he was furious with her uncle, although Buddy didn't seem to catch on to this. She could also tell that Sean hadn't shared her own secret fears with Buddy. She wasn't surprised by this; she trusted Sean implicitly. He was an honorable man and would never do anything that might harm her. When he'd told her he loved her, she *felt* his sincerity.

At that moment, Sean was the only person Prim truly trusted other than Remy, who had been like a big brother to her for as long as she could recall. Everyone in her family had lied to her from the day she'd been born. What had happened to her aunt when she'd been sixteen had evidently spilled over to Prim. Except for the conversation they'd had when Prim was thirteen, Prim honestly couldn't remember the woman ever telling her that sex was bad. Yet, Myrtle must have said or done something to make Prim feel such fear at the thought of having a man come into physical contact with her. At least now she understood why Myrtle had such an aversion to therapists.

When Sean left her uncle's house, Prim waited for a minute then crept back to the front. Once she was certain Sean was nowhere in sight, Prim hurried back to the Aurora family home.

She walked through the house, switching on the lights in each room and pulling all the drapes. Once every light was on, she returned to the front door and stood contemplating her next move. She dug into her purse, withdrew a hair tie, and then pulled her hair into a ponytail. As she did so, she decided she was going to go through each room in the house with great care and dissect any memories she had that might pertain to what Buddy had said or to her own irrational fears.

As she changed into jeans, a sweatshirt, and tennis shoes, Prim reflected that it had been for the best that she and Sean hadn't gotten around to starting her clearinghouse project. She'd discussed her plans with him the month before, but he'd been busy with Kensington business and she'd been busy with Prim's Corner business, Aurora Hardware business, and Aurora town business. They'd agreed to start going through the Aurora home the first Sunday in October, which was that upcoming weekend. She'd hated to put it off, but now she was happy that they'd had to wait.

Prim started with the formal living room. It didn't take her long to look through the drawer of the antique writing desk and examine the furnishings and portraits. She soon moved on to the kitchen.

Every dish, pot, glass, serving bowl, baking sheet, and utensil was removed from its resting place and spread out on top of the worn table. When she ran out of room, she began to put things on the floor. This took quite some time, as the old kitchen was large. When all of the white cabinets and drawers had been emptied, Prim walked slowly through the maze of items and examined them. She thought of the time she'd spent in the kitchen, cooking with her aunt and uncle, and tears flooded her eyes.

Feeling conflicted and alone, Prim suddenly found she was filled with rage. She took the ceramic pitcher she held in her hands and threw it across the room. It shattered when it hit the floor.

Once she got started, she couldn't stop. Soon, anything breakable that had existed in the Aurora kitchen lay in pieces. Prim stood, shaking and breathing hard, as she surveyed the damage. She experienced an odd sense of triumph, combined with anguish, as she scanned the floor. All of the cookware and dinnerware she'd cherished for so many years was no more.

She went to the dining room and proceeded to smash every piece of china before moving on. She didn't bother going into the family room. She had redone that room when she'd moved back into the old home the previous year and knew exactly what was in it. There would be no answers in her furniture, entertainment center, electronics, CDs, DVDs, or books.

Pausing, Prim stood outside the downstairs bathroom and wondered if she should proceed upstairs or go out to the enormous two-car garage and storage area that sat behind the house. She chose the latter and was soon sorting through decades of clutter. She was both frustrated and amazed at the sheer volume of what had been crammed into the place. No wonder no one had been able to park in the garage since before she'd been born.

By the time she left the old building, the sun was up. Going back inside, Prim crunched across the debris in the kitchen and got two bottles of water out of the refrigerator, taking them up to the second floor with her. She made quick work of the two bathrooms before going to what had once been her grandparents' bedroom. The maple furniture was over a hundred years old and was in wonderful shape. She painstakingly went through the drawers of the nightstand, the little desk in the corner, the large dresser, and the armoire. She found unimportant papers that related to business and personal matters, Bibles, and little else.

Moving on to what had been her uncle and aunt's room when they'd come back to the Aurora home, Prim performed a methodical search. She went through everything Buddy had left when he'd returned to the little house he and Myrtle bought after their marriage. They'd lived there until Prim's birth then had rented the place out for the next twenty-three years until Myrtle's death. Buddy hadn't taken much with him when he'd gone.

Prim sighed. There was nothing outstanding in their room either. She went back to her dead mother's bedroom and looked through everything. She'd already seen the trophies and medals and photos, but she hadn't gone through Sandra's drawers. Again, there was nothing remarkable there. It wasn't until she looked under the bed that she came across a book resting against the wall.

The pink, leather-bound book was covered in dust. It had probably fallen back there while her mother was still alive and had been pushed into oblivion by the dust mop Myrtle always used for cleaning under the beds. Prim blew the dust off the cover and sneezed before the imprint in the leather caught her eye: Diary.

Prim sat on the quilted peach bedspread and stared at the journal. Barely able to breathe, she opened it and read:

Dear Diary,

I've never had a diary before, and I don't know if I'll keep this one up. I figure I'll try since it's my eighteenth birthday, and my sister, Myrtle, gave it to me. I appreciated the gift. I know she finds it hard to be around me. I know why, but no one else in Aurora seems to have figured it out. I wonder who my daddy is, but I'll never ask Myrtle. If she can't even look at me when we're alone, then I'm thinking it was some boy who forced himself on her. If I was Uncle Buddy's baby, then she'd love me.

Everyone in town thinks my grandparents are my parents. I don't know how they could be so <u>stupid</u>. I mean, come on! I don't look anything like either of them and don't look like Myrtle. I guess I take after my daddy, whoever he was.

Whatever. It doesn't matter about any of it, because I'm going to go to school this year and then move away to Atlanta. I want to be a singer. Everyone says I have the voice of an angel. It makes me smile, because I don't like to act like an angel. I like to party with my friends, to sneak out at night, and to sleep with boys. I know how to use my body to make them and me feel so good.

Today for my birthday I gave myself a special present. We had a family dinner with a cake and presents. Then I went out with Mae, LouAnn's little sister. She's about as naughty as I am. Ha! We split up at a party, and I ended up doing something I've never done before. I had sex with a MAN. It was so cool and amazing! He knew what he was doing and made me feel so awesome! We did it FOREVER. I didn't want it to end.

I got home late and got yelled at for that. I didn't care. It was totally worth it. It was my best birthday present ever!
Sandra

There was no date on the next entry, but Prim didn't need a date. It read:

Dear Diary,
It's been less than a week since my awesome birthday, and I got another present. Myrtle, Momma, and Poppa all went to see some old cousin out of town, and I made up an excuse not to go. Buddy was here working on the house, and I walked into Momma and Poppa's room in my robe and wearing nothing underneath. Buddy may be older but he's certainly not old and is in great shape. I've always thought he was hot and figured why not see if he'd want to do it with me? Well, he did, although at first he said he couldn't. I can be <u>very</u> convincing. We did it all day in Momma and Poppa's bed, which gave me great satisfaction. I made sure to change the sheets afterwards. <u>They</u> probably haven't done it since Momma got pregnant with Myrtle. They think sex is just something people do to keep the human race going. They're so crazy when it comes to the way they think things should be. I feel sorry for them.
I am kind of jealous of Myrtle though. I wish I could sleep with Buddy every night, although he says that what we did was a mistake and we can't ever do it again. We both promised we'd never tell anyone. Myrtle may not love me because of how she got me, but I don't want to hurt her by telling her I slept with her husband.
Like I said, it was so totally amazing. To think I've slept with two MEN in one week. It's so different from sleeping with boys. I can't wait until I move away and can have sex with real MEN more often. Wow.
Sandra

The next entry read:

Dear Diary,
I bought one of those tests from the store, and it says I'm pregnant. I guess I got a bigger surprise as a birthday present than I'd counted on. I told Momma and Poppa and got a HUGE lecture on sin. I almost laughed in their faces. If they only knew what I'd done to get my baby! I don't even know which man is the

48

father! I'm not going to tell anyone about who my baby's daddy might be. Let them wonder. Everyone at school knows how I like sex, so every boy in my class will be a suspect. Ha!

I'm going to have my baby and take her away from here with me. I know it's going to be a girl; I can tell. I already have a name picked out for her. I'm going to call her Primrose and nickname her Prim. I've never known anyone with that name or read about anyone with that name, so it will be extra-special just like she'll be. I can't wait to feel her moving inside me and to have her and hold her in my arms. She's going to be beautiful.

Sandra

The following entry read:

Dear Diary,

Very bad news. I've been crying for days. Old Doc Stanford says I have leukemia. I have to start treatment right away if I want to live. But if I do that it'll slowly kill my Prim. How could I torture my baby like that? That would be HORRIBLE!

Myrtle actually told me to have an abortion so I'd have a chance to live. Maybe she does love me in some way. I won't do it, but I thought it was nice of her to care.

Momma and Poppa agree with me that I can't have an abortion. I knew they would. God's will be done and all that. I don't care about God's will. I'm Prim's mama and have to protect her. So, I won't have any treatment or anything until after she comes. Then we'll see. I hope I don't die, but the important thing is that she lives. I love her.

Sandra

What followed were dozens of entries detailing Sandra's deteriorating condition and bittersweet joy over the upcoming birth of her daughter. The final entry read:

Dear Diary,

My beautiful baby, Primrose, is here. Doc Stanford and the other doctors say it's too late for me. Oh, well. I've cried a lot about it. I want to see Prim grow up and raise her the way I want, but I guess I won't get the chance. I can only hope that she doesn't get all mixed up by Momma, Poppa, and Myrtle. Buddy will make sure she's taken care of, especially since he doesn't know if she's his daughter or not.

My Prim is so perfect. She's my baby. I don't understand how Myrtle couldn't love me no matter what my daddy did. It wasn't my fault he hurt her. I wish she could have seen that.

I pray that Prim will grow up smart and sweet and find a nice man who'll love her for her beautiful self. I want her to know real love, not just sex. I want her to have both. I think love and sex together would be the most wonderful thing a man and woman could ever have. I wish I'd had it.

I wish I'd had longer to write in you, Diary. I've almost filled you up. I could have bought more diaries and filled them with stories about my little girl. Maybe someday she'll find this and know how much I loved her and how I didn't ever want to leave her.

There was no signature on the final page. Prim's shoulders shook as she cried. She shut the diary lest her tears smudge the ink.

Holding the book against her chest, Prim went to her own room and lay on her bed. She felt so sorry for her mother and for herself. What a cruel twist of fate that Sandra had slept with so many boys only to get pregnant the week of her eighteenth birthday and then to die the week before she turned nineteen. She'd left her daughter in a seemingly stable household that was really a place filled with oddness and deception.

Rising from the bed, Prim slipped her mother's diary into the drawer on her nightstand and went to her closet. She pulled out her old toy box and opened it. Perhaps looking at some of her favorite childhood toys would make her feel comforted.

She knelt on the floor and began to take out the toys one by one. There was a Raggedy Ann doll, some Hello Kitty paraphernalia, a few Hot Wheels cars, a stuffed unicorn, a rubber ball, a teddy bear, a princess doll, and Kim and Tim.

Kim and Tim were Barbie and Ken rip-offs. Prim wasn't certain where they'd come from, but she had loved playing house with the couple. She smiled as she remembered the imaginary world they lived in where Kim was a teacher and Tim was a veterinarian. They'd lived in a house Buddy had built for them that had long ago gotten buried in the junk heap in the garage. In Kim and Tim's world, their little house was filled with love and lots of animals.

Prim instantly felt as though she'd been slammed into solid rock. She was five years old and decided to change Kim and Tim's clothes from their "work" outfits to their "casual" outfits. Something made her stop when the dolls were undressed, and she stared at the plastic figures. A friend of hers in kindergarten had told her that men and women liked to kiss and touch without their clothes on. Well, that's what her friend's older sister had told her. So, Prim decided Kim and Tim should do this, since they were married and lived happily with all of their animals in their little house.

Prim was suddenly jerked up by Aunt Myrtle, who demanded to know what she was doing. Although she was never overly demonstrative, her aunt had never gotten angry with her in the past, and Prim began to cry. Myrtle roughly shook her and repeated her question. When Prim explained what Kim and Tim were doing, her aunt actually yelled at her and said that all men wanted to do when they touched women was to make themselves happy and that it didn't matter if it hurt the women or not. She said that even if a woman begged for a man to stop hurting her, he might not and then there would be terrible pain. She cried that she didn't want any man to ever hurt Prim. The normally gentle woman was screaming, and Prim was terrified. Myrtle ordered Prim to remember what she'd said. Then she practically dropped Prim on the ground and fled the room, leaving the little girl bruised and sobbing.

Prim blinked and was back in the present. She'd always questioned people she'd seen on television who'd said they'd blocked out traumatic memories and had then spontaneously recalled them. She wouldn't doubt anymore. She had actually *been* five again and had just relived the entire harrowing event.

Prim stared down at Kim and Tim. How had her brain managed to eradicate the incident with her aunt? How could she not remember it every time she played with the dolls or changed their clothes? Her mind had obviously protected itself very well from the disturbing episode with Myrtle.

Prim left the toys on the floor as she got unsteadily to her feet. There was one room she hadn't explored, yet. It was the only place in the house she'd still never been. Her aunt and uncle had always told her it wasn't safe in the attic and that she shouldn't ever go there. Prim had heeded those words – even after she'd become an adult. She was now done with being obedient to those who had lied to her and frightened her.

She went out into the hallway and walked to the door at the far end. She opened and closed it; then she switched on the light so she could climb the steps that led up to the attic. Prim was terrified, but she pushed herself to keep putting one foot in front of the other and ascend.

The place was cluttered and dusty. Prim began to open boxes and remove their contents. When she reached an over-sized weathered trunk in one of the farthest corners of the room, she lifted the lid and screamed.

Chapter Five

It had been a stressful Friday for Sean at the Kensington Academy. He'd been forced to expel a student for bringing drugs on campus. He'd also been compelled to immediately suspend a teacher for making an inappropriate comment about a student's ethnic heritage until the Board of Directors could investigate and make a final determination about the teacher's career at the school. Maureen had called in sick that morning, so that had slowed him down immeasurably. Plus, he hadn't been able to reach Prim all day.

Sean had phoned her at lunch, but the voicemail at Prim's Corner picked up after the fourth ring. He'd left a detailed message, asking that she call him back. When he still hadn't heard from her by 3:00, he'd tried again and had gotten the voicemail once more. He'd then tried her cellphone but got that voicemail as well. A part of him wanted to believe she was so busy with work that she hadn't had time to return his calls before he left the campus at 5:30, but another part of him was worried. Prim *always* called him back, even if it was only for a quick chat.

They were supposed to meet for dinner at LouAnn's at 6:30. Sean drove straight home, changed into jeans, a long-sleeved shirt, and tennis shoes before walking to the Town Square. As he approached the restaurant, he saw Remy and hailed him.

"Where are you headed?" Remy asked him once they were close enough to talk.

"I'm supposed to meet Prim at LouAnn's in a few minutes."

"Really? I figured she was sick or something. Her shop was closed all day." When Sean remarked he hadn't known this and explained that he'd been unable to contact Prim, Remy asked, "You think she's okay?"

"I don't know. I've had a bad feeling ever since lunch. Prim always calls me back when I leave her a message, and she didn't today. Maybe she is sick or hurt and needs help. I think I'll make sure she hasn't been in LouAnn's and then head over to her place."

"I'll come with you."

"You don't have to do that."

"I've known Prim her whole life. I want to make certain she's all right."

After LouAnn verified she hadn't seen Prim all day, the two men thanked her and headed for the Aurora family home. As they walked, Remy asked, "You have a key?"

"No."

"I didn't think so, but I figured I'd ask."

"What do you mean you didn't think so?"

"My little brother went out with her a few times. He told me she wouldn't even hold hands with him, much less kiss him. He said she was like that with all the boys. They still asked her out, but they knew nothing romantic was ever going to come of it."

"And nobody thought that was odd?"

"They just accepted it. I personally wondered if someone had molested her, but that was pure supposition on my part. I was her classmate's older brother. What was I going to do, go to the police and tell them what I thought even though there wasn't a shred of proof?" He shook his head and went on, "Prim is sweet, smart, pretty, and giving. I was so glad when the two of you got together and then I'd see you walking hand-in-hand and thought that maybe you'd managed to break down whatever barriers Prim had put up to keep men away."

"But?"

"But I haven't seen the two of you kiss or hug and decided you hadn't been able to wear down her defenses enough, yet. I've been praying you could reach her. You're probably the best friend I've ever had, Sean. Prim's been my friend for years. I want to see both of you happy."

"Thanks. I want that, too. I wish you could find a special someone."

"Someday, I hope."

When they reached the front door of the Aurora home, Sean knocked. No one responded. After a few minutes of knocking, the two men agreed to go around to the back and see if they could get better results there.

"Try the door handle," Remy suggested.

"The front door was locked. What makes you think this one will be open?"

"It's a small town. Some people have a false sense of security."

Prim was obviously not one of those people. The door was locked.

"What do you want to do now?" Remy asked. "Even though the curtains are drawn, you can see cracks of light everywhere. Prim's car is here. Do you want to call the police or just break in?"

"What?"

"We could just break in. It'd be easy."

"How do you know that?"

"Because I did it a couple of times when I was in high school and my drunk parents were too out of it to notice we had no food. I broke into a couple of places and stole some food for my brother and me, although I'll deny it if you ever tell anyone that. I never got caught, and no one suspected me, the school geek and model student, of being a thief."

Sean pondered his options for a few seconds then said, "Do it."

Remy took off his Oxford shirt, removed the t-shirt he was wearing underneath and passed it to Sean before donning the shirt again and buttoning it. He did not tuck it in. He then took the t-shirt back from Sean, wrapped it around his right hand, and brought it up to the pane of glass that was just above the door handle. The third time he hit the pane, it shattered. Carefully using his wrapped hand to push out any remaining glass, Remy explained to Sean that shards could be extremely damaging.

"I think you did this more than a couple of times," Sean said wryly.

Ignoring this remark, his friend said, "Let's hope the locks don't require a key to be opened from the inside." Remy eased his hand through the hole and reached down then smiled and said, "We're in luck. Both of them can be turned manually."

Once this task had been completed, Remy withdrew his hand and painstakingly unwrapped it before dropping the t-shirt onto the ground beside the steps. Then he turned the handle and pushed. Both men heard the sound of broken...something being moved back as the door was forced open. They stepped inside and stood stunned as they viewed the condition of the kitchen.

"Holy crap," muttered Remy. "What happened here?"

"Prim!" Sean called out, as he began to race forward. When Remy grabbed him by the arm, he growled, "I have to find Prim! If someone broke in here while she was home, then she could be hurt or worse!"

"And if they're still here, then they could do the same to us and that wouldn't help Prim any." Bending down, Remy lifted a steak knife and a carving knife from the pile of utensils and handed the former to Sean before saying, "We should stick together."

The two men hastily searched the first floor. As they approached the stairs, Sean said, "Why all the destruction in the kitchen and dining room but nowhere else? If someone was out to loot the place, they would have taken stuff and not destroyed it all. And why not take or smash the electronics Prim has in the family room?"

"I know. It doesn't make any sense. The formal living room didn't look that bad, and the bathroom seemed untouched."

They found the scattered papers and other articles in the upstairs bedrooms and the toys on the floor in Prim's closet. Sean wondered aloud where Prim could be, and Remy suggested they try the attic. If she wasn't there, then he proposed they go out to the garage.

They went to the only door they hadn't opened, and Sean reached for the handle. His heart was pounding, and he and Remy held their knives at the ready in case intruders lunged out at them. None did.

"At least the light's working," commented Remy in a hushed voice. "Man, I'm shaking like a leaf."

"Me, too," Sean whispered back. "But we've made it this far without running into any madmen wearing Halloween masks, right?"

"Thanks for the mental picture," Remy grumbled, as he followed Sean up the stairs.

At first, the attic appeared deserted. There were numerous boxes, but neither man saw or heard anything moving. Sean edged forward, glancing nervously around as he went. He was halfway through the room when he saw Prim's profile in the dim light.

She was sitting on the floor staring straight ahead with her back resting against a box. Sean rushed towards her as quickly as he could and called out to Remy that he'd found her. He heard the man close behind him and knew that at least someone would be there to help him fight off any attackers who might be hiding nearby.

Sean knelt beside Prim and gently murmured her name. She remained silent. Remy crouched on her other side and asked her if she was all right. She shook her head very slightly and said flatly, "There's a dead person in the trunk."

The men looked at one another then back at Prim before slowly scanning the attic for a trunk. They saw it at the same time. The lid was closed.

"We have to look," Remy declared without much conviction in his tone.

Sean nodded, glanced at Prim, and said, "We do have to look, but I know I don't want to and neither do you."

"How about if we do it at the same time?"

Prim, who was still staring straight ahead, said quietly, "He's been dead for years. There's no blood or anything. It's just bones and clothes."

"We should get Prim out of here," Remy urged.

"After we look. We have to see what she saw before we call the police."

"You don't believe me," Prim said dully.

"I do," Sean insisted. "That's why I have to see."

He and Remy stood and walked over to the old trunk. With shaking hands, they reached out and lifted the lid.

"Oh, my God," Sean breathed. "Who? Why?"

"We probably shouldn't have touched the trunk," Remy said, his voice barely audible. "I am not believing this."

"Me neither." Sean looked at Prim and said, "We'll leave the trunk open and get her downstairs."

"Then we can call the police."

"Not yet."

"What do you mean not yet?"

"I want to talk to Prim first." Gesturing towards the trunk, Sean said, "He's not going anywhere. I want to find out what happened in the house today before we decide whom to call and when."

Remy considered Sean's words for a time; then he nodded and went back over to Prim. Crouching beside her again, he asked if she wanted help standing. She shook her head and continued to sit and stare at nothing in particular.

"I think she's in shock," Sean offered, as he sat beside her. He wanted more than anything to take her in his arms and to brush the hair from her eyes. As he studied her, he noted that her skin and clothing were smudged with dirt and something resembling oil.

"Were you in the garage, too?"

She nodded then said, "I remembered what made me afraid of men, Sean."

The two men looked at each other over her head, but there was no verbal exchange between them.

"I remembered," Prim repeated.

"That's good," Sean said reassuringly. "That'll help."

"I think it already has. I want to…I want you to hold me."

"Are you sure?"

"I want to try. Will you let go if I can't do it?"

"I'll do whatever you ask."

Prim looked up at Remy and inquired, "You won't tell anyone anything, will you? I don't want you to leave either, but I don't want anyone to find out about anything…about my…about what happened."

"I won't tell and won't leave."

She thanked him as Sean edged closer to her. He brought one arm around her shoulders and lightly rested his hand on her upper arm. She was trembling but didn't push him away. Instead, she turned towards him and pressed her cheek against his chest while tucking her arms and legs close to her body. Sean brought his other arm around her and cradled her against him while she sobbed and told the two men everything, from the conversation she'd accidentally overheard the previous night between Sean and Buddy to her search of the house and what she'd found and remembered.

As she talked, Remy dropped his head and stood. Then he walked back over to the open trunk. Sean watched him as he continued to hold Prim. The man was studying the corpse, even though Sean could tell the sight was repugnant to him. He realized that Remy was trying to discern the cause of the man's death and wondered if there were any visible signs.

Sean looked down at Prim and reached across to push some of the errant strands of strawberry blonde hair away from her face.

He'd expected her to protest but was pleasantly surprised when she reacted by lowering her knees and placing her hands on his chest. When he kissed the top of her head, she slipped her arms around his waist and tightly hugged him.

Offering a silent prayer of thanks, Sean looked up at Remy, who was smiling at him. The man came back over to where he and Prim sat on the floor and tentatively laid his palm on the back of Prim's head before telling her that everything would be fine and that she was going to be all right now. She sagged against Sean.

"We have to call the police," Sean told her. "Do you want us to call Buddy?"

"No," she said quietly. "I can't see him right now."

"He's probably going to try to come explain things to you," Remy pointed out. "He'll want to tell you his side of the story."

"I can't see him. If he comes, then I'll want him to go away."

"What about Caleb? He's always good in a crisis situation."

"No. I don't want anybody else."

"I think we should call Dr. Stanford," Sean told her. "You've had a bad shock and might have hurt yourself in the kitchen or garage. He needs to check you out."

She told him she didn't want to go to Dr. Stanford's office and couldn't stay in the Aurora family home any longer. The problem was that she didn't know where else to go.

"I have a guest bedroom," Sean reminded her. "You can stay at my place and sleep in my room, and I'll take the guest room. I'm sure Dr. Stanford would come to see you there."

Prim agreed to this but declared she needed Remy to stay with her, too. When he suggested that he could sleep on Sean's couch, she relaxed slightly and told him how grateful she was to have a friend like him.

The two men helped Prim to stand, and she leaned heavily against Sean as they went down the attic stairs to the second floor. At her request, Remy went to her bedroom and removed the diary, placing it in her purse. Sean sat with her on the couch in the family room while Remy called the authorities and the doctor.

The Chief of Police, Byron Peters, was at the Aurora home within minutes. Byron was an African-American man who was probably younger than Sean. He was not overly chatty but personable and seemed to have an excellent ability to direct his men and coordinate their activities. According to Remy, he was also very adept at calming distraught crime victims.

Byron took one look at Prim and assessed her physical and mental condition before taking a seat across from her. He asked her in a soft, congenial tone if she needed anything before they started talking about what had happened in her house. The tension in Prim seemed to ease somewhat, and she told Byron everything she'd told Sean and Remy, excluding the finding of her mother's diary and the recollection of the blocked memory.

"People trust Byron," Remy told Sean later. "They know he'll do his job without gossiping. He'll make something a matter of public record if need be, but he'll keep everything else confidential. Unless he decides to move on, he'll most likely be Aurora's Chief of Police until he retires."

Dr. Stanford arrived as Byron was standing to check on the progress of his men and to meet with the coroner, who was up in the attic with the mystery man's body. The two men shook hands before Byron excused himself from the room. Then the internist came over to Prim, taking in her appearance and the fact that she was practically clinging to Sean.

"Prim? What happened here?"

"Could you talk to someone else? I'm so tired."

"How about if I give him an overview?" Remy volunteered. "He and I can talk in another room if you like."

Remy led the man out of the room. Sean knew that his friend would take the good doctor on a tour of the house so he could see what Prim had endured for the past twenty-four hours. It was the right thing to do. After all, Dr. Stanford was her physician and would need to know how best to approach his patient's overall care.

When they returned an hour later, Prim was sleeping in Sean's arms. The exhaustion had finally won out, and Sean was relieved she was resting and that she showed no signs of reverting back to being fearful of having him touch her. He whispered this to Remy and Dr. Stanford, who sat in the two chairs across from the couch.

"She's been through hell," Stanford remarked. "I need to examine her. However, I don't think she should stay here any longer than she has to. Remy said you're taking her to your house and that the two of you are going to stay with her. I'll drive the three of you over there and then check her out. Has anyone called Buddy, yet?"

"Buddy's one of the last people she wants to see at this moment."

"Byron will be heading over there after he leaves here," Remy pointed out. "I think he's going to want to know if Buddy can explain the dead man in the attic."

"I do," Byron confirmed, as he stepped into the room. "We're getting everything ready to move the body, but we're leaving it in the trunk, which may contain valuable evidence. The Medical Examiner is going to have a look but will probably call in someone from Atlanta. He estimates the man's been dead for at least twenty years."

"And the cause of death?" Stanford asked.

"Officially undetermined until further examination. Unofficially, it looks like he suffered a blow to the head, but I want someone who's well-qualified to sign off on the exact cause." Facing Sean, he said, "You should get Prim out of here before we bring the corpse downstairs."

Sean gently woke Prim. Remy retrieved her purse, as Sean guided her to Dr. Stanford's SUV. He sat in the back with her while Remy took the passenger seat up front. Within two minutes the doctor was pulling his car into Sean's driveway. He drove around to the back, parking behind Sean's garage.

They entered the house through the back door and went straight to the living room. Dr. Stanford performed a cursory examination of Prim and noted that she had multiple scratches on her arms and one on her neck. She couldn't tell him what had made the marks, and they all speculated she'd sustained the wounds during her exploration of the cluttered garage. The internist then asked if his patient felt she was well enough to shower so he could examine her more thoroughly and make certain he wasn't missing anything that might be covered by dirt or oil.

"I don't have any clean clothes with me."

"Byron said I could pack some articles for you while I was upstairs," the doctor told her. "I brought the little carry-on I found in your closet in with my medical bag. What's inside should get you through the weekend. While you shower, I'm going to run to the office. After being scraped up, you'll need a tetanus shot."

While the internist was gone, Prim showered and Sean put fresh sheets on his bed. The doctor returned as Prim came out of the bathroom wearing a pink robe. She went with the internist to the guest bedroom for a quick exam and emerged fifteen minutes later, rubbing her arm.

"That arm may be stiff for a day or so," Stanford was telling her. "Everything else looks good. Just continue to put the antibiotic ointment on those scratches and cuts until they've healed. If any of them start to look infected, don't hesitate to call me. I'll be checking on you tomorrow anyway, but that doesn't mean you can't call me during the night if you need to."

As Sean escorted Dr. Stanford to his car, he asked, "Is she okay?"

"Generally. We'll see how she is emotionally as the days pass. Physically, she'll be fine."

"Did you give her any special instructions or limitations?"

"Eat, drink, and try to relax all weekend. I gave her something to help her sleep."

"Thank you for everything."

"I'm relieved you and Remy are watching over her. Remy's been sort of a big brother to her ever since she was little, and she trusts him." Opening the driver's side door, he added, "She loves you, Sean. Remember what I said the other day. Be careful with her, especially now. She's in a very precarious place."

Sean returned to the house and found that Prim's eyelids were heavy. He took her to the master bedroom and helped her remove her robe. She was wearing a long, white nightgown underneath. She climbed into the bed, and he covered her with the sheets and comforter. The medication took effect so quickly that she was asleep within seconds.

When Sean went back to the kitchen, he discovered Remy had made them each a peanut butter and jelly sandwich. The two men sat at the dining room table with their food and glasses of milk and ate without speaking. The clock chimed midnight as they put their dishes and glasses in the sink.

"I'm going to stay in my room with Prim," Sean told his friend. "I don't want to leave her alone in there. I'll put my sleeping bag and a pillow on the floor. You take the guest bed."

"Are you sure?"

"Yes. You and I are almost the same size. You can wear some of my pajamas to bed, unless you'd rather sleep in your clothes."

"I'll take the pajamas." Pausing, Remy said, "I don't know what to do about tomorrow."

"What do you mean?"

"If Prim wants me to stay here, then I will. If she doesn't, then I don't know whether or not I should open my shop. What happened tonight regarding the discovery of the dead man is going to be all over town by mid-morning tomorrow. Byron will be tight-lipped about everything, but Prim's neighbors will have seen the police and coroner. If I don't open, then they may speculate that things are worse than they are. If I do open, then they'll be asking me what's going on." Sighing, he admitted, "I'm more concerned about dealing with Buddy. He's going to want to talk to Prim and smooth this over, and I honestly don't know if he can."

Sean reflected on this and said, "She'll want a DNA test and rightly so."

"What if he is her father?"

"What if he's not?"

They listened to the silence of the night as they pondered the ramifications of each scenario. Finally, Sean said, "I guess we'll have to see what the tests show. I'm also wondering who the guy in the trunk was."

"You're thinking the same thing I am," Remy suggested. "You think it's Sandra's father."

"What if it's Prim's father?" Shaking his head, Sean said, "I'm wiped. You want to shower tonight or tomorrow morning?"

"I'm ready to crash," Remy admitted. "I'll just get those pajamas and fall into bed if it's all the same to you."

"I think I'll shower now. Let me get us some pajama bottoms and undershirts. Will you watch over Prim while I do that and shower? Then we can both sleep."

Within thirty minutes, Remy lay sleeping in Sean's guest bed, while Sean lay awake in the sleeping bag on the master bedroom floor. He was beyond tired but couldn't shut off his brain. Too much had happened. There were too many unanswered questions. Eventually, he drifted off to sleep.

"Sean?"

Prim's voice instantly brought Sean awake. He told her he was there and stiffly got to his feet. Switching on the small lamp beside the bed, he squinted in the soft light. Prim looked fuzzily up at him and asked for some water. He'd been prepared for this request and had put a glass on the nightstand before he'd gotten into the sleeping bag. He helped her to sit up and drink. Then he lowered her back onto the pillow.

"Where are you sleeping?" she asked, as he put the glass back on the coaster. "Where is Remy?"

"I'm in a sleeping bag on the floor. I told Remy to take the guest bed."

"You can't sleep on the floor," she protested. "Will you sleep with me?"

"I don't think that's a good idea. You're medicated and have had a really traumatic day. I'm not going to take advantage of that. This isn't the time anyway."

"I don't mean I want to *sleep* with you. I can't go there, yet. But I would like to have you hold my hand while I sleep and not have you sleeping on the hard floor. I need you to take care of me for now."

Sean smiled down at her and said, "*That* I can do."

He retrieved his sleeping bag and walked around to the other side of the bed. Then he climbed onto the comforter and pulled the bag on top of him. The moment he took Prim's hand in his, she fell back to sleep.

Prim looked so beautiful and fragile, and Sean alternately adored and detested it. Part of him wanted to envelop her in a protective embrace and never let go. The other part of him was hard and ready and wanted to bury itself deep within her.

Remember what Dr. Stanford told you, he reminded himself. *Even when you do make love to her, it's going to be dicey. How is she going to react to your touching her like that much less –*

There was a knock on the front door of his house. Sean glanced at the clock and saw that it was a few minutes after 6:00. He got up, padded through the house, and then peered out the front window. Byron stood on the porch, and Sean immediately opened the door and invited the man inside. Byron's expression was grim, and Sean's stomach muscles tightened. He asked Byron to have a seat, and the police chief suggested they talk in the dining room.

Once they were seated, Sean asked the man to tell him the reason for his visit.

"I'll start with the easy part," Byron told him. "I had my men clean up Prim's house. It's taken them all night, but the broken stuff has been picked up and taken to the curb for the garbage men. I'm glad today's garbage pick-up in this area of town. There was a heck of a lot of broken ceramic and glass."

"That was nice of you."

Byron shrugged and said, "Prim's only a few years younger than me. She's a real sweet girl, but everyone knew that as nice as the Auroras were, something was wrong in that house. The fact that she wouldn't let any boy touch her made anyone who knew her wonder, but no one ever did anything. She was so good-natured and likable that everyone sort of pretended it wasn't wrong somehow."

"Did everybody in town know about Prim and her inability to be touched by guys?"

"No. It was only when she was in high school and was asked out on dates that her classmates found out. My brother went out with her off and on for over a year, but he knew they were just hanging out." When he saw the expression on Sean's face, he asked, "You don't think black boys date white girls?"

"I'm a city boy, and I've dated white, black, Hispanic, and Asian girls. It wasn't a big deal where I lived. But in Aurora? I wouldn't have figured small-town Georgia would be that liberal even today."

"Aurora's a little different. If it wasn't, then a black guy like me wouldn't have become Chief of Police at age twenty-seven. I want to take care of everyone in our town to the best of my ability."

"I can see why Remy said so many people like you. You really care about your neighbors." He went on, "You didn't come over here this early to tell me about cleaning up the mess at Prim's."

Byron looked solemnly back at him and said, "No, I didn't. After I left the Aurora home, I went over to Buddy Brown's place to talk to him about the man in the trunk. I may not know the identity of the corpse, but I talked to the M.E. about the blow to the head. He said it looks like the man had been hit with the claw end of a hammer. He said he'd studied a case in medical school where the wound was similar and a claw hammer was the weapon used to kill the victim. So, I'm thinking Buddy's family has been in construction since the dawn of time and that he runs a hardware store. I'm thinking Buddy might have a real good idea about how this guy died and who he was."

"Did he?"

"I don't know. When I got to his house, he wouldn't come to the door. I went around to the back and knocked, and he didn't answer that door either. However, that door was unlocked. So, one of my men and I went in to make sure he was all right. We found him on the floor of the kitchen. The M.E. will have to do an autopsy, but it looks like he had a heart attack to me. He could have swallowed pills, but we didn't find any bottles in the house other than over-the-counter medications. You never know." Shooting a glance at the doorway, he said, "I called Dr. Stanford. He met with the M.E. at Buddy's. He'll be coming here next. I think I should be the one to tell Prim, but I wanted you, Remy, and her doctor here when I do. With everything that's happened in the last couple of days, I don't know how Prim's going to react to this. Dr. Stanford's her physician, and Remy's been like a brother to her since she was little. It's pretty clear how you and she feel about each other." Looking hard at Sean, he asked, "You're not going to disappoint her and bail, are you?"

Sean replied indignantly that he had no intentions of "bailing" on Prim.

"I had to ask," Byron said quickly. "You're the principal at the Kensington Academy, and I didn't know how you felt about all this and your career."

"In the first place, I care more about Prim than my career. Second, how would any of this affect my career anyway? It's not like my girlfriend killed the man in the trunk. He's probably been dead longer than she's been alive."

"Some rich people don't want any idea of scandal, no matter what the circumstance is. After what happened with the last principal, they're kind of jumpy from what I understand."

"I was hired to fix that, and I've been doing a damned good job of it. If the Board even tried to approach me about this and suggest that my association with Prim was somehow damaging to the school, then they'd be in for a legal battle that would blow their minds. I really don't think they're that stupid. I'm a fixer, and they know I wouldn't do anything that might tarnish their image."

"What if you had no choice? What if they told you it was Prim or Kensington?"

"I'd resign."

"That's what I wanted to hear. I had to make sure you were on the up and up."

"I'll wake Remy so we can both be dressed and ready when the doctor arrives."

"Good idea. I'm going to make a few calls while you do that."

Remy was unsurprisingly stunned when Sean told him about Buddy. As the man reached for his jeans and one of Sean's shirts, he said, "I'm definitely not going to work today. Jeez. This is like something out of an episode of *CSI*. I feel so bad for Prim."

Sean quietly went into his room and withdrew clean jeans from his dresser and a shirt from the closet. He stopped on his way out of the room and looked at Prim, who was sleeping peacefully in his bed. Grimacing at the thought of what lay ahead for her, he took his clothes to the guest room and dressed while Remy showered. He suspected it was going to be a difficult Saturday.

Chapter Six

As Byron told her that her uncle was dead, Prim sat on Sean's couch with Sean and Remy flanking her and Dr. Stanford sitting in the recliner. She was too numb to shed any tears. All she could do was to listen as he explained. When he finished speaking, she asked, "Did he suffer?"

"If he did, it wasn't for long," Dr. Stanford commented. "It looks like he had a stroke or heart attack and went quickly."

"That's good. I wouldn't want him to suffer." Clearing her throat, she inquired, "Can you tell if he was my daddy even though he's...gone?"

"The Medical Examiner's already taken samples from Buddy," Byron told her. "All we need is a cheek swab from you, and then we can send the materials to a lab for the DNA test and genetic profiling."

"Will you do DNA testing on the man I found in the trunk?"

"We're going to have to. I'll use the results and compare them with yours and Buddy's."

"Can you tell what killed the man?"

"It looks like a blow to the head." Chagrined, he asked, "I really hate to push you right now, but do you remember anything from when you were small that might have to do with this? Any altercations in the house or talk of an incident?"

"No. I was always told by Aunt Myrtle and Uncle Buddy not to go up in the attic because it wasn't safe, but that was it."

Byron stood and said, "You know how to find me if that changes. My men should be finished at your home by the end of the weekend. You can go back after that."

"I'm not going back," Prim said firmly. "I'll never be able to live there again. I don't want to."

"Are you planning on moving into Buddy's house?"

"I couldn't ever live there either. I think I'm going to move into the apartment above Prim's Corner and the hardware store. Remember when I redid that last year when the shop area was renovated? The apartment is over two thousand square feet and is plenty big for me. I had planned on renting it out, but I hadn't gotten around to it. Now, I'm glad I didn't."

"What about the old house and Buddy's place?"

"I know Uncle Buddy left me his house in his will. I'll sell both houses and invest the money until I decide what I want to do."

"Prim, let me advise you not to make any hasty decisions," Dr. Stanford remarked. "You're shocked, hurt, and probably very angry right now. This isn't the time to be making any life-altering changes."

"This is the perfect time. I just found out my whole life has been based upon lies. My grandparents and aunt, who was actually my grandmother, were obviously nice enough to others but were somewhat mentally unstable. Everyone excused their eccentricities because they were descendants of the founders of this town. I don't want any more to do with the Auroras' 'proud' heritage. I just want to be normal and to be able to let someone love me."

"Everyone in Aurora loves you," Remy told her. "You're an integral part of this town. You can't leave."

"I don't plan to leave. I love Aurora. That doesn't mean I don't want to be free of some of the worst parts of my family's history."

"What are you going to do with the hardware store now that your uncle's gone?" Sean asked. "That, Prim's Corner, and LouAnn's are sort of the social hub of the community."

"What about Caleb?" Byron proposed. "He's been talking about quitting the feed store for a while and is looking for something closer to the church. He knows his way around a hardware store and knows how to run a cash register. Plus, he knows everyone in town. Since he's a widower and never had kids, his only other obligation is to his congregation. I bet he'll jump at the chance."

"That sounds like an excellent idea," Sean volunteered. "You like Caleb, and I'd hope you'd trust a pastor with your money."

Prim thought about this and said, "It'd be perfect if Caleb's willing."

As she brought her hands up to massage her throbbing temples, she noted her fingers were shaking. The others obviously noticed it too.

"She has to eat," Dr. Stanford declared. "If what she told me last night was accurate, then I calculate she hasn't had any food in about forty hours now."

"I don't feel like eating," Prim announced. "My stomach hurts, and I feel dizzy and sick."

"Because your stomach is empty and your blood sugar is low," he countered. "Sean, do you have any soup?"

"I always keep a couple of cans of chicken noodle in the pantry."

Byron received a call from one of his men and had to leave, but Remy went to heat the soup while Sean held Prim as Dr. Stanford quickly checked on her various scrapes and took her temperature. His own cellphone rang, so he excused himself to take the call. He returned to the room and apologized, saying he had to leave to see to someone else's medical emergency. Before he departed, he made Prim promise to eat the soup and then return to bed once her food had time to digest.

"What about the shop?" she asked Sean and Remy after she ate. "I can't keep the hardware store and my shop closed indefinitely."

"No, but you can close both of them for a week," Sean told her. "People will understand, and your customers will come back."

"But how will I sell everything and the houses and run things and –"

"Prim, stop," Sean ordered gently. "We can help. You're not alone."

"But you have work and Remy has his own store and –"

"And we'll handle things with you," Remy said reassuringly. "Don't worry about anything except yourself."

She asked Sean if he would lie next to her again as she slept. Remy stayed with her while Sean went to put on his pajama bottoms and undershirt again. Then, Remy left to return to his own place but promised to come back with dinner later. He also promised to phone Caleb and give him general details about the body in the trunk and the death of Buddy Brown. His final promise was to go by Aurora Hardware and Prim's Corner to hang signs in the windows that declared both stores were closed for the week. Prim handed him her keys before he set off for the Town Square.

"Everyone's going to descend on him and want information," she told Sean once Remy had left. "I feel bad that I had to do that to him."

"You didn't do anything," he reminded her. "You're the victim here."

He led her to his bed and helped her to lie back on the pillow. As he prepared to climb on top of the comforter, she stopped him and asked if he would lie underneath the covers and hold her in his arms. When he asked her if she was certain that this was what she really wanted, she insisted, "I need you to hold me."

"Are you telling me that what you remembered about your aunt's outburst has somehow cured you of twenty years of fear regarding men and sex?"

"No. I'm still afraid of how I'll react to you kissing me or us…doing more. But you can touch me, Sean. You can hold me, kiss my head, and stroke my hair and it doesn't scare me at all. You can't imagine what a relief that is and how much it makes me think I can eventually do those other things with you. I *want* to do them with you, and I'm so afraid you won't wait."

"Prim, we've known each other for less than two months. Just because we fell in love quickly doesn't mean I think we have to have sex right away. Please, quit worrying about this." Kissing her on the forehead, he murmured, "I love you. That's the important part. Everything else will work itself out."

He gathered her up against him, and she fell asleep, feeling comforted and safe. When she woke, Sean was sleeping deeply beside her. She knew he had to be thoroughly exhausted. She didn't want to move much for fear of waking him.

Prim lay in Sean's embrace and reveled in the simple act of being that close to the man. Having her body so near to his was almost intoxicating. He shifted slightly in his sleep and mumbled her name. She smiled and then froze as she realized that her long nightgown had somehow crept up in her sleep and the naked flesh of her thigh was draped across the front of Sean's hips. She could feel his erection through the cotton of his pajama bottoms.

A part of her was terrified, while another part was intensely curious and excited. She had only seen a naked man in person

71

once when she'd taken an art class as an elective in college. The professor had live models come in for the sketching portion of the class. The female model was rather large and not conventionally beautiful, but she possessed an aura of loveliness that transcended society's traditional ideas of beauty. The male model, however, appeared to be the embodiment of sensuality and was tall, had well-defined muscles, shaggy black hair and dark eyes, and a large penis.

Prim's easel just so happened to be in the front row of the class, and she had a perfect view of every inch of the man's magnificent body. She'd found herself barely able to breathe as she'd sketched and had pretended to refine her work long after she'd finished in order to continue her scrutiny of the model. She had left the class, wondering what the large penis would look like when erect and what it would feel like inside of her. But then she became frightened and tried to push the notion from her mind.

Sex is normal, she reminded herself. *People obviously like it or else they wouldn't be so eager to do it. Your girlfriends have told you how great it is, and your mother certainly seemed to like it. Stop being afraid. You know Aunt Myrtle's the one who scared you because she was raped, so try to let it go. Sean won't hurt you like Aunt Myrtle was hurt.*

It was easier said than done, of course. She lay vulnerable in Sean's arms, wondering whether she should move away and risk waking him or stay as she was and try not to worry about what was resting underneath her thigh.

As she struggled to make up her mind, Sean came awake. Prim quickly pretended to be asleep and waited to see what Sean would do. For a long while, he did nothing. Then he said her name, and she pretended to wake but didn't lower her leg.

"You should move so I can get out of bed," he said tightly. As she did so and he swung his legs over the other side of the mattress, he told her, "I don't think I'll be able to sleep in the same bed with you anymore until we're ready for true intimate contact."

"I am," she insisted.

"You're not, and I refuse to take advantage of you. I'm not going to have sex with you when we haven't even kissed. We need to do this right, especially since you've never done any of it before. I have to do the right thing."

"That's part of why I love you." She paused then asked, "Have you ever loved anyone before me?"

"No."

"How many girls have you slept with?"

He twisted back to face her and said, "I'm not promiscuous. I don't have sex with every woman I date."

"I'm glad, but I actually want you to have experience. I've never even kissed a man before, remember? I don't know how to do anything."

"I've been with about a dozen women since I was fifteen."

"Were any of them virgins like me?"

"Two."

"And?"

He gave her a half-shrug and said, "The first girl was my first real girlfriend. Neither of us had had sex, so we were both clueless. We'd been told what to expect by more experienced friends, but we still weren't really ready. I hated to hurt her, and we didn't get any pleasure out of it at all. After she healed, we were still clueless but at least we enjoyed…exploring."

"And the other girl?"

"That was in college. I didn't know she was a virgin until we were in bed together, but she said she wanted to have sex with me and was ready. Again, neither of us enjoyed it, and I never slept with her after that."

"I've had friends who've told me what will happen. They said it only hurts the first time."

"Because of your past, maybe you should get a doctor to take care of that surgically before we're together. That way, I won't have to hurt you and you won't be as afraid."

"I should be able to have sex like every other girl."

"You're not like every other girl."

"I want to be, at least when it comes to this. Can you understand?"

He nodded but didn't look happy about the prospect of deflowering her. This made Prim feel bad for him, but it also made her feel even more certain that Sean was a truly good man who only had her best interest in mind.

"I'm going to Tallahassee for Thanksgiving," Sean said suddenly. "Do you want to come with me? I'd really like for you to meet my parents."

"I'd love to, especially with Uncle Buddy…with…him being gone. I have no family anymore." She wiped at her eyes and asked, "Do your parents know about me? They won't mind if I come?"

"Of course I've told them about you. They'd love to have you over for Thanksgiving."

"Will your sister be there?"

"Probably not."

"I'm sorry."

"Me, too. I don't know what to do about Debra. It's her life, but I hate having to stand by and watch her destroy it. Mom and Dad don't really understand and will be upset that Debra's not there for the holiday. She didn't come last year either."

"Are your parents coming here for Christmas?"

"That's the plan. Debra's already turned me down."

Remy arrived at 7:00 with food sent by LouAnn and other concerned townspeople. As they ate, he told them of the men and women who'd asked how Prim was doing and to inquire about recent events. He explained his responses and said everyone had been sympathetic.

"I talked at length to Caleb. He'll come by after the second service tomorrow and see what you need from him. I asked him about the hardware store job, and he was very interested."

Prim thanked Remy for all of his help and then asked the two men if they'd mind going to the Aurora family home the next day to remove all of her clothing and personal effects. She needed her things taken to the apartment over Prim's Corner and Aurora Hardware. She also wanted her car and a photo album that was in the family room.

"What about the rest of your things?" Sean asked.

"The apartment over the shop is furnished to my taste since I'm the one who supervised the renovation. I'll have almost everything I need there. What I don't have, I'll purchase. I don't want most of what's in the old house. I think I'll have an estate sale. I'll do the same thing with Uncle Buddy's place. Someone else can handle it."

"Are you sure you can stay by yourself in the apartment?" Remy asked worriedly.

"I'm a big girl. I know I have 'issues' but actually think I'm going to be able to deal with them for the first time in my life now that I know the truth."

"But you still don't know the whole truth," Sean pointed out.

"Not all of it, but I know so much more. Maybe once the coroner identifies the dead man, it will all make sense. Either way, I move ahead."

"Does this mean you'll talk to a therapist?"

"No. I don't want to start down that road, yet. I'd rather start here with you." Turning to Remy, she added, "And you, if you don't mind my being a little more needy than I was before all of this."

"I've missed being needed since my brother died."

"I'll never stop needing you," she declared. "You were a wonderful big brother to your own brother and to me for as long as I can remember."

Remy thanked her and excused himself from the table. Prim and Sean listened as he went out through the back door and into the yard.

"He was always great," Prim confided. "His parents were so messed up and didn't take good care of him and his brother. Remy did it all. It's kind of like you."

"Except it's completely different," Sean argued. "My parents loved us and were there for us like clockwork. They just didn't have the ability to do it all."

"Remy's mother and father loved their kids. He told me once that when he was little, they were really fabulous parents. It wasn't until they got mixed up with drinking so much that they lost sight of everything else."

"Are they still alive?"

"After his brother died, they divorced. His daddy died of liver cancer around the same time as Aunt Myrtle last year. He asked Remy to forgive him when he was on his deathbed, and Remy did."

"And his mother?"

"She didn't come to the funeral. I don't know where she moved to after the divorce. I don't think Remy's talked to her in a long time. She's probably ashamed and afraid."

Sean moved some green beans around on his plate and said, "People used to ask me when I was growing up how I could deal with having retarded parents."

"What'd you tell them?"

"That *they* were retarded. I had loving, sweet parents who were always there for me and my sister. How many kids have that?"

Prim touched his cheek and said, "I know I didn't."

Sean looked startled, and she wondered why. He obviously knew about her past and wouldn't be surprised by what she'd just told him. However, as he wrapped a hand around hers, she understood the reason for his surprise. She had reached out to touch him with no hesitation or fear whatsoever. She hadn't even given it a second thought.

"Kiss me," she directed quietly.

He kissed her palm and said, "After Remy leaves."

When Remy returned to the house and announced he was going to head back to his place, Prim hugged him and thanked him again for everything. He departed, promising to call her and Sean first thing in the morning so they could coordinate her move to the apartment.

Once he'd gone, Prim helped Sean clear the table and put the dishes in the sink. She expected Sean to lead her to the living room, sit her on the couch, and kiss her. Instead, he took her in his arms where they stood and kissed her lightly on the mouth. When she didn't draw back, he deepened the kiss.

Prim responded by slipping her arms around his neck and pressing her body against his. The way Sean kissed made her want more. She felt herself grow wet with desire and almost began to weep with joy.

"You can't know what it's been like," she told him when they paused for a few moments. "I knew it wasn't normal, and I wanted to be touched but couldn't allow that. It was so lonely." Lifting her lips up to meet his, she said, "Do it again. It feels so good."

She thought he might laugh at her naïveté, but Sean didn't laugh. He responded to her request by kissing her passionately and pulling her closer to him. She felt one of his hands slide downwards, and she moaned softly.

Sean suddenly broke away from her and stood breathing heavily, facing the counter. When Prim asked him if she'd done something wrong, he shook his head and admitted that they needed to take a break or else he wouldn't be able to stop himself from going further.

"But I want to go further," she said earnestly.

"You don't jump from your first kiss to sex in one night," he reminded her. "Although we do seem to be on the fast track for everything now that you're not afraid to be touched anymore."

"I have lots of catching up to do," she offered. "Is that so bad?"

"It could be. If we really, truly love one another, we'll wait to have sex until at least after Thanksgiving. By then we'll have known each other for several months, and what's happened in the last few days will be somewhat behind us. We can set some boundaries now and stick to them for the next couple of months."

"What kind of boundaries?"

"We only kiss or touch with our clothes on until we agree to make love. We don't sleep in the same bed until that time. We use some sort of birth control when we do decide we're ready to have sex."

Sean guided her until her back was against the wall then kissed her again. His hands moved to the front of her shirt, and he cupped her breasts through the material and her bra. As they continued to kiss, Prim felt his palms slide along her waist. He told her that he loved her as he took her face in his hands and pressed his hips against hers. She begged him to touch her lower even if it was through her clothing. He hesitated before refusing. He insisted if he touched her there, that sex would inevitably follow.

"Tonight, we're going to sleep in separate rooms," Sean declared. "I won't be able to stand it any other way."

She assented, knowing he was right and that they should wait. As much as she ached for him, she was still scared of being naked and open to him and of that first time when they'd have sex. It would be better for them to not rush into things.

On Monday, Prim would go to Dr. Stanford's for the cheek swab that would help to determine whether or not Buddy Brown had been her father and if the man in the trunk had been related to her. She would also make an appointment with her GYN so she could get a prescription for birth control pills. She and Sean may have agreed to wait at least a couple of months before having sex, but she might as well be prepared. She suspected that birth control pills would not prevent pregnancy immediately and wanted no surprises.

Aunt Myrtle got pregnant with my mother because she was raped, and my mother got pregnant with me because she wasn't careful. If I get pregnant, I want it to be because it's right for me and for Sean. No secrets. No lies. No fear. I want any children we might have to come out of love and hope.

Prim slept better that night than she ever had in her life.

Chapter Seven

Sean stood dressed in his tuxedo in the center of the banquet hall and admired Prim as she chatted with a group of men and women at one end of the room. She'd accompanied him to the Kensington Academy's 14th Autumn Silent Auction and the formal dinner that followed. She'd donated several antique pieces from the Aurora family home for the event, which had gone exceedingly well and was winding down. He was amazed at what a natural she was when it came to unobtrusively soliciting funds from parents, alumni, and other donors. The same demure temperament and innate beauty that had drawn him to her the first day they'd met attracted others to her like bears to honey. He wondered if she was aware of the effect she had on people and utilized it in conjunction with her business savvy or whether that was simply serendipitous.

Prim looked lovely in her pale blue satin evening gown. The color of her dress matched her eyes, and Sean did *not* think that was a coincidence. The gown had a square neckline and wasn't revealing. Yet, he could see the men's gazes lingering when they looked at her, and this both pleased him and made him feel possessive.

"She's quite charming and lovely."

Sean turned and saw Tony Eichstadt, the Head of the Board of Directors and one of the school's leading donors. The Kensington graduate who'd made his fortune on Wall Street had retired to Atlanta five years ago at the age of fifty. He'd been married to his wife for thirty years and was a stickler for ethics and a proponent of philanthropy. He and Sean had gotten along famously from the moment they'd met at Sean's first interview.

Sean agreed with Eichstadt that Prim was, indeed, very charming and lovely.

"She's also a good businesswoman," Eichstadt went on. "She's very young but knows her stuff. She and I had a lengthy conversation about best business practice and economics. It's my understanding that she has some family money but also runs her own shop, oversees the running of the family hardware store, and retains ownership of a large building with business and residential tenants."

Not certain where Eichstadt was going with this line of conversation, Sean verified that what the man had said was correct and added that Prim was also involved in community affairs and liked small children and animals. Eichstadt laughed and said he didn't doubt it. Glancing across the room at Prim, the older man asked, "Would you step outside the hall with me for a moment?"

Eichstadt led Sean to a private room that held two leather chairs and a small table. There was a roaring fire going in the fireplace beside them. It reminded Sean of an upscale version of the reading area in Remy's bookshop.

Both men took a seat and placed their drinks on the table between them. Although Eichstadt appeared completely relaxed, Sean knew that this informal meeting was anything but inconsequential. Outwardly, Sean was cool and collected, but he was inwardly tense. Whatever the Head of the Board of Directors was about to tell him would directly affect him and his career.

"I wanted to talk with you one-on-one to feel you out about a couple of things," Eichstadt said. "The members of the Board are all Kensington graduates and are all relatively young. We intend to be around for a long time in order to see the school maintain and further develop its reputation. That's one reason why we chose you to handle the aftermath of your predecessor's indiscretions. You emerged from the onset as the frontrunner and the consummate fixer for Kensington. Since school started, we've been summarily impressed with your performance and with your initiative."

"Thank you. I like to do my job and do it well."

"We've noticed, and so have our supporters. The parents and donors you've met with have substantially increased their contributions over the past few months and have brought it to our attention that they believe you're the best principal this school's had in decades. You're fair but decisive. It's what the school needed in order to revitalize."

"I love what I do and have always had a fondness for Kensington. I wish I'd been able to attend it as a young man."

"Which leads me to our next topic of discussion. When we asked you during your interviews what were the top two things you wanted to see changed in our school, you suggested greater accessibility for disabled students and the foundation of two scholarships that would allow for funding of tuition for four years for two underprivileged students, one male and one female. I believe your response was what immediately caught our attention. Most applicants blathered on about nonsense. They said what they thought we as Board members wanted to hear, not what they felt in their hearts. You offered your honest opinion, and that garnered instant respect and positive attention from the men and women on the Board." Eichstadt lifted his glass of champagne and took a sip before continuing, "You were right about both. It's past time the Academy became truly diversified. We're fortunate enough to have a student body that has representatives from all over the United States and several foreign countries, but we've never had a student who was blind, in a wheelchair, deaf, or possessed any other true disability. People of all classes have children who fall into those categories and would love to attend places like Kensington. We'd like to focus on welcoming disabled students and not simply because it will make us look good."

"And the scholarships?"

"I'm going to fund the initial two. We'll develop guidelines and see how those need to be adapted or expanded." Taking another sip from his glass, Eichstadt said, "I do have a request for you though."

"Certainly."

"I want you to select the names of the scholarships since they were your idea."

Sean didn't hesitate.

"The Kenneth Proper Scholarship and the Tiffany Proper Scholarship."

"Your parents?"

Sean nodded.

"Did they want to attend the school like you did?"

Sean smiled and said, "No. My parents are developmentally delayed. They had no idea that such a place as Kensington existed until I told them I was applying to come here when I was in eighth grade."

Eichstadt sat up a little straighter and repeated, "Developmentally delayed? That must have been challenging. Are they high functioning?"

"They both work but can't balance a checkbook to save their lives."

"How long have you been taking care of the family business?"

"Since I was nine and my little sister was three."

"Damn. No wonder you're so good at what you do and no wonder you have such determination. Your parents are obviously still alive. Are they in good health?"

"They're only in their fifties and continue to work full-time."

"I'd like for them to come to our annual holiday party. That's when we'll announce the institution of the scholarships. Do you think they'd be willing to attend?"

"They'd love it, although they've never been to that kind of event before. It might be interesting."

"Interesting is good. By all means, ask your sister to come, too."

"I will." Sean, who'd had a glass of champagne much earlier in the evening, sipped his water and said, "I can't thank you and the Board enough for considering and acting upon my suggestions."

"It's our pleasure." Placing his glass of champagne back on the table, Eichstadt said, "This brings me to something of even greater importance. As I told you, everyone is extremely pleased with you and your work. The contract you signed was for one year and gave us the option to extend, depending on your performance. You've made it clear that you enjoy your role here and have obviously settled into your life in Aurora. You seem to be very much in love with Miss Primrose Aurora, and I'm assuming you'd like to remain near to her and that she'd be loath to leave her hometown."

"Yes."

"We want to extend your contract for four more years. If your performance continues to be as outstanding as it has been so far, then I don't see why we wouldn't offer you a new four-year contract when this renegotiated one ends. This would ensure your employment and allow you to remain in the vicinity."

"It's not a strike against me that I don't want to live in a fancy house or move to some trendy suburb in Atlanta?"

"Not at all. We want you for *you*. It's refreshing to find a man who works so well with the rich but doesn't care about being rich, not that we're paying you a pittance by any means. I get the impression that we could be, and you'd still do the same outstanding job. The fact that you're not one of us is part of what makes you so damned good."

Sean had been praying for some solution that would keep him in Aurora. Even if it hadn't been for Prim, the place had felt like home the moment he'd found it. He wanted to stay.

When he and Tony Eichstadt returned to the party, Sean immediately went to find Prim. She was sitting with a group of very well-appointed ladies at a round table in the almost-empty banquet hall. Some of the women were definitely inebriated and were laughing uproariously. Prim was smiling and appeared to be enjoying herself, but she was more reserved than her companions.

"Sorry I had to disappear for a few minutes," Sean told her, as he bent to kiss her. "It was unavoidable. I can't wait to tell you about it."

"Then we should go," she said casually, as she reached for her evening purse. Turning to the women gathered at the table, she announced, "Ladies, it's been a pleasure. I hope to see you all soon."

They protested her departure but promised to come to Aurora to visit Prim's Corner in the very near future. Sean bid the women a goodnight as he put his arm around Prim's waist and led her towards the door. She impulsively kissed him on the cheek and said, "Tonight was magical. The event was great. Most importantly, I got to dance with you, hold your hand, kiss you, and have you hug me and wasn't scared at all!" She laughed and said, "Plus I think it was great for your school and my business."

When they were in the car, she pressed him to tell her about the important meeting that had taken him away from her at the party. As he reviewed his conversation with Tony Eichstadt, Prim was obviously stunned and pleased, although she remained silent as he spoke. He finished by saying, "If the members of the Board of Directors are willing to go to these lengths to keep me, then my future at Kensington is definitely secure, providing these members remain or that new ones are of the same mindset."

"I'm so proud of you," Prim declared. "Your parents are going to be so proud, too! Will you call them tonight and tell them?"

"No. We'll be driving to Tallahassee tomorrow for the holiday. I think I'll surprise them and tell them on Thanksgiving. We go around the table and say what we're thankful for when we sit down to eat. My turn will be a little longer this year."

"That's a really nice tradition."

"We've been doing it since I was a little boy."

"We never did anything like that when I was growing up."

That sentence was one Sean had come to expect from Prim over the past several weeks. Her seemingly stable upbringing had turned out to be anything but. As Prim had begun to talk about what life in the Aurora household had been like during her formative years, both he and Remy surmised that things had been very wrong between Myrtle and Buddy. Their abnormal marriage and example had certainly been detrimental to Prim.

Remy speculated that Myrtle might have been bipolar, but Sean suspected Prim's aunt had merely been the victim of overly devout parents and then of the psychiatrist who'd raped and impregnated her. Her mental instability and the sexless marriage had evidently pushed Buddy away, although he seemed to have loved his wife despite her problems. Sean had heard from some of Buddy's friends that Buddy had sought out physical intimacy with ladies "on the east side of town," although no one seemed to be aware of his indiscretion with Prim's mother. Sean didn't enlighten them.

As for that encounter, it had not resulted in Prim's conception. The genetic profiling had proved that Buddy Brown was in no way biologically related to Prim Aurora. It had, however, proved that the man in the trunk was related to her, although he wasn't her father. Prim, Sean, Byron, Remy, and Dr. Stanford suspected the murder victim was Sandra's rapist father, especially since Byron had found out during his investigation that the psychiatrist had mysteriously disappeared from Atlanta twenty-three years earlier. Had Buddy Brown killed the man or had it been someone else? And why had the man been at the Aurora home in the first place?

Sean reached across the seat and wrapped his right hand around Prim's left. The past month and a half had been stressful for her, but she'd handled things well. Her hectic schedule had definitely provided a distraction. Not only was she gearing up for the holidays at her own business and with the hardware store, but she'd also insisted on continuing to work with Caleb to organize the Christmas Festival. She'd overseen the sale of both houses and both estate sales, keeping only a few choice items from the Aurora home and from her aunt and uncle's house.

Making the apartment over the shop truly her own had given Prim great pleasure. She'd mixed modern furnishings and antique pieces in such a way that it made for a perfect balance of old and new. She definitely had an eye for blending styles to get the maximum effect out of every article in her home, which included an open living, dining, and kitchen area, a walk-in pantry, three large bedrooms, and two full bathrooms.

Her evolving relationship with Sean had also given her great pleasure. No longer fearful of kissing or touching, Prim begged Sean to school her in how to do everything related to physical contact. He'd insisted on retaining the boundaries that he'd set the weekend that her world had been turned upside down, and she'd respected that, admiring his self-control. She knew he wanted to make love to her but was aware that she still wasn't ready. Despite the fact that she now thoroughly reveled in their kisses, hugs, and caresses, Sean knew she remained fearful of sex. That hadn't stopped her from beginning to take the birth control pills that she'd gotten from her doctor.

The morning following the Kensington fundraiser, Sean rose at 7:30 and prepared to leave. A light snow had fallen during the hours he'd slept, but it was already melting by the time he arrived at Prim's apartment a few minutes before 9:00 and loaded her suitcase into his trunk. They would only be gone from Wednesday through Sunday and had packed medium-sized rolling suitcases. Once Prim had locked her apartment, they hurried to the car and removed their coats as the heater blasted them with warm air.

"It is *so* cold!" Prim exclaimed. "Do you mind if we drive through the first Starbuck's we see so I can get a salted caramel hot chocolate? I'm chilled to the bone!"

"I'm with you there. I didn't eat breakfast, so I think I'll grab a scone or something, too."

"Mm. A scone would be tasty even though I already had some cereal earlier."

"How do you do that?"

"Do what?"

"You eat what and when you want, whether it's good or bad, but your weight never fluctuates. Do you have an eating disorder I should know about?"

She told him no, that she'd been blessed with the ability to eat whatever she wanted at any time without gaining any weight.

"My friends have always been envious of that, but I can't help it. I used to get teased about it but in a good-natured way. My nickname in school was Pixie."

Sean could definitely see why Pixie would be an *apropos* nickname for Prim. His little sister had been fascinated by faeries, pixies, and sprites when she'd been a child, and he'd read countless stories to her about those supernatural beings and others. With her slim form, delicate bone structure and graceful movements, Prim did resemble a fairy creature. He wondered if she knew that pixies were generally thought to be helpful to those in need and had a great love of horses.

"Do you know how to ride a horse?" Sean asked curiously.

"Remy taught me when he taught his little brother. It was the summer when we were ten, and he was nineteen. He was home from college and decided we should learn how to ride."

"Remy went away to college? I thought he took care of his brother because of their drunk parents."

"He did. He drove back and forth to college in Mount Berry. He had this old, rusty, run-down truck that had belonged to his grandfather before he passed, and Remy pretty much ran that thing into the ground. He attended college each fall and spring but would work summers to help pay for gas and other necessities. I don't know how he did it all. His mom and dad were in really bad shape by that time. I mean *really* bad. But he did it. I never asked him how he paid for school. I was younger, so it didn't seem right for me to ask. He just did it."

"What did he study?"

"English with a minor in business. He'd always said he wanted to open a bookstore here in town, and he did about a year after he graduated and has done really well with it." Sighing, she said, "I just wish he had someone to share his life with."

"Did he ever date?"

"He had a girlfriend throughout high school, but she wanted to move away when they graduated. He said he couldn't leave his brother, so they broke up after their senior year. He's dated some since then but not much. I know he's lonely, just like I used to be." Leaning across the seat to kiss Sean on the jaw, she said, "I'm so glad I'm not lonely anymore."

Sean pulled the car over to the side of the road, put it in Park, and kissed her. He wanted to make love to her so badly that it hurt, but he chastised himself for even considering such a thing when she still wasn't ready. He hoped she'd be ready soon. It was getting more and more difficult for him to show restraint when it came to Prim and physical contact.

The drive to Tallahassee took longer than they'd anticipated. Traffic was extremely heavy, and it was sleeting off and on. Then, as they approached the Georgia-Florida border, they heard a loud noise that sounded like a horn but couldn't figure out where the sound was coming from. As they drove further on, they realized it was coming from a car that had been completely demolished. It appeared to have somehow crossed multiple lanes of traffic as well as a wide, grassy area and then smashed into an SUV. The horn on the car was stuck. The accident must have happened only moments before, and people on that side of the Interstate were getting out of their cars and heading slowly towards the vehicles. One of the SUV doors was open, and Sean and Prim could clearly see someone's leg sticking out through the opening.

"My God," Sean muttered, feeling sick and numb.

"Oh, Sean," Prim said in a tremulous voice. "There are dead people in those cars."

He nodded and fought the urge to throw up. There was no way anyone could have survived the crash.

"We should say a prayer for them and their families," he suggested.

"I already did," she confided. "How horrible. Can you imagine having to go to their families and say that they're not coming for Thanksgiving because of that?"

He nodded and tried to wipe the image of the man's leg protruding out of the open door from his mind. What if he and Prim had been on the other side of the road minutes earlier? They would now be dead, and someone would be telling his parents no one would be coming for Thanksgiving.

Both he and Prim were badly shaken and said little for the remainder of the drive to Tallahassee. It was only when he turned the car onto the appropriate exit that Sean began to relax slightly. He pointed out landmarks to Prim as they neared his parents' place.

Kenny and Tiffany Proper lived in an apartment complex that had been built forty years earlier. Not much had been done to upgrade, but at least the buildings had been maintained. Sean and Prim put on their coats then Sean lifted their suitcases from the trunk and asked Prim to follow him.

As they walked, he greeted the people he knew who happened to be outside. Children were playing in the small playground and called out to him by name as he and Prim passed. When they reached the landing, Sean lowered the suitcases and knocked on the door of #4468.

"Who is it?" he heard his father ask.

"It's me and Prim, Dad."

Sean listened as the locks were turned. The door was flung open, and Kenny threw his arms around his son and called out, "Tiffany! Sean's here. His girlfriend's here, too!"

Kenny Proper was several inches shorter than his son but had the same brown hair and eyes. He wore glasses, had a slight paunch, and was dressed in tan corduroy pants, a green flannel shirt, and tennis shoes.

As Kenny hugged Prim and welcomed her to their home, Tiffany hurried out from the kitchen and cried, "Sean! We're so happy you're here! And we're happy to meet your girlfriend, too!"

Sean grinned as his mother hugged first him then Prim. Shorter than his father, she wore a long jean skirt, a fluffy sweater that had a turkey design knitted into it, and penny loafers. Her long brown hair had been plaited into a braid.

Sean brought in the suitcases and then hugged both of his parents again before bringing his bag into his old bedroom and putting Prim's into Debra's old room. By the time he returned to the living room, Prim's coat hung on the coat rack in one corner, and she was seated on the faded couch with a cup of hot apple cider in her hands.

"It comes out of a bag," Tiffany confided. "Kenny's boss at the grocery store gave him a whole box for Thanksgiving as well as a turkey, some stuffing, cranberry sauce, and even a green bean casserole. He's so nice. He does it every year and says it makes his Thanksgiving even better. He's been doing it since before Sean and Debra were born."

"Don't forget about the pie!" Kenny told her. "He gives us a pie each year, too."

"That's a surprise each time," Tiffany said with a smile. "The rest of it stays the same, but we never know what kind of pie we'll have. Kenny and I wonder about it every time. We don't look to see what kind it is until after the Thanksgiving dinner."

They had a Stouffer's lasagna plus garlic bread for dinner and some brownies from the grocery store bakery for dessert. Prim learned during the meal that Sean's mother had never been a good cook, and the children had grown up eating frozen dinners, boxed macaroni and cheese, hot dogs, spaghetti and meat sauce from a jar, and the like. Kenny had no interest in preparing food, only in eating it.

After dinner they played simple board games and Go Fish. Prim said exactly what Sean had expected her to say, that her family had never done things like that when she'd been growing up. She seemed to have a wonderful time and to be genuinely happy participating in those activities with him and his parents.

Later that night, Sean lay awake in the twin bed in his old room, trying not to think about the dead people they'd passed on the Interstate. He was so grateful to be with his parents and Prim but wished that Debra had been there to make the family holiday complete. What was she doing to celebrate Thanksgiving? Was she at a company party with her current alcoholic boyfriend listening to him berate her for not doing something the way he wanted? Had she wanted to come home for the holiday but had been afraid that the jerk would leave her if she did? Did she even care that he and their parents were disappointed that they hadn't gotten to see her for another year?

He thought of Prim, who was hopefully sleeping peacefully in Debra's twin bed. She'd told him how happy she was with him. But he wondered if he could keep her happy.

He'd asked Remy to join them on their trip to Tallahassee, but the man had insisted that his store needed the revenue it generated on Black Friday and the Saturday that followed. Sean knew that this was true, but he regretted that Remy hadn't been able to come. He pictured the man sitting at home alone, eating a peanut butter sandwich for Thanksgiving and reading or playing video games by himself all day.

You and Prim are going to call him. That will brighten his day a little bit. Or, it might make him more depressed.

Sean sighed deeply and rolled onto his side. He eventually fell asleep and dreamed of a time when he and Debra had been young and were climbing on the monkey bars at the playground downstairs. He woke the next morning to his mother's gentle kiss on his forehead and her whispered words of "Happy Thanksgiving."

"Happy Thanksgiving, Mom."

She was sitting on the edge of the bed and took his hand in hers before saying, "Your Dad and I like Prim. She's a real sweet girl. It's sad that she didn't have a real Mom and Dad to raise her. Dad and I know what that's like."

Sean nodded. Both of his parents had been turned over to the State by their parents when they'd been diagnosed as being delayed and had grown up in foster care and group homes. They'd been fortunate to have caring people to look after them and safeguard their welfare.

"Do you love Prim?" his mother asked seriously.

"Yes. I want to marry her, but don't tell her. I was going to ask you and Dad today if you'd go with me tomorrow to pick out an engagement ring."

"That would be fun! When will you give it to her?"

"I don't know, yet. When I do, then I'll tell you and Dad so you'll know it won't be a secret anymore."

"Okay." She bent down to kiss his forehead again and said, "Your Dad and I love you, Sean."

90

"And I love the two of you, Mom."

"We love Debra, too. Why doesn't she come to see us anymore?"

"I don't know. She doesn't come to see me either. It makes me sad."

"It makes me and Dad sad, too. We miss her."

"Me, too. Maybe if Prim and I get married, she'll come to the wedding and start being part of the family again."

"I hope so." Squeezing his hand, she suggested, "Why don't you get up and come help me with the turkey? It's a big one, and you can help me put it in the oven. It's so heavy!"

He and Prim spent the morning talking with his parents and watching the Macy's Thanksgiving Day Parade with them. They ate hot dogs and chili for lunch. They called Remy, who informed them that Lou Ann had invited him and Caleb to her house for a holiday meal. That relieved both him and Prim greatly. When it came time for them to sit down to their own holiday dinner at the worn Formica table, it was 6:00.

Kenny reached first for his wife's hand and then his son's. Sean took his father's hand then held out his free hand to Prim. His mother did the same. Prim seemed not to know what she should do and looked uncertainly to Sean, who explained that they were all going to hold hands while his father said Grace before the meal. She looked embarrassed and quickly took his hand and his mother's. Then she bowed her head while the prayer was offered.

They ate the food donated by Kenny's boss. It was nothing outstanding, although Sean's parents were thrilled with the feast. When they were finished, Kenny announced it was time to go around and say what everyone was thankful for; then they would see what kind of pie they had for dessert.

"Why don't you start this year, Mom?" Sean directed. "I started last year, and Dad started the year before that."

"Okay. I'm thankful for my wonderful husband and my two beautiful children. And I'm thankful to meet Prim and for the fact that none of us is sick with anything. And I'm thankful for all my friends at work and at home. And I'm thankful for all of our blessings." Turning to Kenny, she said, "You go next!"

"I'm thankful for my great wife and my great kids and my friends everywhere and my job and that we have so much. I'm thankful that Sean found Prim and brought her here to be thankful with us." Looking across to Prim, he asked, "How about you take a turn?"

"I'm thankful that Sean and I found each other and that he asked me to come along with him to spend Thanksgiving with you. I'm thankful for all of my friends and that my business has done so well. I'm thankful for lots of other things, too." She turned to Sean and said, "Your turn."

"I'm thankful I found Prim and to have two of the greatest parents in the world and a beautiful little sister. I'm also thankful because I love my new town and friends and my new job and because my boss has asked me to stay for at least four more years after this. I'm also thankful because the people who run the school thought about some of my suggestions and decided to take them. They're going to accept some disabled students and have two scholarships for kids who can't afford to go to school there but want to attend. They're going to call them the Kenneth Proper Scholarship and the Tiffany Proper Scholarship." After explaining in more detail, Sean said, "They want you to come to the big holiday party where they celebrate and will talk about the scholarships. It'll be at Christmastime when you come to see me."

Both of his parents immediately rose to hug and congratulate him and said they were so excited for him and for themselves. They then hugged Prim, who was smiling but seemed sad at the same time. Sean wondered what Thanksgiving with Buddy and Myrtle had been like for her.

That night when it was time for bed, Sean went with Prim to his sister's room and kissed her goodnight. He told her he had to take his parents on an errand the following morning and wanted to know if she'd like to go to the mall with them or stay at the apartment and relax while they were out. He'd suspected she would want to avoid the malls on Black Friday, and she confirmed this. That had been part of his plan, and he was pleased he hadn't miscalculated.

"I don't think we'll be gone more than a couple of hours. We'll pick up some lunch from this great sandwich shop not far from here and be back before you know it. Mom and Dad want to visit with both of us as much as they can while we're in town."

"You were right about how sweet and kind they are. You're very lucky."

"I am."

"Sean?"

"Hm?"

"Kiss me again."

He did. When he returned to his old room, it took him some time to get his emotions and body under control. He knew he was going to have to act soon when it came to sex with Prim for both their sakes. Now that Thanksgiving had come and gone, she would press him to proceed even though she remained fearful.

Sean was afraid of setting her back and of causing her to withdraw from him completely after their initial sexual encounter. He'd been reading books about children who'd grown up in unstable households and the damage that resulted. His reading had helped, but it had also raised more concerns and questions.

Turn off your brain for once and get some sleep, he commanded himself. *Tomorrow you'll get the ring and then see what happens. You could wait until after you're married to have sex, but look what happened with Buddy and Myrtle when they did that.* Giving a mental groan, he reminded himself, *You're not Buddy, and she's not Myrtle. You'd insist on working things out and not just turn to prostitutes or promiscuous young women.*

He prayed for guidance, shut his eyes, and slept.

Chapter Eight

After Sean and his parents left to run their errands, Prim showered and then returned to Debra's room to dress. Once she'd donned a pink sweater and jeans, she stopped and looked around. It was the first time she'd taken a moment to truly examine the bedroom.

There wasn't much to see. Prim assumed Debra had taken most of her things when she'd moved out, but she'd left behind a blue-and-white flowered comforter and matching curtains that Prim deduced Tiffany had sewn for her daughter. The bedroom furniture resembled all of the other items in the Proper apartment in that it was older but well-cared for. Sean had told her he'd offered to buy his parents new things. But they'd refused, saying they loved all of their belongings because of the happy memories attached to each article.

Prim went to Sean's room. She imagined not much had changed in the room since he'd moved out after college. His matching comforter and curtains were a black-and-tan pattern that had random red lines running throughout. Two M.C. Escher prints hung on one wall, and a shelf above an old desk showcased trophies and medals for different track and field events, which came as a surprise to Prim. A framed photo of the family sat on the desk.

Prim moved to Kenny and Tiffany's room. Their homemade comforter and curtains had stars, suns, and moons imprinted on a dark blue background. There were quite a few pictures of the family hung on the walls and awards for Kenny and Tiffany from their respective jobs. Each had been employee of the year more than once. A desktop computer rested on a corner desk that had two chairs placed side-by-side in front of it.

Prim went to the kitchen with its old appliances, cabinets, and countertops and then into the dining room with the Formica table. The living room contained a faded plaid couch, a rectangular coffee table, and an old-style entertainment center that held a bulky television set, a DVD player, an ancient VCR, and a CD player.

Mountains of DVDs, VHS tapes, and CDs were stacked on the floor. The bookcase at the end of the room was filled with books for elementary and middle school readers.

These books are Kenny's and Tiffany's, Prim realized. *They obviously love to read, watch movies, and listen to music as well as play board games and cards.*

There was a small patio beyond the sliding glass doors that was just large enough to hold the two lawn chairs the couple had placed outside. It was freezing, so Prim didn't linger long as she scanned the quadrangle below. She returned to the living room, got her coat, took the extra key Tiffany had given her in case she needed it, and left the apartment, locking the door behind her.

She walked to the playground where she sat and watched a group of children playing on the swing set and slides. Prim lost track of time as she studied the boys and girls. The frolicking children all looked so happy and normal.

Just like I used to look when I was little. I wonder how many of them are really unhappy at home and good at hiding it. Maybe they don't realize how weird their home lives are. I didn't. What if I do have children and screw them up, too?

"Prim?"

She turned and saw Sean standing beside the bench. She hadn't even been aware of his approach. He sat beside her and wiped at her wet cheeks with the sleeve of his coat before pulling her against his chest and stroking her hair.

"I wish my mother hadn't died," she said quietly. "I wish I knew who my daddy was."

"I know." Kissing the top of her head, he said, "You're freezing. How long have you been out here?"

"I don't know. Did you get your errands done?"

"We did. Mom wants you to go with her after lunch to help her buy a dress for the Kensington formal party. She's never had an evening gown of any kind and is both excited and nervous about it. I told Mom that I'm paying for her dress and Dad's tux and that I don't care how much either of them costs. So, if you'll pay for the dress, I'll reimburse you afterwards. I'm going to take Dad to get a tux while you shop with Mom."

"Do we have to go today? The mall will be crazy."

"I think everyone will be home sleeping by the time we go to the department store and the formalwear shop. It shouldn't be bad."

"And if they're so excited, then we should go now no matter what," Prim said with a slight smile. "Maybe I'll find a dress for myself while we shop."

They returned to the Proper apartment and enjoyed the sandwiches Sean and his parents had picked up on their way home. Kenny showed Prim the two books he'd bought at the bookstore, and Tiffany displayed the elf hat with a bell at the top she'd bought to wear to work for the next month. While Prim admired their purchases, she told Sean's parents how much she was looking forward to going shopping with them later.

By the time they got to the mall at 3:00, the crowds had thinned considerably. Sean led Kenny towards the men's formalwear shop, while Prim and Tiffany went into the nearby department store and located the evening gown area.

It didn't take long for Prim to figure out what Tiffany liked. Everything the woman selected was brightly colored and had either rhinestones or sequins on it. She confided to Prim that she'd never had a fancy dress before and wanted it to be sparkly.

"I think these might be a bit too sparkly for the type of party we're attending," Prim told her. "What size do you wear?"

"Twelve."

"Let's ask the salesperson for help. Maybe she'll have some suggestions, since that's her job."

"Okay!"

Within the hour, Tiffany had found the dress of her dreams. It was a long, silver taffeta gown that had tiny black fake pearls edging the high neck, the cuffs of the sleeves, and the hem. The salesclerk brought Tiffany some low-heeled silver shoes that matched her dress perfectly. With the addition of silver earrings and a silver evening purse, the ensemble was complete.

Prim selected a V-neck, long-sleeved burgundy satin dress that had a fitted bodice and a flowing skirt. She told the salesclerk she already had shoes and jewelry at home and then paid for everything before calling Sean on his cellphone.

"Dad and I have been long gone from the tuxedo shop. We're now across the mall, looking at something Dad wants to buy Mom for Christmas. Do you mind doing some more shopping with Mom for a while?"

"Of course not."

"Thanks. Love you."

"Love you, too."

After she'd disconnected the call, Prim told Tiffany that Sean and Kenny were having "guy" time and asked if she minded having some "girl" time with Prim. Tiffany was overjoyed by the prospect.

The salesclerk at the store promised to hold their purchases for them while they continued to shop. As they wandered through the ladies' department, Tiffany asked if they could go look at nightgowns. They were soon standing in the lingerie department.

"What kind of nightgown are you looking for?" Prim asked.

"Something with a reindeer on it. I want to buy it for Debra as a Christmas present."

Prim doubted they'd find nightgowns with reindeer on them at the upscale store, but she quickly discovered she was wrong. Tiffany located a long-sleeved flannel nightshirt for her daughter that had a dancing reindeer pattern on it and declared it was perfect. Prim glanced at the price and told Tiffany how much the gown cost, but the woman said it didn't matter because it was just right. Prim debated about calling Sean, who would no doubt think the price was too high but would also be torn by his mother's wish to buy the gift for his little sister. In the end, she decided not to interfere and see how things played out.

Because it was Black Friday, the normally exorbitantly priced nightgown was on sale for twenty dollars. Inwardly breathing a sigh of relief, Prim hung back and watched as Tiffany happily paid for her daughter's present. She thanked the clerk several times as the man gave her a gift box and tissue paper.

"Do you like reindeer?" Tiffany asked, as they meandered through the department. "I like snowmen."

"I'm more into gingerbread cookie designs," Prim confided. "I actually like to eat gingerbread, too. I think it's delicious."

"I like gingerbread," Sean's mother told her. Suddenly, she said, "Prim, this is so pretty. I bet it would look beautiful on you."

Prim went back to where the woman was standing and looked at the short, sheer, pale green baby doll nightgown she was admiring. It was very attractive, totally revealing, and unabashedly sensual. Simply looking at it made Prim feel scared.

Tiffany frowned and took her hand before saying, "You're afraid."

Prim swallowed hard and nodded as she blinked back tears. She'd thought she was doing so much better, but she obviously wasn't if the mere sight of the lingerie was enough to frighten her. The older woman led her into a dressing room and then shut and locked the door behind them. She gently directed Prim to sit on the long bench in the room, asking, "What's wrong?"

Prim shook her head and told Tiffany she didn't want to burden her with her problems, but Sean's mother put an arm around her shoulders and assured her it was all right, that she was a good listener. Prim began to cry and talked of Myrtle's rape, her mother's birth and death, and the way her aunt had scared her about men and sex. She described her overwhelming relief at her recent ability to kiss Sean, to dance with him, to hold his hand, and to hug him. However, she explained that the mere thought of sexual contact terrified her even though she wanted it.

"What your aunt did to you was wrong, but I don't think she could help it," Tiffany said earnestly. "I'd expect you to be scared after that." Pausing, she asked, "Do you love my son?"

"Yes."

"Do you trust him?"

"Totally."

"Then it's okay to be scared, especially the first time. I don't believe in lying, so I won't tell you that it doesn't hurt the first time. But if you love and trust the man you're with, then you know it'll be okay after that and then it'll be amazing! Sex feels really good, so you shouldn't be scared. If you love someone, then it makes you feel more love than you ever had before." Handing Prim a tissue, she said, "Why don't you do this: Buy that pretty nightgown and put it away? When you're not scared, then you'll have it when you want to wear it."

"But what if I'm always scared?"

"That's why you buy the nightgown. Just by buying it you're saying that there'll be a time when you won't be scared. Maybe it will help you to not be afraid."

Prim hugged Tiffany and thanked her for listening and giving her advice.

"Kenny and I may be slow, but we're not stupid," Sean's mother said. "You need a mom right now, and you don't have one. I can be like your mother if you want."

"I'd like that. Would you come with me to buy the nightgown?"

"Yes, but don't you think you should try it on to make sure it fits?"

"I don't think I can."

"But you have to," Tiffany insisted. "I'll wait outside and look at robes while you do."

Prim reluctantly returned to that rack of nightgowns, selected one in her size, and then took it back to the dressing room. She then removed everything except her bikini underwear. She slipped the gown over her head, bit her lip, and forced herself to turn and look at her reflection in the mirror.

Someday you'll surprise Sean by wearing this, she thought. *The first time you're not afraid at all, you can wear it. That will make both of you happy.*

Prim had just paid for the lingerie when her cellphone rang. It was Sean, telling her that he and his father were done shopping and wanting to know if she and his mother were ready. They agreed to meet in the evening gown department so the men could help them carry their purchases to the car. As Prim and Tiffany walked in that direction, Prim suggested she bring Tiffany's dress, shoes, purse, and jewelry back with her to Aurora since she and Sean had plenty of room in the car.

"That'd be a big help," Tiffany told her. "Kenny and I don't drive and will take the train to Atlanta. Sean will pick us up there. I don't want my dress to get all rumpled."

They were soon back at the Proper apartment and ate Thanksgiving leftovers for dinner. Tiffany showed her husband and son the nightgown she'd bought for Debra, and they both approved of the gown and the price. Prim did not, of course, share her lingerie purchase with either man, and the two women said they were not going to let the men see their eveningwear until the night of the party.

Both of Sean's parents had to work the following day, so he took Prim on a tour of Tallahassee. They stopped by the supermarket where Kenny worked and were given the grand tour by Kenny himself. Then they went to the laundry where Tiffany worked and were welcomed by her and the other employees. Sean and Prim ended up at a Greek restaurant named Mr. Spiro's for dinner.

Mr. Spiro was a seventy-something-year-old man with a larger-than-life personality and a busy restaurant. He greeted Sean with a hug and was then introduced to Prim. He seated the couple himself and proceeded to proclaim Sean's praises for the next twenty minutes.

"Such a good boy and such a hard worker!" Mr. Spiro declared. "He came to me for a job when he was fourteen, and I had him bus tables. He became a waiter, a cashier, and a host as he went through high school and college. Sean was always on time, willing to stay late and willing to do what needed to be done!" Clapping Sean on the back, he said, "I am so proud of this one! He's a fine young man!"

Prim smiled as she wholeheartedly agreed. Mr. Spiro announced that their dinner was on the house that night and said he had a surprise dessert made especially for Prim. When she protested, he dismissively waved his hand and made his apologies as he was summoned to the kitchen by one of his employees.

"He's quite a man," Prim told Sean. "If anyone ever embodied the word *gregarious* it would be him."

Sean grinned and said, "Yes, he is very enthusiastic about everything. He's also very kind-hearted and is dedicated to giving his customers quality food and service. He's given his life to serving people. When he dies, the restaurant will definitely close. Someone else could take it over but it wouldn't be the same."

Prim had never had such delicious Greek food. She enjoyed every bite and made certain to tell Mr. Spiro when he came over to their table as their empty plates were being removed by a server.

"Now it is the time for the surprise dessert!" he announced.

"I think I'm too full."

"But you must!" he insisted. "Trust me. You have never had a dessert like this in all of your life! It is one you will never forget!"

Prim looked to Sean and asked, "Will you share it with me?"

He smiled and said, "I'd love to."

Mr. Spiro vanished and returned moments later with a plate that had a shiny metal dome resting on top. He placed it in front of Prim on the table and said, "Especially for you." Then he lifted the dome and stepped back.

Prim stared at the plate. Resting in its center was an open ring box that held a stunning pear-shaped diamond engagement ring. For a few moments, she forgot to breathe. Then she looked at Sean, who was smiling across the table at her.

"Primrose Anastasia Cassandra Aurora, will you do me the honor of marrying me?"

She nodded and said, "Yes. Definitely yes, but –"

"No but's," he interrupted. "'Yes' is all I need to hear."

He rose, coming around to her side of the table. Then he removed the ring from the box and got down on one knee. She giggled and blushed as he slid the ring on her finger. Mr. Spiro called for everyone in the dining area to stop what they were doing and congratulate the newly engaged couple. They did, and Prim and Sean laughed and kissed.

As they drove back to his parents' apartment, Sean explained that one of the errands he and his parents had taken care of the previous morning had been to go to a local jeweler so Sean could select the diamond and setting for her engagement ring. He'd wanted his parents to be with him for the most important purchase of his life. They'd helped him select the beautifully cut diamond, which the jeweler had set while he took his parents to the bookstore down the street.

"It's perfect," Prim said. "Your parents are really good at keeping a secret. They're wonderful."

"I'm glad you think so, since they're going to be your parents after we get married."

Prim hadn't thought of it that way, and it made her feel good to know that Kenny and Tiffany would be *her* Mom and Dad someday.

"When do you want to get married?" she asked.

"Whenever you want, although I think the summer would be better because of my work at Kensington. It could be this summer or next summer, unless you want to elope sooner. I'd rather not though. I'd really like for the family and friends to be there when we get married and to have a real honeymoon."

"I don't want to elope either. I want your parents there and our friends. It would be nice if your sister could come."

"Yes, it would."

"Do you mind if we think about setting a date and not decide right away?"

"Not at all. I'm just thrilled that you accepted my proposal."

"Did you doubt I would?"

"I was hopeful, but one can never be sure. If you'd said, 'No,' then I don't know what I would have done."

"Did anyone else know about this besides your parents and Mr. Spiro?"

"Remy knew I wanted to propose, but I hadn't told him I was thinking about doing it this weekend." As Prim rummaged through her purse, he asked, "What are you doing?"

"Looking for my phone. We have to call him!"

They phoned Remy, who congratulated them both and said he couldn't wait to see the ring and congratulate them in person. He told them Black Friday and that particular Saturday had been his highest grossing business days ever and that he was celebrating by heading to dinner at LouAnn's Café. They congratulated him on his own success and told him they'd see him the following evening.

When they returned to the Proper apartment, they were welcomed with hugs and well wishes from Tiffany and Kenny. They played board games for an hour and then ate the last of the blackberry pie. Afterwards, Prim went to pack her suitcase and put the negligee at the top before she closed it. When she got home, she would wash it and put it in a drawer for the day she'd wear it for herself and for Sean. She hoped that day would come soon.

Chapter Nine

It was the middle of December, and Sean had been in great spirits since the night of the silent auction at the Kensington Academy. His contract had been renegotiated, and he was making an even larger salary. His job as the school principal was secure. His own personal goals regarding the school were coming to fruition, and he was looking forward to the upcoming Kensington holiday gala. Most importantly, he was engaged to Prim and found that his love for her seemed to grow with each passing day.

The Aurora Christmas Festival had begun and was turning out to be a wonderful experience replete with a visiting Santa Claus, winter games, caroling, and the lighting of the enormous tree in the center of the Town Square. Sean had never been to such an event and found it charming. He promised to help coordinate the following year's festival with Caleb and Prim.

Sean's parents would be coming soon for their vacation, and Sean was eager to share every facet of his new life with them. He knew they would love Aurora and was secretly hoping they'd want to move to the town when they retired so that they could be closer and he could take better care of them. It would be good for him, Prim, and them to have a normal family life.

But not everything was going smoothly. Prim refused to set a wedding date until she was able to overcome her fear of sex, and that had yet to happen. Debra had been dumped by her boyfriend and had immediately found another emotionally abusive alcoholic to replace him. The investigation regarding the dead man in the trunk remained open, but no progress had been made.

Still, things were generally going well. Aurora was decorated beautifully for Christmas, and everyone was in a good mood. Sean felt more at peace in his new hometown than he had anywhere else.

That Saturday night, he was headed to Prim's with dinner that he'd picked up from LouAnn's. Prim had been swamped at the store and had asked him to come to her apartment with food at 6:00, since she hadn't been able to take a break all day. He had offered to relieve her for at least a half hour so she could sit and eat, but she'd declined, saying that he was not a shopkeeper and had Kensington work occupying him at home. Both of those statements were true, so he hadn't argued. He promised to bring her whatever she wanted from LouAnn's, and she'd told him to surprise her.

When he arrived at her door, she had already showered and put on old-fashioned flannel pajamas that were light blue with fluffy clouds on them. Her hair was still slightly damp from the shower, and she was obviously tired but happy.

"Talk about a great day," she told him as they sat down to dinner at her espresso-colored dining table. "It was insane but in a good way. Thank goodness, I ordered that extra inventory. Oh, my God. I can't wait to find out how much business Caleb and Remy did. I'm surprised LouAnn didn't run out of food before you got there."

"She did say she's had to adjust her orders from her suppliers. I think she's loving it but is kind of overwhelmed." After taking a sip of his tea, he went on, "Remy's in heaven about it and isn't concerned at all. He's got a 'bring-it-on' attitude regarding the surge in business and hopes it lasts forever."

Once they finished the meal, Sean insisted on clearing the table while Prim went to sit on the couch. When he joined her there a few minutes later, she snuggled against him and said, "You know I feel really at home here. I love the old building and all the exposed brick and old wood floors. It makes me feel like I'm connected to history."

"You didn't feel that way in the old family home?"

"Yes, but it was different. Because nothing had changed in so long there, I sort of felt trapped by the house and its furnishings. Here, I have the feel of the past but my more up-to-date style. It's a nice balance, and I'm making my own history."

Hopefully, we'll be making our own history together soon, Sean thought, as Prim asked him to tell her about the upcoming theater production of *Rent* at Kensington. He described the students' preparations and the drama teacher's talent and suggested they attend the opening night performance, which was the next Friday at 8:00.

"They're giving three performances so interested parents can come then take the kids home with them after the last one Saturday night."

"What do the kids do who don't go home?"

"There's a small staff that stays on campus. They'll have a party and various activities. I feel bad for those kids though. Why wouldn't their parents want them home? They have the money."

They sat in silence for a long time before Prim said impulsively, "I want to try something."

"Okay. What?"

"I want to see you naked."

"Are you sure?"

"Yes," she said in a small but firm voice.

Sean disengaged himself from her and closed the wooden blinds that ran along the front of the building in the open area that encompassed the living, dining, and kitchen space. He then paused and asked Prim if she wanted him to remove his clothing or if she was going to do it for him.

"Maybe you should do it this first time."

Sean removed his sweater and undershirt. He undid his belt then his jeans and finally kicked off his shoes before pulling off his socks and jeans and tossing them on a chair along with his other clothing. He looked at Prim, who appeared expectant but fearful.

She asked, he thought. *It took a lot of courage for her to do that. Don't try to dissuade her. She's not asking you to have sex with her. She just wants to see your body. It's a step in the right direction.*

Sean pulled off his boxers and added them to the pile of clothes. He smiled at Prim and inquired as to whether or not she wanted him to do a 360 degree turn. She shook her head and asked if she could touch his skin. He nodded.

Prim rose from the couch and came to stand in front of him. She ran her hands along his shoulders, chest, and belly and examined his tattoo. Putting her arms around his waist, she asked about the colorful wings, what they meant, and why he'd gotten them on his chest and not his back. As he slipped his arms around her, Sean hoped he didn't come on the spot.

"I had the tattoo done when I was sixteen. I was really struggling emotionally but knew I couldn't let things get to me. It

105

wasn't only my future at stake; it was Mom's, Dad's, and Debra's, too. I had to keep everything going. If I didn't, then the consequences would've been disastrous. So, I decided to do something for myself that would remind me every day that life might be a bitch, but I couldn't give up and break or it'd be much worse for everyone else I held close to my heart. I found a tattooist I liked, lied about my age, and explained to him what I wanted. I've looked at that tattoo every day for the last fourteen years, and it makes me appreciate that I've never let anything break my wings."

"Did it hurt to have the tattoo done?"

"Yes. I knew it would, but I didn't care. I needed one thing that was just for me."

Prim looked up at him and asked, "Can I touch your hips and legs?"

"You can touch me anywhere you want."

She ran her palms along his hips and butt and then slid them down his thighs and calves. Then she slowly brought them up and touched what hung at the apex of his thighs. He exhaled sharply, and she asked if she'd hurt him.

"Not at all. It feels so good. Just don't be surprised if I come soon."

"Do you want me to stop?"

"No."

"But what if you come?"

"Then I come, and I enjoy it."

"But we wouldn't have had sex."

"Do you think that sex is the only time people climax?"

"No, but I figured it wouldn't be as good alone."

"It's always good."

Prim's hands shook as she explored the shaft and tip of his cock. Her fear kept him from coming, although he certainly got great pleasure from her touch. He asked her if she had any questions.

"I feel so dumb," she admitted. "I feel like any questions I ask will be stupid ones."

"Prim, there are no stupid questions about this."

Blushing, she said, "It looks so big. I don't feel that big inside. What if I can't take you in me when we make love?"

At least you know she's touched herself, Sean thought. *That's promising.*

"It should be fine," he assured her. "Your body should...adjust when I'm in you."

Taking her face in his hands, he kissed her and told her that everything was all right and that she was doing well.

Prim stood wide-eyed before him and asked, "Would touch me like I touched you?"

Sean slowly undid the buttons on her pajama top and then removed it. He slipped his fingers into the waistband of her pajama bottoms and pushed downwards until they were around her ankles. She stepped out of them and left them where they were.

Sean studied her naked body and was awed by how perfect it was. His fantasies about seeing her nude had been extremely accurate. She did have the body of a fairy-like creature who possessed round, firm breasts that were tipped with beautiful light pink nipples. The triangle of hair that pointed downwards was the same strawberry blonde color as the hair on her head. She was delicate, exuding femininity.

Sean touched her cheek. Then he took her in his arms and kissed her. She was shaking against him but responded to the kiss and put her arms around his waist. He caressed her as they kissed, and then he cupped one breast in his hand. She moaned and pressed her body closer to his.

He suddenly thought of some unsolicited advice Remy had given him during their most recent Game Night. They'd been taking a break and sharing a pizza, and Sean was telling Remy about his worry regarding how he would handle his first sexual encounter with Prim. Remy was the only person in the world he felt he could talk to about that, and it helped him simply to say aloud how unsure he was about what might happen when she finally agreed to have sex.

"Get her to come before you do it," Remy had suggested. "Show her what an orgasm feels like before you actually enter her and cause her pain. That way, she'll know how good sex can feel when you do it in the future."

"Let's go to your bedroom," he told her. "We don't have to have sex if you don't want to, but I do want you to be comfortable while we touch."

He could sense her anxiety, but she agreed. They sat together on the edge of the mattress and kissed until Sean felt Prim begin to relax. That was when he laid her back until her head rested on one pillow. She suddenly looked panicked and asked him to stop. He immediately drew away from her and sat up.

"I'm scared," she told him, her blue eyes shining with tears. "Tell me everything will be all right."

"Everything will be fine, but I can get dressed and leave instead if you're not comfortable with this. We could try again soon."

"No. I want to be touched and to touch you."

Sean stretched out next to her and took her in his arms before kissing her again. She clung to him and gave a little cry of delight when he took one nipple in his mouth and slipped his fingers between her legs. The fearful shaking stopped instantaneously, and her hands came up to cradle his head as he moved his mouth to the other nipple. After a few minutes, he could tell that she was on the verge of climax and prayed she'd allow herself to give in to it. Soon, she was crying out his name, arching her back, and shuddering under his touch.

She'd barely finished coming when he heard her say, "Do it now, Sean. Do it now, so we can both enjoy sex together after tonight. Please." Before he could ask, she said, "I won't change my mind. Please."

Sean moved to kneel between her open thighs. When he went to touch her, she automatically drew one knee towards the other as if to block him. He gently rested his palms on her inner thighs and reminded her she wanted this and that it would only hurt this once. He asked her one final time if it was what she wanted. Although she was trembling slightly, she nodded and forced herself to spread her knees further apart.

She was still wet from her recent orgasm, and this helped him ease into her. Despite her fear, he could feel her desire for him as she pulsed around him. Everything went well until he reached the point where he could go no further.

Barely able to form a coherent sentence, Sean asked, "Are you ready?"

"Just do it as quickly as you can; then hold me."

He prayed that perhaps the flesh would tear easily and it wouldn't take much effort on his part or cause her great pain. Unfortunately, that was not the case. As he pushed deeper into her, Sean was forced to bear down with all of his weight. The inner barrier refused to yield without difficulty, and he heard Prim cry out in pain as she dug her nails into the flesh of his back.

When he finally broke through, he felt enormous relief for both Prim and himself. Unable to hold back, he climaxed inside Prim and then sagged on top of her.

After withdrawing, he took her in his arms and held her against him as she shook with residual fear and emotion. He murmured that he'd hated to hurt her.

"But you came afterwards, didn't you?"

"I couldn't help myself. Just looking at you makes me want to come. There was no way I could be *inside* you and not climax." Kissing her on the temple, he said, "I can't wait to feel you climax when I'm in you."

"Me neither. I think I'll be scared again when we have sex until that happens. My doctor says I might hurt for a while after my first time. She said I should wait at least two weeks to have sex again. Is that okay with you?"

Sean fingered her hair and assured her he would wait as long as she needed. He was simply relieved that she was all right and had overcome what had been her greatest fear.

"I was only able to do it because I trusted you implicitly, loved you so much, and knew you felt the same about me."

When Prim went to use the restroom, Sean thanked God for what had just happened and that it was finally done. He prayed that Prim wouldn't find new fear because of the intense pain he was certain she'd felt during intercourse. He also prayed that she'd have an orgasm the next time they were together so she could simply relax and enjoy sex.

He held her all night. In the morning, he got up, showered, and dressed in the clothing he'd worn to her apartment the evening before.

When Prim emerged from the shower, he asked, "How are you feeling?"

"It hurts – but not as bad as did during the night."

After breakfast, she took some ibuprofen before retrieving her datebook from her purse.

"What's that for?" Sean asked.

She smiled at him and said, "I was thinking we could talk about setting a wedding date. Remember, I told you I'd set one once I'd finally been able to have sex. Well, it's done. Now, we can move on."

They decided to marry at the end of June and were soon on the phone calling Sean's parents, Remy, Caleb, and LouAnn with the news. Sean was going to go home and e-mail his sister, but Prim suggested he call her instead. He debated for a while, but then he decided to go ahead and phone her.

"All she can do is hang up, right?" he asked rhetorically.

Prim told Sean she was going to work on her laptop while he made the call. Once he'd dialed, he listened as the phone rang several times. Sean wondered if Debra's voicemail would pick up. That was when he heard his little sister say, "Hello?"

"Hi, Debra."

"Sean? What's the matter? Are Mom and Dad okay?"

"They're fine. Nothing's the matter. I was calling because…well, I wanted to tell you that I'm getting married in June and want you to come."

She hesitated and said, "I – I don't know if I can. When is it?"

His heart sinking, he said, "The last weekend in June. I'm getting married here in Aurora. My contract's been extended at the school, and I'm really happy here. I want you to come be part of my wedding and get to know my fiancée. You'd really like her, and I know she'd like you."

"I – I'll have to – to check my calendar," she stammered. "I'd love to come, but I'll have to make certain I can."

"You mean you'll have to check with your boyfriend."

"No, I – I just don't know about work. Really. I'll look first thing tomorrow and see. I want to come, Sean. I miss you, Mom, and Dad."

"You could still come for Christmas. Mom and Dad will be here for two weeks. You're only three and a half hours away."

"I know, but I really can't."

Feeling sad and desperate, Sean said, "We love you. We miss you. Mom and Dad don't understand and –"

"Mom and Dad don't ever understand," she said quietly. "They never will, and you've always been so busy that you can't comprehend how I feel about having parents like ours."

Sean felt as though his little sister had socked him in the gut. As tears blurred his vision, he said, "You're right. I've been busy. I've been so damned busy trying to keep our family together that I forgot to ask you if you wanted to remain a part of it. I guess I should have asked you about that before the social workers wanted to take us away when I was nine and you were three. I should have asked you if you'd rather be placed with some strangers who probably wouldn't have given a crap about anything except a check and maybe beating or molesting you. I should've let them take us away and break Mom and Dad's hearts. *That's* what I should've done instead of doing everything I could to keep us together! Did you forget that we were all happy, Debra? Did you forget how much fun we used to have when we were living with Mom and Dad?"

"They wanted to take us away?" Debra asked, her disbelief evident in her voice.

"Why'd you think I started taking care of all the business? Mom and Dad could work and care for us, but they couldn't handle paying the bills and all that. So, I started doing it, making sure we had enough, and got a job as soon as I could to help out with anything extra we needed. Remember the year Mom got that lump in her breast that had to be removed? There were a lot of medical bills and deductibles that had to be met. Guess who made sure it was all paid?"

"Sean, I didn't –"

"Did you think I did everything just for fun? Why do you think I worked so hard to get a good education for both of us? If I hadn't, then we'd still be living in the Section 8 housing working at some local convenience store or with Mom at the laundry or Dad at the supermarket."

"I never thought about it," Debra admitted. "I just sort of figured everything was okay."

"Because that's the way you were supposed to feel as a kid. I figured at least one of us shouldn't have to grow up too fast."

"I had no idea. I wish I'd known."

"If you had, would things be different now? Which guy was it in high school who made you start to feel ashamed of our parents? You can feel ashamed of them because of how they were born, but you don't feel ashamed of being the victim of a string of insecure, drunk, emotionally abusive losers?" When she started to cry, he said, "You're smart and pretty and deserve more than –"

She hung up. Sean switched off his cellphone and placed it on the end table beside him.

"Sean?"

Prim was standing at the edge of the room, looking concerned. He was going to tell her that the call could have gone better. However, when he tried to say this, all he could do was choke out a sob. Prim was instantly on the couch next to him. She took him in her arms and held him tightly as he cried. The way she reacted reminded him of his mother, who was the only other woman who had ever seen him cry. He buried his face against her neck and wrapped his arms around her as his shoulders shook.

He eventually stopped crying but stayed exactly as he was. Prim was rubbing his back, telling him things were okay and that he didn't have to do it all alone anymore. She reminded him she was with him now and that she could help him with his parents and maybe with Debra, too. She kissed his temple and whispered that she loved him more than anything in the world.

"I want my little sister back," Sean said, his voice muffled by Prim's neck. "One of those bastards is going to seriously injure Debra one day. What am I going to do then?"

"If it happens, we'll deal with it together. You can't change Debra. You can only be there for her."

"She'll never talk to me again after today."

"She will. She can't be happy with her life. She'll come back to you and your parents someday."

Sean said nothing in response to this, and Prim refrained from verbally attempting to reassure him further. Instead, she simply held him. He prayed that Debra would decide to change her life, just as Prim had worked to change hers.

The next week passed quickly. By Friday, he, Prim, and Remy were all exhausted but were determined to attend the opening night performance of *Rent* at Kensington. Maureen was also planning to be there, and Sean was looking forward to introducing his wonderful administrative assistant to his fiancée and best friend.

The production was excellent, and the students were deservedly proud of themselves. Sean, Prim, and Remy walked to the building where the opening night reception was to be held. On the way, they ran into Tony Eichstadt, who said he and several other members of the Board of Directors had come in early in preparation for the Christmas function that coming Sunday. Sean quickly introduced him to Remy, and the two men shook hands and chatted until they arrived at the reception.

"Sean and Prim, congratulations on your engagement!" Eichstadt suddenly exclaimed. "I don't know where my brain was. I should have said *that* before I said anything else. My wife is home sick, and I must have left my head back there with her."

"No worries," Prim said. After thanking him for his well wishes and then filling him in about the wedding date and the fact that she and Sean had no idea yet as to where they were going to honeymoon, she said, "If you'll excuse me, I need to freshen up."

Eichstadt made his apologies after Prim stepped out of the room. Sean and Remy munched on hors d'oeuvres and talked with the drama teacher about the excellent musical production. Prim appeared but looked paler than normal and seemed shaken.

"What's wrong?" Remy asked worriedly. "Are you going to be sick or something?"

She looked distraught, and Sean took her arm and asked if she wanted to sit down. Shaking her head, she said, "I think maybe we should just go."

"Why?" Remy asked. "What's –"

He froze and stiffened. Sean followed his gaze, which led straight to Maureen. The older woman wore a rust-colored dress and had uncharacteristically curled her shoulder-length gray hair. She looked extremely nervous.

"That's Maureen Hendry, my administrative assistant," Sean volunteered. "I was going to introduce you."

"There's no need," Remy said tightly. "We've met."

"You have? Where?"

Remy clenched his jaw as Maureen approached. She went straight towards the bookstore owner and stood in front of him before saying, "I'm so sorry."

"You're sorry?" Remy hissed. "What is there to be sorry about, *Maureen*?"

The older woman looked pleadingly at Prim, who looked as though she would rather be anywhere else except where she was. Prim bit her lip then said, "Hello, Miss Carrie."

"You look beautiful, Prim. You're all grown up." Turning back to Remy, she said, "You look so handsome, but you're too thin."

"What the fuck do you care if I'm too thin?" Remy asked very quietly.

Sean was shocked and at a complete loss as to what was behind the exchange that was taking place between his best friend and his administrative assistant. Before he could ask, Maureen said, "I care. I've changed."

"Obviously, Miss Hendry," Remy said with more than a hint of sarcasm in his voice. "You care so much and you've changed so much that I haven't seen or heard from you in six years. It was very noble of you to stay away."

Remy stalked out of the building. Sean, who was completely confused, looked between Prim and Maureen and told them to stay where they were while he went after the man. He retrieved both of their coats and jogged in Remy's wake. By the time he caught up to him, Remy was almost at the stables.

"Wait up!" he called to his friend. "It's freezing, and you have no car! Plus, you're headed away from the main road. Where do you think you're going to go?"

Remy turned, and Sean saw in the light provided by the moon that tears were streaming down the man's cheeks. He handed him his coat and put on his own before asking, "Will you tell me what the hell is going on?"

"She's my mom," Remy said thickly. "Before the divorce, she was Carolyn Maureen Hendry Artigue. I guess she decided to drop the first and last names afterwards. No wonder I couldn't find her. I haven't seen or heard from her since my little brother's funeral."

"Oh, my God. I obviously had no idea. I can't...if I had known...."

"It's not your fault," Remy insisted. "You couldn't know."

"Prim must have seen her when she went to the bathroom," Sean speculated. "I guess Maureen didn't see Prim." Feeling divided, he said, "I'm not defending your mother or anything, but I only know her as a nice woman who's the best secretary I've ever had. She must have turned her life around after your brother's death."

"She must have. Good for her. Too bad she didn't love me enough to let me know she was alive or that she cared! All my folks did after they got into drinking was think about themselves. They didn't give a fuck about me or my brother or the fact that we had little food, a piece-of-shit house, and no heat in the winter! I did everything I could to make it right, and look how things ended up. My brother and father are dead, and my mother doesn't give a rat's ass about me! I let the girl I love leave because I had to be the parent for my brother! So, I'm a successful thirty-three-year-old bookshop owner with no family and no woman in his life, and I hate it! I hate my parents for what they did to us!" Covering his face with his hands, Remy said, "But I love them too, Sean. What am I going to do?"

Sean put his arms around his friend in a brotherly hug and said, "I don't know what to tell you. Why don't you come back to the reception and just tell your mom that you can't talk to her, yet?"

"What if I can never talk to her?"

"Then you can't."

Remy nodded and wiped at the tears on his face. The two men returned to the party. Sean half-expected Maureen to have gone, but she was standing near Prim in a corner, looking distressed. Remy walked directly towards her, and Sean prayed there wouldn't be a scene at the reception. It wouldn't be fair to the students, and it wouldn't reflect well on Maureen, who was an integral part of the school's staff.

Remy came up beside his mother and said, "I can't talk to you now."

Maureen wiped at her eyes and said, "I understand. I'm just…it's only that it's such a relief to see you. After I left, I didn't know how to come back. I assumed you'd never want to see me or your father again."

"I didn't. What you and Dad did destroyed all our lives."

She nodded again, refusing to look at him.

"That doesn't mean I don't love you, but it also doesn't mean I can have you in my life right now."

"You still love me?" she asked incredulously.

"You're my mom. I remember what you were like before you started drinking. Of course I still love you. I also hate what you did."

"I deserve that. Your father and I were terrible parents for so long. We put you through hell, and I really am sorry, more sorry than I could ever say. I love you, Remy."

He nodded and said, "I need to go."

"Be safe."

"You, too."

The ride back to Aurora was awkward, but Sean had little to offer in the way of consolation. Prim had known Remy her whole life and would no doubt be having a conversation with their friend regarding what had happened at the reception. Sean was certain she would handle things better than he. Perhaps she could talk to Remy while Sean was in Atlanta, picking up his parents from the train station. Perhaps if Remy spent time with Sean's parents, it would nudge him towards a reconciliation with his own mother. Sean cared about Remy and Maureen and hoped they could have some sort of relationship despite their past problems.

After he and Prim dropped Remy at his apartment, Sean drove towards the town Square and asked Prim, "Was Maureen – Carrie – really that bad when you were young?"

"She and her husband were out of it most of the time. I wasn't supposed to go to their house, although I often did and just didn't tell where I'd been playing. The condition of the place was deplorable. Like I told you before, I was small, so I didn't really ask Remy questions about how they survived. I do know that Aunt Myrtle and Uncle Buddy used to send some kind of food back with the boys when they'd walk me home from school every day. Aunt Myrtle used to say that it looked like they never got to eat anything, and Uncle Buddy did talk to someone once about taking the kids away and putting them in foster care. Nothing happened that I know of."

Sean digested this information before saying, "I have a question that's been on my mind since I first moved here." When she looked quizzically at him, he asked, "What was Remy's brother's name and why doesn't anyone ever say it?"

Prim turned to look out of the car window and said, "Remy kind of lost it after the accident. He blamed himself for not being able to stop his brother from becoming an alcoholic like their parents and then for not being able to stop him from driving drunk and hitting that tree. Remy blamed his parents for it all, too. He became...suicidal. Dr. Stanford finally convinced him to take antidepressants and talk to Caleb about his guilt. He got better after a few months, but those of us who knew him best agreed that we wouldn't talk about his brother unless he brought it up and that we'd never say his name."

"Which was...?"

She looked back to him and said, "Sean."

"Yes?"

"You misunderstand." Reaching over to touch his arm, she said, "Remy's little brother's name was Sean."

"Oh. God. What a freaky coincidence. What was he like?"

She smiled and said, "You, only my age. Physically, he and Remy looked a lot alike with the same black hair and build. They were very close."

"What was Sean going to do after graduation?"

Prim looked at her lap and said, "He wanted to be a high school chemistry teacher. He would have been so good at it. When he talked about science, it made you excited about it, too."

"Did you love Sean?"

"Sean and Remy were like cousins or brothers. I did go out with Sean on a few dates, but we were buddies." She flashed him a sad smile and said, "Sean took me to the Senior Prom because he knew it would be the only way I'd get to go. Even though boys asked me out, they knew how I was about not being able to be touched. No one would have asked me to the prom. Sean did, even though I knew he wanted to go with another girl. He insisted he wanted to go with me."

"Can I see your prom picture when we get back to your place?"

Sean was soon sitting beside Prim on her couch, looking at pictures of her with a younger Remy look-alike. Although it had only been six years before, Prim looked younger than eighteen in her bright pink prom dress. It was evident in the photos how comfortable the boy and girl were with one another but not in a romantic way.

"How long after this did Remy's brother die?"

"About six months. It was horrible to watch him become like his parents. Remy tried everything from hauling him out of bars to taking him to a nearby town for AA meetings. Nothing worked. I wasn't shocked when I heard about the accident. I was just grateful no one else had been injured in the crash."

"Will you talk to Remy tomorrow about what happened at Kensington tonight?"

"Of course." She shut the album and turned to kiss Sean before saying, "I'm glad we saw Miss Carrie. Remy needs his mom, especially if she's sober now."

Sean put his arms around Prim's shoulders and kissed her deeply before asking how she was feeling. He knew it was too soon but wanted very badly to make love to her right then.

"It's better, but I think my doctor's right. I think it'll take another week for me to be all well."

As they kissed again, she startled him by reaching down to rub the bulge at the front of his pants. His breathing quickened as she unbuckled his belt, unzipped his fly, and freed him from his boxers. When he asked her what she was doing, she giggled and inquired, "Am I that bad at it that you can't tell?" I thought it was pretty self-explanatory."

She was soon kneeling before him and was rather clumsily taking him into her mouth. He didn't correct her on her technique or try to make suggestions. She might be a novice, but that didn't mean he wasn't thoroughly enjoying her ministrations. He slipped his fingers into her hair, closed his eyes, and concentrated on her every movement.

He warned her when he felt his climax approaching. He wasn't certain how she'd react if he came in her mouth, but she didn't pull away and drew harder on him. He felt the ecstasy of the orgasm wash over him and groaned with the pleasure.

"Did I do all right?" Prim asked him afterwards. "I wanted to make it good for you."

"It was great," he assured her, as he pulled her upwards and slid his hands under her skirt.

"What are you doing?"

"Turnabout's fair play."

Soon it was *she* who was sitting on the couch, and Sean was kneeling between her spread thighs. Her underwear lay on the floor, and her skirt was bunched up around her waist. Sean started out very tenderly then proceeded to devour her with his mouth. By the time he was finished, she had climaxed three times.

"Will I do that when we have actual sex again?" she asked him breathlessly.

Sean grinned and said, "What we've been doing on the couch *is* actual sex, Prim."

She blushed as he sat beside her and took her in his arms then said, "I know it is, but you *know* what I mean. Will it feel that good when you're in me?"

"It should feel at least that good and hopefully better."

"That was unlike anything I could have ever imagined."

"I hope you mean in a good way," he teased.

"In a fabulous way. Maybe we could –"

"No. One more week."

She pretended to pout but agreed they should do as her doctor said and wait. Neither of them wanted to rush their next encounter with intercourse and risk undoing the progress they'd made.

Sean left her with a kiss and a promise to call her the moment he arrived with his parents in Aurora the following day. She assured him that she was going to talk to Remy and reminded him to drive safely. As he drove past the front of the building, he saw Prim standing in the window, waving and smiling down at him. All was well with his world.

Chapter Ten

Prim was in-between helping customers in her shop when her cellphone rang. It was Sean. His parents' train had been delayed and they wouldn't get into Aurora until at least 7:00 p.m. Prim glanced at her watch. It was almost 4:00.

"Call me when you get to the house," she instructed. "Maybe you can bring them and meet me at LouAnn's for dinner. I'm sure we'll all be hungry."

"That's a great idea. I'll talk to you soon. I love you."

"Love you, too."

Due to the number of people searching for last-minute Christmas gifts, Prim was unable to close her shop until 5:30. She walked to the hardware store and found that Caleb still had customers. She helped him to usher those remaining out with their purchases and then count the till. She asked him if he wanted to join her, Sean, and Sean's parents at LouAnn's for dinner, but he declined, saying he was tired and needed to go home and get some rest before his morning sermons.

After they left the store, Prim walked to The Book Nook and rapped on the window until Remy emerged from the back and unlocked the door for her. He looked exhausted and unwell, and Prim wondered if he'd slept at all the previous night.

"You need to eat," she told him. "Come with me to LouAnn's. I'm meeting Sean and his parents there in a while."

"I don't feel like it, but thanks."

"Remy, I understand that you're upset about seeing your mom last night but –"

"It's fine," he said abruptly. "I saw her. It's over."

"It's not fine. I was in shock, so I can only imagine how you felt. It's so not over."

"Prim, leave it alone."

"You wouldn't leave it alone if it were me in the same situation."

He sighed and said, "No, I wouldn't."

"Are you still taking the antidepressants Dr. Stanford prescribed for you after the accident?"

"I accepted a while back that I'll probably always need to be on them." Shaking his head, he said, "Caleb told me after the accident that only a weak man refuses to admit when he needs help and that I was not a weak man. I've never forgotten that. I'll keep taking the meds."

"Great. Now, come with me to LouAnn's. It'll be good for you."

By the time they met Sean, Tiffany, and Kenny at LouAnn's Café it was 7:30. After she'd kissed Sean, Prim hugged the older couple and introduced them to Remy.

Both of Sean's parents hugged her and Remy, who seemed surprised but pleased. Tiffany patted Remy on the arm and said, "You should sit down. You look real tired, and you're so skinny!" Looking to her husband, she asked, "Kenny, have you ever seen anyone so skinny before?"

"Never," Sean's father answered. "You should eat more."

Remy smiled and visibly relaxed. Then he told Sean's parents that he appreciated their concern. For over an hour, the five of them chatted, laughed, and ate. LouAnn was a frequent visitor to their table. When they left the restaurant at 9:00, Remy announced that he was heading home but would see them all at church the next morning. Tiffany and Kenny hugged him again, telling him how much fun they'd had at dinner. Remy grinned at Sean and said, "You were right. You do have great parents."

"Do you have great parents?" Kenny asked earnestly.

Remy sobered and said, "No." He explained that his parents had been heavy drinkers and had been very bad parents, that his father and brother were dead, and that he didn't have contact with his mother.

"That's sad," Tiffany said. "I could be your mother, just like I told Prim I'd be hers. Kenny could be your father. We're good at being Mom and Dad."

"I'd like that," Remy said quietly. "I'd like that a lot."

After Remy had departed for his apartment, Sean and his parents walked Prim to hers. Tiffany and Kenny were highly enamored of Prim's place. They remarked on how much they liked it and how nice Sean's rented house was.

"The whole town's so pretty!" Tiffany exclaimed. "It's like an old-fashioned kind of town."

"I like it here," Kenny agreed. "Sean asked if we could come live here, but we have to work at our jobs for now."

"Maybe in the future," Prim suggested.

"I'd like to live here near you and Sean, "Tiffany proclaimed. "Sean says everyone is real nice."

"They are. You'll meet a bunch of them at church tomorrow."

"And then the fancy party is tomorrow night," Tiffany said with a smile. "I can't wait to wear my pretty things."

"And I get to wear a tuxedo," Kenny added. "Mine has a plaid belt that looks like Christmas."

Sean grinned and said, "It's called a cummerbund, Dad. It does have Christmas colors in it."

Kenny and Tiffany hugged Prim before they left and told her they'd see her at church in the morning. Prim kissed Sean before closing and locking the door behind him.

She walked to the front and looked out of one of the windows. As Sean's car passed, she smiled and waved as she always did when he left to walk or drive home. This time, Sean wasn't the only one waving and smiling up at her. Tiffany and Kenny were doing the same, laughing and pointing at the window.

Prim gazed at the Town Square. White lights were strung all over the gazebo, and there was an enormous tree positioned in the open area of lightly snow-covered ground that sat across from it. The tree was gaily decorated with multi-colored lights and a bright, glowing star on top. A realistic-looking nativity scene had been set up on the lawn in front of the church, and this was highlighted by a small spotlight. Snowflake-shaped lights hung on all of the old-fashioned lamp posts in the Square. Everything combined in order to make for a picturesque setting that fit perfectly with the feel of the town.

Kenny and Tiffany must be loving this, Prim thought as she shut the blinds. *What a great way to make a good impression on them.*

Prim surveyed the main living area of her apartment, which was devoid of Christmas decorations. She'd been so focused on decorating the shop that she'd neglected to put up a single holiday item in her own home. Also, setting up a tree, lights, and decorations had been something that she and her aunt and uncle had done as a family each year, and she felt odd about doing it without them.

Despite everything that had happened, Prim missed Buddy terribly. Although she loved and missed her aunt, who she now knew had really been her grandmother, she'd always been closer to Buddy. Looking back at her past with new insight, she suspected that this was the result of Myrtle's reticence towards Sandra and her child and Buddy's suspicion that he was really Prim's father. He had been a good-enough surrogate parent, although it was clear to Prim as she ruminated on her childhood that Myrtle had struggled mightily with her own demons and had never truly recovered from the trauma of being raped and giving birth to Sandra.

And I got to suffer for it, too, she thought sadly. *What if I'd never met Sean?*

Deciding she should stop pondering the "what if's" and be thankful for what she had, Prim went to her bedroom and removed her dress, stockings, underwear, and hair clip. She stared at her naked body in the standing full-length mirror in the corner. She was reminded of how she'd done this same thing in the Aurora family home the previous August. She looked virtually unchanged, but she knew there was one major difference that wasn't visible but made everything else different, too. She smiled, got ready for bed, and was soon sleeping soundly.

As Prim had expected, everyone at the Aurora Community Church was instantly accepting of Sean's parents, who were eager to hug all of their new friends. Remy's mood seemed to brighten the moment he saw the couple, and he immediately accepted Tiffany's request that he sit between her and Kenny. He also agreed to join Sean, Prim, and Sean's parents for lunch at Prim's apartment. He was smiling when he said his goodbyes at 3:00 p.m. and headed home.

Sean and his father returned to Sean's house to dress and prepare for the Kensington gala, while Tiffany remained with Prim so they could get ready together. Once the two women were alone, Tiffany asked, "Can we talk a little before we get dressed?

Prim nodded and asked Tiffany to join her on the couch. Once they were seated, Tiffany began by asking, "Are Sean and Debra having a fight?"

"What makes you think that?"

"Because I'm their mom. I know when something's wrong between them even if I don't get to talk to Debra anymore. I can tell when Sean's upset. He's sad about Debra."

"Yes."

"Did he cry about it?" When Prim nodded, Tiffany said, "He cried about it two times in front of me. I told him it would be all right, even though I really don't know. That's what moms are supposed to say to make their kids feel better."

"That's kind of what I did."

"I'm glad he cried in front of you. He keeps so much inside."

"I've been thinking maybe Kenny and I should move here before we get old. I want to be close to Sean and you and now your friend who needs a mom and dad. Do you think you'd want us to live near you?"

"Why wouldn't I?"

"Because we're not so smart and don't want you to think you have to take care of us like Sean thinks he does. I know we don't know how to do our bills and stuff, but we're not babies. If we lived here, then we wouldn't be seeing you every day. You and Sean need to have private time just like Kenny and I do. But it would be nice to be close and to see each other at least once a week."

"I think we'd all like that."

Prim and Tiffany dressed, fixed their hair and make-up and put on their jewelry. Tiffany was so excited that she could barely contain her anticipation. Prim told the woman she looked beautiful, which she did. She was an attractive, middle-aged woman, wearing a lovely silver gown with black beading and had her hair coifed in a stylish up-do. Anyone passing her would never suspect that she had below-average intelligence.

Prim wondered if Kenny and Tiffany's parents were still alive somewhere and if they ever regretted turning their children over to the State. Perhaps their parents had felt they didn't have any options. It had been a different time period, and people had looked upon those with developmental delays in a different light. Maybe their parents hadn't had the means or wherewithal to care for them. Perhaps their families had pressured them to give up their "retarded" children. Prim didn't know and couldn't judge, but she felt bad for them and for Tiffany and Kenny.

When Sean and Kenny arrived, they showered the women with compliments. Kenny kissed Tiffany, and Sean kissed Prim and murmured that he loved her burgundy dress and loved the way she looked in it. When she asked him if he thought the V-neck was too low-cut, he smiled and said he wished it were cut lower. Then he pulled her close to him and passionately kissed her. She could feel how hard he was through the material that separated their flesh and ached to touch him again.

"Do you like my hair pulled up like this?" she asked in an attempt to divert their attention away from their physical desire.

"I like your hair up, down, or in a ponytail," he admitted. "You have the most beautiful hair. Of all the girls I dated before I met you, I never went out with anyone who had strawberry blonde hair. They were all brunettes. I guess I didn't know what I was missing."

"Do you like my belt?" Kenny asked Prim as he proudly displayed his cummerbund.

She grinned and told him it was the most festive cummerbund she'd ever seen.

"We have to go," Sean announced. "If we don't leave now, we'll be late."

"I don't want you to get in trouble," his father said worriedly. "We should hurry."

They arrived at Kensington in time for Sean to drive slowly through the campus and point out the different buildings to his parents. He promised to bring them back during the daytime while they were visiting and give them a more extensive tour.

"It's such a pretty place," Kenny told Tony Eichstadt not long after they'd been introduced. "I can see why Sean wanted to come here to school. We didn't have the money, and I'm glad he didn't go away. We would have missed him. But he would have done real well here."

"I'm sure," the Head of the Board of Directors agreed. "Your son is an excellent principal. More importantly, he's an ethical man."

"What does that mean?" Tiffany asked with interest.

Eichstadt smiled but his expression was in no way condescending. He merely said, "To be ethical means to do the right thing no matter what."

"That's Sean," Kenny observed. "He's always been a good boy. His mother and I love him a lot."

Prim watched throughout the evening's festivities as Sean's parents brought joy to everyone they met. She had expected some of those gathered to be put off by having to interact with someone who wasn't rich or smart. On the contrary, the men and women in their expensive finery at the ostentatious event appeared to be genuinely pleased to talk at length to Sean's parents. She caught a glimpse of Sean once when he'd been standing unobtrusively near the piano and saw that he was watching his parents and was both grinning and wiping at the corners of his eyes.

Everyone ate, danced, and listened to Tony Eichstadt's speech about the school and the upcoming changes regarding Sean's extended contract, the school's new commitment to broadening their student body in order to include disabled students, and the Kenneth Proper Scholarship and the Tiffany Proper scholarship. Kenny and Tiffany were each given plaques commemorating the institution of the scholarships that were to be awarded in their names. As they stood on the stage, holding their plaques and smiling, a photographer snapped their picture with Eichstadt and Sean. Then Eichstadt surprised everyone by asking Kenny and Tiffany if they would like to say anything to the crowd.

Tiffany stepped up to the microphone on the podium and asked, "I just talk into here?" When Eichstadt told her "Yes," she looked back at those seated at the round tables that had been placed in the ornately decorated school museum and began, "My husband and I are so happy to be here. We're so proud of our son and of our daughter, even though she couldn't come to the party tonight. We're proud of Prim, who'll be our daughter soon. We're proud of you, too." When everyone exchanged bewildered looks, she said, "Some people don't know how to act around those of us who don't have lots of money or book learning. Kenny and I don't have lots of money, but we work real hard and like our jobs. We both got a special diploma that says we went to school and finished our learning there. I hope if you ever meet other people like us or

126

people who have even less money or smarts than we do that you'll treat them just the same as you treated us. We love all of you and hope you have a happy holiday season!"

There was total silence in the room, and several guests were dabbing their eyes with tissues. Kenny stepped up to the microphone and said, "My wife's a better talker than I am, but I just wanted to say that I'm glad you folks are...." Turning to Eichstadt, he asked, "What's that word you said before?" When Eichstadt told him, Kenny said, "Ethical. Everyone should be like that and do the right thing. So, if you see someone in need, you help them – whether it's someone in your family or a total stranger in the street. That's what makes us good." Glancing down at the plaque in his hands, he said, "I'm going to thank you for the boy who's going to get this scholarship first. He needs to have a good education but also needs to learn to be a good man at your school. It's not only about book learning; it's about learning about life. Have a very merry, happy holiday time, and a happy New Year."

Prim swallowed the lump in her throat and pulled a tissue from her purse. She wished the Propers' daughter had been there to see her parents. She rose and went over to one of the videographers.

"Will there be a DVD of this available for purchase?" she asked the man.

"No, but there'll be a montage of the evening's festivities on the website. I'm sure there'll be a special link for the two speeches that were just made. That was awesome."

She thanked the man and decided she would have to bide her time. Once the video had been uploaded, she'd find a way to get the link to Debra. Maybe it would bring her home to her family. Even if it didn't, she needed to see it.

By the time they arrived back at Sean's house, it was after midnight. His parents hugged Prim goodnight and told Sean they planned to take off their fancy clothes and get ready for bed. He explained he was going to Prim's for a while, suggesting they go to sleep if they were ready before he got back.

"That was the most wonderful event I've ever attended," Sean told Prim once they'd entered her apartment and removed their coats. "It was so gratifying."

"I think everyone who was there would agree with your opinion."

"I wish Debra had come."

"I know." Slipping her arms around his waist, she said, "I had an idea about that."

As she explained, Sean brushed some ringlets of hair from her face. When she finished, he told her that he liked the idea and would find out when the footage of the evening's program was available on the Kensington Academy website. Then he kissed her, and Prim forgot about everything else.

"I should go," he told her. "It's late, and you have to open the shop at 9:00."

"Stay a little longer," she pleaded. "Kiss me some more."

Shaking his head, he said, "If I stay, then I'll want to make love to you, and it's still too early. Just a few more days."

His hands glided over the front of her satin gown and slid down her hips. When she asked him to touch her, he took one index finger and lifted it to her neck then drew it slowly down over her exposed flesh to the point of the V that rested between her breasts. Then he lifted her chin, kissed her again, and insisted that he had to go.

Someday, he'll be able to stay forever, she thought. *Soon.*

Chapter Eleven

Sean stood beside Prim on the steps of the Aurora Community Church and looked out over the Town Square. It was a beautiful Christmas morning. The sun was shining; the air was crisp; and there was a light dusting of snow on the ground. People were dressed in their Sunday best and were smiling and hugging each other just a little more than usual. Sean's parents were already seated in a pew, saving seats for him, Prim, and Remy.

"Maybe Remy overslept," Prim proposed. "We were up pretty late last night, playing board games with your parents and decorating the tree at your house."

"Have you ever known him to be late for church?"

Prim frowned and said, "After the accident. It was before he started taking the antidepressants. He quit coming to church altogether for several weeks."

"Maybe I should go to his apartment."

"He seemed to be so happy last night with us and your parents. I'm sure that he's fine. He'll be here soon."

She sounded very certain of herself, so Sean decided to let go of his worry for a while. Prim had known Remy longer and better than Sean. If she wasn't nervous about the man's absence, then he supposed he shouldn't be either.

Sean and Prim huddled together for warmth. Their coats were "marking" their places in the pew next to Tiffany and Kenny.

"I can't wait until we open presents after church," Sean told her.

"You're like a little kid," Prim teased. "What if you don't get what you asked Santa to bring you?"

"I've got everything I need, except having Debra in our lives. It's just fun to open presents and see how excited everyone is and to have the surprise of finding out what people thought you'd like and if they like what you got them."

"Hi, guys!" Remy called out, as he jogged over towards them. "Sorry I'm late."

"We're just glad you made it in time for the service," Prim said with a smile. "Merry Christmas."

He hugged her and said, "Merry Christmas, Prim." After giving Sean a quick hug and wishing him a Merry Christmas as well, he announced, "I decided to look up the number and call my mother this morning before I left for church. That's why I was late."

Prim and Sean asked simultaneously how the call had gone. Remy admitted it had been brief and strained but that he was glad he'd decided to phone his mother. She'd told him she'd never had a better Christmas present.

"Are you going to talk to her again soon?" Sean asked hopefully.

"I don't know. It was really difficult for me to pick up the phone and dial it this morning."

"But you did," Prim pointed out. "You may find it's easier next time."

"Or not," Remy hastened to say.

"Or not," Sean agreed. He didn't want Remy to feel as though they were pressuring him in any way, although Sean was encouraged that his friend had reached out to Maureen.

The three of them went into the church and took their seats. The building was packed, and the service was both moving and invigorating. Caleb's sermon was solid, standard Christmas fare, encouraging peace, love, and goodwill towards mankind and the environment. After the service was over, everyone stayed for a half hour of Christmas caroling.

"That was so much fun!" Kenny told LouAnn as they all exited the church afterwards. "I liked that!"

LouAnn grinned and said, "Me, too. We've got a great group of people here, and Caleb's such a good pastor. He knows how to reach everyone."

"Is he married?" Tiffany asked. "He seems like such a nice man that you'd think he'd be married to a nice lady."

"He was married for fifteen years," LouAnn confided. "His wife died not too long ago of cancer. She was a generous woman, always willing to help anyone in need. She and Caleb loved each other a lot."

"Did they have any children? If they did, then I bet they're nice children."

"No children. Rumor has it that she had female problems and couldn't get pregnant."

"LouAnn, Christmas isn't the time for gossiping," Remy chided gently.

The blonde woman looked embarrassed and said, "You're right. I shouldn't have said that. Please don't tell Caleb. He's a dear friend and a wonderful pastor."

"We won't say anything," Kenny promised. "It must be hard for him. Does he have family to go to? He could come to Sean's with us."

"And you could too," Tiffany offered.

LouAnn thanked them but said her sister had invited her over to spend Christmas day with her and her family. Caleb was going to visit his siblings and other relatives in Atlanta after the second service. She bid them all a blessed day before hurrying off.

Sean suggested they walk back to his house and get warm. Then they could heat up the food he'd bought from LouAnn's Cafe for their Christmas lunch. Everyone set out, except Prim. Remy jokingly asked if she was coming, and she shook herself as if she'd been daydreaming and was returning to reality. Sean frowned and asked if she was all right. She nodded and murmured that something had just occurred to her before going past him and taking Tiffany's hand.

Sean turned to Remy, who shrugged and gave him a look that said, "Don't ask me what that was about. I've got no clue."

When they arrived at the house, everyone took off their coats and hung them on the hooks near the back door. Sean turned on the oven and put the chicken pot pies and broccoli casserole in to heat before withdrawing the Caesar salad and dressing from the refrigerator. Prim and his mother set the table; then his father put the rolls Remy had brought and the pecan pie and chocolate cake Prim had baked on the shelf of the hutch.

The phone rang, and Remy, who was the only unoccupied person at that moment, offered to answer it. He came into the kitchen with the cordless receiver held against his chest and said, "Sean, it's your sister."

Sean felt an urge to throw the bowl of salad at the wall. Not sure why he was reacting that way, he stopped mixing the lettuce and dressing and nodded before accepting the receiver. Forcing himself to sound cheerful, he wished Debra a merry Christmas and asked how her holiday was going.

"It's good," she lied unconvincingly. "How about yours?"

"Great. Mom and Dad went to church with me, my fiancée, and best friend this morning. It's a beautiful day here. How are things in Nashville?"

"The weather's pretty bad. I guess it's good I didn't make the drive to Aurora. I'll probably spend a quiet day at home."

Sean struggled not to make a comment about her latest excuse and said instead, "We haven't opened our gifts, yet."

"I know. It's before lunch. It's only...well...this is the best time for me to call."

The jerk of the month must have gone out for a few minutes, Sean thought.

"Thank you so much for the gold locket," Debra was telling him. "I love the little picture of Mom and Dad on the one side and of you and me when we were little on the other."

"I'm glad you liked it. Do you want me to go open my present now so I can let you know how much I like it? You know I will but –"

"No," she interrupted. "I should talk to Mom and Dad before...before I need to go. I wanted to wish them a merry Christmas and tell them thank you for the reindeer nightgown from Mom and the Santa Claus coffee cup Dad sent."

"Well, I'm glad you called. I love you, Debra."

"I love you, Sean."

He took the phone to the dining room, but his parents weren't there. Prim was lighting the two candles that had been placed on the table and told him Kenny and Tiffany were on the front porch with Remy, enjoying the beauty of the day.

"Debra, I'm going to get Mom and Dad. Why don't you talk to Prim, my fiancée, for a minute until they come in? Hang on."

Before his sister could protest, he handed the phone to Prim and left the dining room. He would have to apologize to Prim later for putting her on the spot but wanted Debra to make some connection to the woman he loved and didn't know how else to do it. He could hear Prim introducing herself in a light-hearted tone and asking Debra if she was having a happy holiday season.

He went onto the porch and told his parents that Debra was on the phone and wanted to talk with them. They became very excited and hurried inside. Sean stayed out on the porch with Remy. He wanted to cry but didn't.

After a few minutes, Prim came to the front door and told him that the kitchen timer had sounded. He and Remy returned to the house, where his parents were having an animated conversation about their time spent on the phone with their daughter and how nice it had been to hear her voice. Sean felt sad and rather sick as he went to the kitchen to take the food out of the oven.

As he reached for a pot holder, Prim came up behind him and put her arms around his waist. She laid her head against his back and asked him if he was all right.

"I'm sorry I surprised you like that. I wanted you to meet her somehow and didn't know what else to do."

"I'm glad you did. We had a nice, albeit superficial, conversation. She was very pleasant."

"Debra should have been here today," he said quietly. "She should be with us."

"She called, Sean. That was a big step for her, wasn't it?"

"Yes, but she was doing it while her current loser boyfriend was out and –"

"And nothing. If she had been too far gone, then she wouldn't have phoned whether the boyfriend was home or out. She'd be too intimidated to do anything without his permission."

He saw the logic in what she was saying and told her it made him feel better. Prim released him and came to stand in front of him then kissed him. When they broke apart, he hurried to take the food out of the oven before it burned.

After lunch, everyone adjourned to the living room in order to open presents. The Proper custom was that Santa came in the morning when there were small children, and family gifts were exchanged after lunch. They had already been informed weeks ago that family members got one box from each person. Tiffany explained to Remy and Prim that Kenny was the official "Present Hander-Outer" and would pass out all of the gifts under the tree then each individual would have a turn to open his or her presents in front of the others.

"We always start with the youngest and end with the oldest," Kenny added. "That's only right. The younger ones are usually the most excited and want to open their presents first. Even if Debra was here, Prim is still the youngest since Debra turned twenty-five in September and Prim won't be twenty-five until the end of May."

"Kenny knows everyone's birthdays," Tiffany proudly proclaimed. "Kenny, tell everyone while you hand out the presents."

As Kenny handed Prim her gifts, he said, "May twenty-eighth." Moving on to his son, he announced, "Sean will be thirty-one on January first. He makes every year a happy new year!" While handing Remy his gifts, he said, "You told me you'll be thirty-four on your birthday, which is February twenty-ninth and doesn't come every year. Too confusing." As he handed his wife her presents, he said, "Tiffany will be fifty-two on August fifth." As he collected his own gifts, he added, "And I'll be fifty-four on June thirtieth."

Prim was soon thanking Tiffany for a flannel nightgown with gingerbread men printed all over it and Kenny for a gingerbread man mug. She also thanked Remy for the wok she'd been talking about buying but had never gotten around to purchasing. Then she opened the box from Sean.

"An iPhone? But I don't have a data plan for an iPhone and my current cellphone contract doesn't run out until next month and –"

"And I got iPhones for us and put you on my plan. A successful businesswoman needs to have an iPhone in today's world, right? I picked out a case, but if you don't like it, you can return it and get something else."

Prim lifted the pink case that had white flowers decorating it and declared that she loved the design. She hugged and kissed Sean before asking him how she was going to ever figure out how to use it.

"I think we'll all be learning together."

Remy looked suspiciously at him and said, "What does that mean?"

"Open your gift from me."

"We can't go out of turn!" his mother protested. "You have to go next, Sean."

The first box Sean opened held a knit pajama top and bottoms that displayed X-Men Wolverine characters with claws extended all over them. He smiled and thanked his mother, who said they reminded her of when he'd been Wolverine for Halloween many years earlier. He promised her that he'd thoroughly enjoy wearing them.

His father had purchased him a mug that had a blackboard, ruler, and apple design. On the blackboard was a message that instructed the reader to go to the principal's office. Everyone laughed, and Kenny was very pleased.

The box from Debra held a dark wood nameplate and stand. *Sean Proper, Principal* had been etched in a bold script with some sort of laser. It was very elegant and had a slight lacquer finish to it. Sean loved it and said he'd have to e-mail his little sister and let her know how much he appreciated it.

Remy's gift to Sean was a signed copy of a hardcover book by one of Sean's favorite authors. Sean was immensely pleased and profusely thanked him before looking around for a box from Prim. There was none.

Everyone smiled when he asked what was going on. Prim excused herself from the living room and went through the house and out the back door. Remy was quick to follow but told Sean to wait where he was. Moments later, the back door opened again, and Sean heard what sounded like rubber rolling along the old wood floors.

Remy came in ahead of Prim, who was pushing a men's red bicycle. A sleek, black helmet hung from one of the handlebars.

"Your mom and dad said you and Debra never had bikes as kids and that you always wanted a red one. I know this one doesn't have a banana seat, but I hope you like it."

Deeply touched, he told her he loved it and went to examine the bike. The red finish had a metallic tint to it that made it seem to shimmer even in the light of the living room. He remarked that he couldn't wait until the weather would allow him to take the bike out for a test ride.

"I already have a bike, so we can ride together," Prim told him. "Mine actually has a basket in the front, so we could even bike to the park and have a picnic or something."

Or something, he thought, as he imagined making love to Prim in the countryside somewhere when the temperature was warmer.

Kenny urged Remy to open his presents. He received a plush, dark brown blanket from Tiffany, who told him it would help to keep him warm since he was so skinny. His mug from Kenny had books all over it, and he declared he would keep it at The Book Nook and use it every day for his afternoon cup of Chai tea. Prim gave him a video game that he'd wanted. It had come out only two days earlier. And Sean gave him an iPhone with a black case.

"Sean, you can't do that," Remy declared. "It's too much, and I don't have a cellphone plan, period. I only have landlines."

"You're on my family plan, too. After all, you are part of our family now, right?"

"You have been talking about getting rid of your land phones and going to a cellphone," Prim pointed out. "Just do that and pay Sean for the monthly charge."

Remy seemed uncertain and asked Sean how much his portion of the plan would be. When Sean told him, he said, "That's not much more than I pay for my home phone. I have to keep the business phone separate, but I could cancel my landline at the apartment." He considered for a moment before saying, "Okay. Thanks, Sean."

"It's Tiffany's turn next," Prim said quickly before Remy could change his mind.

Tiffany loved the sweater Prim had bought for her. It had abstract designs in varying colors all over it. She told everyone gathered that she was going to wear it the next day and couldn't wait to wear it to work when she got home.

The box from Remy held a gift basket that was shaped like a sleigh and was filled with potpourri, scented soaps, and a Mrs. Claus sachet. Tiffany was fascinated by the creative design of the gift basket and its contents and told Remy it was one of the most unusual presents she'd ever gotten.

Sean had purchased his mother a cellphone, but it was not an iPhone. She was thrilled and loved the little flower charm that hung from the top.

"That way you always know it's your phone," Sean told her. "You don't have to worry about paying the bill because it's on my plan, too."

Debra had sent her mother a DVD set of every well-known animated Christmas show ever made. Tiffany was very happy with her daughter's selection and suggested they could watch the shows during the remainder of their holiday visit. Sean remarked that he didn't know if there would be enough time, but he assured her that they would try.

Kenny had bought his wife a long, white robe with polka dots on it that zipped up the front. He had also purchased matching slippers and pajamas. Tiffany remarked that she would match all over.

Kenny received the same cellphone from Sean; but his had a star hanging from the top to denote that it was his. He too was ecstatic with the new phone and thanked his son. He asked Sean to show him and Tiffany how the phones worked, and Sean promised he'd go over it with them until they knew exactly how the phones functioned.

Remy gave Kenny a board game that Sean had told him that Kenny didn't own. Kenny wanted to play the game right away, but the others convinced him to wait until later.

Prim's gift was an official Green Bay Packers sweatshirt. Sean had told her the Packers had always been his father's favorite football team, although even Kenny didn't know why he'd become a fan. No matter what the season was like, the Packers were his team. He never missed a game on television if at all possible.

Debra had given her father a DVD about the history of the Green Bay Packers and an official NFL knit Green Bay Packers cap. He asked Prim if she and Debra had coordinated their gifts, and she informed him they had not. It was a nice coincidence.

The box from his wife held a heavy, plaid jacket with a thick lining. Kenny tried it on, declaring he was going to go outside to try it out. In a few minutes he was back, announcing that it was the best everyday jacket he'd ever had.

When Kenny took his seat beside his wife, Sean said, "I have one more present for you, Mom and Dad."

"But we only give one box with gifts in it per person for grown-ups," Tiffany remarked. "That's our tradition."

"I know, but this is a present for you and Dad. I couldn't split it in half, so you get a present together this year."

He went to his bedroom, returning with the box Prim had wrapped for him back in August. His parents laughed at the funny paper and the quirky, curved Christmas tree topper. Tiffany carefully removed it and said she wanted to save it. Then she and Kenny unwrapped the box.

When they took out the statue of the family playing the board game at the table, both of Sean's parents commented on how real the people looked and how much they resembled the Tiffany, Kenny, Sean, and Debra of years past.

"Such happy times," Tiffany murmured. "We have to put this where we'll see it a lot."

Turning to his son, Kenny said, "Sean, this is so special. You're the best son in the world. Come give me and Mom a hug."

Sean told his parents that he was glad they liked their joint gift and went to hug them. As he did so, he noticed that both Remy and Prim looking rather sad. There was nothing he could do about it. He couldn't go back and change their childhoods and lack of family.

For the rest of the afternoon, they played the board game Remy had given Kenny. Prim cooked homemade spaghetti and meatballs for dinner, and Sean showed Prim and Remy the basics of the iPhone as he had been shown by the man at the store. Then he helped his parents learn how to use their new cellphones.

By midnight, everyone was tired but happy. Sean offered to drive Remy and Prim home, and both accepted. His parents declared they were very sleepy and were going to bed. They hugged Remy and Prim and thanked them again for their presents and the fun they'd had with them all day.

"This has been the best Christmas I've had since I was five," Remy said, causing Sean's parents to hug him once more.

"This is the best Christmas I've *ever* had," Prim announced, which made the older couple hug her again as well.

Once Remy and Prim had collected their presents and put on their coats, they hurried with Sean through the freezing night air to Sean's car. They drove through the empty streets of Aurora until they reached Remy's place, which was in one of the oldest apartment buildings in town. It was a nice, historic building that had once been a small hotel. Remy said he liked it because it had character and lots of architectural detail. He liked not having to be responsible for a house as he had been for so many years when his parents were unable to do anything except drink themselves into an alcoholic stupor. Sean liked the place and was intrigued by the building and its history.

"Before I get out, I have a question for you, Sean."

"Okay."

"Why didn't you give your parents iPhones, too? Did you think they were too complicated? I mean, I know it's a lot to learn, but I see little three-year-olds using their parents' phones."

"Little three-year-olds who've been raised on them. Their brains conform and learn, depending on what they're exposed to from birth." Sighing, he admitted, "Yes, I did think it would be a challenge for Mom and Dad, especially since they've never had a cellphone, period. Also, I was worried about what kind of things they might download onto the iPhone. They don't really understand money and might buy all sorts of apps they don't need or that would add up to a lot. They wouldn't get that there's a limited amount of space in the phone. I've had to clean their computer more than once, and it hasn't been pretty."

"Makes sense. Thanks again for everything and the ride home."

Sean drove to Prim's apartment. Once they were inside and had deposited the presents onto the dining room table, Prim told Sean she had another present for him and asked him to sit on the couch and wait for her.

"I wanted to give you this here," she declared, as she handed him a small box, artfully wrapped in gold paper with a plethora of ribbon. As she joined him on the couch, she said, "I want to start our own tradition of opening special gifts for each other after everything else is over and we're alone."

"I like that idea." While he undid the bow, he asked, "Is it breakable?"

"No. Just old."

Sean lifted the lid of the box and peered inside. Nestled in some white satin fabric was a small misshapen silver coin.

"It belonged to my great-great-grandfather, the one who founded this town," Prim told him. "It's from 70 A.D. or so. I had a coin expert examine it once. I have the papers that explain who the ruler was and everything, but I didn't want to stick all that in the box."

"So, this coin is almost two thousand years old?"

"Yes."

Sean lifted the coin and studied it more closely. He was awed by the fact that the little piece of silver he held had been hand-made so many centuries in the past and that the ruler's impression was actually clear on the tiny coin.

"This is amazing. I can't wait to read about it."

"I'm glad you like it. I have history but no family. You have family but no history."

Sean replaced the coin in the box and put the lid back on before taking Prim in his arms and kissing her. She was very responsive and voiced her disapproval when he stopped and sat back.

"We can kiss some more, but first I have a present for you. Evidently, we had the same thought about exchanging gifts privately." Rising, he went to his coat and withdrew a small, square, gold box that had a tiny pink bow on top. He handed it to Prim, as he sat next to her again.

She lifted the lid then removed a delicate bracelet from inside. The bracelet was silver and had three charms on it with each one separated by tiny detailed beads. Prim declared it was beautiful and asked him to explain why he'd selected those particular charms.

"The first one is a pixie, because that's what you remind me of every time I look at you. You're delicate, magical, and beautiful." Pointing to the next charm, he continued, "The heart is because I love you so much." Fingering the last charm, he said, "The key represents that we hold the key to our future." As she admired the charms, he said, "We can add the rest throughout the years, but I wanted to start with the things that linked us just like the little beads link the charms."

Prim asked him to put the bracelet on her. Her smile broadened when she saw it on her wrist. She kissed him and told him it was lovely and that she appreciated the thought he'd put into the gift and the symbolism of each part of the bracelet. Then she kissed him again.

Her hands slid under his sweater and rubbed against his bare flesh. She told him she wanted him to make love to her, and he didn't argue. They moved to her bedroom and undressed. Sean almost groaned aloud at the sight of her slender body, the hard nipples that tipped the firm breasts, and the triangle of strawberry blonde hair. She seemed so alive and alluring, yet so fragile. He could see that she was trembling slightly but didn't hesitate to step forward and slip her arms around his neck. Then she moved her fingers up into his hair.

For a long while they simply kissed and touched. Then Prim pulled him towards the bed. After more foreplay, Sean moved between her legs. He could still sense fear within her, although it was not nearly as great as it had been the last time. However, when he made to enter her, she performed the same movement she had the first time and tried to bring one leg across to block his entry. Catching herself, she smiled weakly and apologized.

"Never apologize for being afraid. I hope after tonight you won't be afraid anymore."

"Me, too. It hurt so much the first time that I guess I'm still scared."

"No more pain, remember?"

Prim nodded and slowly parted her knees. Sean drew on his fifteen years of experience in order to make her relax and truly want him inside of her. She was soon urging him to enter her body with his.

But she automatically tensed as he slowly sank into her. It wasn't until his cock was completely encased by her slick, hot passage that she allowed herself to stop shaking and release the tightness in her limbs. She smiled up at him, and he smiled back.

"Are you okay?"

She nodded and asked him to make love to her as he would to any other woman.

"I can't do that. I never loved any of the others like I love you."

"You know what I mean. I want to know what sex is really like for you and me."

As her hands and mouth explored his flesh, he allowed his palms and fingers to roam over her breasts, belly, waist, hips, and thighs. He felt the pulsing of her around him and thanked God that she was reacting normally to his touch. She made small moaning noises as he stroked her and licked and sucked on her nipples. When he added rhythmic thrusting, she murmured his name. She didn't ask him to stop, so he didn't.

Prim cried out as she came. She ground her hips against his, driving him deeper into her. Sean was on the verge of climax but wanted to watch her come. He raised himself slightly and savored the sight of her experiencing such pleasure for the first time with him in her. Her lithe body writhed beneath his, and he gave in and came. The intensity of orgasm was nothing new to Sean, yet this climax was different from any other he'd ever had because he'd had it with Prim.

"That was…fabulous," Prim said with a tender smile as he withdrew and lay beside her on the mattress. "Was it okay for you?"

Propping himself up on one elbow, Sean echoed, "Okay? Prim that was the most beautiful sex I've ever had with anyone."

"You're so amazing, Sean. You're dedicated, handsome, and…good."

"I could say the same things about you, except I'd call you beautiful instead of handsome, of course."

"Why would you call me beautiful? I'm not."

Sean frowned and asked, "What makes you think that? Who told you that?"

"No one had to tell me."

"Prim, you're naturally gorgeous. All I've heard in town is how every boy wanted you but knew you couldn't be touched so no one tried. Every man who meets you now tells me how drawn he is to you and how envious they all are of me."

She was silent. Sean was at a loss as to how to proceed.

Remy, he thought later as he drove back to his house. *Maybe Remy can give me some advice.*

"It was probably Mr. and Mrs. Aurora who poisoned her mind," Remy told him the next day when Sean dropped by The Book Nook, which had only been closed for business on Christmas Day.

"You mean Myrtle's parents?"

"Remember I told you how crazy religious they were? Mrs. Aurora was a big believer in women not enhancing their feminine attributes. She thought it was prideful and that vanity for either sex was a sin.

"You've told Prim all the right things. You've made love to her. I don't know how else you can convince her that she's a truly attractive woman." As he moved some books to a nearby shelf, he said, "I always used to tell her what a pretty pixie she was when she was younger and had that nickname. I suppose she thought it was just talk. Part of it was, since she was kind of like my kid sister and I wasn't thinking of her in a sexual way. But I was also being serious."

"It's so frustrating! How can I change what's ingrained in her brain?"

"You can't. Only Prim can."

"Thanks a lot."

"It's the truth. You can't make Prim have a better self-image or straighten out your sister's self-esteem issues any more than I could make my parents or my brother stop killing themselves with alcohol. All you can do is give positive reinforcement and hope they come around. I know you're used to fixing problems. It's in your nature, just like it's in mine. You have to accept that you can't fix everything or you'll self-destruct. Trust me. I've been there."

Chapter Twelve

"Happy New Year!"

Prim laughed with joy and turned to kiss Sean as the fireworks exploded above the crowd gathered in the Aurora Town Square. Before she brought her lips up to his, she said, "Happy birthday, Mr. Proper."

He grinned and thanked her then pulled her close to him and kissed her with such intensity that it took her breath away. They hadn't had sex since the morning after Christmas, and Prim wanted to leave the festivities in the Square and go straight to her apartment and make love to Sean. She wanted to feel him in her again and to begin to learn how to please him as well as herself in a variety of ways.

"Happy birthday, Son!" Kenny exclaimed from beside where Prim and Sean stood kissing. "Can Mom and I give you a hug?"

Sean smiled and hugged first his father, then his mother. When Kenny suggested they get hot chocolate, the two men excused themselves, promising to return moments later with cups for the four of them. Prim and Tiffany watched as they made their way through the crowd.

Tiffany took Prim's gloved hand in hers, squeezed it, and said, "My little boy is so grown up. Every year I can't get over it. He's such a miracle."

"Do you believe every child is a miracle?"

Tiffany grew serious and said, "Yes, but most aren't miracles like Sean."

"What do you mean?"

"If I tell you, then you can't ever tell Sean. I'm not asking you to lie. I'm just asking you not to tell about when he was born." Tiffany frowned and said, "I don't know if you know this or not, but it hurts worse than anything to have a baby."

"So I've heard."

"When it was time for me to have my baby, we had to go to the hospital for poor people, and the doctors weren't so good there.

144

Kenny stayed with me the whole time, which was a long time. There were problems, and when the baby finally came out, he was dead. The people at the hospital said it was a sad thing but that it happened sometimes to babies being born. Kenny and I cried and cried and asked to hold him. He was all cold and blue, but we wanted to hold him and kiss him. The nurses told us how sorry they were. We asked them to check him again to make sure he was really dead, and they did. We were so sad."

Prim felt chilled to the bone, and it had nothing to do with the cold January air. She wanted to say something but felt it wouldn't be right. Tiffany needed to tell her this story in her own words without being directed or pressured.

"He was born at 11:25 p.m. on New Year's Eve, and we held and kissed him for a long while. He was so still." Tiffany blinked back tears and said, "My poor little baby. He was dead but looked so peaceful. Kenny and I said there must be a reason for God to take our son while he was being born but prayed for God to change His mind. All of a sudden, the baby moved a little and made a noise. Everyone had left us alone in the room, and Kenny ran out to tell them that the baby was alive. They thought because we were slow, we didn't understand he was really dead, but Kenny told them to come and see. When the doctor came back in, the baby was all pink and warm and crying. The medical people got real excited and took him and checked him out again. They said they couldn't explain it because he'd been dead and was dead for a long time after he came out. The doctor said he was going to put the time the baby was born right then because he hadn't been alive before. So, it said on the papers that he was born at 12:01 a.m. on New Year's Day."

"My God," murmured Prim. "Why didn't you ever tell Sean?"

Tiffany looked in the direction of her son, who was standing in line with his father and said, "We didn't want to scare him or make him feel like something was wrong with him. We thought if we told him he was born dead and then came to life that he might think about it too much. The doctors had told us he might be slow like us or even worse because his brain hadn't had any air for so long, but he turned out to be smarter than most people. We were so grateful and happy. That's why we named him Sean."

Barbara Cutrera

"I don't understand."

"We went to the priest at our church and told him what happened. We said we wanted to name our baby something that meant God was kind to us. He looked up some names and told us Sean meant that God was gracious. He said *gracious* was another word for *kind*. So, we named him Sean."

"I knew that Sean was a special man, but I had no idea how special. What about Debra's birth?"

"She came quick and didn't have any problems being born. She's a smart girl, but she's not as smart as Sean. We never told her that though. We always loved and treated them the same, as much as any parent can do that with their kids. Every kid is different and wonderful." Looking sad, she said, "We miss her. I wish she'd be with us again."

"Sean wishes that, too."

"He's always wanted the best for all of us. Kenny and I know it was hard for him to take care of things because we were slow, but he never complained. He never complains, but he worries a lot about everything. He keeps it all inside, and that's not good for anyone. It makes me worry about him. That's why I was so glad when you told me he cried in front of you. He should do that more. I get the idea he talks to Remy about things, and that's good. He needs to talk to another man who's not his dad and who's as smart as he is."

"Remy needs that, too," Prim pointed out. "I suspect that's why he and Sean became such good friends so quickly. Plus, you and Kenny have been great for Remy during your visit. You've made such an impact on him."

"Do you think he and his mom are doing all right meeting tonight?"

"I hope so. He wants what Sean has with you and Kenny, but things with his mom were so bad for so long that I don't know if he can have a close relationship with her."

"At least they're both trying." Sighing, she said, "I'm really going to miss it here. It's so nice. I'll miss Sean like I always do, but I'm going to miss you, Remy, and all these other great people, too. I hate to leave tomorrow."

"We're going to miss you and Kenny as well. We'll talk on the phone and through e-mail."

146

"It's not the same." As the men approached with their drinks, she said, "I want to be like your mom for real. You need a mom who's here and can love you all the time in person."

Prim's eyes misted over with tears, and she hugged Tiffany and told her that she wanted that very much.

"The hot chocolate is delicious!" Kenny proclaimed. "You have to try it!"

The women stepped apart and accepted their cups. Lines creased Sean's forehead, and Prim knew he sensed her sadness and his mother's. She forced a smile and then sipped her hot chocolate.

"It *is* delicious!" Tiffany exclaimed. "I think this is the best hot chocolate I've ever had!"

"It's LouAnn's secret recipe," Prim confided. "I don't know what she does to make it taste so good."

"It's nice that lots of people come out to celebrate and see fireworks for New Year's Eve," remarked Kenny. "That was real pretty."

"I'm so glad you and Tiffany got to see it," Prim told him. "It's great you were able to be here for the Kensington holiday party, Christmas, New Year's Eve, and Sean's birthday."

"Kenny, I don't want to go," Tiffany volunteered. "I like Aurora, and I want to be near to Sean, Prim, Remy, and all these nice people."

"We've talked about this. I want to move here, too. We can't right now. We have jobs and our life in Tallahassee."

"Being close to our children is more important," Tiffany insisted. "We'll find jobs here."

"What if we can't? I won't live with our children. That's not right."

"I didn't say it was. Sean would tell us if we couldn't make it."

"I don't want him to have to tell us what we can and can't do all the time. He's had too much on his shoulders since he was little."

"Mom and Dad, please stop," Sean interrupted. "It's my birthday. You two hardly ever fight. Don't do it today."

Kenny apologized and told Tiffany that they could talk more about it on the train and then when they got back to their apartment. The couple kissed and smiled at Sean.

"I'm tired," Kenny announced. "I think I want to go back to Sean's and go to bed. We can all sleep late tomorrow and then have Sean's birthday dinner."

"I have some business to take care of early in the day, but I'll be over to Sean's as soon as I'm done," Prim reminded them. Turning to Sean, she said, "Why don't you walk home with your parents? I'm going to go upstairs and hopefully get some sleep."

"Are you sure?"

"Sean, I live right across the street. I can walk home in two seconds. I appreciate the chivalrous attitude, but I'll be fine."

He reluctantly agreed, kissed her, and waited until she'd hugged his parents before setting off with them towards his house. When they were almost out of sight, Prim heard Caleb say her name.

"Happy New Year, Caleb," she said with a soft smile.

"I wanted to wish you the same. You don't look very happy. Do you want to talk about it?"

"No, but thank you."

He nodded but looked disappointed and told her that she knew where to find him if she needed anything. She thanked him again then excused herself and walked across the street and around the corner.

Remy was sitting on the step in front of her door. She asked him if he wanted to come inside, get warm, and talk. He nodded and followed her in.

Once they'd hung their coats on the coat rack, Prim asked her friend if he wanted some tea before beginning to cry. Remy put his arms around her, and she could tell that he was crying, too. She hugged him and buried her face against his chest.

Eventually, Prim asked, "It didn't go well with your mom?"

"It's like I'm talking to a stranger," he admitted. "I want my mom back, the one I had when I was small. Maureen is nice, caring, and sober. All of that is great, but I remember her playing games with me and teaching me to read and...and...it's just been too long and too much has happened. I'm glad to know her now, but she's not Mom. She's Maureen."

"It's better than it was not knowing anything, isn't it?"

"Yes, but I guess I always hoped that someday she'd come back and be the same person she was before the drinking and the disappearing act. That was stupid of me."

"It's not stupid. It's human nature."

Still holding her, he asked, "Why are you upset? Did something happen at the celebration tonight?"

"Tiffany said I need a mom around to love me. She's so right. I want *my* mom and wish I could have known her. I hate everything that happened before I found out the truth. I hate the way things were and didn't realize how wrong it all was. I never had a real mother, and I want mine. Instead, I killed her."

"You didn't kill Sandra any more than you killed the man in that trunk. Leukemia killed her."

"But if it hadn't been for me, then she could have gotten treatment. The odds of her surviving would have been really good. Because of me, she died. It's my fault."

"It was Sandra's choice." Remy stepped away from her and asked angrily, "Do you really believe you're to blame? You were responsible for some man's raping Myrtle and bringing Sandra into existence? You were responsible for Sandra's sleeping with every boy she knew who attracted her? You were responsible for her sleeping with a man the night of her eighteenth birthday and getting pregnant with you? You were responsible for her getting leukemia? You were responsible for her deciding not to have an abortion? You were an innocent! Can't you see you were the one good thing that came out of that whole mess in the Aurora household? The fact that you turned out to be sweet, smart, and beautiful to boot can't be an accident."

"I'm not beautiful," she mumbled, as she stared at her feet. "Sean thinks I am, but it's only because he loves me. I'm not pretty at all."

"That's a load of bullshit your grandparents and Myrtle put into your head!" he growled. "You probably don't even remember them brainwashing you. They were crazy. You've always been pretty, which is why every boy in this town who was anywhere near your age wanted to date you. You have beauty and this way about you that makes men want to protect you and fuck you all at the same time."

"Remy, don't say that!"

"I'm saying it because it's the truth! You refuse to see it and I hate that! I've always loved you like a sister and can't stand it when you downplay yourself. Sean thinks you're beautiful because you *are*. Everyone sees it but you!"

"How can I see it? I want to believe you and Sean, but I can't force myself to see what I never thought was there!"

Remy shook his head and announced that he was going to the restroom. Prim pulled several tissues from the box by the couch, wiped her cheeks, and blew her nose. By the time she'd drained a glass of water, Remy returned to the main living area.

"I should go," he said. "I'm sorry that I yelled. I was upset because of my mother and then I lost it when you said that about being responsible for your mom's death and not being pretty. I shouldn't have gotten so angry. I just worry about you."

"Like Sean worries about Debra."

"Exactly. There's nothing either of us can do about what we see is a huge problem. I wish I could make you perceive yourself the way others do. I pray that you will at some point."

"Do you still blame yourself for your brother's death?"

"No."

"But it took you a while to recognize that it wasn't your fault."

"Yes."

"So, it's going to take me a while to sort out my own feelings about lots of important things in my life."

He nodded and came over to hug her. Then he kissed her forehead and told her to get some sleep. As he put on his coat, he said, "I'll see you at Sean's tomorrow night for the party."

She thanked him for being her oldest and closest friend. He told her the feeling was mutual.

"I thought Sean was your best friend."

"Guy friend," Remy clarified. "There is a difference, Prim."

She smiled and said, "I love you, Remy Artigue."

"And I love you, Pretty Pixie."

Once Remy had gone, Prim shut off the lights and went to her room. She removed her shoes, pants, heavy sweater, bra, and underwear and then slipped on the flannel nightgown Tiffany had given her for Christmas. She smiled at the gingerbread men on the nightgown and went to her bathroom. When she flicked on the light, she blinked in surprise.

I AM A PRETTY PIXIE.

Remy had taken a tube of lipstick and had written the words on the mirror above the sink. When Prim stared at her reflection, the words were right in front of her. She said them aloud.

Nothing happened. There was no blinding flash of light, no instant recognition of her own attractiveness. However, Prim noticed that she did feel *something* deep inside when she read the words aloud. She said them again, and she liked what she felt when she did so.

Prim left the lipstick on the glass. She decided she would be mindful of the words every time she looked in the mirror and would say them aloud. If she reached a point where she believed what she was saying, then she'd clean them off.

The following morning, Prim repeated the words on the mirror as she brushed her hair. She'd already prepared Sean's birthday meal the previous day. Tiffany had offered to cook and was planning on heating frozen pizzas and buying a birthday cake from the store. Despite his willingness to eat whatever his mother prepared, Prim knew how much Sean loved home-cooked meals and had asked her future mother-in-law if she could do the cooking and baking. Tiffany had thought it was sweet and hadn't objected.

Prim left her apartment and drove to Mae Lane's house. Mae was LouAnn's little sister and was forty-two, the same age Sandra would have been had she lived. According to Sandra's diary, Mae had been with her on the night of her eighteenth birthday. Prim had realized as she stood on the steps of the church on Christmas Day that Mae might hold some key to the mystery of her paternity. Prim had called, asking if they could meet, and the woman had suggested New Year's Day since LouAnn would be visiting her deceased husband's family and Mae's husband and sons would be out hunting.

The Lane country home was forty-five minutes east of Aurora. When Mae opened the front door, Prim had to fight to hide her shock. The blonde woman was at least seven months pregnant. Mae smiled, greeted her, and explained, "Our two sons are eighteen and seventeen. We hadn't planned on having any more children, but life had other plans for us. It was a pleasant surprise."

As she took her seat on the sofa in the enormous living room, Prim accepted Mae's offer of a cup of hot tea and a cranberry-orange muffin, which turned out to be delicious. She asked Mae if she'd baked it herself, and Mae confided that LouAnn had brought four dozen the day before for their New Year's Eve party.

"I'm not a great cook like my sister. I'm a great wife, mother, and hostess and know how to please my husband in bed. When you can do those things, you don't have to be a great cook. You simply have to know where to find good food." Looking intently at Prim, she said, "My sister's kept me up-to-date about Aurora residents and business since I left twenty-four years ago. She tells me you're engaged. Congratulations."

"Thank you."

"You told me you wanted to talk about your mama," Mae said as she broke off a piece of muffin and then put it in her mouth. Prim noted the perfectly manicured nails, the expertly coifed hair, and flawless make-up job. Her maternity shirt and pants were certainly designer, as were her shoes. Prim felt extra-plain compared with this woman.

"You and my mama were best friends in high school?"

"We were quite the party girls. Our parents would have died if they'd known about half of what we did. Hers especially. Mr. and Mrs. Aurora were overly pious. They made her start dying her hair when she was a little girl because they thought redheads were more prone to sin." Glancing at Prim, she asked, "You did know your mama was a redhead, didn't you?"

"I'd heard that from a few people in town."

"She had the prettiest red hair, and they made her dye it. They wanted her to be a brunette like them, but she demanded that if they were going to make her dye her hair, she wanted to be blonde. They gave in. They usually did with Sandra. I got the impression they didn't cave with Myrtle as much when she'd been growing up."

"What was my mother like?"

"Kind of like me but more brazen, I suppose. We were good at sports and school. We liked the attention we got from boys and started having sex with them when we were freshmen in high school. We used our natural attributes and enhanced them to get what we wanted from boys. We had a lot of fun, but we weren't rash. We were …careful about not getting pregnant. That's why I was so surprised when Sandra got pregnant with you. She'd had sex so many times without ending up pregnant." Looking down at her own rounded belly, Mae said, "I guess we all miscalculate sometimes."

"But the night of her eighteenth birthday, she went to a party with you."

"Yes, she did. It was at Dempkey's Bar, which was pretty wild even back then. We were there for a while. Then Sandra came over and told me she had to leave. I knew by the way she was talking that she was going off to have sex. I wished her a happy birthday again, and then she was gone."

"Did you see whom she left with?"

Mae shook her head and said, "Honey, I don't know who your daddy is. Your mama told me the next time I saw her that she'd had the best sex of her life with an older man, but she wouldn't tell me who it was. All she'd say was that he was a man who knew how to do it better than any of the boys we'd been sleeping with."

"She didn't tell you anything else about him?"

"Well, she did tell me *about* him, just not his identity. She said he was older than we were, that he was blonde, that he was sexy and smart, and that he was very good in bed."

"Did she tell you what they did?"

"She did, but you don't need to hear it. You shouldn't have someone telling you about all the ways your mother had sex. All you need to know is that it was nothing immoral." Laughing, she said, "I guess it depends on your definition of *immoral*. One could say that both of us were loose girls. We were, but we never did anything terrible. We simply liked sex, and neither of us felt that was a bad thing."

"What happened after my mother told you she was pregnant?"

"She wanted to get you away from her parents and sister. She said they were crazy. She was going to go to Atlanta after you were born and be a singer. She planned to stop dying her hair. She wanted to enjoy raising you, living life, and having sex. Then she found out about the leukemia."

"Did she consider having an abortion?"

"Never. She said you were her baby and that it was her duty to protect you. She knew you were a girl and said you were going to be smarter, prettier, and sweeter than she'd ever been." Mae reached across the table and touched Prim's hand before adding, "She never regretted her decision, not even towards the end."

"What happened after I was born?"

"Sandra wouldn't let you out of her room. She said she wanted to spend every last moment of her life with you. She did. All of her waking moments were spent holding you, talking to you, and playing with you. I went to see her every day that last year of her life. We thought she would die holding you in her arms, but Buddy insisted that they put you in your crib when she lost consciousness for the last time. He was right to suggest that. She was already gone, and you didn't need to be next to her when she died."

Mae dabbed at her eyes with a napkin and said, "Sandra loved you so much. She was my best friend, and I still miss her."

"I wish I'd known her."

"Me, too."

"Did my mother ever tell you *why* she didn't want to reveal my daddy's identity?"

"No."

Prim sighed but thanked Mae for her honesty. Before rising from the table, she asked, "Do you know why she named me what she did? I know about the Primrose part. Cassandra was her given name, so that makes sense. But what about the Anastasia portion in the middle?"

Mae stared into her teacup and said, "When we were girls, we watched a movie about Grand Duchess Anastasia and the murders of the Russian royal family by the Bolshevik secret police in 1918. Sandra was deeply affected by it and said she identified with Anastasia, who was supposedly a very bright and impish girl. Kind of high schoolish, but I thought it was very poetic. Sandra was always one to try to help lost causes."

"Why do you think that was?"

Mae stood and said, "Because I believe she thought of herself as a lost cause. She wanted you to be happy, something she never really was. She knew how to have a good time, but things weren't happy at home. She knew she wasn't loved, which was a terrible thing. Looking back on it, I suspect that's why she slept with so many boys. She wanted love from someone."

"And you?"

"I had a happy home. I just liked the power that came along with sex."

Not quite certain what Mae meant by this, Prim thanked her for her time and left the Lane home. She drove back to her apartment in Aurora, went to her apartment, loaded all the food for the party into her trunk, and drove to Sean's house.

Sean and Remy helped her bring everything in, and she put the macaroni casserole in the oven and the shredded barbecue roast in the microwave. Tiffany placed the marinated vegetable salad and the pasta salad on the table, while Kenny placed the cake on a shelf of the hutch. Remy warmed the biscuits in the oven once the casserole had been removed, and they all sat down to eat.

Everyone complimented Prim on the food, and they proceeded to eat and then to have second helpings. Prim was pleased by this, but her mind was on her conversation with Mae. After dinner, they adjourned to the living room so Sean could open his birthday presents.

His parents gave him a digital camera, and he protested that they'd spent too much.

"You needed a good camera to take pictures of your new hometown and the school and of your fiancée," Kenney said.

Tiffany pointed out, "You'll want it to take pictures of your kids someday."

"The man at the store said this camera was the best one for a person who wanted to take good pictures but wasn't a real photographer," Kenny declared. "You should have the right camera for what you need."

Prim knew that Sean wanted to push the issue of price with his parents but simply smiled and thanked them. He assured them he would enjoy using the camera and that it would be a good catalyst for him to explore the surrounding areas. This led to an explanation of what the word *catalyst* meant.

Remy's gift to Sean was a fishing pole. Since Sean had told him he'd never been fishing, Remy said it was high time he learned. They would go as soon as the season permitted. He declared he was also going to teach Sean how to ride a horse, just as he'd taught Prim and his younger brother. Sean was eager to learn and thanked his friend.

Prim gave Sean a framed photo of him, Prim, Sean's parents, and Remy. The picture had been taken the week before by Caleb as he'd been snapping photos of the decorated Town Square to submit to *The Aurora Town Talk*. The little group had been admiring the Christmas tree when he'd asked if he could take their picture. Later, Prim had called him and asked if she could get a copy. She'd enlarged the print to an 8 x 10 and had put it in a nice dark frame that could go in Sean's home or office.

It was a wonderful picture of all five of them, and one could tell how happy they were. The tree provided the perfect backdrop, and Caleb had gotten a nice close-up of the group. Sean smiled and declared he was going to put it in his office as soon as he returned to school. Prim was thrilled he liked it but knew what he was thinking – that Debra should have been in the picture, too.

"I have another present for you at my place," she told him as she cut the cake later that evening. "You have to wait until you get back from Atlanta tomorrow afternoon to get it, though."

"The picture was perfect. I don't need anything else."

"Let me surprise you. After you get back from bringing your parents to the train, meet me at LouAnn's Café for dinner. Then you can come back to my place to get your special gift."

"I will on one condition."

"Which is?"

"Open your mouth," he directed mischievously.

Feeling rather embarrassed although she wasn't sure why, Prim complied. Sean took the middle finger of his left hand and lifted one of the icing rosettes Prim had formed on top of the cake. He offered it to her, and she didn't hesitate to use her tongue to catch some of the frosting that was about to fall then wrap her lips around the end of the finger and slowly pull back. Sean literally groaned, although he did so quietly. Prim bent to cut another piece of cake and smiled a satisfied little smile.

To think I couldn't even hold Sean's hand back in August, she thought. *Look at me now!*

When Sean joined Prim at LouAnn's the following evening, he ordered tomato soup and a grilled cheese sandwich. She proclaimed the combination sounded delicious and decided she'd have the same thing for dinner. Sean was stunned when Prim told him she'd never eaten the two together. Before she could utter the words, he said, "We never did that when I was growing up."

"Do I say it that often?"

When he nodded gravely at her, she looked out of the window at the Town Square and said, "Remy and I had a pity party for a little while after I came home from the fireworks. He wrote something on my mirror, but I didn't discover it until after he went back to his place. You'll see it tonight. I'm leaving it up and trying to believe it. I hope you won't laugh."

"I won't."

"You don't even know what it says."

"It doesn't matter. I still promise."

Once they were in Prim's apartment, Sean asked, "When Remy was here night before last, did you have an argument?"

"Sort of. He got angry because I said I was responsible for my mother's death and that I wasn't pretty. He disagreed. He also told me I had this thing that made men want to protect me and...have sex with me."

Sean snorted and remarked, "Remy's more direct than that when he gets upset. I'm sure he probably said men want to protect you and fuck you. He's right. There's making love; there's sex; and then there's fucking."

"What do you want with me?"

"All three." He paused and added, "And to love and protect you, of course."

Sean excused himself to use the bathroom. Prim took the opportunity to shut the wooden blinds that ran along the front windows. When Sean returned to the living area, Prim asked him what he thought about the message written in lipstick on her mirror.

"I think it's genius. I'm glad you left it up. I hope you come to believe it soon. It's one hundred percent true."

As Sean got himself a glass of water, Prim went to the master bedroom and put on the short, sheer, green nightgown. She felt aroused and ashamed simultaneously and reminded herself the shame was coming from the part of her past that had been so twisted by fate and her relatives. She said aloud, "I am a pretty pixie." Then she returned to where Sean was waiting.

As soon as Sean spotted her in the nightgown, Prim could *feel* his desire radiating from across the room. She shyly looked down and asked if he liked her new nightgown. Speechless, Sean nodded and placed his glass of water on the dining room table as he approached.

He took her in his arms and kissed her while weaving his hands through her hair and then lowering them to her back. He moved his mouth to her neck, and Prim found herself throbbing in anticipation and wishing he would unzip his fly and enter her right there. When he stopped and drew back, she thought he might do exactly that. He didn't.

"What is it?" she asked rather breathlessly.

"I just...I want to look at you for a moment. You're so beautiful. The nightgown is perfect for you and makes you look even more like some sort of fairy creature." Grinning, he said, "Maybe a woodland nymph tonight."

"I want you," she said softly as she felt the blush creep up her cheeks. "I want to please you and myself."

Sean kissed her then took one of her nipples in his mouth through the sheer fabric and slid his hands up under the hem of the gown. Prim moaned and said his name as he gently rubbed his fingers between her legs. When he moved his mouth to the other breast, she came. Sean supported her with his one arm as she climaxed, but he never stopped sucking on her nipple or touching her with his fingers.

"Enter me," she demanded. "I *need* you to come in me."

"Then take me in you," he said in a very low, quiet voice.

She removed his sweater and unzipped his jeans. Then she stopped, took his hand, and led him to her bedroom. Once there, he stepped out of his shoes and slipped out of his socks, jeans and boxers. She urged him to lie back on the bed and scrutinized his body just as he'd scrutinized hers. He didn't blush or look away. He stared up at her as she stared down at him.

Prim climbed onto the bed and bent to kiss Sean. He immediately began to gently squeeze her breasts as she awkwardly prepared to take him inside of her. He moved his hands to her waist and held her immobile. She was instantly and inexplicably terrified. Her emotions must have been evident in her expression, because Sean hastened to reassure her that everything was fine.

"If everything's fine, then why are you holding me like this?"

"Because the way you were about to take me inside of you would have hurt us both. I want to show you a more…pleasurable way." As she tried to stop shaking, he asked, "Do you want to call it quits for tonight?"

"No. Show me."

He was soon fully embedded in her and explained different ways she could move on top of him to make both of them come. Prim began to try some of the moves. She reveled in the feel of his large shaft stretching her and the exquisite sensations she felt as she undulated her hips, raising and lowering herself on top of it. Sean's breathing became ragged as he allowed her total control and watched her moving on top of him in her sheer green gown. His hands never stopped caressing her where he was able to reach.

She could somehow tell that he was on the verge of coming. Continuing to move her hips, Prim quickened the rhythm and slid her hands up into her hair. She had no idea why she did this, but it seemed like it was the appropriate thing to do. She watched and felt Sean climax as she surrendered to her own orgasm. Just when she thought she was finished, Sean rubbed his thumb over the spot below the triangle of hair, and she experienced a brief but intense resurgence of sexual ecstasy.

Tired but overjoyed, Prim soon lay next to Sean, who drifted off to sleep. Prim sat up and gazed at the naked man who was so alive and so loving. She thought of Tiffany's story about Sean's birth. Neither Tiffany nor Kenny was deceptive about anything, and Prim believed every word the older woman had spoken. She imagined the heart-wrenching scene in the delivery room. She pictured the stillborn baby, the grim-faced doctor and nurses who probably secretly thought it was better that the delayed parents not have the responsibility of raising a child, and the grieving mother and father. She imagined Tiffany and Kenny crying as they held and kissed their dead little boy and prayed to God. He had certainly interceded, but why? Was it because of the parents, because of the eventual existence of Debra who would need him, or because Sean would one day be meant for Prim? Was it because of Mr. Spiro at the restaurant? Or was it because of Remy? Perhaps it was because of every child Sean had helped in his vocation as a principal. Perhaps it was all of the above or someone whose life Sean hadn't touched, yet. She suspected it was a combination of everything.

Sean had definitely been given a second chance at life for a reason. There was no way a baby could be clinically dead for over thirty minutes and not suffer any detrimental consequences. Yet, Sean was healthy and highly intelligent. He was, indeed, a miracle.

Prim got into bed and pulled the covers up on top of both of them. She snuggled against Sean and enjoyed the warmth and feel of his body. The thought of him as a newborn baby who was cold and blue was frightening to her, and she saw the wisdom in Tiffany and Kenny's decision never to reveal the truth to Sean. If thinking about it scared Prim, then how would Sean feel if he knew he'd been born dead and had remained so for an extended period? He could never know. He worried too much about everything and everyone as it was. Prim would never tell.

Chapter Thirteen

Sean was exhausted but happy. His day with the students at Kensington had been extraordinarily rewarding, and he was glad he'd made time to spend one day each week with those who hadn't been able to go home for the holidays. He had gotten to know those eleven boys and girls particularly well and to bond with them on a different level from that of the general student populace. Since these children were ones who had more complicated and often troubled home lives, this was important to him.

The majority of the students at Kensington seemed to like and respect him. Their acceptance of him did make his job easier and more enjoyable, and he'd appreciated it. It was something he didn't take for granted.

When he got home, Sean forced himself to lift weights; then he took his customary hot bath before donning the Wolverine pajamas his mother had given him for Christmas and getting ready for bed. He fell asleep as soon as he'd laid his head on the pillow.

The ringing of his iPhone woke him at 8:00 the following morning. He groaned and reached for it. He still had a few more days of vacation and had been looking forward to sleeping late. When he glanced at the display and saw that the caller was Tony Eichstadt, he was instantly awake and answered as if he'd been up for some time.

"Sorry to call during your holiday," said the Head of the Board of Directors apologetically. "I wanted to know if I could meet you for lunch."

"Of course. Where? Atlanta?"

"No, I was thinking I'd like to visit your adopted hometown. Would you mind giving me a tour?"

Sean doubted that Eichstadt had decided to drop by for a visit "just because" but replied nonchalantly that he would love to show the man around Aurora. He wasn't lying but wondered what Eichstadt's motive was even as he rose from his bed and suggested they meet at noon at LouAnn's Café for lunch.

Sean put on a nice pair of jeans, a long-sleeved white shirt, and a cream-colored cable-knit sweater. After slipping on socks and shoes, he washed his face and combed his brown hair; then he phoned Prim and told her of Eichstadt's call and the unexpected lunch date.

"Maybe he's really gay and is attracted to you," she teased. "He wants to pour out his heart to you over cheeseburgers and fries."

"Thank you for that mental picture," Sean grumbled. "Now I'm going to have to *not* think about that while we're talking about whatever business he wants to discuss."

"Sorry. Just trying to make you not worry. I'm sure it's something good. He really seems to like you and has been one of your biggest proponents since you've been the principal at the school."

"I'll definitely bring him by Prim's Corner during our tour."

"I'm wearing a blue dress and black shoes. Do you think that will be okay?"

"You always look beautiful, no matter what you wear."

"I am a pretty pixie," she recited, but he could tell she still didn't believe it. When he commented on this, she said, "At least I'm trying. I say it every time I look in the mirror. I just said it to you, and I'm in the kitchen. So there."

He smiled and told her he was proud of her.

"I'm proud of myself. I love you, Sean."

"And I love you. See you in a few hours."

Sean read until 11:40. Then he donned his coat and walked over to LouAnn's. He was engaged in a conversation with some of the locals regarding the state of education in Georgia when Tony Eichstadt arrived. Sean immediately introduced the man to everyone present, and they greeted him and welcomed him to their town.

Eichstadt removed his coat as he and Sean took their seats at a table in the middle of the crowded restaurant. He was dressed in khaki pants and a black sweater and seemed thrilled to be in the midst of the throng. When he ordered a cheeseburger and fries, Sean pretended to cough in order to hide his grin. Sean ordered a bowl of creamy potato soup that came with a buttered roll.

They ate and spoke about their individual holiday experiences. Sean talked of time spent with his parents, Prim, Remy, and of his interactions with the students who'd remained at Kensington over the break. Eichstadt had taken his wife, daughters, and in-laws on a three-day cruise and then had returned to host a New Year's Eve fundraiser in Atlanta. Both agreed that they'd enjoyed their time off.

When they finished their lunch, Eichstadt insisted on paying the bill. The two men donned their coats and began their tour of the Town Square area. They stopped in various places and conversed with locals, including Byron, Dr. Stanford, Remy, and Caleb.

"What an odd and lovely place," Eichstadt said, as they walked towards Prim's Corner. "An old-fashioned town with almost New Age mentality. I've never been to a place where the pastor of the church runs the local hardware store."

"He used to work at the feedstore," Sean said with a quick smile. "His theology is solid, and he's extremely approachable."

"So I gathered."

When they entered Prim's shop, she was helping a young man who appeared to be looking for a birthday present for his girlfriend. She smiled and nodded to Sean and Eichstadt but continued to help the man. He eventually selected a fluffy zebra-striped blanket that was folded and tied with a large white satin ribbon. Sean showed Eichstadt around the store while the man paid for his gift and Prim wrapped it.

"This is a truly unique shop," Eichstadt told Prim when she came over to where he and Sean were standing near the Sock Monkey section. "It reminds me of Aurora – a curious mixture of past, present, and future."

"I like that description," she told him with a smile. "It fits."

Sean and Eichstadt stayed at Prim's Corner for an hour and discussed everything from town business to Prim's business. They all left together at 5:00 and walked *en masse* to Prim's apartment. Eichstadt was suitably impressed by the place and the interior design. He readily accepted Prim's suggestion that they order a pizza and eat at her home.

Once the pizza had been consumed, Eichstadt sat back and sighed contentedly.

"It's been a long time since I've had food delivered from a local pizzeria. That Supreme pizza we just ate was better than any I've had in years."

"I'm glad you enjoyed it so much," Prim remarked. "I'll pass your compliments on to the owner, who was one of my best friends throughout elementary and high school."

As he accepted a glass of red wine from Prim, Eichstadt said, "Well, I was going to wait to discuss why I came here until I was alone with Sean, but I think now would be more appropriate. Do you mind? It's about Sean's parents."

"What about them?" Sean asked. "Is there a problem?"

"Quite the contrary. I want to start by reiterating what a joy it was to have them at the holiday party. They're both so warm and genuine." After taking a sip of his wine, Eichstadt continued, "Everyone was deeply moved by their speeches. Quite a few persons present contacted me the next day and made significant contributions to the two scholarship funds and to the school itself. The future of the scholarships is permanently secured."

"That's great to hear," Sean said sincerely. "It makes me happy, and it'll make them happy, too."

"A link to the speeches will be posted on our website tomorrow. I thought you might want to share it with them and with your sister, especially since she couldn't attend the party."

"I'll definitely tell all of them. I can't wait to see it again myself."

"Me neither," Prim put in. "There are a lot of people here in town who are eager to see it, too."

Eichstadt stared at his glass of wine for a while before saying, "I know that you brought your parents out to the school last week to spend the day with the students who were left behind for the holidays."

"They had a wonderful time, and so did the kids." Cocking his head, Sean asked, "Is there an issue? Did someone complain?"

"Not at all. I've gotten reports from the staff and students who were present regarding what a rewarding experience everyone had." Looking directly at Sean, he said, "And you went back by yourself yesterday. You really do care about the students."

"I've always cared about my students, no matter which school I was heading."

"Yes, I know. You continue to impress and surprise the Board of Directors. Keep it up and you'll retire from Kensington, if that's what you want."

"I like the sound of that, but I know there's more you have to say. Please, just say it."

Placing his glass on the table, Eichstadt announced, "I have a proposition for your parents, but I wanted to discuss it with you first because of their unique situation."

"Go on."

"You want them closer to you, but they don't want to be intrusive in your lives."

"They also like and need to work and want to keep working as long as they can."

"I think we Board members may have a solution regarding everything."

"I'm listening."

"We believe your parents could be a real asset to the school, and I don't mean in a monetary way. You and I have discussed true diversity. Even if we have the male and female scholarship students who are underprivileged and students with disabilities, I still believe the children could benefit from greater exposure to all types of people. What your parents said was true. Most human beings don't know how to treat those who don't fit society's ideal mold."

"So, what exactly do you have in mind?"

"What if your parents work at the school in more than one capacity?"

"I don't follow."

"The laundry at Kensington will be losing one of our employees in March when she and her husband move to another state. Therefore, we'll have an open position in that area. We also need help with the facilities, grounds, and the horses. Your father likes working inside and out at the grocery store and would probably transition well to that. Your parents could work at the school and even live on campus since they don't drive. They would be supervised in their jobs as they are now. Their meals would be provided nine months out of the year because of the cafeteria available to the students and the on-campus staff. All of it would give them a chance to interact with the other employees

165

and the students on a continual basis." Smiling, he admitted, "Actually, the Board would like to start a cooperative program that would bring the students and all staff together routinely."

"That would be excellent."

"Do you think your mother and father would be interested in such a change and a chance to be located closer to you?"

Sean did but merely said guardedly, "It's a possibility."

"We're not out to exploit your parents. I know what you're thinking: Because of them we've gotten a huge increase in donations and want to milk the opportunity. But that's simply not true. We'd like to help them, you, and the students. Those children are away from their families and need love. Your parents seem to have a great capacity to love. It might help all involved if this works out. We on the Board are well-aware that if it doesn't, we could lose you as our principal, and we definitely don't want that. This will be a big risk for Kensington. We had quite an extensive discussion about this before deciding to get your thoughts on the subject. If you're against it, then we'll drop this with no hard feelings. If you think it could work, then I'll review things in more detail and let you approach your mother and father regarding the positions and options."

Before Sean could say anything, Prim asked Tony Eichstadt if she could have a word alone with Sean.

"Take as long as you like. It's nice to simply *sit* for a while."

Prim led Sean to her bedroom and directed him to sit on the edge of the bed. He was rather confused but did as she asked and waited as she paced beside it. Finally, she stopped in front of him and stated frankly, "You need to do this."

"I'm not sure about the entire proposal."

"I am. You were destined to take care of your parents and to be loved by them and to love them. This would be the most optimal scenario they could ever hope for. They'd be paid a good wage and wouldn't have to worry about housing. They'd have decent meals provided for them most of the year. No more frozen dinners or canned chili every day. They'd be surrounded by people almost all the time. Plus, they'd be close to us but not too close, which is what they're worried about. And on top of all that, the kids and staff at Kensington would watch out for them, care about them, and be cared for by them. They'd have purpose, which they crave in everything they do."

"What if something happens and I leave my position there or my contract's not renewed?"

"The Board of Directors wants you. So, they will want me, your sister, your parents, Remy, or anyone else you need in order to keep you where you are."

There was no denying that she was right about the entire idea. What Eichstadt was suggesting made sense from a business perspective as well as from altruistic and personal standpoints. The Board wanted Sean. Keeping his parents close would keep *him* close. He was concerned that some Board members might eventually view this arrangement as a means of leverage should they feel the need arise. It wouldn't sway him if there was an issue he disagreed with, and his parents would understand if he had to make a choice between doing something unethical and remaining at the Kensington Academy because of them. They would support his decisions no matter what.

Sean also understood that Prim desperately wanted to have parents, and his parents were perfect for a woman who had been alone her entire life. He'd tried to imagine what growing up without any mother or father would be like, but it made him too sad to consider for very long. She needed his mother and father as much as he did.

Debra needs them, too, he thought. *Maybe if they were in closer proximity to her, she'd return to the family. Perhaps she would go back to being the Debra she used to be.*

"I think you're right, although I do have some questions for Eichstadt." As he pulled her into his lap, he said, "Right now, I have a question for you. What did you mean when you said that I was destined to take care of my parents, to be loved by them, and to love them?"

"God sent you to them for a reason. What other child could have done what you did? They would have lost custody of you and Debra if you hadn't taken on the responsibility of keeping things together. I'm sorry it all fell on you, but I feel like God gave Tiffany and Kenny the perfect child for them." She kissed him and said, "You don't know what a miracle you are, Sean Proper."

He was instantly aroused by her nearness and love and wished they could have sex before returning to the main living area. Knowing that this would not be prudent, he resigned himself to kissing her again and murmured that *she* was the miracle in his life. He'd never shared himself with any other girl or woman the way he had with Primrose Aurora.

"What you're suggesting sounds fantastic," Sean told Tony Eichstadt when they returned to the couch. "I do have a few questions."

"Ask away. I have plenty of time and want to burn off that glass of wine I had before I get behind the wheel."

"Where would my parents live on campus?"

"The quarters behind the stables. They were originally built for the stable master, but we updated everything during our renovation of the campus several years ago. Now the stable master lives in the apartment that was added on the side of the barn. The old quarters are vacant and include two bedrooms and two bathrooms as well as an open-concept living area much like this one, only smaller. There's also a porch on the back that overlooks the hills."

"I know the stable master lives at Kensington year-round, but who else is out there? I wouldn't want them to be all alone for three months each summer."

"Several of our dormitory staff live on-campus twelve months out of the year. Kensington *is* their home. The Board feels more comfortable having someone occupying the buildings and being on the grounds year-round."

"When would you like for me to talk with them?"

"At your earliest convenience. The laundry position must be filled at the beginning of March. The start date for the other position is more flexible, although I'm sure your parents would want to start at the same time."

"I'll talk with them as soon as possible and let you know on Monday when I return to work. I think they'll be thrilled but a little scared. They've been in the same apartment and with the same jobs for decades. They want to move here but will be nervous. I don't think it'll take a lot of convincing, but who knows?"

Eichstadt stood and thanked Sean for his consideration of the Board's suggestion and for his tour of Aurora before adding, "And thank you Prim for your hospitality. Would you both come to Atlanta for a Valentine's Day fundraising event where all proceeds will go towards fighting illiteracy? It would mean a lot to my wife and me." When they readily accepted, he told Sean, "I'll e-mail you the details at work and look forward to seeing the two of you very soon."

Sean walked with Eichstadt to the man's Mercedes, which was parked in the lot behind LouAnn's Café. Once he'd seen the man off, he returned to Prim's apartment. He felt as though he was in a state of shock and said so.

"You probably are," Prim remarked. "Do you want to call your parents from here or from your place?"

"I think I'm going to drive to Tallahassee to explain all of this to them. I don't think they'll quite get everything over the phone. If I'm in shock, then imagine how *they're* going to react."

"But that's a six-hour drive, and they have to work tomorrow. It'll be Friday, and traffic will be bad."

"So, I'll drive down when I know I'll miss rush hour in Atlanta and present this to them after dinner. I'll spend the night and drive back Saturday." When she looked disappointed, he said, "It'll be better this way. Trust me." Taking her in his arms, he said playfully, "I'll bring you back a surprise from Tallahassee."

He caught a flicker of a forced smile and asked her what was bothering her.

"What if they say 'No'?"

He realized then how frightened she was by the prospect that his parents would choose to remain where they were. He slipped his fingers into the strawberry blonde hair and looked into the wide blue eyes before saying, "They'll come, Prim."

She nodded uncertainly. Sean kissed her, but she didn't respond to him the way she usually did. Her heart wasn't in the kiss, and he suspected her mind was worrying too much to allow her to relax. He almost gave in and called his mother and father right then in order to allay her fears, but he knew that would be a mistake. If he didn't talk with them in person, they might actually refuse.

Sean walked home and phoned his parents to let them know that he was coming to see them the next day and would be spending the night. He told them he had some exciting news that he wanted to share with them when they were all together.

"Debra's coming home?" his father asked hopefully.

It took Sean a moment to recover before he said, "No, Dad. Not yet."

"You're getting married sooner?" his mother speculated.

"No, Mom."

"Prim's not pregnant, is she?" his father asked. "You should be married before she has a baby."

"No baby, Dad. You're both just going to have to wait until tomorrow night to find out."

His drive to Florida proved uneventful, and Sean was thankful. There were no accidents along the way and no major traffic jams. He arrived at his parents' apartment at 4:00 and talked with the neighbors until his mother and father got off the bus at 5:40. They hugged him and immediately asked what his exciting news was.

"After dinner," he promised. "Let's go to Mr. Spiro's restaurant. When we get home, I'll tell you everything."

Mr. Spiro effusively greeted them and chatted with them off and on during their meal. By the time they left, it was almost 9:00, and all of them had full bellies and smiles on their faces.

They had barely gotten into the apartment when Sean's father asked, "What's the news? Tell us, Son."

Sean reviewed what Tony Eichstadt had proposed to him and Prim the previous evening. His parents listened with interest but didn't ask questions as they typically did. Once he'd finished, his father said slowly, "I don't know, Sean. It all sounds so good, but…well…I'm kind of scared. Your mom and I have lived our whole lives in Tallahassee and have worked at the same places for so long. We want to be closer to you and Prim and to Debra, but what if we do the wrong thing? What if we don't like it out there?"

"Then you get other jobs and a place to live in Aurora. Or if you don't like it in Georgia, you could move back to Tallahassee."

His father looked around the apartment and stated, "But our home will be gone by then. Someone else will be living here."

"We should move, Kenny," his mother said firmly. "Nothing is more important than our children. Sean wants us to be near to him. Maybe someday Debra will, too. Even if they didn't, Prim needs us real bad. The poor child has never had parents. We both know what that's like, but at least the people who took care of us treated us like we were their kids when we were growing up. I don't think she had even that. She was nobody's little girl after her mother died. She needs us to treat her like she's our little girl."

His father thought about this for a while and said, "You're right, Tiffany. All of our kids need us to be not so far away, and Prim will be one of our kids soon. Remy could use a mom and dad, too. We talked about being there for him when we were visiting at Christmas. If we could help our kids and him and then all those boys and girls at the school who don't have moms and dads around, then that would be a very important thing." Looking to Sean, he asked, "How do you think we should go about this? Should we go in to work Monday and tell them we're leaving in February? I know a lot of people wait until just before they quit, but I don't think I can do that. They should know."

Sean was well acquainted with his parents' bosses and knew that neither his mother nor father would lose their jobs prematurely if they shared their plans to move. He reassured them that they could tell whomever they pleased and asked them if they wanted to come up to Kensington to see their new home before the move.

"I don't think we should take time off since we'll be quitting," his father told him. "Could you send us pictures or a video?"

"Sure. We'll have movers bring whatever you want from here when it's time for you to actually move."

His mother looked around and declared, "I think we should leave all of our furniture here for people in the apartment complex who need it. Some of them have almost nothing. Our stuff is old, but we love it. Still, there's no need to take it to Georgia. I just want to bring our things like the books and DVDs and CDs and all of our things that have to do with our good memories." She looked expectantly at her son and asked, "Do we have enough money to buy new furniture and curtains and bedspreads once we get to our new house?"

"Yes, Mom. We can all go shopping together."

Later that night when his mother and father had gone to bed, Sean called Prim to tell her the good news. He didn't share with his fiancée that one of the deciding factors had been his parents' sorrow over her predicament as a parentless child. She was thrilled they'd accepted and sounded as if she wanted to cry with relief. Tears stung Sean's eyes as he listened to her telling him how happy she was for all of them.

Once he'd finished his conversation with Prim, Sean hung up and called his sister. He expected to get her voicemail. Instead, a man answered the phone.

"May I speak to Debra Proper?"

"May I ask who's calling?"

"Sean. I'm Debra's brother. And you are…?"

"Patrick. I'm Debra's boyfriend. I'm a lawyer at the firm where she works." He paused then said, "Your sister is a very smart and beautiful woman."

Sean agreed and wondered whether or not Debra had finally found a man who would treat her well. He asked to speak to her and was told to hold on for a minute while Patrick went to get her.

When she picked up the phone, Debra asked, "Sean, are you all right? Are Mom and Dad okay?"

"We're all fine. Why do you always think something's wrong when I call?"

"Because I do. It's 10:00 p.m. my time but 11:00 p.m. your time."

"I know. I'm sorry to call so late, but I had some news I wanted to share with you."

Sean described the events of the past two days and explained about their parents' move to Georgia. Debra sounded genuinely happy for their mother and father and told him she hoped they would love their new location and employment opportunities.

"Maybe you and Patrick could come visit us once they move," Sean offered. "You know Mom and Dad would like to have you check out their house. I don't think they ever thought they'd live in a house."

"Maybe we will," his little sister replied with enthusiasm. "They move in late February?"

"Yes."

"That would be nice. I could meet your fiancée, and you could meet Patrick. He's wonderful, Sean."

"I'm pleased to hear it. He sounds nice. How long have you two been together?"

"We met at the company Christmas party. We started talking and found that we had a lot in common." Lowering her voice, she confided, "I know it's only been a short time, but I think he may be *the one*."

"I hope so. Just take care of yourself."

"You, too. I love you, Sean."

"And I love you. Call anytime, Debra."

Sean didn't tell his parents about Debra and Patrick. He prayed that the man was sincere, but he felt it was too early to get his hopes up. He'd been let down too many times in the past.

He returned to Aurora and Prim on Saturday. His surprise to her was a cooler filled with Greek food from Mr. Spiro's restaurant, and she was thrilled. They froze some of the food, refrigerated the rest, and ate it for lunch on Sunday after church.

Sean returned to Kensington on Monday. Maureen seemed subdued, and he finally asked his administrative assistant if something was wrong.

"My holidays were difficult," she admitted. "I was so thankful for Remy's call on Christmas and for our visit on New Year's Eve. Yet, so much has happened, and there were so many bad years. His father and I weren't good parents once we became alcoholics. He seems like such a spectacular man, but it's like I'm talking to a stranger, not my son. And, of course, the holidays make me think of my younger son who was killed in the drunk-driving accident. They also remind me of my ex-husband, whom I still loved even though we divorced. So much pain because of our addiction. I went to Alcoholics Anonymous meetings every day during our vacation. I needed them. It was a real struggle, and I'm glad to be back at work. Here, I have more control."

"Remy loves you, Maureen."

She smiled sadly and said, "He loves me the way I was before the drinking. I haven't been that person for decades. Thank God, I'm sober and productive now, but I know what my husband and I did damaged both of our children. If only we could turn back the clock."

"Remy wants to know you."

"Any relationship with my child is better than none, but I wish it could be different. I wish I could take the pain I caused away. All I can do is make amends and try to forgive myself. I hope he'll forgive me one day."

"I think he has. I know he forgave his father before the man died."

"Did he? I don't think so. If your father had wronged you terribly but was lying on his deathbed, begging you for forgiveness, then wouldn't you give it to him even if you didn't really mean it?"

The phone rang, and she excused herself to answer it. Sean thought about her words long after she'd left his office. Wishing that life could be a little less complicated, he turned to his work and began the second half of his first school year at Kensington.

Chapter Fourteen

Dr. Stanford came into Prim's shop late Tuesday morning looking for an anniversary present for his wife. It had been a slow day at Prim's Corner, and there was no one else in the store at that moment. Prim had been relieved by the lack of customers. She'd awakened at 5:00 a.m. with a mild case of nausea and a pain in her stomach. She was not at her best and wasn't in a cheerful mood.

Prim said nothing to the doctor about how she was feeling. If she got worse, she could always walk across the street or call him. He was there as *her* customer, and it was up to her to assist him.

After she'd helped the man choose a lovely framed print that talked about the beauty of couples sharing their lives together, he paid for it and waited as she found a box and wrapped the gift. As she selected a bow for the top of the box, he asked, "Have you thought any more about seeing a therapist?"

Prim stopped what she was doing and turned to face him. He seemed very serious, and she frowned. When she reminded him that she wasn't afraid to be touched by Sean any longer, he nodded but told her that wasn't the only reason she needed to talk to a therapist.

"Does everyone in today's world have to see a therapist to live their lives?" she asked with a slight edge in her voice.

"Of course not. But some people benefit more than others. Remy prefers to talk to Caleb, as you know. That's fine as long as the counselor has training, which Caleb does. The counselor needs to be experienced, and the person who needs help has to continue to be making progress."

"I'm making progress," she said defensively. "I'm stable."

"Yes, but you've had some huge adjustments in the last few months. There are still so many childhood issues you need to sort through, and you've lost Buddy. Buddy was like a father to you, and I get the impression you've swept your grief for him under the rug because of your anger over all the lies. I just wish you'd talk to someone about everything. Please don't discount the benefits of sharing your burdens with someone who's trained to help."

175

Continuing to feel queasy, Prim placated the doctor by telling him she wouldn't rule it out and attached the bow to his wife's present. Once he'd gone, she flipped the sign in the window, went in the bathroom, and threw up. She felt better afterwards and sipped some water, used a small amount of the mouthwash she kept in the back room, and then returned to the shop.

When 5:00 arrived, Prim shut down her store and walked to Aurora Hardware. Caleb had pulled the shades in the windows and was counting the till. He informed her that the store had done a great business all day.

"It's all of those people who had New Year's resolutions," he suggested. "They had long lists of household projects that they've been putting off."

"Good for us," Prim remarked. "I hardly had anyone today. I think my customers are still recovering from the holidays."

He agreed and asked her where Sean was that evening.

"There's a staff meeting and dinner at Kensington. I think it will be a little different than when Sean went out there with his parents and then by himself to spend time with the students who were left behind during the holidays. No video games or pizza party tonight." Shaking her head, she mused, "I don't understand how those parents can leave their children at school during the holidays. They're gone nine months out of the year. Why wouldn't they want them to come home every opportunity they could get?"

"Things at home may be bad, and the parents believe they're sparing the child pain. Some parents simply don't have the capacity to love. Some want to be good parents but don't know how." As Caleb placed the money to one side, he told her, "Almost a century ago, my grandmother died, giving birth to my mother. My grandfather had no idea what to do with the baby and said he couldn't look at her without thinking of her mother. He knew she needed him but was incapable of being a loving father. He hired nannies for her and tried his best but ended up sending her to a boarding school for girls when she went to kindergarten."

"Kindergarten! How could anyone send a five-year-old away to boarding school?"

"My mother said it was the best thing that ever happened to her. The nuns were good and kind, and they loved her as if she were their own child. Her fellow students were like her sisters. She was lucky. I know that not all boarding schools have good atmospheres be they secular or parochial."

"So, your mother was at boarding school for thirteen years?"

"Yes. She got a fantastic education and learned how to love herself and God. She also learned to love her father for who he was and to accept him. They were never close, but she understood."

"Is she still alive?"

"No, she died when I was about your age. I was the youngest of five, and she had me when she was forty. She was a wonderful woman."

"What did she do?"

"She was a religion teacher at a parochial school from the time she graduated college until she retired at sixty. It was she who got me interested in being a pastor."

"Was she unhappy because you didn't become a priest?"

Caleb grinned and said, "I have a doctorate in theology, Prim. I was a priest."

She blinked in surprise and asked, "For how long?"

"About a year. I realized early on I had a calling but that the priesthood wasn't for me. I left the church on good terms and eventually followed my vocation on a somewhat parallel road when I became the pastor of the Aurora Community Church over twenty years ago. I'm sure my mother would have been disappointed that I left the priesthood, but she would have continued to love me. My siblings had a hard time at first but accepted it after a few years. We never stopped talking, but I know they wished things would've been different. My father never understood, but he also never stopped loving me. He passed three years ago."

"Did your wife know you used to be a priest?"

"Of course. She knew everything there was to know about me." Putting the money that rested on the counter into the bank bag and then locking it, he added, "I still miss her greatly. I doubt if I'll ever remarry. My wife was the love of my life. I can't imagine being with another woman after her, although God may have other plans." Gesturing around the shop, Caleb asked, "Who would have ever thought I'd be running Aurora Hardware? When

I was a boy, I was going to be an astronaut. Now, I'm a pastor and a shopkeeper. Go figure."

Prim giggled at first, but then she began to cry. She turned her back to Caleb as she gave in to the tears, but he came around the counter and stood in front of her before asking what was the matter. When she cried harder, he took her in his arms and held her as she wept.

Prim wanted to tell Caleb everything, but she found that she couldn't. It didn't make sense: She was unable to confide in him about any of it – her family secrets, her sorrow over never having parents present in her life, her fears about having children of her own, and her grief over the death of her uncle. She knew that he sensed her inability to share her concerns and was troubled by this. It made her feel worse, and she cried harder. She felt awful both emotionally and physically, wishing that Sean were there to make it better.

"Whatever burden is weighing you down can be lifted," Caleb said soothingly.

"I wish I could believe that," she declared before breaking away and running for the back of the store. She went out the door that led to the parking area behind the building. Within seconds, she was in her apartment.

Prim stood, shaking and miserable near the front door. She didn't know what to do next. Before Prim realized it, she had the phone in her hand. Tiffany answered on the second ring and offered her a warm greeting. All Prim could do in response was cry.

"I'm so sorry you're sad," the woman said sympathetically. "Whatever it is will be okay. You just go ahead and cry. I'm right here."

Prim wept uncontrollably for a long time. Occasionally, Sean's mother would tell her that everything was going to be fine. Eventually, Prim cried herself into exhaustion and stopped weeping.

"I want you to pretend like I'm right there, giving you a big hug," Tiffany told her. "There. Is that better?"

Prim assured her that it was and thanked the older woman for being there for her. She suddenly felt the urge to throw up and told Tiffany she was going to be sick. Tiffany instructed her to go ahead but to call back and let her know that everything was all right afterwards. Prim hung up and hurried for the bathroom. She made it just in time.

She called Tiffany back as soon as she was able and told the woman she was not feeling quite so sick.

"Get some sleep. Call me back if you want to or need to. You'll feel lots better in the morning."

"Thank you. I needed to hear that."

"I wish I was there with you."

"Me, too."

"Sean would come to you if you called him."

"I know, but he's got a meeting at work tonight. I don't want to get him sick."

"Can I ask you a question before we hang up?"

"Sure."

"Will you call me 'Mom' after you and Sean get married? I'd like that."

Her eyes filling with tears, Prim said, "I'd love it."

"Will you practice now?"

"Okay."

"Goodnight, Prim."

As tears trickled down her cheeks, Prim said, "Good night, Mom."

It was the first time in her life that Prim had ever uttered those words, and it made her both happy and sad. After hanging up the phone, Prim put on the long gingerbread men nightgown that Tiffany had given her and went to bed.

She woke during the night, drenched with sweat and feeling much more nauseated than she had the previous day. Her belly hurt, and she knew that she was running a fever. She staggered to the bathroom and threw up what little remained in her stomach then tried to stand. She couldn't.

Prim sat shivering on the bathroom floor for two hours, as she wondered what to do. Aunt Myrtle had always told her that a person shouldn't wake others during the night unless it was a true emergency such as a fire in the house. If one got sick, then one toughed it out until morning.

Crawling back to the bedroom, Prim reached for her iPhone and looked at the time. It was only 2:14. She was doubled over with pain and knew she couldn't make it until dawn. Too weak to dial, she used the voice command on her phone to call Sean.

"Prim?" he answered sleepily. "What time is it?"

"A quarter after 2:00. I'm so sorry to wake you, but I couldn't wait. I don't feel well and need you to come. Please, come."

As a wave of nausea threatened to overcome her, Prim disconnected the call and crawled back to the bathroom. She made it halfway across the floor before deciding she could go no further. She lay on the cool tile, praying that Sean would arrive soon.

She had never felt so ill in her life and had no idea what was causing her so much pain. She knew she wasn't pregnant, because she'd been taking the birth control pills every morning without fail. She thought of a childhood friend whose mother had suffered an intestinal blockage and wondered if that might be the culprit. She also considered that perhaps she was suffering from a severe case of the stomach flu.

Sean was suddenly there, stroking her hair and telling her everything would be fine. Remy appeared not long after. Byron came next and then Dr. Stanford. Caleb was the last to arrive. Prim dimly wondered what they were all doing in her bathroom and wished the pain would stop and that everyone except Sean would leave. She was so tired....

Dr. Stanford performed a cursory examination before directing the others to help Prim roll onto her back. They ignored her protestations and did as he asked. The internist took her temperature, checked her pulse, and then listened to her chest and belly with his stethoscope. As he pressed in various places on her abdomen, she cried out and asked him to stop.

"When did you start feeling sick?" Stanford asked, as he sat back on his heels.

"Yesterday morning."

"Why didn't you tell me when I was in your shop?"

"I thought it was a virus. It wasn't like this."

"Obviously not. When did it get like this?"

"A few hours ago."

"Why didn't you call me right away?" Sean asked softly.

"We didn't do that when I was growing up," she mumbled wearily. "I didn't want to wake anyone. I was trying to wait until morning."

There was silence for a moment in the bathroom, and Prim realized this must be yet another thing that was not normal for most families. She fought the urge to cry and wondered how she could ever have children and raise them well when she didn't know what "normal" families did.

"When is the last time you ate anything?" Dr. Stanford asked.

"I ate a piece of toast for breakfast and some plain grits for lunch, but I threw up a lot earlier in the day and then again before you all got here."

"And the last time you had anything to drink?"

"I had some water before I went to bed." She thought for a moment and said uncertainly, "7:00?"

Withdrawing his cellphone, the doctor hit one of the speed dial buttons then said, "Don, it's Philip. I have a problem here and need your help. Yes. I've got a twenty-four-year-old patient in Aurora whom I suspect has acute appendicitis. No, otherwise in good health. Yes. How soon? I'll get her there right way. Thanks." As he hung up, Stanford remarked, "One of my good friends who just so happens to be an excellent surgeon."

"Surgeon?" Prim echoed, as she struggled to think clearly through the haze of pain.

"You're presenting with all the symptoms of acute appendicitis," the internist told her. "My friend's meeting us at the hospital to perform an emergency appendectomy. This is a life-threatening situation. You don't get to choose the course of treatment."

The pain worsened, and Prim moaned and asked why it seemed to move from one spot in her belly to another. As Dr. Stanford explained that it was indicative of appendicitis, she nodded and asked for a glass of water.

"Nothing until after surgery," he told her. "We need to get moving and get you fixed up as soon as possible."

Under the internist's direction, Remy went to find socks and put them on Prim's feet while Byron spread a heavy blanket on the floor beside her. Caleb ran a washcloth under the tap and wiped her face with it, while Sean stayed beside her and held her hand. Once everything was arranged, the men worked in unison to transfer her from the tile to the blanket.

Prim was swaddled like an infant. She whimpered as Sean lifted her, carrying her out of the apartment and down the stairs to Dr. Stanford's waiting SUV. Aurora was too small to have its own hospital or ambulance, so Sean eased Prim into the backseat and buckled the middle seatbelt loosely across her waist before going around and taking the seat where her head rested. He lifted her up slightly, cradled her head in his lap and then secured his own safety belt. Dr. Stanford took his position behind the wheel, while Remy sat in the passenger seat. Caleb rode with Byron, who was going to drive in front of them in the squad car with the siren on in order to clear the way if there was any traffic on the roads and get them to the hospital a little more quickly.

"Why am I so cold?" Prim asked, as she shivered uncontrollably.

"It's cold outside, Pixie," Remy told her. "It's actually starting to snow. You'll be warm again once we get to the hospital."

Prim appreciated his comforting words although she suspected that the reason she was shivering had more to do with her inflamed appendix than it did the weather.

"How far is it to the hospital?" Sean asked evenly.

"About thirty-five minutes without an escort," Dr. Stanford replied. "With Byron leading the way, I've made it in twenty on other emergency trips."

Prim began to see black spots across her field of vision and verbalized that she felt as though she was about to lose consciousness. The three men urged her to fight to stay awake, but she could feel herself slipping into the darkness. Dizziness overtook her as Sean announced, "I can see the hospital."

Snowflakes drifted onto her face as she was removed from the backseat of the SUV. People were surrounding her, and there were bright lights and the antiseptic smell that always seemed to pervade medical facilities.

Remy kissed her forehead, and Caleb and Byron took turns giving her hand a quick squeeze as she was wheeled down a hallway. Sean bent to kiss her and told her that he loved her. She found herself incapable of responding to any of them.

Dr. Stanford never left her side. He explained that he was going to stay with her and be present in the operating room. After patting her on the shoulder, he excused himself to put on scrubs and sterilize his hands.

When a nurse approached Prim with scissors, she screamed. Misunderstanding, the nurses assured her that they were not going to use the scissors on her. Prim managed to tell them she knew this and begged them not to cut off her gingerbread men nightgown.

"We have to, Sweetie," one of the older nurses told her. "We don't have a choice."

Prim cried as the scissors sliced through the fabric and the gown was cut away. The nurses transferred her to another gurney where her underwear and socks were removed. She was covered with a sheet and rolled into what she assumed was an operating room. An IV was inserted into her left arm.

Dr. Stanford appeared and introduced her to his surgeon friend. The anesthesiologist was telling her to count backwards from twenty. Then everything went black and quiet.

Chapter Fifteen

Sean stood beside Prim's hospital bed, wondering how to proceed. He was still shaken by Dr. Stanford's conversation with him, Remy, Caleb, and Byron. According to the internist, the surgeon barely had time to remove Prim's appendix before it had ruptured in his hand. If it had burst within her, Prim could have died because of the toxins released into her body. She'd been moments away from a possible slow, painful death. As it was, she was on IV antibiotics and was expected to recover completely.

"That was too close for comfort," Stanford had told them. "If she'd called any one of us earlier, then it would've spared her hours of suffering alone and risking death. We've got to figure out a way to get her into some sort of counseling."

Once Prim was moved to a regular room, all of them had gone directly to see her despite the fact that she remained unconscious. Byron and Caleb left not long afterwards, promising to come back later that day. Remy stayed but had gone to the cafeteria to allow Sean some time alone with his fiancée.

Sean studied Prim as she slept. She was so pale and looked so frail in the hospital bed. She stirred and struggled to open her eyes. Sean instructed her to lie still and rest. She mumbled something about her nightgown, but he couldn't make out what she was saying before she drifted back into unconsciousness.

Sean walked to the nurses' station and asked the first woman he saw, "Could you tell me what had happened to the clothing Prim Aurora was wearing when we brought her into the hospital?"

"I'm not sure. Wait here while I check with some of the other staff."

She returned minutes later with a heavyset nurse who had short gray hair and a sympathetic expression.

"We had to cut off her nightgown," the woman told him. "She begged us not to, but it was an emergency. We assured her that we didn't have a choice, and she didn't fight us. But she cried the entire time. I felt so bad, but we had to do it. I'm glad she's going to be all right."

After thanking the nurse for everything she'd done to help Prim, Sean excused himself and went to a nearby waiting room. It was almost 8:00 a.m. He phoned Maureen at the office, explained about Prim's hospitalization, and told her he wouldn't be in to work that day. When she asked him if there was anything she could do for him or Prim, he told her no but thanked her. He promised to call her later with an update.

Next, he phoned his parents. They were understandably upset and concerned. They wanted to take the train right away to come up to be with him and Prim. His first impulse was to tell them to stay put, but he needed his mother and father. So he asked them to come. As much as he wanted them there, he suspected Prim would need them even more.

Sean spent the following half hour purchasing their tickets and setting up a taxi to take them to the station. Once all of the arrangements had been made, he telephoned his parents again. His father answered.

"I'll get someone to pick you up in Atlanta," Sean told Kenny. "Keep your cellphones on, and I'll let you know who's coming."

"Sean?"

"Yes, Dad?"

"You need to calm yourself down a bit. Prim's going to be okay."

Sean hadn't realized how tense he'd been until that moment. His chest was tight, and he had a terrible headache. He made himself take a few deep breaths and thanked his father for reminding him not to overstress.

"You do that a lot. It's not good for you."

"I can't help it, Dad."

"Try. Mom and I want you to not be so worried all the time. That makes people have heart attacks and other bad things."

Sean agreed that his father was right and promised to try to remain as calm as possible despite what was going on. Then he asked to talk to his mother.

"It's going to be okay," Tiffany told him the moment she got on the phone. "We'll be there soon."

"I'm glad. We need you and Dad here."

Sean went back to Prim's room and found Remy gazing somberly down at Prim. When he asked his friend what was bothering him, Remy said, "I was just thinking about her when she was little. I remember her and my brother playing hopscotch, marbles, and hide and seek. I taught her how to ride a bike and a horse. I was the one who took her with me and my brother to the Community Church when she said she wanted to go and Buddy and Myrtle wouldn't take her."

"How old was she?"

"About eight. It was the first time she'd been in a church since Mr. and Mrs. Aurora had been alive. She was too little to remember that, thank goodness. Their kind of religion was toxic, if you ask me."

"So, Buddy and Myrtle weren't church-goers?"

"After Myrtle's parents were gone, neither of them ever went as far as I know. They didn't object to my taking Prim with me and my brother, which was good. Prim liked it and said she felt safe there." Closing his eyes, Remy said, "When I was younger, I used to lie awake at night and work out plans to run away and take my brother and Prim with me. I figured if I could just get them far enough away, everything would be all right. I talked myself out of it every time. Sometimes, I wish I hadn't."

"Most likely, you would have been found, charged with kidnapping, and the kids would've been returned home," Sean pointed out. "They would have grown up without you. Things would've been ten times worse for them."

"That's what Caleb tells me when I beat myself up about not following through." Opening his eyes, he said, "My brother's dead, and Prim almost died today. Maybe I should've taken the risk."

"You knew something was really off in the old Aurora house, didn't you?"

"I told you I did. The Auroras typically never invited people into their home. Myrtle and Buddy didn't start that. I guess it began when Myrtle got pregnant with Sandra, and then it just continued. All I could do was watch out for Prim as best I could and try to keep her out of that house as much as possible, just like I tried to keep my brother out of ours. Buddy and Myrtle seemed more than happy to let me play the role of big brother and shepherd her from one activity to another. That right there told me that something was wrong. What parent in his or her right mind would let some young guy be responsible for his little girl? Why wouldn't he be doing those things himself?" Sighing, he continued, "Thank God, I wasn't an evil boy interested in molesting her. If I had been, she would've been easy prey. That was another reason I stayed so close. Buddy and Myrtle simply weren't present in her life outside the house unless she was at the hardware store with them or if something at her school happened that called for them to attend. Someone could've harmed Prim if I hadn't been looking out for her all the time. She was so trusting and naïve."

"Did she have girlfriends? I hear her talk about having other girls as friends when she was growing up, but she doesn't have any really close female friends that I've seen."

"I'm not sure what happened. Prim's always been everyone's friend, and she did have close girl friends when she was in elementary and high school. When she moved to Atlanta, I don't know how things were for her. When she came back, she reconnected with people, but most of her old girl friends had either permanently moved or stayed but were already married and were having babies. As much as she was a huge part of the community, Prim was pretty isolated."

"Like you."

"Maybe I wasn't as good of an example as I should've been."

"You were better at being a parent to the two kids than any of the adults. I don't know how you did everything and kept your sanity."

Sean went over to stroke Prim's hair. She opened her eyes. She appeared still drugged, but looked truly awake for the first time since her surgery.

"Hey there," Sean said with a smile. "How do you feel?"

"Okay."

She didn't sound "okay," and Sean asked her if she was in pain.

"A little. My side hurts."

"That's because you had surgery there. Do you remember last night?"

She nodded and said matter-of-factly, "We can't have any children now."

"Of course we can. They only took out your appendix. Everything else is fine."

"Nothing is fine. That's why we can't have any children."

Sean frowned and glanced at Remy, who took Prim's hand and told her that she was going to recover and could have as many children as she wanted after she and Sean got married.

"No, I can't."

Sean and Remy looked at each other. Sean knew Remy was thinking the same thing he was, that Prim remained under the influence of painkillers or the lingering effects of anesthesia.

"Will you still love me if I can't have children with you?"

"I love you and intend to marry you. We're going to have children."

She insisted that she couldn't and began to cry. Sean bent low and took her face in his hands, and she tried to slip her arms around his neck. The IV tube prevented her from succeeding, and she whispered that she was sorry over and over and asked him to forgive her.

"There's nothing to forgive," he said soothingly. "Prim, you'll be all right. *We'll* be all right."

A nurse came in and declared that Prim needed to rest. When Prim protested, the woman told her it was time for more medication and injected something through the IV tube. Once Prim was unconscious again, the nurse turned to the two men and told them her patient would be asleep for some time and suggested they leave the room and get some fresh air and something to eat. She eyed Sean and asked if he was feeling well.

"You take him out for a while," she said to Remy. "Maybe go outside the building for a minute."

Once she was gone, Sean asked, "What was that supposed to mean?"

"It means you look terrible and need to take a step back from the situation. You're shaking, Sean. I've never seen you like this."

"I've never been like this." Rubbing at his throbbing temples, he asked, "What am I going to do?"

"Right now, you and I are going to take the nurse's advice. Then we're going to try to figure out what to do about Prim."

"The first thing I have to figure out is who's going to pick up my parents at the train station this afternoon. Maybe Caleb would do it."

"Call him."

Caleb readily agreed to pick up Sean's parents in Atlanta and take them directly to the hospital. Remy then suggested that they go to the cafeteria, get some breakfast, and talk. Sean reluctantly agreed to leave Prim and went with his friend.

"I wish I understood what she meant about not having kids," he admitted after pushing himself to eat some oatmeal and drink some juice. "There's nothing biologically wrong with her that we know of. Maybe she was still drugged and got mixed up."

"She was lucid enough," Remy told him. "And I understand completely. Even if I find the right woman, I'd probably never have children with her."

"What? Why not?"

"For me, there are two reasons. One, I already raised two kids, my brother and Prim. I know that sounds stupid, but it's pretty true. I spent most of my life being a parent and don't know if I want to start from scratch again."

"It would be different. You're older and would have a partner to help you. You wouldn't have to worry about where your next meal was coming from or keeping your kids out of the house to protect them. Plus, they'd be *your* kids, the product of love between you and your wife."

"True."

"What's the other reason?"

"My formative years were good, but the rest of it was terrible. I wouldn't know what to do with kids in a stable home." After taking a sip of his coffee, Remy said, "I think that's what's scaring Prim out of her mind. She doesn't know what a normal childhood is, so how can she be a good parent?"

"That's ridiculous. She's great with kids. I've seen it."

"Other people's kids. She interacts with them and then they go home. When it's her kids, she'll be responsible for them and their sense of security." Sighing, he said, "You forget that I've known Prim since she was born. When it comes to this, I can tell you what she's thinking."

"Okay. What's she thinking?" Sean snapped.

189

"She's imagining she'll lose you if she refuses to have a family." Pausing, he asked, "Will she? Don't be quick to answer. Think about it. If Prim won't get help or have kids, would you still love her and want to spend the rest of your life with her?"

Sean straightened indignantly and said, "I love Prim no matter what. I'm a fixer. I'll figure it out."

"Prim's not an administrative problem or a high school kid with a bad attitude. You can't fix Debra, but you're going to fix Prim? It's not up to *you*; it's up to *them*."

Sean squeezed his eyelids tightly closed and asked, "So, how can I help them? It's consuming me."

"I believe it, but I don't know what to tell you. There has to be a way to get Prim to really open up about life in the Aurora home plus a way to get her to feel comfortable with the idea of having children and being a good parent. I'm not sure what that is, since she won't get counseling."

"And Debra?"

Remy shrugged and said, "Maybe if I knew her, I could give you suggestions. As it is, I have nothing to offer other than to keep doing what you're already doing."

God, a little help would be good right about now, Sean prayed. *Something. Anything.*

Nothing came to him. Feeling dejected, he followed Remy outdoors and stood behind the hospital in the freezing January air for a few minutes. It was a beautiful day, and they gazed at a stunning view of woods, hills, and a brilliant blue sky dotted with fluffy clouds. He wished Prim was standing outside with them enjoying the view.

"Better?" Remy asked when they returned to the warmth of the building.

Sean nodded. He did feel better, although he was still stewing over the problem of what to do about Prim and this new declaration of hers. As he pushed open the door to her room, he was hoping she'd be fully awake and wouldn't remember anything she'd said earlier. Perhaps Remy was wrong about her fear.

Prim's room was empty. Sean and Remy looked at one another in surprise then turned their attention back to the bed. The IV bag was still there, and the tube dangled from the hook at the top of the stand.

Remy dashed to the bathroom and peered in. He looked back at Sean, shook his head, and swore. Both of them darted out and down the hall. After informing the nurses that Prim was not in her room, the friends began a frantic search. They were stopped by a security guard when they reached the cafeteria. The man informed them that they'd located Prim and asked them to follow him. The guards wanted their assistance in getting her back to her room without startling her or disrupting activity in the hospital.

Prim was standing barefoot in her hospital gown in front of the window of the nursery. She was staring at the newborns as if transfixed. When Sean said her name, she didn't acknowledge him.

"Pixie, you need to get back to bed," Remy gently urged. "You shouldn't be walking around so much after surgery."

Prim didn't move.

"I'll carry you," Sean told her. "It's too soon for you to be up."

Prim slowly turned to look at him and said, "They're so little and so beautiful. They're all so helpless and innocent." When he agreed, she admitted, "I want to have babies with you."

"We're going to have babies, Prim. You're going to be a great mother someday."

"How? How can I be a great mother when I don't know what normal parents do with their children? I'll hurt ours without even meaning to. They'll hate me for it and so will you."

"That's not going to happen," Sean assured her. Taking her by the shoulders, he suggested, "Why don't you let me carry you back, and we'll figure out a way for you not to be scared?"

He lifted her and walked through the hallways until they'd reached her room. He laid her in the bed and then stepped back so the doctor and nurses could examine her. Her IV was reinserted, and he and Remy were asked to step outside for a moment so a more thorough examination could be performed.

Once the attending physician told them Prim hadn't done any real harm to herself during her unscheduled walk, Sean and Remy were allowed back in.

"I'm not going to leave you alone until I know you're truly all right," Sean vowed.

191

Prim, who had been given more painkillers, mumbled, "I'll never be truly all right. I'm nobody's child. I should never have been born."

Before Sean and Remy could dispute this, she was unconscious again. Sean's iPhone rang, and he glanced at the screen. It was Tony Eichstadt. He didn't want to, but he took the call, figuring it might distract him for a few moments.

"I called Kensington to talk with you, and your administrative assistant told me about your fiancée. I'm relieved to hear that she'll recover fully. Is there anything I can do?"

"No, but thank you for the call. I'm hoping she'll be released tomorrow, but she had a little setback today."

"Take off the rest of the week, Sean. You haven't missed a day of school, yet. They'll survive without you for a couple of days."

"My parents are coming in. I'll see how it goes."

"Call if you need anything. Tell Prim I hope she's feeling well soon."

"I will. Thank you again."

When he ended the call, Sean phoned Maureen and told her that he wasn't going to be in to work the next day and would keep her posted. She asked him if Remy was with him, and he told her he was. She then requested to talk to her son. Remy reluctantly accepted the iPhone.

"Yes. Yes. I know. Yes. I appreciate it, Maureen. I will. You, too. Goodbye."

Sean didn't ask his friend to explain the conversation. The man's tone had been casual, but there was still hesitancy there. At least he'd agreed to talk to his mother.

Sean's parents arrived with Caleb at the hospital that evening. Prim was awake and had been encouraged by Sean and Remy to eat a cup of cherry Jell-O. When she saw Kenny and Tiffany enter the room, she burst into tears. Both of them came over and immediately hugged her.

"They cut off my gingerbread man nightgown," Prim cried, as she hugged Tiffany. "They said they had to, but I didn't want them to."

"I'll find you another one," Tiffany assured her. "Your life is more important than a nightgown."

"But it meant so much to me," Prim sobbed. "You can't know how much I liked it."

Tiffany comforted Prim as Kenny went over to give Sean and Remy each a hug. Caleb came forward and quietly asked how things had gone in his absence. Sean merely shook his head, and Caleb sighed.

"Would all of you men mind leaving me and Prim alone for a few minutes?" Tiffany asked. "I want to talk to her with no one else around."

"We'll be in the waiting room down the hall," Sean told his mother. "Just come get us when you're ready for us to come back."

While they waited, Sean and Remy filled Kenny and Caleb in on the day's events. They discussed what Prim needed and how to help her, but they couldn't seem to agree on how to reach her.

Tiffany entered the waiting room after an hour. She walked straight over to her son, gave him a hug, and said, "Prim's not so scared anymore. She's sleeping now."

"What do you mean she's not so scared anymore?"

"She told me how she wants to have babies but is scared about raising them. So, I told her how Dad and I didn't know anything about babies when I got pregnant with you, and we took parenting classes. We learned a lot and kept taking them until you were about four. We learned how to do things like change a diaper and feed you but also how to do things like deal with temper tantrums."

"Sean had temper tantrums?" Remy asked with a grin.

"For a while when he was two," Kenny replied. "We didn't know what to do about them, so we asked at our classes, and they told us. It helped."

"Parenting classes," Caleb muttered. "What an excellent idea. She'll gain confidence and learn how parents and children are supposed to interact."

"That could also cause problems," Remy pointed out. "She's going to learn what *wasn't* done for her that should've been."

"Prim needs to know," Sean reminded him. "Maybe she'll agree to get professional help or talk to Caleb as a result."

"One can hope," his friend commented.

"Well, I didn't get to give you a hug," Tiffany told Remy. "Come here, You."

As his wife hugged the man, Kenny asked, "Sean, do you want me and Mom to stay here while you, Caleb, and Remy go home for a while? You all look real worn out. You could take a shower and get some sleep and then come back later. Mom and I will sit in Prim's room until you get back. I don't think Prim should be all by herself right now."

"I agree." Turning to his pastor, he asked, "You've had a long day, too. Byron should be coming back in a while, but I'm sure he's exhausted after last night and then working all day."

"We all need rest," Caleb remarked. "But I don't know –"

"I could stay."

They turned to stare at Maureen, who was standing across the room.

"You didn't have to come," Sean protested.

"I wanted to. You and Remy both sounded so exhausted when I spoke with you earlier that I knew I had to be here. I'll stay with Prim and your parents while you take a break."

"That's a good idea," Tiffany concurred. "Thank you."

"It would be my pleasure. I want to help."

Sean thanked his assistant before adding, "I'll set my alarm for midnight and come back. Mom? Dad? I know you usually go to bed earlier. Is that okay with you?"

"We'll be fine," his father told him. "When you and Debra were little and got sick, Mom and I used to stay up all night with you if we needed to. We can do the same for Prim."

"It might be good for her to see that people do that," Tiffany volunteered. "I don't think her aunt and uncle did. That was wrong of them."

Caleb drove straight from the hospital to Remy's apartment. By the time he dropped him off, it was 8:00. Sean told Remy not to worry about returning to the hospital with him. He promised that he'd call his friend if there was a problem. Otherwise, he would let him know once they'd gotten Prim home so that he could see her as soon as possible.

As they rode the few minutes to Sean's house, Caleb asked, "How are you holding up?"

"I'll let you know once I figured it out."

"Your mother had a great idea about those parenting classes," commented Caleb. "Sometimes solutions come in unlikely forms."

"I hope the classes are what she needs. They won't change the fact that she feels like nobody ever wanted her."

Caleb sadly shook his head and said, "I wish things could have been different for her. I wish they could have been different for that whole family. Remy's, too. I can ponder 'why' all I want, but it won't change anything. I have to trust that everything happened the way it did for a reason and that God has a plan."

"Usually that works for me, but the situations regarding Prim and my sister have me very confused and frustrated."

"Would you like some company?"

"Not tonight. I can barely keep my eyes open. Maybe in the next couple of days."

As Sean stepped out of Caleb's car, the older man said, "Call me anytime, day or night."

Sean thanked him, entered his house, took a shower, and went directly to bed. He woke with a start at 4:00 a.m., realizing that he hadn't remembered to set his clock alarm. He immediately phoned the hospital and asked if someone could summon one of his parents to the phone, since he didn't want to risk waking Prim by ringing her room. He was surprised when Maureen picked up the receiver.

"Everything's gone smoothly tonight."

"Maureen, you should've called me. I forgot to set my alarm, and I didn't mean to leave everyone stranded at the hospital."

"No one was stranded. Your parents took turns napping on the loveseat in Prim's room. Whenever one of them was awake, we'd talk quietly while Prim slept. They're so wonderful. You're very lucky."

"Thanks. I know. How has Prim done during the night?"

"When she's woken up, she's been so amazed that we're all sitting with her. She said –"

"We never did that when I was growing up," he interrupted.

"How did you know?"

"Remy and I have heard it way too many times. I wish I knew what they *did* do in the Aurora house when she was growing up."

"Be careful what you wish for," Maureen muttered. "Why don't you go back to sleep for a while? We have things under control here. Neither you nor I will be going to work today, so take your time. Just remember to bring Prim something loose to wear home."

"Loose?"

"She's had surgery. She'll be uncomfortable if you bring her jeans and a close-fitting shirt."

"I see your point. Thanks. I've never had surgery myself and wouldn't have thought about that."

Sean ate a protein bar, paid some of his bills online, lifted weights, and then took a long, hot bath. Once he was dressed and ready, he put on his coat and drove to Prim's apartment in order to get her something to wear home from the hospital.

He went straight to the master bedroom and entered the walk-in closet. Prim had plenty of dresses, but it was below freezing outside so Sean was concerned about her being cold. He selected one long dress that felt as though it would be warmer than the rest. Then he added a pair of drawstring knit pants and a sweatshirt to the pile. After choosing a pair of black shoes and a pair of tennis shoes, he placed the clothing in one bag and the shoes in another. Realizing that she would need underwear, Sean went to the dresser and pulled out a pair of panties, a bra, and some socks and added them to the bag of clothing. He caught a glimpse of the green negligee during his search and stared at it for a few moments before shutting the drawer.

As he prepared to leave, Sean stopped and placed the two bags on the floor near the front door. He went to the coat rack and got Prim's coat, scarf, and knit hat. Once those items had been draped over the back of a barstool at the counter, he went to sit on the couch for a while to collect his thoughts.

It was the first time Sean had been alone in Prim's apartment, and it gave him an odd feeling. He sat for thirty minutes and alternated between praying and trying to formulate different strategies that might aid Prim in her own struggles. He then went to use the master bathroom before leaving for the hospital. As he washed his hands, he stared at the lipstick message Remy had written on the mirror many weeks earlier. I AM A PRETTY PIXIE. Would Prim ever believe it?

Sean withdrew his iPhone and called his sister, knowing it was an hour earlier in Nashville and that she was probably getting ready for work. He wasn't surprised when he got her voicemail.

He left her a message, simply telling her that he loved and missed her and hung up before gathering Prim's things and heading for the stairs.

Chapter Sixteen

Prim put on her lip gloss and said the words, "I am a pretty pixie." Frowning at her reflection, she pulled her hair back into a clip and repeated the words. There was no epiphany. She was still plain Primrose Aurora. She was beginning to despair of ever accepting what Sean and Remy kept telling her.

As she inserted earrings and fastened her charm bracelet around her wrist, she thought of Tiffany and Kenny. They'd stayed with her and Sean for over a week after Prim's release from the hospital. They had only been gone for one day, and she missed them already. She'd been awed by their attentiveness and by how helpful and caring they'd been during her initial recovery.

"That's what families are for," Kenny had told her. "We love you, so we love doing it."

Before their departure the previous day, Tiffany had given her a full-length white flannel nightgown that had colored hearts printed all over it.

"There weren't any more gingerbread men ones," she'd explained. "It's January, and it's too long after Christmas. All the Valentine things are on the racks now, so I got you something with hearts when Sean took me to the Wal-Mart in that town down the road. You'll be covered with hearts and can think about how much Kenny and I love you even though we're going back to Tallahassee for a few weeks."

Prim had hugged her future mother-in-law and told her how much she appreciated the gift and the visit from her and Kenny.

"I guess it all worked out that I had to have surgery," she told the older woman. "We were able to spend more time together, and you got to go with Sean to the Kensington Academy to see your new house. I'd like to have gone with you."

"I wish you hadn't had to have surgery, but I'm also glad we got to be here and see our new place. We really like it. You'll see it soon. You just be careful. You're already overdoing it, Prim. I really don't think you should open Prim's Corner for at least another week."

"I can't keep the store closed any longer. I promise to sit in-between customers."

"I just worry about you," Tiffany told her. "You're so special. You have to take care of yourself."

I'm special all right, Prim thought as she prepared for her return to the hospital for the first parenting class. *Really special but not in a good way.*

Prim sighed then left her bathroom and went back to her closet.

"Uh-uh-uh!" Sean called out from the bedroom. "Don't you dare bend down to get your shoes." As he stepped up behind her, he added, "I don't even think we should be going to the class tonight. You should be resting."

"I have to go or I'll lose my nerve," she protested. "We'll be sitting anyway. What's the difference between sitting there and sitting on my couch?"

"There's a big difference, but I know you're not going to listen, so I won't bother arguing with you about it. Tell me which shoes you want, and I'll get them for you. It's 6:15. We need to leave."

When they reached the hospital, Sean dropped Prim off at the front door and went to park his car. After asking for directions at the front desk, they walked hand-in-hand to the Resource Center, which was where all classes and meetings took place.

Prim nervously glanced around as she and Sean entered. There were eleven chairs arranged in a circle on one side of the room. One couple and a single man were already seated.

"I'm here with you," Sean reminded her. "Don't be afraid."

He led her to the circle, and they each took a seat before saying "hello" to the others. A single woman joined the group a few minutes later. Another couple came in just after the teacher entered and took her seat in the chair marked "Head of the Class."

"It's five minutes to seven," she pointed out. "We have one more couple coming to join us. Then we'll get this show on the road."

Once the last couple had arrived, the instructor, an older woman, began, "Welcome to our Sunday night parenting class. I've been doing this longer than most of you have been alive." Sitting back in her chair, she said, "What we're going to do now is go around the circle and give our first names and tell why we're here. My name is Patty, and I'm the instructor."

Prim happened to be sitting directly to Patty's right, and she prayed that Patty wouldn't pick her to go first. The woman turned to the left and asked the man beside her to begin.

As they went around the circle, they learned that two of the couples were newly expectant parents who simply wanted to do all they could to acquire good parenting skills. Another couple was going through a divorce and was concerned about raising their two-year-old son in separate households and keeping him well-adjusted. The single man had recently been widowed and was now raising a five-year-old daughter and a three-year-old son alone. The single woman was there because there had been a court order issued requiring parenting classes if she was to remain in contact with her seven-year-old son.

When it was Sean's turn, he said, "My name's Sean. I'm here tonight because my fiancée and I are talking about having children after we get married this summer. I want to learn good parenting skills in case we do."

All eyes turned on Prim. She decided that honesty was the best policy and said hesitantly, "I'm Prim. I'm here because I never had a mother or father and am afraid to have children of my own. Sean's mother suggested we take parenting classes and said it might help me not to be afraid."

"How can you not have a mother or father?" the single woman asked. "Everyone has to have parents."

"My mama died when I was a baby, and she never told anyone who my daddy was. I was raised by my aunt and uncle, but my aunt had…emotional problems and my uncle always deferred to her." Looking at Patty, she asked, "How can I be a good parent when I don't know what 'normal' parents do?"

Patty smiled gently at her and said, "Everyone here wants to learn how to be a good parent or how to become a better one. We're going to talk extensively, have hands-on learning, watch DVDs, and read books. Everything you learn during our classes will assist you in becoming comfortable with the idea of being a parent. If you have any questions, then you go to the head of the class. That's me."

"Hence your chair," offered the single man.

Patty grinned and confided, "A former student gave me this chair. I thought it was a wonderful gift. I've been told I'm a walking library when it comes to all things parenting."

Each person in the circle was given a book on child development. It reviewed appropriate parental responsibilities and actions throughout a child's life. Patty told them she expected everyone to read the book, but the main theme in it was to love one's child and do one's best. She asked them to read one chapter per week so that they could engage in conversation about the material during following meetings.

"Tonight, we're going to talk about basics like conception and prenatal development. Good parenting begins before birth."

After the lesson for the night was over, Patty asked if there were any questions. Not surprisingly, the expectant couples had a long list, but Prim didn't mind. She had never learned so much about the topic in any science class and hadn't known the particulars regarding fetuses and how they reacted to things in utero.

"Any other questions?" Patty asked before they ended the first meeting.

Prim awkwardly raised her hand.

"Yes, Prim?"

"Do unborn babies feel pain?"

"There's debate about that. Some people believe a fetus can experience pain after the first nine weeks. Many studies show that a fetus doesn't feel pain until after twenty weeks or more."

Prim thanked Patty, who then declared that the lesson was over and told them she would see them the following Sunday. All of the class members stayed, chatted for a few minutes, and then dispersed. Both lost in thought, Sean and Prim rode in companionable silence back to Aurora.

"So, what did you think?" Sean asked, as he walked up the stairs with Prim to her apartment.

"Once Patty started teaching, I was enthralled. I learned the basics in biology, but this is so much more informative. It was an amazing night."

"I thought so, too. To think of how complex it all is bowls me over. Every baby really is a miracle."

"Some more than others," remarked Prim, as she opened the door and walked in. "Some less."

Depositing her keys on the side table, Prim removed her coat, hat, and scarf. As she hung them on the coat rack, she turned towards the doorway. It remained open, and Sean stood just outside the threshold.

"Sean, it's freezing. Come in."

He walked deliberately forward, shut and locked the door behind him, and strode over to her. He appeared troubled, and she asked him what was wrong.

"What did you mean by some more and some less?"

"Nothing. It's not important." Starting to turn away, Prim suggested that Sean take off his coat and enjoy hot tea and cookies with her. He stopped her, took her in his arms, and pulled her to him. He kissed her and then repeated his question.

"You're the product of such love and faith," she told him. "You're a true miracle."

He looked perplexed but merely asked, "And what do you think you are?"

"An accident. My parents had some great sex, and I was the result. There's no miracle there, just lust and biology."

He pulled her closer, and she rested her cheek against his chest. The material of his wool coat felt odd under her soft skin. He stroked her hair for a while then asked, "Why were you so interested in finding out if unborn babies experienced pain?"

"I used to have nightmares when I was a teenager that I'd felt my mama's pain while she was pregnant with me."

"What did Buddy and Myrtle do when you had the nightmares?"

"I never told them." Suddenly feeling exhausted, she said, "I'm really tired. I think I need to go to bed."

"You're pushing yourself way too hard."

"So you've told me."

"So everyone's told you. You shouldn't be opening the shop."

"We've been over this already."

"You need to hire someone to work with you. That way, you'd have a back-up if you were sick or wanted to take a day off."

"Thank you, Mr. Entrepreneur. I'll take it under advisement."

He kissed her and said he was going to go back to his place and let her get some rest. Although she wanted him to stay longer, Prim didn't ask. She was worried that they would get into a discussion about the prospect of having children together and how she would manage to run the shop and raise a family if by some miracle she allowed herself to get pregnant. She wasn't ready for that conversation, yet.

The next morning, Prim opened Prim's Corner as usual. Business was steady, mostly because townspeople had heard about her emergency surgery and wanted to check on her. By lunchtime, she considered that perhaps she should fall prey to disaster more often. It was good for business. Those who came in were buying at least one article before they left, and she had one sale that was well over a thousand dollars.

Sean phoned at 1:00 to find out how she was feeling. After assuring him she was fine, Prim told him of her profitable morning and promised him she was sitting on a stool behind the register between customers. He observed that she should be lying in bed or on the couch in her apartment instead of sitting in her store.

"I'm okay. You don't have to sound so tense."

"I love you. Worrying about you comes with the territory."

Momentarily speechless, Prim was uncertain as to how she should respond. She eventually managed to stammer a goodbye and hang up. When Sean immediately called her back, she didn't answer the phone.

Prim spent the remainder of the afternoon helping customers and wondering if Sean loved her at all or if he merely wanted to protect her or save her from her own life. By 4:00, she was light-headed, so she decided to close the shop early.

When she returned to her home, Prim undressed and put on the flannel nightgown Tiffany had given her. She was slightly dizzy, and her healing incision was sore. She ate a bowl of cream of wheat and then retrieved the book on child development and good parenting that she'd received the previous night and took it to the couch.

She'd only planned on studying the introduction that reviewed the material Patty had explained in the first class and then going on to the next week's required reading. However, she found that once she started, she couldn't stop. She finished the book after midnight and placed it on the coffee table before deciding she should go to bed.

As she rose from the couch, Prim's mind was clouded by the discrepancies between what she'd just read and what she'd experienced during her own childhood. She absently checked her iPhone and saw that Sean had left her three voicemails, and Remy had left her two. There was also a message from Caleb.

Sean's first message was, "Prim, I'm sorry. Whatever I said wasn't meant to be anything negative. I love you."

His second voicemail said, "Prim, please call me. I love you."

In his final message, he had admitted, "I don't know what to say here. Call me. I want to talk to you. I love you."

Prim deleted all three messages without checking the times the calls had been received. She also deleted Remy's voicemails, which expressed his concern for her and his need for her to call him to talk. Caleb's message offered support and guidance and was also hastily deleted.

Prim switched off her phone and went to bed. As tired as she was, she was unable to sleep. She continued to think about the book and her life and how wrong things had been for her. She envisioned having children and raising them the way she'd been raised, despite her efforts to do things properly. She pictured her sons and daughters hating her and Sean leaving her and taking the children with him.

In the morning, Prim dragged herself out of bed and got ready for work. She did not repeat the words written on the mirror and had to push herself to eat a piece of toast simply because she needed something in her stomach in order to take her daily birth control pill. Once she arrived at the shop, she went through the motions of helping her customers, but her mind refused to stray far from the incongruity of what was supposed to be in parent-child relationships and what had been in hers. She didn't answer her iPhone when Sean, Remy, and Caleb called.

The door to the shop opened at noon. Prim turned towards it, expecting either a customer or one of the three men who had been trying to reach her via the phone. Instead, it was LouAnn.

The short, blonde woman was holding a plastic bag obviously filled with containers of food. The fact that she looked very worried made Prim feel both appreciation and annoyance. As

LouAnn walked forward and placed the bag on the counter near the register, Prim greeted her and asked, "Who sent you?"

"Nobody sent me, Honey. Caleb and Remy were in for breakfast this morning, and I overheard them talking. They're real concerned about you, and they said Sean is beside himself but doesn't know what he did wrong or what to do to make it right. They said you haven't returned any of their calls since yesterday. They were very upset." Pausing, she added, "I haven't seen Remy this down in a while. I decided to come check on you."

"At noon? LouAnn, this is one of the busiest times of day for you."

"And it's also when you should be eating. My staff can handle things without me. If there's a problem, then they can call me on my iPhone."

"You have an iPhone?" Prim blurted out before she could stop herself.

LouAnn grinned and said, "I may be a small-town widow but I'm also a businesswoman. I've had an iPhone for a while. I've been learning the computer a lot over the last few years and finally decided to set up a Facebook Fan Page and a Twitter account. I've been thinking about setting up a website, although I may need help with that."

"I had no idea. I'm sorry if that sounded condescending."

LouAnn smiled at her and assured her there was no need to apologize. She then took Prim's hand and said, "Honey, you do look real tired and sad. Close the shop, and let me walk you back to your place and sit with you while you eat."

When Prim politely refused, LouAnn suggested that she take the food to the back room and eat while LouAnn minded her shop. Prim, who was feeling light-headed again, relented and carried the bag to the back of the store. She ate slowly and then returned to the sales floor. After thanking LouAnn for the beef noodles and the baked apples, she told her she would save the pie for later and offered her gratitude for the woman's thoughtfulness and for the break.

"You call me anytime," LouAnn told her. "I'm only a hop, skip, and a jump away."

By 3:30, Prim was once again feeling faint. Once she'd completed a transaction with a customer and the woman had gone,

Prim closed the shop and left through the back door carrying the container that held her piece of pecan pie. She slowly climbed the steps to her apartment, gripping the rail with one hand to help steady herself. She planned to strip off her clothes and go directly to bed as soon as the pie was put away.

The first thing she saw when she opened the door was Sean sitting on her couch. For a second, Prim thought she was hallucinating. It was not quite 4:00, and he was rarely back in Aurora before 6:00.

"Sean? What are you doing here?"

"Waiting for you. You haven't been answering my calls since yesterday, and I've been going crazy, wondering what I did to make you angry. I've also been worried about you."

"I wasn't angry." Putting the container on the breakfast bar, she went on, "And you worry about me way too much. I'm wondering if maybe our entire relationship is a mistake."

"A mistake," he repeated flatly.

When Prim asked him to leave and declared that she needed time, he got to his feet and said, "No way."

"Just leave!" she demanded. "I don't know what to think about us anymore and don't even know if you really love me or if you just want to fix me. Well, you can't fix me! The parts of me that are broken were broken before I was even born!"

"What in Heaven's name are you talking about?"

"Please go away for a while."

Ignoring her demand, he urged, "Explain what you just said to me about being broken before you were born."

"No!"

"Tell me!" he shouted, startling her. "What sort of crap did Mr. and Mrs. Aurora tell you that made you so afraid?"

"Just go! I don't want you here right now!"

He went. Feeling miserable and depressed, Prim started for the bedroom. She had taken two steps before she lost her balance and fell. Mercifully, she passed out before she hit the floor.

She regained consciousness and groaned. The left side of her head throbbed, as did her shoulder and hip. She reached up to rub the area above her ear and felt a small lump. It was tender to the touch.

Prim attempted to sit up and failed. She checked the time and deduced that she couldn't have been unconscious for long. She considered trying to crawl to the bedroom and maneuver herself up onto the mattress.

I need to call Sean, she thought. *That's what a normal person would do. It doesn't matter that you just sent him away or that you were brainwashed into thinking that a person shouldn't ask for help when she's sick. That's wrong. Make it right. If you're not willing to try, then you might as well just give up and die right now.*

Prim reached into the pocket of her dress and withdrew her iPhone. She used the voice command to call Sean, praying he'd answer. Perhaps he would play the same senseless game she'd been playing with him, Remy, and Caleb for over twenty-four hours.

"Hi, Prim."

He seemed weary, and tears filled her eyes.

"Sean, I'm so sorry. I'm worn out and scared."

"I know. Me, too. I'm scared you don't love me anymore. I need you."

The fear in his voice was something she'd never heard before. Feeling responsible, she said, "I love you so much, and I need you, too."

"Maybe we could have dinner at LouAnn's and then just watch some TV tonight. You know, regroup."

"I'd love to, but I can't."

"Oh. Okay."

He sounded crestfallen, which surprised her. It made her feel badly for him, but it also pleased her. He really did love and need her.

"Sean, I can't because I'm lying on the floor of my living room. Please don't freak out. I fainted after you left. Will you come back?"

"Will I come back?" he echoed in disbelief. Then he began to chuckle and said, "You're not going to make this easy, are you?"

She smiled and said, "No, but at least I'm finally catching on."

"I think I'm catching on, too. Should I call Dr. Stanford?"

"I don't believe so, but you can decide once you're here. How's that?"

"Good. We're both making progress, right? Neither of us is losing it or getting upset. I'll be there in a few minutes."

"I'm not going anywhere." Pausing, she added, "Don't run. If you do, then everyone in town will follow you up to my place to make sure I'm okay."

"Point taken. I'll walk quickly."

Sean arrived five minutes later. He didn't dash across the room but did hasten over to where she lay on the floor and knelt beside her. He asked her if she was hurt and where. Then he examined the bump on her head.

"Did you throw up when you regained consciousness?"

"Do you see anything on the floor?"

"Smart aleck. Do you feel sleepy?"

"Yes, but I didn't sleep at all last night so I think that's why."

He kissed her. Then he asked, "What kept you awake?"

"I read the book Patty gave us in class. It made me think about a lot of things."

"You read the whole book last night?" He grinned sheepishly and admitted, "I did, too." Sobering, he prodded, "Do you want to talk about it now or after I get you to bed?"

Prim wanted to say she wasn't ready to talk, but she sensed somehow that the days of avoidance regarding discussions of her upbringing were over. If she wanted to be with Sean, she was going to have to trust him with everything.

"I want to talk about it after I'm in bed. Will you lie next to me and hold me while I tell you?"

"You know I will, but first things first. I really do think we should call Dr. Stanford and tell him what happened. It would make me feel better if he said you were all right. I also want to call Remy and Caleb and let them know that you're safe and that I'm with you."

He helped her into a sitting position and held her against his chest while she fought vertigo. Then he lifted her from the floor and carried her to the master bedroom.

"It's a good thing you lift weights all the time," she mumbled, as he put her down. "Most men wouldn't be able to lift somebody off the floor and carry them around like this."

"I've been working out since high school when I was on the track-and-field team. I never thought I'd have to use my muscles for something like this."

He kissed her forehead and instructed her to rest while he phoned the M.D., Caleb, and Remy. Once he'd made his calls, he told her that the doctor was coming to check her out after he'd seen his last patient of the day.

Forty minutes later, Philip Stanford appeared with his black medical bag. After examining Prim, he chastised her for returning to work too soon and for not taking proper care of herself. He ordered that she spend the rest of the week in bed or on the couch and then return to work part-time for two more weeks.

"But I'll lose the shop!" she protested.

"No, you won't. I stopped by LouAnn's before I came here. She's going to cover for you for the rest of this week and then she'll work the half days you can't for the next two weeks. Give me a set of your shop keys, and I'll take them to her on my way home. I'll also give her your cell number so she can call you if she has any questions or problems. You can take the calls, but you have to swear to me that you won't go downstairs to the shop when you're supposed to be resting."

Once the doctor had gone and Prim had called LouAnn to thank her for everything, she phoned Remy and Caleb and apologized for not returning their voicemails. She explained what was happening and asked them to come to see her the following evening. Both men seemed cheered after talking with her, and she thanked them for being so understanding.

"I called my mom and dad while you were on your phone," Sean told her. "They're glad you're okay and that you're agreeing to take it easy. They were happy we went to the parenting class."

"We have to go this Sunday," Prim insisted. "I can't miss the class no matter what."

"That'll be our weekly outing. Maybe if you're compliant until then we'll be able to eat out for dinner that night, too. Either that or one of the pregnant women might have a pickle or two to spare in her purse."

Prim was instantly gripped by fear and said, "I'm really scared all of a sudden."

Sean immediately stripped off everything except his boxers, got under the covers, and then lay next to Prim, who had put on the flannel nightgown with Dr. Stanford's help. Sean took her in his arms and assured her that she was safe.

"You're shaking," he muttered. "Why?"

"I don't know."

"Just start talking. Talk about anything and everything. It doesn't have to be in order or make sense. Just talk. It'll get easier to share your experiences that way. Tell me what it was like to grow up with Buddy and Myrtle raising you. How was it in the house?"

"I was like a piece of the family china. They took care of me and valued me, but I was ignored a lot of the time."

"Were they cruel?"

"Uncle Buddy was sweet with me, but he wasn't around a lot. He was either working at the hardware store or out after dinner."

"And Myrtle?"

"She wasn't mean, but it was like she didn't know how to act around me."

"Did either of them read with you or play with you?"

"Uncle Buddy did when he was home. Aunt Myrtle took care of the house and the business accounts, but she never really played games or dolls with me. We *did* all used to cook together. That was the most fun thing we did as a family. At least that's what I used to think before I found out the truth."

"Is that why you smashed all the dinnerware and china the night you overheard Buddy talking to me about how he thought he might be your father?"

Nestling against him, she nodded.

"Prim, you have to tell me what you meant about being broken before you were born. What did Mr. and Mrs. Aurora tell you that made you think you were less of a person than anyone else?

Pressing herself closer to him, she said in a small voice, "I was only three, but I understood that what they were saying was serious and still remember every word. I didn't really understand until I was older. I didn't realize what they meant until after Uncle Buddy died and the truth came out."

"What did they say?"

"That my mama died because God was punishing her, and that they hoped maybe she'd redeemed herself by giving up her life for mine. That my daddy was a devil who'd pay for his sins with his soul and that I was a child of sin by a child of sin and was tainted and destined to...to fall prey to wickedness."

"Please, tell me you don't believe what those ignorant zealots said."

"I was little, and I wondered for years if I was going to be evil because my parents had sinned and my father was supposedly a devil. I kind of took it literally."

"When did you realize that you weren't guilty by association?"

"When I was eight and started going to the Community Church with Remy and his brother and heard Caleb preach about a God who was loving, not vengeful."

"But what your grandparents said left an impression on you."

"Definitely. I guess it's always in the back of my mind somewhere."

"It wasn't an accident that Sandra got pregnant with you the night of her birthday. You were meant to be. You were meant to save me." Running his fingers through her hair, he continued, "I've had a Type A personality since the day I was born. I've always been driven, always needed to take care of everything and everyone, and always had to be the best. The women I was with liked that about me. They wanted me to take care of them, but none of them ever tried to take care of me. You've been different. You want and need me, but you've fought me every step of the way because you were afraid. You want to take care of *me* because you love me. I'm in awe of you, and yet you can't seem to understand how amazing you really are."

"If you keep telling me, then maybe someday I'll accept it."

"I'll keep telling you as long as I have breath left in my body. You are my fairy princess, after all."

"I am a fairy princess. I am a pretty pixie." Beginning to cry, she said, "I want to believe it. I really do."

"You will in time. Trust me."

"I do." As her tears trickled down her cheeks and across Sean's bare chest, she admitted, "I miss Uncle Buddy so much."

Sean comforted her as she talked of the good times she'd shared with her uncle and of how she missed having him in her life despite what he'd done and what he'd failed to do. She fell asleep in her fiancé's arms, feeling relieved, safe, and loved.

Chapter Seventeen

Sean firmly shook the hand of the ninety-year-old alumnus of the Kensington Academy and thanked him for his time. He had known going into the Friday lunch meeting that persuading the wealthy, cagey, elderly man into donating money to the school would be tricky. No previous principal or board member had ever succeeded, but then none of them had been Sean Proper.

After escorting the man to his waiting limousine, Sean bid him farewell and headed back to his office. He was looking forward to his daily call to Prim and was thinking about the literacy fundraiser that they were to attend the following evening in Atlanta. He was also considering how best to approach the director of the equestrian program regarding a student's complaint that she'd been unfairly removed from an upcoming competition. Then there was the matter of the meeting he was scheduled to attend in order to discuss final plans for the annual Parent Weekend, which was to be held at the beginning of March. His parents were moving to Kensington the last week in February, and he needed to call and confirm with the moving company one final time.

He opened the door of his office and was surprised to see Maureen standing behind his desk. She was holding the framed photo of him, Prim, his mother and father, and Remy that Caleb had taken in the Town Square the week before Christmas almost two months earlier. Maureen looked across the room at him and commented, "Remy seems so happy in this picture. I was thinking about him when he was a small boy. He was very boisterous and so intelligent."

"He really wants to be close to you."

"I know. It's not his fault. It's mine. All we can do is keep trying."

"Prim and I are planning a birthday party for him at her place. We're going to have it on his actual birthday since it's a Leap Year this year. Would you like to come?"

"I'd love to, but I think it would be awkward. I was going to ask him if I could take him to dinner, but I'm not certain if he'll be

213

comfortable with us celebrating his birthday together. I'll just have to ask and see what happens. Maybe I'll call him tonight. That would give him a couple of weeks to consider it."

"If you change your mind, you're welcome to come to the party."

"Thank you." Cocking her head, she asked, "How is Prim? Has she fully recovered from her surgery?"

"She's healed now and doing fine."

"Good. Did she hire someone to help her at the shop?"

"Yes, a woman named Tammy Lynn. Prim said they were close in high school. She seems nice and competent."

"I know her," Maureen admitted. "She'll do well at Prim's Corner." Replacing the frame on the desk, she said, "I've taken up enough of your time about this. How did your lunch meeting go?"

"We'll find out eventually. He's a crafty old guy. I gave it my all. We'll see if he makes a donation. If not, then at least I tried my best. Prim says I'm too hard on myself, so I'm attempting not to stress as much. It's tough for me to change, but I guess it's tough for each of us, isn't it?"

As he drove home, Sean reflected on how well things had been going for Prim since the night she'd fainted in her apartment. Something had changed that night, and he believed it was their attendance at the first parenting class and her reading of the book that had planted the seed. Once she'd begun talking to him and Remy about life with Buddy and Myrtle, she hadn't been able to stop.

From what they'd learned, Myrtle had taken care of the Aurora business accounts, the house, Buddy, and Prim – in that order. Everything was neat, tidy, and detached. The woman hadn't been intentionally cruel or neglectful. She'd simply been unable to connect with her family on a deep emotional level. Prim credited her with teaching her how to be a good businesswoman and how to clean house, but those were the only accolades she gave Myrtle.

Things had been different with Buddy. When he'd been at home, he was the one who had interacted with Prim in a more normal parental fashion. Of course, he'd suspected Prim was his child, so that was only natural. He insisted that he, Myrtle, and Prim cook dinner together and made at least that time spent in the kitchen enjoyable for the threesome. However, he would often leave after dinner and not return until well after Prim had been put to bed by Myrtle, who always instructed her that she should never disturb anyone during the night unless the house was on fire. Prim had said she would often lie awake at night, waiting for her uncle to come home and wishing that her mysterious father would climb up a ladder to her bedroom window and take her away to live with him.

Prim's happiest moments seemed to have been those she experienced at school, with her friends, with Remy and his brother, and at the Community Church. She was at ease everywhere except in her own home alone with Myrtle. The older she got, the more excuses she found to stay away. She had volunteered and joined every club and activity she could think of so that she could be gone from the house – except when it was time to cook dinner or to help Buddy with yard work or home projects.

Neither Buddy nor Myrtle had been overtly demonstrative with Prim. Buddy would always give her a quick hug and a kiss on the forehead before he left the house, and Myrtle would pull the covers up to Prim's chin and pat her on the shoulder each night. Prim had wanted to sit in their laps or to be kissed on the cheek or hugged all the time but was discouraged from this by Myrtle. Buddy deferred to his wife regarding limiting physical contact in the household, much to Prim's dismay.

Sean thought of his own parents and of how much they loved to hug and kiss him and Debra. How many times had the children sat in their parents' laps either to be read to or to read to them? He smiled as he thought of how often they would all pile onto the old couch and lean against each other's shoulders while they read or watched television together. Then he frowned as he thought of Prim's growing up without those experiences and that feeling of real love.

When he arrived at his house, Sean changed into jeans and a sweater before grabbing his coat and walking to LouAnn's Café. Remy, Prim, and Caleb were already there, waiting at a table. The moment he saw Prim, all he could think about was seeing her in her formal gown the next evening.

"I'm not going to show you," she'd informed Sean when he'd casually inquired after she'd purchased the gown. "There has to be *some* mystery in a relationship, don't you think?"

Sean didn't point out that much of Prim's life was a mystery. He knew what she meant. He also knew that he was very ready to have sex with her, which was something they hadn't done since her emergency appendectomy.

"No intercourse for four to six weeks," her surgeon had told them before Prim had been discharged from the hospital. "For one thing, the body needs time to heal properly. For another, Prim missed two doses of her birth control pills and was given antibiotics, which may reduce the effectiveness of oral contraceptives. If you have sex without some other form of protection before you give yourself enough time, you could get pregnant."

That warning had scared Prim into abstinence more quickly than anything else the man could have said. Although the parenting classes were doing her a world of good, she remained uncertain as to her own ability to be a good mother. She was trying to convince herself that it was possible, just as she was trying to convince herself that she was truly attractive.

Sean watched Prim as she ate her tomato soup and grilled cheese sandwich. She was so innocent and pure. How could anyone have thought her mother's sexual escapades were punishable by death and that her father had been a devil?

"You want to know what I think?" Remy asked him as the two men walked back to Sean's house after dinner. "I think that subconsciously Prim didn't want to stand out because she was trying to stay under the radar. If she didn't draw attention to herself then perhaps God or Satan or whomever her crazy grandparents made her afraid of wouldn't notice her and would pass her over for damnation."

"Do you know if she ever told Caleb about any of that junk?"

"He's a man of God. How do you tell a man of God that you're afraid your father was one of Satan's minions and that you were tainted by your own conception? She knows it's not true, but she probably worries about it anyway." When they reached Sean's front porch, he asked, "Would you mind if Maureen came to my birthday party?"

Sean grinned and said, "Not at all. You want me to invite her or would you rather do the honors?"

"You can call her."

Sean did as soon as his friend had left. Maureen tearfully thanked Sean for the invitation and for sharing the information with her that it had been offered at her son's request.

Sean picked Prim up at 9:00 the following morning. The fundraiser they were to attend was to be held at Tony Eichstadt's house in Atlanta, and he'd requested that Sean and Prim stay in the guest quarters on his estate. He wanted them to have lunch with him and his wife at a posh downtown restaurant and then relax before the evening's main event. They would have brunch with the Eichstadts the next morning before driving back to Aurora.

The Eichstadt home reminded Sean of a grand manor in some fairy tale of olden days. It was enormous, built to appear rustic, and set back in a wooded area far outside of Atlanta's city limits. Of course it had all the modern conveniences hidden within the seemingly bucolic setting. The guest quarters, which was situated approximately a hundred yards from the main house, reminded Sean of cottages in pastoral tales, except that the house had such amenities as heated flooring and a chef's kitchen. It also had large exposed beams and furnishings that appeared to be hundreds of years old, but the rustic décor had been blended with the contemporary touches. The television and sound system were state-of-the-art, but were well-concealed from the naked eye.

They rode with Tony Eichstadt and his wife, Gillian, to a trendy section of Atlanta and ate a fabulous meal at an upscale fusion restaurant. Gillian, a tall, plump brunette, was easy-going, witty, and highly intelligent. The foursome lingered for two hours after their meal was over, continuing to converse.

They returned to the Eichstadt estate at 3:00. Tony and Gillian excused themselves to make certain that everything was going according to plan. Sean wanted to suggest that he and Prim have sex but decided against it. Instead, he told her that he wanted to take a walk with her and explore the grounds.

Cobbled footpaths extended from the main house throughout the Eichstadt estate. They wove through the thick woods and around a nearby pond. Sean and Prim remarked on the serenity of the setting and of what a pleasant surprise it was not to see tennis courts, pools, stables, or garages filled with a multitude of expensive cars. Despite the size, furnishings, and obvious cost of the main house and guest quarters, there were no other trappings that one typically associated with wealth.

When they returned to the guest quarters at 6:00, Sean went to shower while Prim made a call to Tammy Lynn to discuss the day's business at Prim's Corner. Sean was dressed in his tuxedo and completely ready by 6:30. But Prim was still on the phone.

He came up behind her and slipped his arms around her waist. He brought his lips to the side of her slender throat and began to kiss it while she instructed Tammy Lynn as to how to correct a problem the woman had experienced while ringing up a sale item. When he slid his hands up under her sweater, Prim told Tammy Lynn she had to hang up and would talk with her further on Monday.

"Sean, stop," she demanded, as she grabbed his wrists and pushed downwards. "I'm already running late, but I needed to talk to Tammy Lynn. She's doing well, but she's still new."

"Don't you want me to touch you?"

Sean regretted the words the moment he'd uttered them. Prim stiffened and asked him to release her. Then she went into their bedroom and shut the door. Moments later, he heard the water running in the shower.

Very smooth, Sean thought with annoyance. *Remind her of how afraid she used to be of having men touch her. What a great way to set her back.*

He paced as she showered. When he heard her leaving the bathroom and entering the bedroom, he went to the door and said her name. She told him quietly that she needed a few minutes alone and would meet him at the main house.

"Prim, I'm sorry for what I said. I didn't mean it *that* way."

"I know," she answered, her voice muffled by the door that separated them. "Don't worry so much. It just caught me unawares. I'll be fine in a little while. Go on to the house. I'll be there soon."

Sean had to work at releasing the tension in his body as he arrived at the back door that led into the Eichstadts' kitchen. He greeted the busy staff as he made his way through and went to the gigantic living room where the hosts and some guests were already lounging and enjoying appetizers and drinks. Since he wasn't driving anywhere, Sean accepted a glass of bourbon and went to work.

Sean was under no illusions that he and Prim were there as guests. They both knew that Tony Eichstadt had requested their presence in order to solicit donations. It was something they excelled at, and the Head of the Kensington Board of Directors had immediately recognized this in the couple. They could enjoy themselves while working towards their goal, but they were there to do a job.

"Where's Prim?" Eichstadt asked when Sean came up to stand beside him. "Not ill, I hope."

"No, just running late. Business to take care of. She has a new employee. She'll be here soon." After complimenting Gillian Eichstadt on her appearance, Sean said, "I know we've discussed the players who'll be attending, but who are the ones you invited but don't expect contributions from?"

Eichstadt verbally pointed out the men and women in question, and Sean nodded. Those would be his primary targets for the evening. After all, he did love a challenge.

"Sorry I'm late," he heard Prim say from behind him. "You know how work can be."

Sean turned and froze. Prim was standing a yard or two away from him and the Eichstadts, looking demure and utterly beautiful. Her strawberry blond hair hung loose, save for a clip of some sort that resembled small fairy wings and had been fixed behind her left ear. The gown she'd chosen to wear had spaghetti straps and consisted of gauzy beige, pale pink, and sage green layers of material that were fitted across the bodice and then hung freely all the way down to a handkerchief hemline that almost touched the floor. Although there was definitely some sort of material under the layers that prevented the gown from being see-through, it was impossible to discern exactly what that fabric was or how it had been stitched. The layers seemed to float with Prim's every movement. Dainty sage green slippers were on her feet. She looked like a living fairy, minus the pointed ears and wings on her back.

With the men seemingly incapable of movement or speech, Gillian Eichstadt stepped forward and said, "You look exquisite.

Those delicate diamond earrings perfectly compliment your dress. But I'm worried you'll be cold!"

"Thank you so much for the kind words. As for me being cold, I wore a heavy wrap to the house from the guest quarters and am warm now that I'm inside. As for looking exquisite, I think you've cornered the market on that."

At some point during the women's exchange, Sean found his voice and remembered how to walk. He went to his fiancée, took her in his arms, and gently kissed her before telling her how fabulous she looked. From behind him, Tony Eichstadt quietly agreed. Had the man not been happily married for so long, Sean knew that he would have had some stiff competition. Literally.

As he glanced around, Sean quickly assessed the situation and understood that every man in the room, including the male servers at the party, wanted Prim. He sensed no jealousy from the women present, only admiration. He found that to be very interesting and intuited that they somehow realized what he had long ago – that Prim was innately sensual but was totally unaware of it.

Sean stared into Prim's blue eyes and wondered how he was going to be able to work the room without being distracted by her presence. She kissed him and whispered that they should get to work. The illiterate children of Georgia were counting on them.

For the next three hours, Sean and Prim mingled with the guests. Whether together or separately, they seemed to be well-received by the wealthy party-goers. As the event drew to a close, Tony Eichstadt pulled Sean aside and commended him for his efforts.

"You and Prim are naturals at this. I thought *I* was good. But you two have outshone me tonight. Not only did you help with this cause, but I've been hearing people talk nonstop about Kensington and Prim's Corner." Looking across the room to where Gillian was talking with Prim, he said, "Gillian told me after lunch that she's extremely impressed by the both of you. My wife is very astute."

"It's nice to be appreciated."

"Appreciate each other. Don't lose yourself in your work."

"Did you ever lose yourself in yours?"

"I did, and it almost cost me my marriage."

"What brought you around?"

The man looked grimly at Sean and said, "Ovarian cancer. They gave Gillian a ten percent chance of survival. I decided the moment I got the news to retire early and spend as much precious time with my wife as I could. That was several years ago. I've never regretted my decision. I loved my work, but the love of my life was more important. She's been cancer-free for almost two years. We work together to help those in need. It's very rewarding."

Once all of the guests had departed, Sean and Prim sat with the Eichstadts and reviewed the night's events. The donations promised were substantial, and Gillian profusely thanked the younger couple for their participation.

"This is my favorite project," she admitted. "My grandmother was illiterate, and I was the one who taught her how to read and write. It made such a difference in her life. No one should have to go through life feeling inadequate because of what she was denied by birth or circumstance."

Prim straightened, and her eyes widened. Sean took her hand and asked her if anything was wrong. She shook her head slightly, but Sean could sense that something of great importance had just taken place in Prim's mind. He wondered if whatever it was would lead to positive or negative repercussions.

Prim excused herself from the conversation, saying, "I'm tired and am going to head back to the guest quarters." When Sean proclaimed he was going with her, she kissed him and then said, "It's not necessary. Stay and visit longer with the Eichstadts. There's ground lighting along the footpaths. I can easily find my way back to the other house."

Sean reluctantly allowed Prim to leave the main house alone. He talked with the Eichstadts for forty-five more minutes before announcing he should join Prim and get some rest. They bade him goodnight and said they would see him and Prim at 10:30 for brunch the next morning.

Sean walked quickly through the cold night air towards the guest quarters. It was dark in the thick woods, but the lighting along the footpath gave off exactly the right amount of illumination for someone to easily see where he was heading. Occasionally, there would be a lamppost that held what seemed to be old-fashioned lanterns holding candles hanging from it, although Sean knew all of the lighting was wired and constant.

When he opened the door to the guest quarters and stepped inside, Sean let out a low whistle. Dozens of white roses filled the living room. There was a card resting against the largest vase which was positioned on a small wooden table near the entrance.

Enjoy your first Valentine's Day together.
-Tony and Gillian

Sean called out Prim's name, but she didn't reply. After a hasty search of the rooms, Sean realized she wasn't in the house at all. He began to panic. Had someone grabbed her as she'd walked back alone or had whatever revelation she'd experienced pushed her over the edge?

That was when he saw the note on the pillow of the bed.

Went for a walk. Follow the rose petals.

Grateful there was no wind that evening, Sean returned to the front door and stared down. Now that he was aware of what he was looking for, he easily spotted the petals scattered on the footpath that led towards the right. He walked in that direction, searching for Prim as he went.

When he rounded a corner near the pond, he saw her standing on the path under a lamppost. She wasn't wearing her wrap and waited in the chilly night air dressed only in her evening gown and slippers. A small smile played on her lips when she saw him.

Feeling as though he was dreaming, Sean stood in the middle of the woods not ten feet from Prim and admired her strawberry blonde hair, blue eyes, full breasts, the slight curve of her hips, the ethereal-looking gown, and her pale skin. He could almost envision the outline of wings behind her.

"Once upon a time, there was a noble knight," Prim began softly. "He carried the weight of the kingdom on his shoulders but was glad to do so. Yet, he longed for someone to take care of him on those rare occasions when he allowed it."

Sean stood mute and still. He had always been the one to tell the fairy stories to his sister and parents when he'd been younger and wanted very much to have Prim tell him this particular one. He had no idea where it would lead or end.

"One cold, clear evening, the knight was returning to his lodgings after helping those in need. An anonymous note directed him to follow a trail of rose petals. He did and eventually came across a pixie who was waiting for him on the path." Prim slowly moved towards him and said, "The knight was enamored of the pixie, although the pixie wasn't quite sure why. Still, she could tell that the knight wanted her, and she wanted him."

Sean could clearly see the top of her dress puckering under the pressure of her hardened nipples. He wanted more than anything to take the pink buds underneath in his mouth and warm them with his hot breath, his lips, and his tongue. He felt as if he was going to explode at any moment, but he refused to surrender to his body's reaction to this fantasy that Prim was creating for him.

"What the pixie didn't know was that the love of the knight would set her free, allowing her to transform into a fairy princess. Although she continued to have doubts about where she had come from and where she was going, she decided that the knight was wise and had the ability to see her for what she truly was. She, in turn, had the ability to see the knight for what he was and to give him what he needed."

"What was the knight?"

"A gift from God to the world."

"And what did he need?"

"To let go of his burdens when possible."

"And what did the pixie want from the knight?"

"To be loved unconditionally." Slipping her arms around his neck, Prim pressed herself against him and murmured, "She wanted understanding, reassurance, and to have the knight inside of her."

Sean groaned and kissed her. He could feel how cold the bare flesh of her arms was against his neck and drew back in order to remove his tuxedo jacket. She stopped him and shook her head.

"You're freezing," he told her.

"I won't be for long."

"What do you want?"

"To go back to your lodgings, my knight," she said coyly.

"You want me to make love to you?"

She shook her head.

"You want me to have sex with you?"

"No."

He absorbed what she was intimating and asked, "Are you sure? I don't know if you're ready."

"I do. I am a pretty pixie," she declared with conviction. "I'm ready to be a fairy princess."

"I don't understand. What changed?"

"No one should have to go through life feeling inadequate because of what she was denied by birth or circumstance," Prim told him, repeating the words Gillian Eichstadt had uttered earlier. "That struck a chord within me. It sort of woke me up."

"I think *I* must be dreaming," Sean muttered, as Prim took his hand and pulled him back towards the guest quarters.

"If you are, then we're both having the same dream."

Prim sighed with relief as the warmth inside the guest quarters surrounded them. Once Sean had closed and locked the door behind them, Prim undid the buttons on his jacket and waited for him to remove it before reaching for the top of his shirt. He put his hands on her shoulders, which were as cold as icicles.

"You'll probably catch pneumonia," he said worriedly. "Why didn't you take that wrap or a coat?"

"Pixies don't wear those things," she pointed out. "And I won't catch pneumonia if you do what we both want right now."

He pulled her to him and kissed her hard. His fingers found their way first into her hair and then moved downwards to caress her body through the material of the gown. She soon had his shirt unbuttoned, his pants undone, and his fly unzipped. His hands moved to the zipper at the back of her dress.

When they were both naked, Sean lifted Prim and carried her to the bedroom. The pressure was building at the base of his spine to an almost unbearable level as he lowered her onto the mattress of the old-fashioned, hand-carved teester bed. He looked down at her for a moment and saw the tender, young, beautiful creature that was Primrose Anastasia Cassandra Aurora. He wanted to do what all men dreamed of doing to her. He desired to safeguard her welfare and fuck her until neither of them was capable of rational thought.

Sean was soon on top of Prim and inside of her. As he used his hands and mouth to warm her cold skin, he thrust deep and hard between her legs, reveling in the feel of being enveloped by hot cushions of flesh that were slick and throbbing. She moved under him and consciously tightened around him. He thrust harder. She climaxed just before he did.

Trembling, Prim told Sean she needed to take a two-minute break for the bathroom. He gave her the two minutes; then he went in as she was washing her hands. He came up behind her and began to caress her and stroke her with his mouth and palms. She whimpered, but he didn't ask her if she wanted him to stop. He didn't have to. She was pushing one of his hands down and bringing the other up to one breast. She shut her eyes with the pleasure as he rubbed between her legs.

Guiding Prim until her hands rested on the edge of the counter, Sean eased into her from behind. She moaned softly as he placed his hands on her hips and began to thrust. He stared at their reflection in the mirror, watched as Prim moved back and forth, watched as her perfect breasts rose and fell with their movements.

"What are you?" he managed to ask.

"I'm Prim," she answered breathlessly.

"Pretty, smart, giving, innocent Prim." As she gripped the edge of the counter, he urged, "Say it! Feel it!"

She said it and had the most intense climax she'd ever had since they'd been together. Sean released in her and fought to stay upright as he did so.

He lost track of the remainder of the night and of how many times they came and of what positions they used. He felt unbelievably powerful. He was Prim's knight in shining armor, and she was his fairy princess. Nothing existed except the two of them together in the magical cottage in the woods.

Sean woke to Prim's kiss. He was unbelievably sore but felt surprisingly refreshed, despite his lack of sleep and his physical exertions. Slipping his fingers into Prim's hair, he asked her if she was all right.

"Very tender but fine. Perhaps we should wait a week or two before having sex again. Well, at least like that. Do you think we'll do what we did last night anytime in the near future?"

"I doubt if there'll be repeat performances of last night. I've never…that was quite an experience. I don't think we could have that marathon session again without killing ourselves."

She concurred but added, "Although doing…that...you know the word I don't like...doing that on occasion would be exhilarating."

"So, you want me to keep making love to you and having sex with you all the time but you only want me to –"

"Sean," she said in a warning tone.

"I don't like the word either, but can you think of a better one for what we did?"

"No."

"Well, then I won't say it but let's agree to surprise each other and do it whenever the mood strikes us. You can do it to me, you know. It's not just a one-way street."

"How could I do it to you?"

He grinned broadly and said, "Try it sometimes and see."

They ate a delicious brunch with the Eichstadts before driving back to Aurora. The first thing Prim did was clean the lipstick inscription from her mirror, which made Sean's heart sing with joy since it meant she finally believed it. Remy had them over to his apartment for an early dinner, knowing they had the parenting class to attend later that evening. Once they'd finished eating, Prim announced that she'd forgotten her iPhone at her apartment and was going to drive back over to get it before she and Sean left for class.

"You did it, didn't you?" Remy asked Sean, as they cleared the table.

"Did what?"

"You know what."

"You can tell?"

"Of course I can tell. Prim's the same but different. She finally looks comfortable in her own skin. Plus, you both look exhausted."

"It was indescribable. I've been with about a dozen other girls in my lifetime, but I've never loved anyone but Prim. It made what we did totally magical. Loving her has made everything totally magical."

226

Remy busied himself with washing a plate and said, "I miss that. I haven't had it since I broke up with my girlfriend from high school. I'm questioning whether or not I'll ever find another woman I love who'll love me."

"You will."

"You can't know that. I'm going to be thirty-four in two weeks. I'm a successful store owner who's lonely as hell."

"Look at me and Prim. Neither of us ever really expected to fall in love with anyone. But look at us now."

Remy nodded but seemed unconvinced. His pervasive melancholy stayed with Sean for the remainder of the evening. When Prim dropped him off at his house after the class, she asked him what was wrong.

"Remy feels like he's destined to be alone forever. I tried to tell him that it wasn't going to happen like that, but I don't think I did a good job."

"I'll talk to him tomorrow. He always gets like this around his birthday."

"He does?"

"Yes. He'll bounce back after the party. I see it every year. Caleb will be more watchful over him for the next couple of weeks, too."

"You think he'll hurt himself?"

"No. That used to be a worry after his father and brother died, but it's not anymore. He just needs extra attention right now."

Once he'd lifted weights and taken his long, hot bath, Sean called his parents and discussed what would be their last week of work at the supermarket and laundry. He assured them that he would be in Tallahassee to supervise the movers and asked how their packing was going. They were excited but understandably nervous. They eagerly told him of the farewell parties their employers were throwing for them before their departure for the Kensington Academy.

After hanging up with his parents, Sean called his little sister. She actually seemed happy with Patrick, the man she'd been seeing since just after Christmas. She talked about coming with him to see her parents' new home once they'd gotten settled. Sean hadn't told his parents. He remained leery but was hopeful that things were finally going well for Debra when it came to relationships. He had a nice conversation with her that evening and told her he loved her before ending the call. She told him she loved him, too. He smiled and went to bed feeling happy, relaxed, and ready for whatever the future might bring.

Chapter Eighteen

Prim woke utterly terrified. Her heart was pounding, and she was shaking. She reached for the phone and prepared to speed dial Sean. Instead, she inexplicably selected Caleb's number.

"Prim?" he answered sleepily. "What is it? What's wrong?"

"I'm scared!"

"Why? What happened? Are you hurt?"

"No! I had a nightmare and...and I'm so scared!"

"I'll be right there. Do you want me to call Sean?"

"No! No, just come. I need to talk to you alone. Please."

"I'll be there as soon as I can."

Prim hung up and reached for her robe. She slipped it on over her long flannel nightgown and wandered from room to room while she waited. As the minutes dragged by, she became more and more afraid. By the time she heard the knock, Prim was beginning to find it difficult to breathe. She hastened to open the door.

Caleb, who was wearing jeans and a plaid flannel shirt, hurried inside and closed and locked the door behind him. He took her by the shoulders and told her that everything was going to be all right. She shook her head and said, "I...I feel like I can't breathe!"

Brushing stray locks of hair from her face, Caleb said gently, "You're having a panic attack. I've seen people have them before. You'll be fine. Just come sit with me and try to let go of the fear. I'm not going to allow anything to happen to you."

He took her to the couch and suggested they sit beside one another. Prim, who continued to have trouble breathing, was able to convey to him that she was too anxious to sit. She repeated that she was scared.

Caleb pulled her close to him, all the while talking soothingly to her. After a time, Prim found that it was slightly easier to breathe and that she wasn't trembling so badly. Caleb loosened his hold on her, sat on the couch, and then pulled her into his lap. He held her against his expansive chest as if she was four, not twenty-four. Prim tucked her hands between her cheek and his shirt and shut her eyes.

She asked in a small voice, "Can we sit like this for a while?"

"As long as you need."

Her fear gradually receded. Caleb didn't say a word but merely held her in his strong arms. Prim sighed and thanked him.

"I think this is what it must feel like to be a child and have a grown-up hold you when you're scared. I always wondered. It's nice."

"God, I'm so sorry you never had that," Caleb muttered and tightened his arms around her. "Do you want to tell me about what made you so afraid?"

"No, but I think I have to. I don't know what to do. I don't know what to believe."

"What did you dream?"

"That I was my mother. That I was in a bar on my eighteenth birthday and had sex with a strange man in a bedroom somewhere. He…changed while we were together." Suddenly terrified again, Prim gripped the front of Caleb's shirt and said, "He turned into a devil, but I didn't stop him. I begged him not to stop even though I knew what he was." Prim buried her face against the man's chest and asked, "What if my grandparents were right? What if my mama died because of what she did and what if my father was a devil? Am I tainted like they said?"

"Tainted? You're *not* tainted," Caleb proclaimed. "Your mother did *not* die because she had sex or got pregnant, and your father was *not* a devil. Your parents might not have loved each other, but you weren't the product of some unholy union. You were the result of passion between two human beings who were lonely and desperate. You were an innocent." Caleb placed a hand on one side of her face and said, "You *are* an innocent. You're one of the most pure-hearted people I've ever met. If you were tainted by evil, then you'd be overshadowed by it. There's not an evil bone in your body." Taking one of her hands in his, he asked, "Why didn't you ever talk to me about this when you were younger?"

"I never dreamed about my parents having sex until tonight."

"That's not what I mean. What I mean is why didn't you tell me about what Mr. and Mrs. Aurora said regarding your mother, your father, and you?"

"I was afraid you wouldn't let me come to the Community Church anymore. I was scared you'd tell me that God didn't care about me and neither did you."

"I would never, *ever* tell you that. I would never believe that. Mr. and Mrs. Aurora were very confused people. It's tragic that they frightened you about something so important. I wish I'd known a long time ago about all of this. I could have made a difference."

"You did every time I talked to you or heard you preach."

"I could have done more. I should have done more."

Prim dozed, waking with a start at some point during the night. She found that she was still in Caleb's embrace, although she was no longer sitting in his lap. Instead, she was curled beside him with her head resting against the center of his chest.

"You're still here."

"Of course I am."

"I'm sorry I called you during the night and kept you up."

"I'm not. I'm proud of you, Prim. You did what a normal person would do in that situation. You needed help, and you asked for it. Think about what happened with your appendicitis. You almost died because of the way you reacted. This time, you didn't hesitate. That's a big step for you."

"It is, isn't it? I didn't even think about it." Sighing, she said, "But you'll be tired for work today and then for Remy's birthday party tonight."

"It doesn't matter. You would have done the same for me or anyone else. Stop expecting less for yourself than you give to others."

"I'm trying."

"And you're doing a wonderful job. I'm very happy for you and for Sean. I couldn't have picked a better man for you if I'd tried."

"Caleb?"

"Yes, Prim?"

"Are you my father?"

It was something she'd wanted to ask him for over a decade. She knew it was irrational. He hadn't even lived in Aurora when her mother had gotten pregnant with her. Still, she'd had a nagging feeling that the man was her biological father since she'd been a freshman in high school. She had to ask.

"Caleb?"

"I think I am, Prim."

Not knowing how to respond, she stammered, "B-but how? You didn't move here until after I was a baby. Nobody ever talked about you and my mama being together."

"That's because nobody knew. After I left the priesthood, I was without purpose for the first time in my life. I became depressed and took odd jobs doing farm work and construction. I felt lost, but I knew that I had to find my way back to what God wanted me to do. I just didn't know how to do that."

"How did you meet my mama?"

"I was passing through the region and ended up at Dempkey's Bar. I was never a drinker, but I was lonely. Lots of lonely people go to bars to talk as well as drink. Your mother was there. She was so beautiful and so sad."

"Did she tell you her name?"

"She said it was Anastasia. She asked that I not say my name, so I didn't."

"Anastasia," Prim repeated slowly.

"I suggested we take a walk. At some point, she shared with me that it was her eighteenth birthday. That was when she started to cry and said she wished she could fly away from Aurora. I held her and told her everything would be all right. She asked me to make love to her." Looking chagrined, he admitted, "I didn't hesitate to take her back to my motel room and do exactly that. I'd never been with a woman before, and your mother was very attractive. We were both lonely. We spent quite a while together. It was a very powerful experience for both of us. At some point during the night, I fell asleep and woke up alone."

"What about after that?"

"I moved on. I eventually found the path that led me back to my vocation as a pastor, although I felt as though God didn't want me to give up the physical work I was doing. It helped to ground me. A couple of years after that night I spent with your mother, I heard through a friend that the town of Aurora needed a pastor and that there was also an opening at the feed store. I decided it was a sign from God and came here. Everything fell into place."

"Did you look for my mother?"

"I wondered about her, but I never ran into anybody named Anastasia or heard of anyone local who had that name. Sandra had died before then, so there was no chance I could have ever seen her after I settled here. Of course, I decided that perhaps she had moved away like she'd wanted."

"When did you first suspect I was your daughter?"

"The summer before you left for college in Atlanta. Remember when you wanted to join that service sorority and asked me to write you a letter of recommendation? You gave me the paperwork that accompanied the request, and it had your full name listed. When I saw that one of your middle names was Anastasia, it struck a chord. It's not a very common name. When I noted your birthdate and did the math, it fit."

"Why didn't you say anything?"

"You were getting ready to leave for college and were so excited. What if I was wrong? The name and dates could have been a coincidence, although I seriously doubted it. However, your mother could also have slept with other men during that same time period. She wasn't a virgin when I was with her.

"What if I approached you, upset you, and then it turned out I wasn't your father after all? Conversely, what if I was? How would either scenario impact you? Would you change your plans and not go away to school, which was what you really wanted? Would you be glad to know, angry, or indifferent?" Shaking his head, he said, "If I'd uncovered the information when you'd been a minor, I wouldn't have hesitated to push the issue. I'd always felt as though things weren't good at home for you, but I had no proof. Since you were eighteen, I thought it might make things worse if I told you what I suspected." Rubbing at his face with one hand, he admitted, "And then there was Remy. In the midst of my own personal shock at what I'd uncovered regarding my possible relationship to you, Remy was on the verge of killing himself. He wasn't my biological child, but I'd treated him as if he were my own son since he'd been a young boy and had come to me for guidance. I really didn't know from one day to the next if he'd succumb to depression and cut his wrists. I wasn't certain if he was going to make it through those few months after his brother's accident. How would he react to speculation that I was your father? Would that be the trigger for his final act of despondency?"

"And what about when he started taking medication and I started college? What about when I came back to Aurora after Aunt Myrtle died?"

"Things seemed more normal for you with only Buddy here. Of course, I didn't know that Buddy had slept with your mother at around the same time I did. I had no idea that he'd always thought he was your father. I was only thinking that your lifelong relationship with him might be damaged.

"During the years after I started to suspect you were my daughter, I spent untold hours praying about what to do. I reviewed the facts with my wife, who said she knew I'd talk with you about it someday when the time was right. I guess that time is now."

"Did you ever find out if it was really my mama you slept with?"

"No. It wasn't as though anyone was carrying the mysterious Anastasia's picture around or displaying it anywhere. No one was ever invited into your home, so there was no chance of me catching a glimpse. It wouldn't have occurred to me that the woman I'd had sex with was one of the Auroras. Once I moved here, all I heard about them was how crazy religious your grandparents were and how reclusive the family had become over the years. By that time, the only sociable adult was Buddy."

Prim got off the couch and went over to the long, low bookcase she had in the living area. She withdrew a photo album that she'd saved from the family home before it had been cleared out and sold. She took it over to where Caleb sat. After flipping through the first few pages, she passed the book to him.

He stared down at the picture of Sandra Aurora, wearing her cheerleading outfit and holding her pom-poms and a trophy. After a minute, he nodded and said, "This was the young woman I knew as Anastasia."

"What do you want to do?" Prim asked uncertainly.

"I want to know if you're my child," he said firmly. "I've wanted to know for the last six years, but I didn't want to mess up your life by being selfish and asking you to take a DNA test. If you don't want to now, I'll understand."

"How could I not want to? My whole life I've dreamed about having parents. I prayed that I'd have a father like you. I just thought it was a silly dream."

"So, you're not angry with me for not telling you what I suspected?"

"No. I understand. It's just such a relief to know that it wasn't that you didn't want me."

"Didn't want you? How on earth could I not want you for my child? I wish I had suspected that Remy was mine, too. I'd love to claim the both of you."

"So, what do we do?" she persisted.

"Get a DNA test."

"But we can't."

"Why not?"

"Because of the church. What if you are my daddy and all of this comes out?"

"If my congregation can't accept what happened long before I became their pastor, then I haven't done a very good job of teaching them what love and forgiveness is all about and wouldn't want to stay on there."

"What about Remy?"

"What about him? He's not suicidal like he was before. Do you think he'll be angry with me?"

"No, but I think he might feel…left out."

"He's thirty-four years old today, Prim. It's not like I'd abandon him if it turns out that you are my daughter. He knows that."

"What about the dead man in the trunk?"

"What about him?"

"The police might look to you as a suspect if they knew you were my father."

"I didn't kill the man. They can question me all they want. I'm not concerned with anything except your welfare at the moment."

She nodded and went to get the papers Dr. Stanford had given her listing the results of the DNA testing performed on the samples from her, the man in the trunk, and Buddy Brown. She glanced at the clock and noted that the Atlanta lab opened at 8:00 a.m.

"We could leave in a little while and be there when they open. They could do a cheek swab on you and compare it to my results. We should know in a week or two."

"What about Prim's Corner and Aurora Hardware?"

"Tammy Lynn can take care of the shop on her own for the day. The hardware store will just have to stay closed."

"What do you want to tell Sean, Remy, and anyone else who asks where we were?"

"That we had business to tend to. It's the truth. I don't think we should say anything to anyone until we get the results. You may not be my father, and no one needs to be talking about it if it turns out not to be true."

"And if it is true?"

"Then I want everyone to know."

They were soon on their way to Atlanta. They arrived at the lab at 10:00 after getting lost twice and fighting morning traffic. Once they'd signed consent forms and paid the fee up front, Caleb submitted to the cheek swab. They ended up at a Cuban restaurant for lunch.

While they waited for their food, Caleb asked, "What led you to believe I might be your father?"

"It was about ten years ago when you organized the Thanksgiving meals for the needy. Everyone who was there was putting the items in bags so that they could be delivered with the turkeys. My partner for the day was your wife. She and I were chatting about this and that. I caught a glimpse of you from across the room and watched you while you worked with your partner. I remember thinking that you and I did things a lot alike and that when you laughed it was the same way I laughed. Maybe it was wishful thinking, but I had the oddest impression we were related. I told myself I was being ridiculous but –"

Her iPhone rang, and she glanced at the display and gave a small sigh before answering.

"Hello, Sean."

"Prim, where are you? I called the shop, and Tammy Lynn said you weren't coming in today."

"I'm in Atlanta with Caleb."

He paused before asking, "Why?"

"It has to do with Aurora family business."

Pausing again, he asked, "Why didn't you tell me you were going?"

"Because I didn't know until this morning."

"O-kay," he said slowly. "Will you be back in time for Remy's party?"

"We're just grabbing a bite for lunch, then we'll be on our way back to Aurora."

"I see. May I talk to Caleb for a moment?"

She passed the phone to the man and waited with interest to see what Sean was going to do. Caleb greeted him and assured him she was fine and that they would be home soon. Sean must have fallen silent, because Caleb shrugged and waited for a full minute. He then sat bolt upright and blinked in surprise.

"I honestly don't know," Caleb said. "That's why we're here." Then, "Please. Thank you. Yes, definitely." Passing the iPhone back to Prim, he said quietly, "He knows."

"You know?" she asked once she'd put the phone to her ear. "How could you know? Caleb and I didn't even figure this out until last night."

"It's my job to fix things, remember? Your question about your paternity was a problem that needed fixing. I wondered from early on if Caleb or Dr. Stanford was your father. Both were men when Sandra turned eighteen and are very protective of you. Both are giving and caring like you are. They have the right coloring to produce a strawberry blonde child if they procreated with a redhead. Although your build is more like Doc Stanford's, I was actually leaning towards Caleb, but the dates didn't work. I suppose you've straightened that out. Will you explain it to me later?"

"Of course. Sean, you can't say anything. We could be completely wrong. No one can know until we're sure."

"You know me better than that. I wouldn't tell anyone."

"Not even Remy," she insisted. "It's his birthday. His mom's coming to the party, and your parents will be there along with us,

LouAnn, and Caleb. It's his special day, and I don't want to take away from it in any way."

"I'm not going to say a word to anyone," he declared. "I love you very much, Prim. I hope it is Caleb. I'll see both of you tonight."

When they returned to Aurora, neither Prim nor Caleb went to work. Instead, they went to the grocery store and picked up the few remaining items Prim needed in order to complete her menu for the evening, which consisted of all of Remy's favorite foods. Caleb helped her carry everything up to her apartment and sat at the breakfast bar and talked with her while she cooked. In the middle of frosting the cake, she began to cry.

Caleb immediately left his seat and came around to take her in his arms. He asked her why she was crying, to which she replied, "I feel like a regular girl talking with her father while she cooks. What if you're not my daddy? I've wanted parents for so long. I know I'll never have my mama, but I so want to have a father."

He tentatively kissed her on the top of the head and said, "I think the test results will be positive, but we'll have to wait and see. If they're not, then I'm going to help you find out who your father really is. If at all possible, you need to know."

He dried her tears with a nearby dish towel and then excused himself to go to his own home in order to shave and change clothes. While he was gone, Prim busied herself with the final preparations for the party, trying not to think about how things might be affected between her, Caleb, and everyone in the community depending on the results of the test. She knew she would be crushed if Caleb was not her father and ruminated on the twists of fate that had led to the sexual encounter between him and her mother.

Stop thinking about this, she told herself. *Whether he is or isn't my father I don't need to be imagining him in bed with my mama.*

The nightmare she'd had the previous night came back to Prim, but now it held no power over her. Caleb could no more be a devil than Prim could be a petunia. She grinned and went to answer the knock at her door.

She'd expected her first guest to be Remy. Instead, it was his mother. Prim smiled and welcomed her inside.

"I know I'm early," the woman told her. "I was too nervous to wait until 7:00."

"You're only a half hour early. Why don't you come in and have a seat? Would you like Coke, Diet Coke, cream soda, or water?"

"Cream soda would be perfect. Thank you." As she sat at the breakfast bar, Maureen asked, "When was the last time you saw Sean?"

"We had dinner last night."

Maureen shook her head and said, "*My* Sean."

A lump formed in Prim's throat. She swallowed it and admitted, "The night he died. I insisted on going with Remy to Dempkey's Bar to try and talk him into letting Remy bring him home. He wasn't drunk, yet. He refused and told us to leave. Remy said 'No,' but the bar owner told us to get off the premises or else he'd call the police. The conversation we were having was drawing attention and wasn't good for business," she said bitterly. "The man actually reached for the phone, so we reluctantly left. Remy was beside himself but didn't know what else to do. He took me home."

"And how did you find out about the accident?"

"From Caleb. He came to the house just as Aunt Myrtle, Uncle Buddy, and I were sitting down to breakfast. Remy had called him from the...the morgue. He'd...." Dropping her head, she said quietly, "The Chief of Police had picked him up during the night to...to go...identify the body. Remy had been...well...Dr. Stanford had been called in and had given him some sort of sedative. Caleb and his wife had brought him to their house and put him to bed." Blinking back tears, she asked, "Could we not talk about this anymore tonight?"

Maureen apologized and said, "We won't talk about it ever again. I'm sorry for bringing it up now. There's just so much I don't remember that it's pathetic. I don't...I don't recall exactly when was the last time I saw my Sean. I was in such bad shape. I do remember the last time I saw Remy though. The hurt look in his eyes has haunted me for years. I failed him."

"Then, yes. Now –"

Someone knocked on the door. Prim hurried to answer it. It was Sean, his parents, and LouAnn. Caleb arrived a few minutes later, followed by Remy.

When Remy and Maureen saw one another, she left her seat and walked slowly over to him. He came inside, and his mother awkwardly put her arms around his shoulders and said, "Happy birthday."

"Thanks for coming, Maureen."

"Thank you for having me."

"This is really nice," Tiffany remarked cheerfully. "It's good to be here in Aurora with all of you and in our new house."

"How are you liking it?" LouAnn asked. It must be such a change after living so long in the same place and with the same jobs."

"It's kind of scary, but we like our new house and our new jobs sound like they'll be good," Kenny answered. "Plus, we'll get to see Sean and Prim and all of you, even though we hated leaving our friends in Tallahassee."

"At least we can still call them," Tiffany pointed out. "And Sean says he'll take us back once in a while to see them and to eat at Mr. Spiro's restaurant."

The evening went well as they talked, ate, and gave Remy his gifts. Remy seemed more at ease in his mother's presence than he had been for as long as Prim could recall. As they all enjoyed cake and ice cream, Maureen withdrew a square envelope from her purse and handed it to her son.

"You don't have to watch this now, but I wanted you to have it. It's a copy of our old home movies from when you were little. I had them all transferred onto a DVD a couple of years ago."

"Can we see?" Tiffany asked excitedly.

"Mom, Remy may want to watch them in private first," Sean advised.

"No, I want to see it now."

He asked Prim if she minded. She assured him that she didn't, although she was nervous about what might happen. She turned on the television and inserted the DVD into the player beside it.

They all sat and watched Remy's young parents' wedding and reception, a trip to Lookout Mountain, Maureen holding a newborn Remy, the boy taking his first steps, his first, second, and third birthday parties, a lengthy recitation by the preschooler of various dinosaurs and all of their characteristics and the time periods when they had lived, Remy's fourth birthday party, and video of him and his parents playing in the snow, swimming in a pool, and camping. The family seemed very happy and loving. Maureen and her husband were energetic and involved with each other and their son. They were nothing like the man and woman Prim had known when she and their younger son had been growing up.

Prim kept giving her friend a sideways glance every now and again. The films were great, but would they make him feel comforted or dejected? He seemed mesmerized and didn't say anything to anyone for several minutes after the DVD ended.

"So, I wasn't romanticizing my early childhood," he muttered. "It really was good."

"It was," Maureen confirmed.

"I think you two should hug," Kenny suggested. "Hugging is good when people fight then make up."

"Dad –" Sean began, but Remy was already on his feet.

Maureen stood and took her son in her arms. He hugged her tightly and asked if she would come back with him to his apartment so they could talk further. After thanking Prim for the wonderful meal and everyone for their attendance at his party and the gifts, Remy left with his mother.

LouAnn departed not long afterwards followed by Caleb. Tiffany and Kenny gave Prim a hug and told her they would see her soon as they left with Sean, who said he was coming back after he brought them home to Kensington. While he was gone, she showered, put on a long nightgown, and slipped her robe on top of it.

When she heard Sean enter the apartment, Prim went to the living area and asked him to sit with her on the couch. They spoke of the party and of how they were trying not to worry about Remy and Maureen. Then Prim explained everything that had happened with Caleb and their resultant trip to Atlanta for the DNA test. They talked of the ramifications of the results no matter what they were.

Sean kissed her before saying, "I hope Caleb turns out to be your father. I can't wait to be able to say I'm your husband."

Pausing, he added, "I want to be able to say I'm the father of our children. You want a baby, don't you?"

"Yes. I'm just afraid I'll be a terrible mother."

"Prim —"

"Don't *do* this, Sean! Stop pushing me!"

She pulled away from him and got to her feet. He stood and told her not to run away from what she wanted.

"Six months ago, I couldn't even hold your hand!" she said furiously. "In the last couple of months, we've made love, had sex, and fucked! What more can you expect from me? What's your hurry? You want me to have a baby now and be a terrible mother so you can leave and take it with you? You want our child not to know her mama like I never knew mine? At least she'd have a father, right?"

Sean was dumbstruck. He shook his head once before saying, "I would never take our child away from you. Ever."

"Would you leave me with our child if I weren't taking proper care of it? Would you stay with me and let our baby suffer?"

Sean's lips parted. He stared at Prim for a while then said, "So, that's what this is about. You're worried that our baby will suffer the same fate as you, that I'd let it be ignored and neglected because of my love for you just like Buddy did with Myrtle."

Prim turned, heading for the master bedroom. Sean was instantly in front of her. He took her by the wrists and said firmly. "You're not going to run away from this. I want you to listen to me. I don't run from anything. You understand?"

"But I'd want you to!" she cried. "I'd want you to take our baby away from me if I treated it the way I was treated! I'd want you to promise me you'd make sure she was loved and hugged and played with and paid attention to! I don't want her to end up like me!"

His arms were around her shoulders, and he whispered to her that he would always be there to safeguard both her welfare and that of any children they might have together.

"You're not Myrtle, and I'm not Buddy," he reminded her. "You're Prim, and I'm Sean. Not only are we different than they were, but we also have a lot of support through my parents, Caleb, Remy, LouAnn, Byron, Dr. Stanford, and everyone else we're close to here in town and elsewhere. Our children will be so blessed. Our children will be cherished."

Prim thought about Tiffany's story regarding Sean's birth. She remembered the chilling description of the cold, dead newborn who miraculously came to life and touched the lives of so many others. If she trusted that the miracle had actually happened then how could Prim not trust what Sean was telling her?

All she could manage to say was that she loved him. Sean kissed her and took her to bed, holding her against him until morning. Neither of them slept.

Chapter Nineteen

Despite the packed pews, there was total silence in the Aurora Community Church. Caleb had announced at the previous Sunday services that there would be a special meeting that Wednesday night at 6:00 p.m. Curious, his congregates had turned out *en masse* and had just finished listening to his speech regarding the events of his earlier life and his confirmed paternity of Primrose Aurora.

Prim was squeezing Sean's hand so tightly that he wondered if his fingers were turning blue. She was trembling and chewing on her lower lip. Although she'd been ecstatic to learn that Caleb was, indeed, her father, she was apprehensive as to how others might react.

"He's such a powerful man in the pulpit," she'd told Sean more than once. "What if he isn't allowed to preach after this? What if people don't think he's worthy of being their pastor anymore?"

"Because he had sex with your mother a quarter of a century ago and you were the result? People here aren't going to judge him for that. They'll talk about it a lot for a while, but they won't judge. That's one reason why I fell in love with this town."

She'd continued to be anxious, and Sean had been forced to provide her with frequent reassurances that everything would be fine as the Wednesday night meeting had drawn closer. He figured that Caleb would lose some members of his congregation, but the majority of them would stay. They were all sinners, as was every human being on the planet. His admission might even help him to reach those who saw pastors as thinking they were "holier than thou." Only time would tell.

People began to shift in their seats. Byron, who was sitting two rows back from Sean and Prim, cleared his throat and stood. He said, "Pastor Caleb, you've been our spiritual leader here for a long time. You're a good man. I think I speak for just about everybody in this church when I say that we don't want to lose you as our pastor because you had a moment of human weakness twenty-five years ago, especially when the result was the creation of such a wonderful human being as Prim Aurora. My family and I will be proud to keep coming to your church as long as you preach here." He paused then added, "And I hope you'll stay on at the hardware store. You're a respected, hard-working member of our town."

Thank you, Byron, thought Sean. *Thank you, God. That should set the tone for everyone's response to what Caleb shared.*

It did. The comments from the Chief of Police were echoed by almost everyone present. Only three members of the church got up and left. The rest stayed, showing their support for Caleb. They also congratulated him and Prim.

Sean had known that Prim herself would make Caleb's startling revelations more acceptable. The townspeople had known Prim since her birth and had commented to him often how badly they felt for the parentless young shop owner.

As Sean watched Prim standing beside her father, he thought of his little sister and of how long it had been since she'd stood next to their father. Although Debra seemed happier with her current boyfriend and continued to promise to come see him, her parents, and Prim soon, she was still making excuses. If things were going so well for her, then why hadn't she come to Aurora and to see their parents' new home at Kensington?

At least Mom and Dad are happy. Being on the campus is working out great for them and the students and staff, and they do love the house. At least I know they're eating better and have people watching out for them all the time. At least they're closer.

Tiffany and Kenny Proper had been in their new home for over a month and loved working at the school. The students were responding well to their presence and enjoyed including them in many of their after-school and weekend activities. Sean made time to see his parents at least once every school day, and he and Prim spent time with them each weekend.

"I think that went really well," Remy said from beside Sean, bringing him back to the present. "That was a wise move on Byron's part. Smart guy."

"Agreed. I'm very grateful. How are you dealing with all of this news?"

"I couldn't be happier for Caleb and Prim. I wish Caleb was my dad, too."

"I know, but I'm glad at least you've reconnected with your mother. The two of you seem to be doing great."

"It's a slow but steady progress. It's been a long time coming."

Sean glanced around at the thinning crowd and said, "There's something I've been wanting to ask you ever since I moved here. I never see Dr. Stanford and his wife at the Community Church. Where do they attend services?"

"To my knowledge, they don't. From what I understand, they believe in God but not in organized religion. I haven't seen Mrs. Stanford in public for a long time. She's been pretty unwell for quite a while."

"That's too bad."

"It is. She's a nice person. Speaking of nice people, where are your mom and dad tonight? I figured they'd be here."

"Me, too. They said they wouldn't know how to answer people's questions about Caleb and Prim and thought it would be better if they didn't come. I was surprised. They don't usually worry about things like that."

"Are they okay with Caleb's being Prim's father?"

"They're so happy for both of them. They want to have a little party for them on their back porch after Easter."

"That would be nice. It's almost April, and the weather will be getting consistently pleasant soon. You'll have to take your bike out more often."

"I plan on it. Prim and I want to start riding each weekend for exercise. Lifting weights is good, but I need a greater cardio workout and so does Prim. She does that yoga stuff but nothing else."

"I need anything. I really don't exercise at all."

Sean grinned and said, "You exercise your hands when you play video games."

"I'm sure Dr. Stanford wouldn't consider that satisfactory."

"So, ride bikes with us."

"I will sometimes. Other times, you'll want to go alone." Lowering his voice, he said, "There's a place you should take Prim that's really beautiful. I'll tell you how to get there. When I was with my girlfriend in high school, we used to go out there all the time and enjoy the scenery and each other."

"Remy, we're in church," Sean admonished, although he couldn't help but smile.

"It'll be a religious experience for both of you. I mean it. The place is gorgeous."

"So, Prim doesn't know about it?"

"It's off the beaten path. You might have to leave markers. It's worth the hike though."

Remy, Caleb, Prim, and Sean went to LouAnn's Café for dinner. Prim couldn't stop smiling and telling the others how relieved she was that things had gone so well. Sean's iPhone rang. He glanced at the display and noted that it was Tony Eichstadt. Excusing himself from the table, he stepped outside and took the call.

"I apologize for phoning you after hours," Eichstadt said. "I need to know if we can have lunch at Kensington tomorrow. It's important."

"Of course. I had another lunch meeting planned, but it can be changed." Hesitating, he asked, "Important in a good way or a bad way?"

"Both. Look, I can't talk. I'll see you tomorrow at noon." Before hanging up, he added, "Don't worry. Your job's not in jeopardy or anything like that. See you tomorrow. Tell Prim 'hello' from Gillian and me."

When Sean returned to the table, he reviewed his conversation and passed along the greeting to Prim from the man and his wife.

"Any ideas regarding what this meeting could be about?" queried Remy.

"No clue. I'll find out tomorrow." Looking between Prim, Remy, and Caleb, he added, "You should all probably get a good night's sleep. What happened tonight at the church is going to drive people to your shops in droves. They're going to be all full of questions."

"Hopefully, they'll want to buy stuff while they're gossiping," Remy said with a smile.

Sean walked Prim home after dinner. She invited him to stay, but he told her she really should get some rest and so should he. The following day was going to be a tiring one for both of them.

"When we're married, are you going to keep the other place so we can sleep apart if we have a big day ahead of us?" she teased. "That could get expensive."

"When we're married, I never want to spend a night apart from you," Sean told her. "But we also won't be having sex every time we go to bed like we usually do now."

"How do you know?" she asked playfully. "Maybe we'll spend the rest of our lives being tired during the day because we're up all night."

Sean left her after they shared a long kiss and told her to sleep well. He waved up at her as he passed her front windows on his way home. She smiled down at him and waved back.

Less than three months, he thought happily. *We'll be married and living together. It'll be so nice to sleep next to her every night and to wake up beside her each morning.*

The following day, the Head of the Board of Directors was early for their lunch meeting. Sean and the assistant principal were almost finished with their daily review of school business, and Sean asked Maureen to escort Tony Eichstadt to the front room where the two of them would be dining and talking. He expected her to return within minutes, but she didn't.

Slightly concerned, Sean left his office and went to the designated room. He came upon his assistant chatting amiably with Eichstadt.

"There you are, Mr. Proper," said Maureen when she saw him. "I hope the two of you have a nice lunch." Inclining her head towards the businessman, she said, "Mr. Eichstadt. Enjoy."

Once she'd left the room and a server had carried in their lunch, Eichstadt said, "Your assistant is a very bright woman."

"She's the best assistant I've ever had."

"Then you made a wise choice when you selected her. I'd expect no less from you." Taking a seat, Eichstadt remarked, "I'm on a tight schedule so I'm going to get right to the point. Do you remember the elderly alumnus you spoke with in February?"

"You mean the one who had more money than God but wouldn't give any of it to Kensington?"

"That's the one."

"Yes, I remember him."

"What if I told you that he died and left his entire fortune to the school?"

"I'd be thankful that I had spoken to him before he died."

The older man laughed so hard that he could barely breathe.

"It doesn't faze you," he said when he could speak without laughing. "Nothing fazes you. If the man died and left us not one red cent, you'd shrug it off. If he died and left us everything, you'd be thankful. Either way, you'd be fine."

"It takes a lot to rattle me," Sean admitted. "It's money. It's important, but it's not what really matters."

Eichstadt sobered, lifted his glass as if in toast, and said, "A truer statement I've never heard."

"You didn't come here because the man left us his fortune, although I'm happy to hear it," Sean stated matter-of-factly.

"No. I came here to tell you that Gillian's cancer is back." Placing his glass on the table, he lowered his eyes and said quietly, "It's everywhere."

After the initial shock had worn off, Sean asked, "When did you find out?"

"A couple of weeks ago. She had a seizure. I didn't know what was happening. They ran tests. The cancer's metastasized to her brain."

Sean shut his eyes and said, "I'm so, so sorry to hear that. How long?"

"Not long. She wanted me to ask you and Prim if you would help me spearhead the literacy project that she and I have been working on for these last two years." Obviously struggling to maintain his composure, Eichstadt said, "She was planning to ask the two of you herself, but she's medicated now a lot of the time. I promised her I'd come today to talk with you."

"You don't give a damn about the elderly man's leaving his money to Kensington either," Sean said flatly.

"No. I want to see the school's future and path secured, which I believe it is. However, Gillian's happiness and dreams are more important to me than my own. The other news was simply coincidental." After taking a sip of his tea, he added, "Thank you for providing me with the laugh. That was an unexpected bonus. I've done nothing but cry, lately. Our daughters are in denial, as are my in-laws. Gillian and I are the only ones who understand

and accept her disease. After I depart from here, I plan to return home and not leave her side until she's gone." Rising, he asked, "Would you and Prim attend the funeral?"

"Of course. Is there anything we can do for either of you now?"

"Pray that she goes quickly. I don't want to see her suffer. There's no hope of recovery."

When he returned to his office, Sean tried to concentrate on work but found it impossible. After an hour, he rose from his desk, told Maureen that he had to take a walk, and left the main building.

First, he went to his mother, who was busily folding sheets in the laundry. She was chatting with her female co-worker and was debating which was better, the original *Star Trek* television series or *Star Trek: The Next Generation*.

"Mom?" Sean interrupted. "I'm sorry, but could I talk with you a second?"

"You can talk with me forever," she said with a smile. "You're my baby."

Sean grinned and apologized to the other woman for taking his mother away from her work. He walked with her to a nearby room, shut the door, and then hugged her.

"What's wrong, Sean? You're upset about something."

He confirmed that he was but told her he couldn't share the details with her.

"You don't have to. I'm sorry you're sad. Can I make it better?"

"You already have. I just needed a hug."

"Dad gives good hugs, too," she pointed out. "You should go get one from him next."

"I will. Thanks, Mom. I love you."

"And I love you, my beautiful boy."

Kenny was working with the stable master, grooming a horse. He was talking to the animal as if it were a person and was asking the horse whether or not it felt good to be brushed. Kenny speculated that it must feel great.

"I'm sure he likes it," Sean offered, as he walked forward. "You're really good at brushing, Dad."

"It's relaxing," his father admitted. "Your mom and I are going to learn how to ride. You should, too."

"Remy and Prim have promised to teach me if I don't learn here." As the stable master wandered off to the other end of the stalls, Sean asked, "Do you have a minute for a hug?"

"I always have time for a hug, especially one for you. God sent us the best son anyone could ever have. I can hug you as much as you want."

As Sean hugged his father, he asked, "Are you and Mom really happy here? I know you say you are, but I worry that you're just saying that to make me feel like I didn't drag you to Georgia."

"Nobody did any dragging. It was time to move, and we're glad we did. This is the best place we've ever lived, and we have so many new friends and a house and really good food and pretty things to look at. Plus, we see you all the time and get to see Prim and the people in town." Patting Sean on the back, he asked, "Did everything go okay at the church meeting last night?"

"It couldn't have gone better. I think it's all going to be fine. Prim is so happy that Caleb is her father."

"I'm sure she is. He's a great man, and she's a wonderful girl."

"I just wish she weren't so scared about us having kids."

Kenny stepped back and said, "You two will have kids. Your mom and I can tell how much Prim wants to have babies. You'll be getting married this summer. Once that happens, I don't think she'll be so scared."

"I wish I shared your confidence."

"You have more confidence than anyone else except when it comes to Prim. If you believe things will work out, then she'll believe it. Keep going to those parenting classes and telling her it'll be okay. You're both going to be great parents someday."

"Thanks, Dad."

"That's what dads are for. You'll tell your kids this kind of thing when you're a dad one day."

Sean returned to his office still feeling sad, but he was heartened by his conversations with his parents. He called Prim but told her he couldn't talk and would explain about his meeting with Tony Eichstadt that evening. He was dreading having to tell her about Gillian's imminent demise and wondered if he should talk with Caleb first.

Unable to focus, he left Kensington early and drove back to Aurora. He arrived at the hardware store just as Caleb was locking up and asked if they could talk for a few minutes.

"I'm sure you're tired of talking," Sean said with a sigh. "The whole town's probably been in here today."

"Pretty much, but it went well. Business was terrific, too." Gesturing for Sean to have a seat across from him, Caleb asked, "What's up? You look troubled."

Sean told his future father-in-law about Gillian Eichstadt and asked the man how he thought Sean should approach Prim regarding the subject.

"She's so happy right now. This is going to make her think of her mother, which will lead her to think of everything else."

"Prim's not a broken doll you can fix," Caleb reminded him. "She's a woman with an innocent heart and a lot of hurt. Think of the progress she's made since you've known her."

"I know. I just want to make her release her fears so she can be truly happy."

"You don't have the power to make her release her fears, Sean. And are *you* truly happy? You're a man who does everything with great forethought and intensity. That's the only reason Prim's protective walls have been knocked away. No one else could have done it, and I'm eternally grateful. However, I also worry that you're going to push yourself into an early grave because of your efforts to make everything better for everyone else. Don't lose yourself to your cause."

"It's my purpose," Sean corrected. "I think it's what I was born to do."

"Perhaps. Just take your own advice once in a while and let go."

Sean left the hardware store and went to The Book Nook. Remy informed him he'd done a great business that day and asked Sean how his meeting with the head of the Board of Directors had gone. Sean told him, and Remy sat down hard in a chair near the fireplace. Shaking his head, he said, "That is so horrible."

"Yes, it is. Now I get to go tell Prim and deal with how upset she'll be."

"Don't overdo it with the talking," Remy advised. "Her mind's going to go wherever this takes it. Just tell her it'll be okay and hold her." Hesitating, he asked, "Did you already talk to Caleb about this?"

"Yes. Why?"

"His wife died of ovarian cancer kind of in the same way not that long ago. I'm sure it's going to make him think of what she went through and bring him down. He loved her so much."

Mentally kicking himself, Sean admitted he'd forgotten all about Caleb's deceased wife and the fact that she'd died of cancer. Remy told him not to blame himself and declared that he'd go talk to Prim's father.

"He's saved my life so many times," Remy said, as he reached for his keys. "He's listened and physically taken care of me when I couldn't take care of myself. I think it's my turn to be there for him tonight. You go to Prim."

Sean hugged and kissed Prim the moment he stepped into her apartment. He told her about the monies bequeathed by the wealthy elderly man as they ate biscuits and a chicken stew she'd prepared in the Crock Pot. She congratulated him on his efforts and then answered his questions about how her day had gone. As they cleared the table, she asked, "What are you not telling me, Sean Proper?"

He took the plates from her hands and put them on the counter before breaking the news to her about Gillian Eichstadt. He held her against him as she cried and said nothing, except that everything would be all right. He listened as she told him she prayed Gillian would go quickly unlike her own mother.

"If your mother had died right away, then you wouldn't be here," he pointed out. "I might not have stayed in Aurora, and my parents would still be in Tallahassee. Caleb wouldn't have a beautiful daughter and might not have formed the bond he did with Remy because Remy might have stopped going to the Community Church if it hadn't been for you and his brother. Remy might have killed himself if you hadn't been there to help keep him going. Maureen would have lost both her sons. I could go on and on with how you've changed the lives of everyone you've met."

"It's a wonderful life?" she asked rhetorically.

"Your mother held on because she wanted you to live and wanted to give you her love for as long as she could. That was her gift to you and to this world."

He spent the night at Prim's, but there was no making love, no sex, and nothing else. There was only tenderness and understanding, and Prim nuzzled against Sean and slept through the night despite her distress. Sean, on the other hand, didn't sleep at all. The only thing he could think about was Gillian's life coming to an end and how alone Tony Eichstadt would be. He held Prim a little tighter, praying that God would give both him and Prim long lives to spend together.

Chapter Twenty

Prim looked down at the sheet cake on the patio table and smiled.

"We wanted something for you and Caleb," Tiffany said excitedly. "That's why we had them decorate it with a fairy princess and a hammer."

"It's perfect," Prim told the woman before giving her a hug. "Thank you and Kenny so much for having this party for us."

"Well, it's a special thing, the two of you finding out about being father and daughter. It's something to celebrate." As Sean came up beside his mother, she gave him a quick hug and said, "Your dad and I couldn't imagine our lives without you and Debra." Frowning, she added, "I do wish Debra would come see us and where we live and work now."

"I know, Mom. I hope she comes here soon. If she doesn't, then at least we know she'll come for the wedding in June. It's only a couple of months away."

Prim had overheard Sean talking with his sister the previous night and knew that he was worried she was *not* going to come soon or attend their wedding. Frustration radiated from him in the hours following the call, and he apologized to Prim, who'd heard him raise his voice in anger at his little sister. Sean refused to talk about the conversation and said he was going to figure out a way to reach Debra that would make her want to have a real relationship with her family once more. Prim had refrained from telling him that he couldn't "make" Debra do anything.

"It's time to blow out the candles!" Kenny proclaimed.

"But it's not a birthday party," Prim pointed out.

"That doesn't matter," Remy told her. "Candles can be for any special occasion. Really, Pixie. It's okay."

Kenny leaned over the cake and put one candle in the spot where the fairy princess's hands were clasped together and the other in front of the head of the hammer. After lighting both candles, he instructed Prim to blow out the one held by the fairy and Caleb to blow out the one in front of the hammer. When Prim hesitated, Maureen counted to three, and Prim and Caleb blew.

Caleb grinned and hugged Prim, who thanked everyone as they clapped. Everyone in this instance included Kenny, Tiffany, Sean, Remy, LouAnn, Maureen, Byron, Dr. Stanford, and Tony Eichstadt.

Neither Prim nor Sean had expected Eichstadt to attend the little celebration. He was still very much in mourning for his wife and looked haggard. Yet, he'd accepted their invitation without hesitation and declared he'd be remiss if he didn't go on living since his beloved Gillian was gone.

Prim was sorry Dr. Stanford's wife hadn't been able to accompany him, but the woman was supposedly out of town visiting a cousin. Byron's wife and children all had colds and were in bed. Prim had promised to send home cake for each of them and was disappointed that they hadn't been able to join in the fun.

"It is so beautiful out here," Dr. Stanford remarked. "It's a lovely setting in which to work and play."

"Tiffany and I know how to ride horses now," Kenny declared. "Sean, too. We're going riding with Prim, Remy, and Sean next weekend if anyone wants to come back and go with us."

The cool April breeze lifted Prim's hair away from her face as she accepted a piece of cake from her future mother-in-law. Tony Eichstadt, who happened to be sitting beside her on one end of the porch, asked where she and Sean were planning to honeymoon after their marriage in June.

"We can't agree on what to do. Sean wants to take this long honeymoon and go around the world, but I can't leave my shop for several weeks. I suggested we rent a cabin somewhere and just enjoy nature, but he says we can do that anytime." Focusing on her plate, she said, "I think he wants to take a trip overseas right away in case we have children."

"It does become more complicated once you have little ones, but Gillian and I did it many times. It's enjoyable either way."

"I guess."

Narrowing his eyes, Eichstadt said quietly, "You don't want children."

"I do."

"But?"

Staring at the candle protruding from her piece of cake, she said, "I don't even know when to blow out candles on a cake. How can I be a good mother? What if I'm terrible and Sean and our children hate me?"

"Prim, you're a gentle woman who will be a wonderful mother."

"I'm not so sure."

Eichstadt placed his plate on the small table beside his chair and leaned closer before saying, "My brother and I had very cruel parents. When I first came to Kensington at age fourteen, I had a terrible idea of what families were like; plus I was a severe stutterer. The principal at the time was a stellar man who saw to it that I got speech therapy. During my four years here, I lost my stutter and gained self-confidence, but I held fast to the idea that I'd never have children. I was afraid I'd turn out to be exactly like my parents or, equally as bad, like my brother, who was brilliant but disturbed and abusive to women and children."

"But you have children. What made you change your mind?"

"I fell in love with a wonderful woman who came from a loving household. I knew they'd help me if I stumbled in my efforts to be a good father. They did. Sean and his family will do the same for you. Your father and friends will as well." Sitting up and retrieving his plate of cake, he went on, "Regarding your honeymoon, how long do you feel you could leave your shop?"

"A week. I wouldn't feel comfortable with having my assistant running it longer than that on her own. I'd lose business if I wasn't there for more than a few days. It is Prim's Corner."

"May I make a suggestion?"

"Of course."

"Place a map of the United States or of the world on the floor. You and Sean each take a turn tossing a penny onto the map. Then you choose one of the two locations where the pennies land."

"That's an interesting idea. I'll suggest it to Sean. Thank you, and thank you for sharing your own experiences about parenting."

"It's not something I tell a lot of people, but I felt you should know."

Prim thought about her conversation with Tony Eichstadt for the remainder of the day, the following morning, during the church service, and as she and Sean rode their bikes down one of the rural roads. She was so distracted by her thoughts that she blindly pedaled after Sean without paying attention to where they were or asking him where they were going. When he slowed his bike to a stop near a large rock, she did the same. As Sean wheeled his bike around the rock and instructed her to park hers next to his, she did so without hesitation or much thought. They hung their helmets on the handlebars, and Prim automatically walked behind Sean as he set out into the woods.

They hiked for a long time, finally stopping in a clearing to drink some water. Once Sean had put the bottle away in his backpack, he took Prim by the shoulders, kissed her, then asked, "Where are you?"

"Me? I'm right here."

He smiled and said, "No, you're not. You've been somewhere else ever since the party yesterday afternoon."

"Tony and I had a talk, and it's made me rethink a lot of things."

"Such as?"

"Well, he had a suggestion about where we should go for our honeymoon."

"That's not what's on your mind. What else did he say?"

"He told me a few details about his life that made me feel I could be a good parent."

"Do you think the parenting classes are helping at all?"

"Definitely, but I've still been scared. What he said was a little more personal and made me feel that maybe it would be okay."

"I'm glad for that. I don't want you to spend our marriage filled with anxiety because either we do or don't have children."

He took her hand and led her through the woods. As they stepped out of the trees, Prim gasped.

"How did you find this place?"

"Remy. He said he used to come here all the time with his girlfriend in high school. He told me if I brought you here that it would literally be a religious experience for both of us."

As she scanned the beauty of the hills and valleys that lay before them, she asked, "Whose land is this?"

"Remy says it's yours. He told me it's part of the property owned by the Auroras. Why?"

"Because I want to build a little cabin on this spot someday and come out here on weekends or whenever we want to get away. This is breathtaking. Our family and friends could stay out here whenever they want, too. It's too pretty not to share it with the people we care about."

They ate lunch, talked, and then made love on a blanket. Afterwards, Prim and Sean reluctantly left and hiked back to their bikes before returning to town. They arrived clean but slightly late for the parenting class. After apologizing to the others, they took their seats.

"As I was saying, we're going to do something a little different tonight," Patty told them. "It's my job as your teacher to give you a variety of experiences, and that doesn't simply include books, DVDs, and Power Point presentations. Tonight, we're going to go to the nursery and interact with the babies. The parents have already given their permission." Standing, she ordered, "Everybody, follow me! We're in luck tonight. This has been a busy weekend. I'm going to take one person or couple at a time and get you settled with your babies. Remember how we practiced with the dolls. I'll be right there to give you instruction or answer any questions."

Sean and Prim were last in line. They waited their turn and watched the others with their assigned babies. The single father was the best out of all of them, but Prim reminded herself that he already had two small children of his own.

"Your turn," Patty said to her and Sean. "I have a very special baby for the two of you."

They walked over to "their" baby. Prim glanced at the card above him. It stated that he was six pounds, two ounces and seventeen inches long. The space for his name was blank.

"Why isn't his name written on the card?" Sean asked Patty.

"Because his mother abandoned him here shortly after she delivered him this morning. He doesn't have a name."

"Abandoned him?"

Patty touched the baby's small head and said, "It happens. Sometimes, they're teenagers who never told their families they were pregnant. Sometimes, they're drug addicts who can't care for their babies. Sometimes, they don't have the money to take care of their children. Sometimes, they just don't want the baby but didn't have the money for an abortion." Smiling down at the newborn, she said, "They tested him for drugs. He's clean. He should be adopted by someone quickly and easily. Right now though, he has no one. He needs to be held, touched, and talked to before they take him to the foster home tomorrow. Our nurses try to give these abandoned babies extra attention, but, as I said, it's been a busy weekend." Turning to Prim, she directed, "Why don't you sit in the rocker and hold him first?"

Prim's heart was pounding as she sat and held out her arms for the nameless baby boy. Patty praised her on her technique when she cradled him against her. Then the woman was called away to assist one of the other class members. She promised to return soon.

"He's so handsome," Prim murmured. "How could his mother leave him here all alone? He's so helpless."

"At least she had him here and didn't just give birth in some back alley and leave him to die. I remember that happened not far from our apartment when I was about thirteen. I never forgot that feeling of horror it gave me. I kept thinking that the mother could've left the baby at a church or anyone's doorstep if she didn't want it. She didn't have to let it die. What a tragedy for the mother and the baby."

Patty returned and instructed Prim to pass the infant to Sean. When the baby began to fuss, she handed Sean a bottle and encouraged him to offer it to the boy, who sucked greedily on the nipple.

"At least he's got a good appetite," Sean remarked. "I hope they find a good home for him."

"May I hold him again?" Prim asked, once Sean had removed the nipple from the baby's mouth.

Placing a burp cloth on her shoulder, she gently lifted the baby up and rubbed his back for a while then lowered him into her lap. As she stared down at him, she wondered where his mother was and if she was sorry she'd had to leave him. Would he ever be told he'd been abandoned at birth or would his adoptive parents keep that from him? Would they even tell him he was adopted?

"Goodbye, Baby," she told him, as she kissed his soft hair then placed him back in his hospital bassinet. "Good luck."

Sean laid a hand on the newborn's back and said nothing aloud, but Prim knew he was saying a prayer for the tiny boy to have a good life despite his circumstances.

As they rode back to Aurora once the class ended, Prim asked, "If we had children, how many would you want?"

"I'd like to start with one and see if we want more."

"Would you prefer boy or girl?"

"I'd prefer healthy."

"We could adopt."

Sean smiled across at her and said, "Prim, we can't adopt that baby. I'm sure there are a lot of other people who are on the adoption list waiting for infants. He'll find a loving family."

"You don't know that. Just because they want to adopt doesn't mean they'll treat him right. What if they're mean to him?"

"We can't adopt every abandoned baby who goes through that hospital."

"I know, but I so wanted to help him tonight."

"We did help him by holding him and loving him, even if it was for a short while."

After a few moments, she asked, "How can I run my shop and have children?"

"There are good daycares. Maybe you could work half days while the kids are at daycare and have Tammy Lynn or whoever your assistant is to work the other half."

"What if I didn't want to work?"

"Then you close the shop altogether or hire people to man it full-time. I think you're putting the cart before the horse. We're not even married and are only now able to discuss the possibility of having kids. You can figure out the rest if and when we have babies."

"I want to have babies with you."

"And I want to have babies with you. Remember, we don't have to have them right away. You're only twenty-four, and I'm thirty-one. We could wait several years if we chose to." Glancing over at her, he asked, "How many kids would you want?"

"I think starting with one is a good idea. I don't care about the sex of the baby either. And no, there's no need to rush."

"Then we agree that if we have kids, we'll start with one, that we don't care if it's a boy or a girl, and that we don't have to rush into parenthood. See, that's not so bad, right?"

"Right."

When they arrived back at her apartment, Sean said, "You never did tell me what Tony's ideas were regarding our honeymoon."

"I'm going to show you. Hang on."

Prim went into the room where she kept her desk and computer and rifled through one of the bookcases until she found what she was looking for. She returned to the living room with a map of the world she'd purchased a year earlier in order to use it as part of a display in one of her shop windows. Going to her purse, she withdrew two pennies from her wallet. After spreading out the map, she gave Sean one of the pennies and explained, "We each toss one; then we pick one of the places where they land."

"We're not getting anywhere just talking about it," he remarked. "I'm game."

They both shut their eyes, counted to three, and threw the pennies. Once they'd heard them land, their eyes snapped open. They burst out laughing. They'd overshot the map.

They repeated the performance, this time making a concerted effort not to toss the coins so hard. When they opened their eyes, they scanned the map.

"The North Pole or Oregon," Sean mused. "Is it going to be Santa's workshop or the West coast?"

"Hm. I've always wanted to see Santa's workshop, but I think he and the elves might be on vacation in the middle of the summer. We should probably go to Oregon."

"Oregon it is. For...?"

"One week. Sean, I can't take off any more time than that and —"

"And a week is fine. It's not like it's the only trip we'll ever take. Will you let me figure out the arrangements and set everything up? It is the groom's job to pay for the honeymoon."

"It is?"

"Yes. Let me spoil you for a week."

"You spoil me all the time."

"No, I love you all the time and treat you the way you should've always been treated. Get used to it."

"I am." Kissing him, she repeated, "I really am."

Chapter Twenty-one

"Mr. Proper?"

Sean glanced up from the pile of papers he was sorting and asked, "Yes, Maureen?"

"May I talk with you for a minute?"

"Certainly. Come in and have a seat." As she did so, Sean asked, "Did you get the wedding invitation, yet? Prim put them in the mail day before yesterday."

"Then it will probably be in my mailbox when I get home. The wedding's only two weeks away. Are you nervous?"

"About the wedding? No. I'm excited. The only thing I'm nervous about is the possibility that my little sister won't show. Prim asked her to be a bridesmaid, but she declined and said it would be difficult for her to get away long enough to drive here for our wedding day." Shaking his head with disappointment, he confided, "I'm pretty much out of patience with Debra. And it takes a lot for me to run out of patience with anyone."

"So I've noticed. I do hope she comes."

"My parents will be crushed if she doesn't, but I can't do anything about that. I've been placating them for a long time. It's up to Debra now. If she doesn't show up for this, then I'm going to stop chasing her."

"I'll say a prayer that she attends the wedding and spares everyone from more heartache."

"You didn't come in here to listen to me whine about my little sister. What's up?"

"I'm worried about your father."

Surprised, Sean asked, "Why?"

"The other day, I was walking across campus and passed him doing some landscaping. He seemed awfully out of breath. He said he was huffing and puffing because he'd been working hard, but I wasn't so sure. I've been debating about whether or not to mention it. Your father's a grown man, but perhaps he needs some direction."

"I know he had a physical last July, and the doctor said everything was fine. Still, if you think there's something to be concerned about then I'll talk to him. I won't mention you told me. I'll just ask him if he wants me to give him Dr. Stanford's number so he can get his yearly physical. He and my mom both do that every summer. Thank you for telling me."

She nodded, but he could sense that she remained worried.

"As a matter of fact, I think I'll go talk to him now," Sean told her. "I won't be gone long. Thanks again."

He found his father happily emptying recycle containers around the campus. He hugged him and told the man he'd been out for a walk. They chatted for a minute before Sean inquired about the medical appointments for both of his parents.

"Your mother already made them with that nice Doc Stanford. They're in the middle of July, just like always."

"You know you can go sooner if you feel bad," Sean reminded him.

"Yes. Your mom and I feel fine. We're getting a little older all the time just like everyone does, but neither of us is hurting or anything. Your mom hasn't had a lump in her breast for years. That was scary."

Sean agreed and tried again by saying, "It doesn't have to be a lump. It could be anything out of the ordinary."

"We're okay, Son. We're middle-aged people. I'm going to be fifty-six not long after your wedding." Grinning, he said, "Your mom and I can't wait for the wedding."

"Neither can Prim and I."

"Don't worry about if Debra doesn't come. We'll all be sad, but it's a happy thing to get married. So, we won't be sad that day. We'll save it for later. Promise me you'll do the same. You don't want to be all hot and bothered on a day when you should be real happy."

"I'll try. It's hard for me not to stress about things."

"I know. Talk about not being healthy! Is your blood pressure okay? Mom and I worry about your blood pressure."

"It's fine. Working out helps to lower blood pressure, which is one reason why I try to do it consistently."

Kenny nodded and said, "Exercise is good. That's one reason your mom and I like to do physical work. It keeps us active."

"That's good, Dad." Checking the time, he said, "I'd better get back to my office. The school year's winding down, and the papers are piling up. I love you."

"And I love you, Sean."

On his way back to the main building, Sean stopped by the laundry and chatted with his mother for a short time. She told him that she and his father were doing fine and were going to see Dr. Stanford in July.

"You worry way too much," Tiffany told him. "Is your blood pressure all right?"

He smiled and assured her it was before telling her he loved her and giving her a hug.

When he got back to his office, he reviewed both conversations with Maureen. She appeared to remain uneasy, and it made him uneasy. However, he couldn't demand that his parents go to the doctor if they insisted nothing was wrong and had their yearly appointments scheduled. Resigning himself to waiting for another month, Sean went back to Kensington business.

The next two weeks went by quickly and chaotically for Sean and Prim. The school year came to a close, and the students left the campus. LouAnn hosted a wedding shower at her restaurant that seemed to involve most of the town. Remy had a bachelor party for Sean that included going to a nice restaurant in Atlanta with Caleb, Byron, Tony Eichstadt, Philip Stanford, and Sean's father. Tammy Lynn held a bachelorette party for Prim at her house that included Sean's mother, LouAnn, Byron's wife, and Maureen.

"I've never been to a fun party like *that*!" Sean's mother had told him afterwards. "It was so funny and we were all laughing so hard that I thought we'd all pee our pants!"

When he'd asked Prim about the fun party, she'd blushed and told him it had been a Fun Party, which meant that they'd eaten foods made to look like sexual body parts and played games that involved intimate details of their physical relationships, past and present. Prim admitted she'd been amazed at how much they'd all enjoyed the rowdy atmosphere, the freedom to talk about what was normally a taboo topic, and participating in playing raunchy games. The representative who was in charge of the party had toys and lingerie for sale afterwards.

Sean was both shocked and amused. He asked Prim if she and the other women had bought anything.

"You go in another room to order so no one gets embarrassed. And yes, I did buy a few things. You'll have to wait to see."

An uncomfortable thought struck him.

"Did my mom buy anything?"

"I didn't ask anyone else whether they did or didn't make purchases. If you see a charge on your parents' account for that night, then you'll know she bought something."

Unable to resist, Sean pulled up his parents' checking account on-line as soon as he returned to his rented house. His mother had made a purchase of over a hundred dollars. Sean tried to imagine what she could've bought. Then he tried *not* to imagine what she could've bought. He was certainly *not* going to ask her.

The day of the wedding started out cloudy and humid. However, by midmorning, the skies had cleared, and a gentle breeze blew almost continually. Birds were chirping, and happy children were out riding their bikes and roller skating.

Since they'd wanted to marry in the gazebo in the center of town, Sean knew there might be a small crowd. As he, his father, and Remy walked towards the Town Square in their tuxedoes at 12:30, Sean realized he was nervous. He wondered if Prim was nervous, too.

When they reached the Square, the three men stopped and gawked. It was as if the townspeople in Aurora were gathered for a parade. Although they were mindful not to crowd the center of the Square that had been cordoned off with white ribbons or to cluster near the gazebo that had been decorated with white bows and flowers, they were everywhere.

"I believe this is the biggest turnout I've ever seen at a wedding," Tony Eichstadt said, as he came up to Sean and shook his hand. "Congratulations early in case I can't get to you through the throng here or at the reception."

"Thanks. Prim and I are so glad you could come."

"I wouldn't have missed it for the world. Gillian's here in spirit, I'm sure."

Sean nodded and smiled, glad to see the man and to see that he looked better than he had since his wife's death.

"We're going to be late for your wedding," Kenny told his son. "We're supposed to be over there already."

The three men edged their way through the crowd. Sean accepted congratulations as they went. They stopped a few yards in front of the gazebo and waited. Sean scanned the area and spotted Maureen, Dr. Stanford, Byron and his family, and a myriad of locals he'd come to know well over the last ten months. His little sister was nowhere in sight.

A hush fell over the crowd. Sean looked towards the church. His mother emerged. She was wearing a light green outfit comprised of a short-sleeved lace jacket with a shell top underneath and a skirt that fell just below her knees. Matching shoes were on her feet. As she got closer, Sean gasped. His mother had cut her long hair to several inches above her shoulders and was wearing it in a trendy style. When she came up to give him a hug, he told her she looked amazing.

"Thank you. I can't wait for you to see Prim."

The church door opened again. This time, it was Tammy Lynn who made the walk to the gazebo. Her dress was made out of the same green material as Tiffany's but was one piece and was cut in a more youthful style. She nodded and smiled at Sean and Kenny; then she grinned at Remy as she walked past him and took her place beside Tiffany.

Sean glanced at the doors of the church in anticipation. Two other church members pulled open the doors and out stepped Prim and Caleb. Caleb was wearing a tuxedo like Sean, Remy, and Kenny. Beside him, Prim stood wearing a wedding gown like none Sean had ever seen.

Prim's gown was white and strapless, which was nothing extraordinary. Everything else about the dress gave it an otherworldly quality. Small satin fabric flowers were clustered across her breasts. Below that, beaded satin had been fitted and curved slightly around to the side of her right hip. Below the bodice were tiers of sheer fabric that looked like petals extending towards the ground. When she turned to pass Tammy Lynn her bouquet, Sean saw the small pearl buttons that ran from the top of the back down to below her hips where flounces of fabric suggested a butterfly was nestled within the white petals.

On someone else, the dress might have been too much. But on Prim, the dress was dazzling. Sean wanted to make love to her in that dress and intended to do so the first chance he got.

Prim's hair was loose and slightly curled. A cornet of baby's breath rested atop her head. She wore tiny hanging pearl earrings that matched the pearl buttons on her dress.

My fairy princess, he thought. *Naturally exquisite.*

Sean took Prim's hand and led her up the steps of the gazebo to where Caleb stood waiting. Prim's father spoke of the love between Sean and Prim and the beauty that came out of true love. Then he performed the wedding ceremony, which was simple but moving. When Sean kissed Prim after they'd exchanged rings, the crowd cheered.

They were sprinkled with birdseed as they left the gazebo and headed back towards the church. The reception was to be held in the hall behind it. Once they reached the large room with its round tables draped with white tablecloths and clusters of white rose bouquet centerpieces, Sean took Prim in his arms and pulled her close against him.

"I want to make love to you while you're wearing this dress, Mrs. Proper."

"I want you to do everything you can think of to me in this dress once we're home."

The reception hall was soon packed, and everyone ate, visited, and danced to the music of the band. Sean threw the garter, which Remy caught. When Prim tossed the bouquet, Tammy Lynn was the recipient.

"What time do you two want me to pick you up in the morning?" Caleb asked as the attendees finally began to leave the party.

"About 6:00," Sean answered. "Our flight doesn't leave from Atlanta until 11:00, but we'll have to drive there, go through Security, and all that jazz."

"I'll see you at 6:00 then." Hugging Sean, he said quietly, "I couldn't be happier for my little girl. I couldn't have asked for a better son-in-law."

Sean hugged Caleb back and thanked him before watching the man go over to Prim and tenderly embrace her. He said something that made her eyes well with tears, but she smiled up at him and nodded even as she wiped at her cheeks.

Everyone wished the couple well on their honeymoon as they left the reception and walked hand-in-hand across the street back to what was now their apartment. Sean's lease wasn't up until August, and he'd decided to let it continue until it expired. That way, his parents could stay in the house off and on all summer when they wanted to visit in Aurora and have privacy.

Prim carefully climbed the steps to the apartment in her wedding gown. Sean unlocked the door and asked her if she wanted him to carry her over the threshold like in the movies. She smiled but declined.

They had barely made it inside and closed and locked the door behind them when Sean took Prim's face in his hands and kissed her. She rested her palms on his chest then slid her hands down and undid his pants. He was quickly naked in the center of the room, although she remained fully clothed.

"Wait," she declared. "Don't go anywhere."

Sean chuckled and asked her where she thought he was going to go. He watched her walk back towards the master bedroom, listened as she moved around in the room, and savored the sight of her walking back to him. He noted she wasn't wearing her shoes anymore and deduced that she was probably not wearing anything else except the wedding gown.

As she slipped her arms around his neck, Prim said, "Make love to me."

"It might ruin your dress."

"My dress can be cleaned."

"What if I tear it?"

"Tears can be stitched."

"What if I tear it off you and it can't be repaired?"

She kissed him and murmured, "I love this dress, and I'm glad you love it, too. But it's a dress. If it gets destroyed because of what we do while I'm wearing it, then I won't regret it. We'll have tons of pictures of the wedding and reception and never forget it or what we did afterwards."

"What do you want me to do?"

"Fulfill your fantasies. Fulfill mine."

"How will I know what yours are?"

"I'll tell you."

"Tell me then. Tonight, let's make it your turn."

"I'm a lonely shopkeeper, and you're a school principal. We fall in love and get married and have children and grandchildren and die old, healthy, and at the exact same time."

"I think we can manage everything except that last part." Sliding his hands to the front of her dress, Sean cupped her breasts through the gathering of small, satin flowers and pressed his hips against her. He asked her again to tell him her fantasies but specified this time that he meant those of a sexual nature. Blushing, she admitted she'd never told anyone about those and would be embarrassed.

"I'm your husband. Nothing you could tell me would ever embarrass me. I'd hope you'd feel the same way. If I'm uncomfortable with one of your fantasies, then I'll let you know and you can just keep it to yourself. You do the same with me. Okay?"

Her blush deepened, but she agreed. She pulled away from him and walked in her fairy princess wedding gown towards the long, dark dining table. Keeping her back to him, she began to speak.

"I'm a princess who's been promised by her parents to marry an old king I don't love. I've sworn not to marry him because I love the man who saved our people from a fierce dragon. That man is cunning, handsome, and brave. It's also rumored that his...that he's much larger than any other man in the kingdom.

"Because I've made it known that I want to marry the dragon slayer and not the old king, I've been locked in a tower. I'm a virgin and of royal blood. My parents don't want anyone to spoil me before my wedding."

Sean's desire was building with every word. He hoped that her story wouldn't last much longer. He wasn't certain if he could.

"The night before my wedding, the dragon slayer manages to scale the tower and climb in through a window. He's so stealthy that even I don't hear him. I'm standing near a table with my back to him. He comes up behind me without making any noise."

Sean padded across the floor as quietly as he could.

271

"The dragon slayer slips one arm around my waist and quickly and quietly tells me not to make a sound, that he's come to make certain I'd only be with him.

"The rest," he said through a haze of arousal. "Tell me how it ends."

"The dragon slayer won't let me turn around to face him. He says I can't until he's entered me for the first time. I beg him to touch me."

Sean guided Prim until she was leaning slightly forward with both palms resting on the table. Then he lifted her skirt and slipped his fingers between her thighs. She moaned.

"How does it end?" he asked, his breathing labored.

"The dragon slayer brings one of my knees up and rests it on the table then pushes his way inside me. There's no pain, only ecstasy. The tower guards hear my cries and burst through the door just as the dragon slayer releases inside me. They watch transfixed as he withdraws, lays me back onto the table, lowers my top, spreads my legs, and thrusts in and out until he and I climax simultaneously."

Sean brought Prim's left knee up and positioned it on the table. Then he eased into her and began to thrust. Both of his hands rested on her hips, steadying them and holding up the sheer fabric petals of her skirt so that he got a perfect view of her backside and of what he was doing to her. She began to cry out, and he envisioned the tower guards bursting in but refused to let himself come, yet. He knew it was physiologically impossible for him to come more than once every twenty minutes. He couldn't fulfill her fantasy if he released in her now.

Sean pulled out of Prim, turned her around, and said, "They're watching us. I'm going to take you in front of them."

Her face was flushed, and her blue eyes were wide. The strawberry blonde hair was framing her face.

Still so innocent, even like this, he thought. *Protect and fuck.*

He unbuttoned the top few buttons on her gown and pulled down the front. He enjoyed the taste of her flesh as she wove her fingers through his brown hair and requested he enter her again. Sean lifted her up until she was sitting on the edge of the table. Then he laid her back and stared down at his naïve and beautiful wife. He pushed up her skirt, parted her legs, and drove into her.

The sight of her twisting with passion and her exposed breasts rising and falling with her movements was driving Sean insane. He glanced down and said in guttural tones, "My beautiful princess. They're all watching us. They're supposed to stop me, but it's too late. They wish they were in my place between your legs."

Prim began to scream. She pushed against Sean as he slid his hands along her inner thighs then moved them around her hips and under her buttocks. He squeezed them as he came, wondering if he'd ever been this deep inside any woman before. Somehow, he managed to stay upright as his climax peaked and ebbed.

Both he and Prim were breathing heavily. Sean climbed on top of the dining table and stretched out beside his wife, who scooted up until she was able to lay her head on his tattooed chest and drape one arm around him. He brought both arms around her and sighed contentedly.

"Oh, Sean," she murmured. "That was incredible."

"For me, too. I am really tired though. I think we may have to explore more fantasies at other times." When she didn't answer, he said, "Prim?"

She was asleep. He smiled, shut his eyes, and joined her.

Chapter Twenty-two

Prim sat beside Sean on Cannon Beach in Oregon and accepted the roasted marshmallow that he passed to her. It was the last night of their trip, and they'd decided to splurge and pay the pricey fee to the hotel that would allow them to participate in the nightly ritual of making S'Mores. The staff was responsible for starting the fires and providing the supplies. The rest was up to the guests.

They were seated with two other couples, one from Hawaii and another from Quebec. Prim had been surprised to find out that her husband was fluent in French. Although he made time to speak to her and the couple from Hawaii, he seemed to be thoroughly enjoying his talk with the husband and wife from Canada who could only manage a few words of English. They appeared grateful to have met someone who could understand them.

"It's their first day here," he told the others. "I was letting them know about the places we've been and what not to miss."

They all chatted then. Sean translated for the Canadian couple, and the six of them had a nice time making their S'Mores, although the wind was strong and cold. Prim was glad she and Sean had worn thermal underwear and the heavy wool sweaters that they'd bought from a local retailer.

An hour later they bid their new acquaintances goodnight and went upstairs to their rooms, which were on the second floor and faced the beach. Their bedroom had huge sliding-glass doors that opened onto a large balcony. There was a fireplace situated across from the king-sized bed. The bathroom was next to the bedroom and had walls made of dark, sliding screens. If one pushed back the screen that faced the bedroom, one could soak in the enormous tub and look out at the ocean view. The third room was small and held only a loveseat, a chair, two side tables and lamps. It was a nice reading room, so Prim and Sean had both spent time reading there during their trip. It was quiet and peaceful in that room unless one turned on the wireless sound system.

In the light of the full moon, the outline of Haystack Rock was clearly visible from their balcony. Prim and Sean had gone out in the middle of the night several days before to take a tour during low tide and hear about the wildlife that inhabited the enormous monolithic rock, which was a 235-foot-high sea stack. They'd learned that the tide pools were home to intertidal animals, such as sea anemones, starfish, limpets, and crabs. Birds, including puffins and terns, had nesting grounds on the rock. The excursion had been well worth the cost and the inconvenience of lost sleep and dealing with the bone-chilling cold.

"I want to go out to Haystack Rock one more time before we leave," Sean told Prim as they got ready for bed that last night.

"Me, too. It's so…mystical."

"This entire honeymoon has been mystical," Sean said with an impish grin.

Prim grinned back. They had explored the surrounding areas very thoroughly, but they had also spent a considerable amount of time in their rooms. Although they'd been having sex for over seven months, Prim found she was now somehow less reserved in bed than she had been before their marriage. She still preferred that Sean take a dominant role in their love-making, but she didn't hesitate to tell him what she wanted or needed from him. He told her that he liked it.

"Make love to me one last time during our honeymoon," she directed. "Let's turn the fireplace on and open the sliders a little and listen to the waves as we make love."

The following morning before they left, Sean and Prim walked to the water's edge and gazed at Haystack Rock. No picture they had taken or seen in any shop could capture its essence. They drank in its power, and Sean wondered aloud if it was the same power that people talked of feeling at Stonehenge, Easter Island, and other famous mystical places.

They reluctantly left the tranquil beach and spent the remainder of the day standing in lines in airports, getting on and off planes, and searching for their luggage on the carousel in the Atlanta airport. Prim remarked it was a good thing they'd had such a peaceful time on the beach, since everything that had followed could have easily been much more stressful if they'd been in a different frame of mind. Sean responded that he already wanted to go back, and she wasn't certain if he was joking or not.

Her father picked them up at the airport and asked them how the trip had gone.

My father, Prim thought, as Sean spoke.

Although it had been several months since the DNA test had confirmed that Caleb was her biological father, it still pleased Prim more than she could have anticipated to put those words beside each other. Years of belonging to no one and of having no parent to protect and love her had brought with them terrible sadness. Despite the fact that she was now twenty-five years old, knowing that her father was with her brought her immeasurable joy. Simply learning that he was not a faceless, nameless devil had relieved her of a lifetime of anxiety about her birth parents and herself.

My birth parents....

There was something Prim was forgetting, and that bothered her. It was something important, but she couldn't remember what it was.

My birth parents, she repeated silently in an effort to help her recall whatever she needed to remember. Nothing came to her. *It'll come later when I'm not trying so hard to remember.*

By the time they arrived back at the apartment, it was 11:00 p.m. They promised Caleb they'd see him at the noon service, and he hugged both of them and said he was looking forward to it.

"Sean, your mom and dad insisted they wanted to go to the store to make sure you two had things to eat when you returned. Remy went with them. It's an interesting combination, but you won't starve."

"That was very sweet of them," commented Prim.

"If I weren't so tired, I think I could actually go for some Vienna sausages or a frozen corn dog right about now," Sean told them. "Is there milk and cereal or just junk food?"

"I believe Remy threw in a few things he knew the two of you would prefer. Perhaps the rest could be donated to our local shelter. They're always in need and would be happy with anything."

Sean woke the following morning, complaining that he didn't feel well and wouldn't be attending the noon service at the Community Church. When Prim asked him what was wrong, he told her he had a bad headache and would take some Advil and return to sleep.

"We'll be going to my parents' house for dinner with Remy, Maureen, Caleb, and LouAnn in order to review the highlights of our trip," he told her. "I want to go but need to get rid of this headache first."

Prim asked, "Do you mind if I go alone to the service?"

"Of course not. Tell Caleb I'm sorry I missed it."

She was sitting in church beside Remy when she remembered what she'd forgotten – her birth control pills. In all of the excitement of the wedding and honeymoon, she hadn't taken them in over two weeks. The fact that she and Sean had had sex at least once a day throughout their honeymoon, which happened to be during the middle of her cycle, did not make Prim feel better. It momentarily terrified her.

I could be pregnant, she thought numbly. *What if I'm pregnant?*

Prim didn't hear anything that was said during the first half of the noon service. All she could do was think about the possibility that she was carrying Sean's baby. A part of her wanted that more than anything, while the other part of her hoped that it wasn't true or that she would miscarry early on.

What a terrible thing to imagine, she thought. *What sort of person would wish for that?*

"Prim? Pixie?"

She turned to Remy and realized that he must have been speaking to her. She apologized for being lost in thought and asked him to repeat whatever it was he'd said.

"I asked you if you felt all right. You don't look so good."

"Actually, I'm not feeling that great. I think I'll leave the service a little early and get some fresh air. Will you explain it to Caleb?"

"You sure you don't want me to walk you home?"

"No, but thanks."

She left quietly as her father began his sermon. The truth was that she didn't want Remy to walk her home because she wasn't planning to go home, yet. She wasn't quite certain where she was heading.

Prim walked through the Town Square and went to her old house. She stood at the gate and gazed at the Aurora family home. She had no regrets about selling it and most of the possessions that had been inside. She hoped the new owners were happier there than she'd been.

Knowing what she had to do, Prim headed to the cemetery where her mother was buried. She'd never been to the gravesite and wasn't even sure where the plot was. It didn't matter. She needed time to think as she wandered in search of it.

When she finally found the headstone that bore Sandra's name, Prim sat beside it and leaned against the marble. She shut her eyes and spoke silently to her mother. She told her everything she could think of, from her earliest memories to her current predicament. There was no sense of time passing as she held this one-sided conversation, only longing and relief. She prayed that her mother would somehow send her guidance and find a way to give her comfort.

"Prim?"

She opened her eyes and looked up at Caleb. He was standing at the foot of her mother's grave in khaki shorts, a tee-shirt, and tennis shoes. He was drenched in sweat.

It was only then that Prim realized how hot she was. Her cotton dress was stuck to her back and chest, and her hair hung in damp tendrils against her neck and face. Her throat felt parched.

As she watched, Caleb withdrew his cellphone from a pocket and dialed a number. When he put the phone to his ear, he waited for a minute then said, "Hi. Yes, I found her. She's okay. No. I'm with her. I'll bring her home. Okay. Bye." Tucking the phone in one pocket, he walked over to Prim and sat on the ground beside her before saying, "You gave us all quite a scare."

"A scare?"

"You left the church about 12:30. Sean called me at 2:00 and asked if you were still with me. I told him 'No,' that Remy'd said you weren't feeling well and had left early from the service. Sean kind of flipped out." Grinning, he said, "He's so cool and collected, except when it comes to you."

"And Debra."

"His little sister?"

"Yes. I think he's given up on trying to reach her and get her to reconnect with him and his parents. He's actually had shouting matches with her on the phone."

"Sean? That's very atypical behavior for him."

Prim nodded and confided, "He cries about her sometimes. Don't tell him I told you though."

"I wouldn't dream of it." Pushing back some of the damp hair from her face, he said, "You look overheated. When's the last time you had something to drink?"

"Before I left the apartment."

"How long have you been out here?"

"I don't know. What time is it?"

"Almost 5:00."

"I walked from the church to my old house and then here. It took me a while to find my mama's grave, but I've been here ever since. I had no idea it'd been that long."

"Sean, LouAnn, Remy, Tammy Lynn, Byron, and I have been looking for you all afternoon. We were starting to wonder if there was foul play involved. It's not like you to wander off." Pausing, he asked, "You want to tell me what's on your mind?"

Turning away from him, she said, "I'm a horrible person."

"You're anything but."

"You don't understand."

"You're right. Make me understand."

Fat tears rolled down her cheeks as she said, "I realized during church that I forgot to take my birth control pills since the week before the wedding. I forgot about them completely. It's been two weeks, and we've...been together a lot. I could be pregnant."

"I see. And that makes you a horrible person how?"

"Because I want to be pregnant, but I don't. I was okay with the idea of maybe having children someday, but it still scares me now. I had a thought that if I was pregnant maybe I'd lose the baby early on. What sort of person hopes for that?"

"Someone who's very afraid." Resting a hand on her back, Caleb asked, "Do you think you're the first woman who's had that fleeting thought? Men have had it, too. Unplanned pregnancies are often cause for fear. That doesn't make you a horrible person. It makes you a frightened human being."

"I may not even be pregnant."

"If you aren't, then life will go on as before. What if you are? Would you have an abortion?"

Prim shook her head. She thought of the infinitesimally small cluster of cells she might be carrying inside of her, ones which would grow and form a baby. If that tiny cluster of cells did exist, then it was her privilege to protect it from harm, not destroy it. Her own mother had given her life for Prim's. How could she do any less for her own child?

Looking to her father, she asked hoarsely, "What do I tell Sean? Should I wait to find out if I'm pregnant first?"

"He's your husband, and you're obviously upset. You can't put him off until you find out. You have to talk to him and then go to the doctor."

"Tell me it'll be okay either way."

Caleb took her in his arms and said, "It will be okay either way."

"I don't know *how* I could've forgotten my pills," she muttered tiredly. "I'm so careful about that."

"Have you stopped to consider that perhaps it was God's way of intervening?"

She actually giggled through her tears and said, "God made me forget about my birth control pills?"

"If God is capable of performing miracles, then perhaps this is one. If you hadn't forgotten the pills, do you think you'd ever have allowed yourself the opportunity to get pregnant? I tend to doubt it. You've been so traumatized by your early life that I think you may have run away from parenthood forever. I think Sean has been hoping you'd change your mind but had pretty much accepted the idea that you were never going to actually have children. He loves you so much that he would have forfeited his own dream of having a family with you if that was how things played out." Pulling her closer, Caleb said, "We can't predict the future. If you're pregnant, then you and Sean were destined to have a child together. If you lose that child, then there is a reason for that. There's a reason for everything. We just don't always understand what it is. Sometimes we feel like things are hopeless and God intervenes."

Prim thought about her husband as a baby, lying dead in his parents' arms. God had definitely intervened and given him a second chance at life. He had touched so many lives and helped so many people, including her.

Feeling dizzy, Prim leaned heavily against her father and said, "If I'm pregnant, then our baby would truly be a miracle because of Sean."

"Sean?"

"Tiffany told me he was stillborn. Something went wrong during the birth, and he was cold, blue, and lifeless for over a half hour after she delivered him. The doctor didn't do anything to try to save him, because he was clinically dead. The medical people told her and Kenny that it was just one of those things. She and Kenny prayed for God not to take their baby. Suddenly, he came to life. No one could explain it. There was no medical reason for his spontaneous resuscitation, and they told them he'd probably be severely delayed because of the extended period when his brain didn't have any oxygen going to it. They were wrong, of course."

"My God," Caleb breathed. "Thank you, Lord."

"Sean shouldn't even be alive. So, if I'm pregnant with Sean's child, then an even greater miracle's happened. I...he...."

Caleb leaned her back slightly and said, "I'm going to take you to the car and give you something to rehydrate you. I think you're on the verge of heatstroke. Pregnant or not, you don't need that."

He laid her on the ground, stood then squatted down to lift her up. She asked him if she was heavier than the sacks of grain he'd had to lift at the feed store for all those years, and he laughed. When he got her to his car, he placed her on the back seat, turned on the engine, and switched on the air conditioning. He then sat beside her and offered her some cool sports drink packed with electrolytes that had been stored in a small insulated bag.

"Not so fast," he directed. "You'll throw it up if you gulp it down."

In-between taking small sips, Prim said, "You can't tell Sean about what happened when he was born. Tiffany and Kenny never told him, and I wasn't supposed to tell anyone. I probably never would have if I hadn't been kind of out of it because of the heat. Promise me you won't say anything."

"I promise."

"Thank you for that and for helping me with...with this."

"I would do anything for you. I'd die for you. You're my child."

My child, Prim thought. *I might be having my own child soon.*

For the first time in her life, that thought didn't terrify her. Quite the opposite. She positively *ached* for a baby.

"Caleb? Would it be all right if I called you Daddy?"

"I'd love that," he said thickly.

"Daddy," she said sleepily. "I've always dreamed about having my father around and calling him Daddy."

She dozed, waking when Caleb reached to unbuckle her seatbelt once they'd arrived at her apartment. She was exhausted but didn't feel faint anymore. She assured her father she could make it up the stairs alone, but he insisted that he climb them with her.

Sean opened the door when they reached the top step. She couldn't tell if he was scared, frustrated, or angry with her. Perhaps it was a combination of all three emotions. However, he didn't say a word but merely ushered her and Caleb inside. Once he'd closed the door behind them, he came over to her and asked her if she was all right. She looked to Caleb, who nodded encouragingly and told the two of them that he was going home but to call him back if they needed him.

"You scared me," Sean said evenly once her father had departed. "I thought maybe someone had kidnapped you or killed you."

"I didn't mean to upset anyone."

"Well, you pretty much scared *everyone.* Mom and Dad were ready to call someone with bloodhounds to look for you. They were convinced that bloodhounds were the only way we'd find you. I guess they've watched a lot of crime shows as well as family shows and sitcoms."

"Oh, my gosh! Your parents. I ruined everyone's dinner plans."

"Prim, are you listening to yourself? You were missing for half the day! As if anyone cared about dinner! Will you tell me what possessed you to disappear for hours without telling anyone where you were going or answering your phone?"

"My phone didn't ring. Oh. I guess I forgot to switch it back on when I left church."

"Will you please just talk to me!"

She nodded and assured him that she wanted very badly to talk with him but needed to eat something and shower first. She hadn't eaten anything since breakfast and felt grimy after her afternoon spent walking and sitting in the sun.

Sean sighed in exasperation and asked her what she wanted to eat. When she emerged from the shower in her bathrobe with wet hair, he had two bowls of dry cereal on the counter.

"I don't need two bowls," she protested.

"One's for me. I haven't eaten all day. I was too busy panicking and looking for you." As he poured the milk, he added, "I already called everyone to let them know Caleb found you. Tammy Lynn is going to run the shop alone tomorrow."

"Okay."

"You're not going to argue with me?"

"No. You and I have important things to talk about, and we'll have an appointment to go to tomorrow anyway."

"An appointment?"

"I'll explain everything after we eat."

They sat at the dining room table and ate their cereal in silence. Once they'd finished, Sean brought the bowls to the sink and ran some water in them while Prim went to sit on the couch. Her heart was pounding in anticipation of the conversation they were about to have.

When Sean sat next to her, Prim asked him to hold her. He draped one arm around her shoulders then stroked her cheek with his free hand. She snuggled against him and sighed.

"Why'd you rush out of the noon service if you weren't coming home?" Sean asked guardedly.

"Because I remembered something I had forgotten."

"You remembered something you had forgotten, and it made you disappear for hours on end? Why?"

"Because it scared me."

"What could you have forgotten that would scare you so badly?"

After a quick silent prayer to God for help, Prim said in a small voice, "My birth control pills. I forgot all about them and haven't taken any since the week before our wedding. I could be pregnant."

Sean froze and was quiet. Prim pulled back from him and tried to gauge his reaction. He looked shocked and wary.

"And if you are? Will you have an abortion?"

"I could never do that."

"God, Prim. I *love* you. I'm your husband. If there were problems, then I'd insist we all get help." Leaning forward, he kissed her and asked, "Did your disappearing act help you to come to terms with the idea of being pregnant?"

"Yes. I went to my mother's grave for the first time ever and unloaded on her. I prayed that she'd send me some guidance. Then Daddy appeared."

Sean smiled and said, "So, you finally did it."

"What?"

"Caleb's been wanting you to call him Dad or Daddy or Papa ever since he found out he really was your father."

"Oh. I didn't know if it would make him feel odd."

"I'm sure he's thrilled. I take it he gave you guidance at the cemetery."

"Yes. I went from being afraid to actually *hoping* I was pregnant."

"Are you still hoping?"

"Yes. That's why I figured we could go to the doctor tomorrow and see if they can tell, yet."

The following afternoon, Sean accompanied Prim to the OB/GYN's office. An exam and blood test confirmed that Prim was, indeed, pregnant but only just. The doctor said she had no way of determining the exact date of conception, but the tests were definitely positive. She suspected that the fetus was two weeks into development because of the internal signs that were apparent during the exam and the hormone levels in Prim's blood, which were admittedly slightly skewed by her use of her birth control pills up until the week before the wedding.

As soon as they were back in the car, Sean asked, "Are you okay with this?"

"A little scared but happy, too. How do you want to do this? Do you want to tell people as we see them or make some big announcement?"

"We have to tell your father, since he already knew you might be pregnant. Why don't we wait to tell the others at my father's birthday party this Saturday? He'd love to get that news as a birthday present."

"Are you going to call your sister?"

Sean looked sad. Then he shook his head then said, "She's avoided us for the last couple of years. She won't listen to me no matter how hard I try to convince her that Mom, Dad, and I love her and need her in our lives. She didn't come to our wedding. I doubt if she'd even care that she's going to be an aunt. It's her loss."

It's everybody's loss, thought Prim, as they headed for the hardware store so she could tell her father that he was going to be a grandfather. *Please, God. Help Debra like you've helped me. Help Sean to reach Debra or find another way. She must be so alone like I was. Amen.*

Chapter Twenty-three

Sean glanced around his parents' living room as his father reached for the birthday present that was from him and Prim. The guest list was typically eclectic – Caleb, Remy, Maureen, LouAnn, and Tony Eichstadt. Byron and his family were on vacation at Six Flags for the weekend; Tammy Lynn's parents were visiting from Florida; and Dr. Stanford was running late that Saturday afternoon due to a patient's medical emergency. Mrs. Stanford was, as usual, a no-show due to her health issues.

Kenny held up the shirt Sean and Prim gave him and read the front. He read it again then said, "I like it, but I think you got the wrong shirt. It should say 'Dad,' not 'Granddad.' Do you still have the receipt?"

Sean smiled and said, "We didn't make a mistake, Dad. Prim's pregnant."

Caleb grinned, while the other guests erupted with excited congratulations.

"Well, this is the best birthday gift I've ever gotten!" Kenny declared. "I have to go put on my present. Then we can take pictures!"

He went into the bedroom and quickly reappeared, wearing his new shirt and then hugging first his son then his daughter-in-law. He asked LouAnn to take some pictures of him wearing the shirt with the two of them flanking him and then with his wife included. LouAnn happily snapped photos of the family using Sean's digital camera.

"I may have a lot of questions for you," Caleb told Sean's parents. "I didn't have the honor of raising Prim, and my wife and I were never able to have children together."

"Tiffany and I will help you sort it out," Kenny said. "Most people think too hard about things. You have to learn the basics and follow your heart."

Philip Stanford arrived at this point and was told the good news. After congratulating the expectant parents and grandparents, he accepted a piece of cake from Maureen and ate and talked with the others. Prim and Sean told everyone about their honeymoon and showed pictures they'd taken on the trip. They also handed out souvenirs they'd brought back for each person and were thanked by all for their gifts and for sharing the experience.

Kenny came over to his son and announced, "Your mom's going to talk here with Prim, and I want to have a talk with you. I want to take a walk with you in the woods out back and tell you some important things."

Sean followed his father away from the house and listened as the man gave him advice on taking care of babies and children and on raising them right. He thought of how simple the man made it sound, and he supposed that for his parents it had been simple. Sean had been the one who'd handled all of the complicated issues in their family.

After they'd been walking for almost forty-five minutes in the summer heat, Kenny grew red in the face and started breathing heavily. Sean asked his father if he wanted a drink of water and offered him the bottle in his hand. Kenny shook his head and said he was just getting old.

"Dad, you're in your mid-fifties. You're *not* old."

"Older," Kenny corrected. "I'll bet you that's what Doc Stanford will say when your mom and I go see him in a couple of weeks."

"Older," Sean echoed, but he was worried. His father looked unwell, and he suggested that the two of them turn around and walk back to the house.

"Okay. I do feel kind of bad."

Alarmed, Sean asked, "Bad how?"

"Kind of dizzy and out of breath. I've got kind of a pain, too."

"Pain where?"

"My left arm, but that doesn't make any sense. I haven't done anything hard with my left arm today."

Sean was about to tell his father that he should sit on a nearby wooden bench when Kenny collapsed. Sean dropped the water bottle in his hand and knelt beside him. He asked him to describe what he was feeling.

"I don't...I feel real bad."

"It's going to be okay, Dad. I'm going to call Prim and tell her where we are and to get Dr. Stanford here right away."

"No, you…you shouldn't worry her. It might be bad for your baby."

"I have to call. I think you're having a heart attack."

"A heart attack? No. I'm…I'm just getting older. I told you already."

"Humor me, Dad."

His hands shaking, Sean pulled out his iPhone and called Prim. He explained what had happened and told her where they were on the grounds of the school.

"I don't know where you're talking about," she said, the fear evident in her voice. "I don't know the grounds like you do."

"Tony will know. Tell him to bring Dr. Stanford here right away."

His father asked him for the phone and said he wanted to talk to Tiffany. Sean told Prim, who handed the phone to her mother-in-law before hurrying to speak to the others.

"Tiffany, I feel real bad. Sean says I'm having a heart attack. Yes, I know he's usually right about everything. Prim's getting help from Doc and Tony. They're…they're coming to help me. I know. That's not up to me. It'll be okay no matter what. God will take care of me, just like he took care of Sean. I love you, Tiffany." Once the call had been ended, he said, "Sean, I have to tell you something important."

"You can tell me while we go to the hospital."

"No, I have to tell you now. I love your mom, you, Debra, and Prim more than anything in the whole world. God gave you to me and your mom as a special blessing, and we've always been so thankful for that. You're a living miracle, and I love you. Will you give me a hug?"

As tears streamed down his cheeks, Sean bent forward and lifted his father up into his arms. He told him that he loved him and that he couldn't have asked for a better father. He encouraged him to hold on as they waited for help to arrive.

"My angel boy," Kenny murmured before going limp.

"Dad!" Sean cried out before quickly lowering him back onto the ground. "*Dad!* Daddy?!?"

He called out for help, even though he knew that Tony and the internist could not be close, yet. He checked his father for a pulse. When he found none, he started CPR, stopping periodically to see if there were any signs of life but getting none. He refused to give up.

"Sean."

He looked up and saw Philip Stanford kneeling across from him. The doctor asked him how long he'd been administering CPR, and he replied that he had no idea.

"When did he stop breathing?"

"I don't know. Five minutes after I called Prim?"

"That was over thirty minutes ago. Let me examine him."

"But we can't stop! You're supposed to do CPR until you get someone to the hospital!"

Tony Eichstadt crouched beside him and said, "We called for paramedics before we left. Maureen's going to lead them out here when they arrive. I gave her explicit directions to this area of the campus. However, they won't be here for at least another half hour if my calculations are correct."

"So, we take turns doing CPR. We can take turns!"

"Sean, he's gone," Philip Stanford said quietly. "We can continue CPR until they come, but it won't do any good. I suspect he died quickly. From the symptoms that you described to Prim, it sounds like he had a massive coronary. If you want us to keep trying, then we certainly will. As a physician, I can tell you that it's too late. If you've been at it for a half hour and we have another half hour to go then another hour or so until we get him to the hospital…."

"But he's my Dad!" Sean cried, his face tracked with tears. "I *have* to save him!"

"You've already saved him for most of the last thirty-one years," Caleb said quietly. "Now you have to let him go peacefully to be with God. Don't traumatize his corporal form anymore. He's in Heaven."

Sean looked down at his father, who appeared to be sleeping contently. He swallowed hard, bent forward, and kissed his father on the cheek then hugged him tightly. As he got to his feet, he asked Remy, "Where are Prim and my mother?"

"At the house with LouAnn and Maureen. We didn't think it would be a good idea for either of them to come out here regardless of how your dad was doing."

Sean nodded and blindly accepted the bottle of water Caleb handed him. After draining it, he said, "I need to go back to the house."

"I'll go with you," Remy volunteered.

Sean nodded and looked between the doctor, the pastor, and the Head of the Board of Directors. He asked them if they would stay with his father until the paramedics arrived. They solemnly agreed to his request. Sean took one last look at his father lying on the ground in the midst of the trees, and then he set off.

They were almost to the house when they saw Maureen and the paramedics hurrying their way. Remy's mother and the three men stopped to ask them for an update. Sean found that he couldn't speak. Remy told them Kenny was dead, and Maureen came over to hug first Sean and then her son. The paramedics offered their condolences.

"I'll take them to where your dad is," Remy offered. "Mom, why don't you go with Sean to talk to Tiffany and Prim?"

Maureen said with astonishment, "You called me 'Mom,' Remy."

"Yes, I did."

She put her arms around him and hugged him tightly before kissing him on the temple and saying, "You won't regret it."

"I know I won't. I love you."

"I love you, too." Turning to Sean, she asked, "Do you want to go to the house now or wait a few minutes?"

"My father's dead. A few minutes isn't going to change that. Let's just go."

As his friend went with the paramedics and their rolling gurney towards the woods, Sean walked with Maureen towards the house. As they entered the living room, Prim looked up at him from where she sat on the couch and burst into tears. He supposed that the truth was plastered all over his face. He hadn't had to say a word.

LouAnn put her arms around Prim as she herself began to cry. Tiffany stood and asked, "Is Dad in Heaven now?"

"Yes, Mom." Going over to her, he gently took her by the shoulders and repeated his father's words, "That's not up to me. It'll be okay, no matter what. God will take care of me, just like he took care of Sean."

Her eyes filling with tears, Tiffany nodded and said, "Dad was right."

"What did he mean, Mom?"

"When he told me he felt real bad, I knew he must be real sick. You know Dad doesn't ever complain about feeling bad. I told him he couldn't up and die, especially now that he was going to be a granddad. He told me it wasn't up to him and that it would be all right."

"What about the rest? What aren't you telling me? And why not?"

"Because you don't have to know everything, Sean. You *shouldn't* know everything. You already take on too many burdens."

"Stop trying to protect me from whatever it is you think I can't handle! I've handled *everything* since I was a little boy!"

"Sean, that's enough!" Prim cried, as she got to her feet and hurried over to him.

"I deserve the truth! My father just died in my arms! I spent an eternity giving him CPR even though I knew it wouldn't do any good! I want someone to tell me what's been kept from me my entire life!"

Without waiting for an answer that he suspected would never come, Sean stalked out of the house and went to where his car was parked. After an hour of driving, he filled up his gas tank at a Shell station in an unfamiliar town. Then he set out again. It was almost 8:00 when he reached his little sister's small, rented house in Nashville. There were two cars parked in her driveway.

He pounded on the front door of the house. It wasn't long before Debra opened it. She was wearing shorts and a light pink tee shirt. Her brown hair and brown eyes hadn't changed, but the bruised cheekbone and swollen lip were definitely recent additions to her appearance. So was her look of shock at seeing her brother.

"Sean? What are you doing here?" Glancing back towards the inside of her house, she said, "You need to leave."

"Why? Because your boyfriend will hit you again if you didn't get his permission to do something first?"

"I fell," she offered lamely.

"Sure. You fell. Did you fall the day of my wedding, too? Is that why you didn't come?"

Sean heard footsteps moving in their direction, and Debra attempted to close the door in his face. He roughly pushed it open, and she jumped back, startled. A blonde man who was approximately Sean's height, weight, and build stood at the edge of the living room. He was wearing jeans, a Polo shirt, dock shoes, and a large gold coin ring on his right ring finger. He looked smug but angry. He demanded, "Who the hell are you?"

"I'm Debra's older brother," he replied coolly. "We spoke on the phone once. You must be Patrick."

"Neither Debra nor I asked you to come here. Get out."

Debra touched Sean on his shoulder and urged, "Please, go. I'll talk to you soon. I'll come see you, your wife, Mom, and Dad."

"No, you won't," he said bitterly.

"I *will*," she insisted.

"No, you won't. Dad's dead. He died in my arms this afternoon. It was probably a massive heart attack. One of the last things he said to me was that he loved you, me, Prim, and Mom more than anything in the whole world. Even after everything you *didn't* do, he was never angry with you. He may not have understood, but he loved you until the end."

Debra began to sob, and Patrick ordered her to shut up. Sean strode over to the man and punched him in the jaw. He heard Debra cry out for him to stop, but he wasn't anywhere near ready to stop.

What his parents, his little sister, his wife, his co-workers, and his friends didn't know about Sean Proper was that he'd been in quite a few fist-fights in his younger years. From an early age, he'd refused to tolerate anyone's calling his parents demeaning names, whether it was to their faces or behind their backs. Bright and resourceful, Sean had taken care of those he considered to be cowardly bullies by waiting until opportune times to confront them. If he could persuade them to cease and desist, then nothing else happened. If they came at him or taunted him by continuing their verbal attacks, then he fought with them until he prevailed. *That* was the original reason he'd taken up lifting weights and participating in track and field events. He had to win, to stop the injustice for those who couldn't stop it themselves.

"I fell while we were playing," he'd tell his parents if he came home with bruises, cuts, or a swollen nose. Since it hadn't happened every day, his parents had easily accepted his explanation. His little sister had seemed to accept it as well. Perhaps she'd realized more than she'd let on and had learned how well it worked, except that she was using it as an adult in order to excuse being routinely abused by cowardly bullies.

Sean lashed out at his sister's boyfriend with every ounce of strength he possessed. The two of them seemed equally matched, which made Sean try even harder to beat the man into submission. He was repulsed by Patrick and by what he'd done to Debra and perhaps to every other woman with whom he'd had a serious relationship.

Debra was yelling for both of them to stop fighting. Neither man paid her any attention. Sean landed a blow that knocked Patrick to the ground, but Patrick quickly rolled and was back on his feet. Sean reflected somewhere in the recesses of his mind that Patrick seemed to have had his share of fist-fights but that they appeared to have been recent. Sean wasn't surprised.

"Sean, stop!" Debra exclaimed. "I'll leave him! I'll get help!"

"Like hell you will!" Patrick growled. "Not while you're having my kid you're not!"

That caught Sean off-guard. He turned towards his little sister and asked incredulously, "You're pregnant by this loser?"

Looking completely overwrought, Debra said, "No! I'm not. I – I just told Patrick that I was because I thought he was going to leave me." Facing her boyfriend, she said, "I'm so sorry, Baby. I was scared I'd lose you." Turning back towards Sean, she began, "I thought –"

There was a loud, cracking noise, and Debra stopped talking and staggered back a few feet. She looked down at her chest. A tiny, red circle began to grow larger as blood spread from where Patrick had shot her with the gun he was now gripping tightly in his right hand.

Debra lifted her head and said, "I should have listened to you, Sean. You were right about everything all along."

He rushed forward and caught her as she crumpled to the floor. He had an odd feeling of déjà vu and cried out her name.

Holding her against him, he twisted towards Patrick and hissed, "You fucking bastard!"

The man pointed the gun directly at Sean's head. Sean realized he was going to die and that his mother would be widowed and childless; his wife would be widowed; and his child would be fatherless all in one afternoon. He prayed for God to take care of Prim, their baby, and his mother as well as Caleb, Remy, and everyone else he held dear.

"Oh, Daddy," Debra mumbled, as she stared at the wall behind Sean. "I missed you so much."

She slumped in her brother's arms, and he howled with grief. Patrick prepared to fire his gun.

"Drop it!" called out a policewoman, as she burst through the open doorway at the front of the house. A male policeman was right behind her. Both of them had their guns drawn.

Patrick automatically moved the barrel of his gun from Sean's direction toward the advancing authorities. The policewoman pulled the trigger of her gun, and Patrick stumbled but didn't fall. Instead, he raised his gun and yelled, "Bitch!"

The male policeman fired off a round, and Patrick toppled over. Both cops kept their weapons at the ready and pointed at Patrick until the policewoman had verified he was dead. While she radioed in a call for back-up, paramedics, and a coroner, her counterpart came over to Sean and asked him if he was badly hurt. He dully shook his head.

"My little sister's dead," he said flatly. "He killed my little sister."

"Let me check her out," the cop suggested. Once he saw the wound, the blood, and found no pulse, he said, "I'm sorry for your loss."

Sean thanked him without any conscious thought. He stared down at Debra's face. He refused to let his little sister go when the Medical Examiner appeared to remove her body from the scene. Paramedics attempted to coax him into allowing them to assess his condition and take him to a hospital. Someone tried to get him to give an official statement regarding what had happened.

"Mr. Proper? Sean?"

Struggling to focus through the cloud of emotional and physical pain surrounding him, Sean directed his attention towards a woman he didn't know. He suspected she was a mental health professional sent in to deal with him. He didn't care who she was, but he knew what she wanted.

"They can't take her," he vowed. "Once they take her, then I'll never be able to hold her again."

"They don't want to take her from you, but they need to. You're hurt, and they want to examine you. Your wife and baby need you to come home to them."

"How do you know about my wife and baby?"

"Mrs. Proper is the one who called the Nashville Police Department. She explained about your father's death earlier today and said she suspected you were headed here to tell your sister. She also told them that your sister was most likely in an abusive relationship. The team that responded knew there might be trouble." Looking down at Debra, she admitted, "They always hope it won't be trouble like this."

"I failed her." As tears blurred his vision, Sean asked, "How can I tell my mother? I already had to tell her about my father earlier. She's a little delayed. I don't...I can't...."

"You don't have to," the woman told him. "Someone else can take care of that."

Shaking his head, he said, "I take care of everything."

"Not this time. Your wife has already been notified. She said she was going to tell your mother."

A man squatted beside Sean and said, "Mr. Proper, we really do need to take your sister now. I promise you we'll take good care of her."

"By doing an autopsy. By cutting her up."

"We treat everyone with respect," the man assured him. "Every person deserves dignity be they alive or dead."

"Can I kiss her before you take her away?"

"Of course," the woman told him. "Would you like for us to give you a minute alone with her?"

He nodded. Once they'd stepped to the other side of the room, he told his baby sister one last story about a girl named Debra who went to Heaven and was happy all the time. When he finished, her cheeks were wet with his tears.

Several hours later, Sean was dressed in a fresh pair of scrubs and seated in a chair in a small room next to a hospital E.R. His mind was blank, and he was fine with that. The door to his room opened, but he didn't turn to see who was entering. People were talking about bruises, stitches, and shock. Then the door closed again. Someone moved towards him. He looked up and saw Caleb. He wondered where Prim was. A sickening thought struck him. Perhaps the events of the day had so traumatized her that she'd miscarried their baby.

"Where's Prim?" he asked, as Caleb took a seat across from him.

"With your mother. Tiffany seemed to be handling your father's death reasonably well, probably because of the conversation he had with her before he died. The news about Debra was totally unexpected. She's very distraught and confused and asked Prim to stay with her. Prim was so torn because all she wanted to do was come to you."

"But she couldn't leave my mother."

"No. Dr. Stanford gave your mom something to help her rest, and Prim, LouAnn, and Maureen are still at her house. Tony stayed with the women at Kensington in case they needed anything. Remy's in the E.R. waiting room. They'd only let one of us come back here at a time. He suggested I go first."

"I killed my little sister," Sean said suddenly. "It never would have happened if I hadn't gone to the house to tell her about Dad. I was so angry and upset that I didn't stop to think about what the consequences might be if her boyfriend was there. I spent all these years trying to save her, and I'm the one who got her killed in the end."

"This is not your fault," Caleb declared firmly. "It's no one's fault except Patrick's. You couldn't have saved Debra any more than you could have saved your father."

"Maureen told me last month that she thought something was wrong with Dad. I suggested he go to the doctor, but he said he and Mom had their appointments scheduled in the middle of July. I didn't push it. I should have. He might still be alive if he'd gone for a physical then."

"You're a very special man, but you're not God. You can't save everyone, especially at the expense of your own mind and body."

Staring at the floor, Sean asked, "Do you know what happened when I was little? I know something happened, but my parents would never tell me. I don't think Debra knew. I think Prim knows, but she won't say."

Caleb nodded and admitted, "She promised your mother that she'd never tell anyone, but the day I found her in the cemetery she was slightly overcome by the heat and told me the story."

"Tell me."

"It's not my place."

"Tell me!" Sean shouted. "Tell me that all of my efforts to do right by everyone haven't been in vain! Tell me that my life has *meant* something!"

Caleb reached forward and put one hand behind his neck and the other on one shoulder before saying firmly, "Your life has been touched by God in a way that most people can't even imagine. It's meant everything to those other lives you've touched."

"I don't understand," Sean said wearily.

"I probably know more than your parents and Prim, so I suppose I should tell you the whole story."

"Why would you know more?"

"Human curiosity got the better of me. When Prim told me the bare essentials last Sunday I was intrigued. I may run the hardware store, but I'm first and foremost a pastor. Miracles fascinate me, and I've actually been doing research on them for the last few decades. Little miracles happen all the time, but the big ones are rare. If what I'd heard was correct, you were definitely a big one. I wanted to know everything, not that I didn't believe Prim or think that your mother hadn't told her the truth. I wanted to hear all the facts for myself."

"The facts? What facts? What miracle?"

Caleb released his hold on Sean and said, "I'll let you listen for yourself in the car on the way home. Let's go."

Caleb helped Sean to stand and leave the room. When Remy saw them approaching, he got to his feet and came over to carefully give Sean a brief hug. He asked him if he'd hurt him, and Sean shook his head and said he still didn't feel anything. Remy took a medicine bottle out of his pocket and said, "They told us to give you one of these every four hours once whatever they gave you wore off. Let me know when you need one."

When they reached Caleb's car, Sean sat in the front passenger seat, while Remy sat in the back. Once Caleb had started the engine, he said, "Remy, there's something very important Sean needs to hear. It's been a secret for many years. He may want you to keep it a secret after you hear it."

"I've kept lots of secrets in my life," Remy said seriously. "I've got room for one more."

Caleb removed a CD from the glove compartment and withdrew it from its paper sheath. He inserted it into the car's CD player before beginning the drive back to Georgia. They listened to what was undoubtedly *not* a professional recording.

"Thank you very much for agreeing to speak to me, ma'am."

"You have to call me Miss Jackie," the woman instructed. "And I couldn't *not* speak to you. When I got the call from my old friend in the records department and she said it was about the baby, I knew I had to talk to you. She said you were a pastor and were looking into a miracle that happened at our hospital thirty-one years ago. I know all these privacy regulations today should prohibit me from telling you what happened, but I think they're a load of hooey. I don't have to use any names, but I want to talk about it."

"I'm very interested. Thank you for meeting with me so late."

"Well, you said you worked until 5:00, and it's a two-hour drive from where you live to where I live. I'm sure you're glad I moved to Georgia last year. Otherwise, you'd have had a long drive to Tallahassee."

"You don't mind my using a digital recorder during our conversation?"

"Not at all. If I could tell the world what I witnessed and have it help more people, that would be wonderful. I've already told a lot of men and women over the years. It was a true miracle."

"Please, tell me how it started."

Sean's pulse quickened as the woman said, "I was working as a nurse in a hospital that served the poor. We were understaffed, underpaid, and had some medical personnel who had questionable standards. I was an idealistic young nurse, who was trying to make a difference.

"Anyway, it was just after midnight on New Year's Eve when I started what was going to be a forty-eight-hour shift," Miss

Jackie explained. "This young couple came in, and the wife was in labor. They were just the sweetest things. It was obvious they were somewhat delayed. They apologized for bothering us but thought that it was time for their baby to be born." Sighing, she said, "The worst obstetrician we had was on duty. He was a cruel, burnt-out doctor, and he examined the mother and told us that he didn't see why they let people like her kind have babies. He told us to call him when it was time for her to deliver and just left her in our care. The other nurses and I were mortified. We gave the couple extra attention and spent time explaining what was happening as labor progressed. They kept thanking us for being so nice." The nurse paused and said, "I wish all laboring mothers could be like that woman. She never complained, even as things got worse, and it got closer to her time to deliver. Her husband stayed with her the whole time and held her hand and gave her ice chips or put a wet rag across her forehead or whatever we suggested might help. The doctor finally came back when we told him it looked like the mother was in the final stage of labor. It had been almost twenty-three hours, and he was annoyed because he thought he was going to miss Dick Clark's countdown on TV." Sounding indignant, she said, "Now here's this poor woman in agonizing pain, trying to give birth, and he's irritated because he doesn't get to see the glowing ball drop in Times Square."

"What time was this?" Caleb asked.

"A little before 11:00 p.m."

"Was that when something went wrong?"

"Yes. The baby just wouldn't come. The doctor should have performed a C-section almost immediately, but he kept saying we didn't have the staff on duty for surgery. We could have managed. We all were thinking the same thing – that he was hoping the baby would die because he didn't think that 'retarded' people should have babies. We nurses were furious, but we had no authority. All we could do was what we were told and help the mother as best we could. It was monstrous."

"And what happened?"

"She finally delivered at 11:25. It was a boy. He was unresponsive, blue, and was cold."

"In other words, he was stillborn."

"Yes. We knew there was no chance of saving him, although he was examined thoroughly again at the parents' request. He'd been gone for a while. If the doctor had performed surgery earlier during the labor, he probably would've been fine. Instead, he was dead. The doctor told the parents that these things happened and went off to watch Dick Clark."

"And the parents?"

"They were so heartbroken. They cried and asked if they could hold their baby. We cleaned him up and wrapped him loosely in a blanket and told them to spend as much time with him as they needed. Then we stepped outside the room and discussed how we were all going to report the doctor to the administration, whether it cost us our jobs or not. We were seething and heartsick for the couple and for that poor baby who'd died for nothing."

"And?"

"And right after midnight the father came running out of the room all excited and told us that their baby had just come alive. We nurses thought that maybe it was wishful thinking. The doctor, who'd returned to the desk once he'd switched off the TV in the lounge at one minute after twelve, said it was impossible. The father kept insisting, and we pressed the doctor to check it out in order to stop the parents from deluding themselves."

"But?"

"But the baby *was* alive! He was warm, pink, and alert. His breathing and heart rate were normal. All of us, including the doctor, were stunned. It was impossible. We knew the baby had been clinically dead for at least more than a half hour. Yet, there he was. The doctor was so astonished. I think he was scared out of his wits, if you want my honest opinion. For all intents and purposes, he'd killed that baby. Now that baby had come back to life. Talk about a wake-up call from God! He told the parents that because the baby had been deprived of oxygen for so long, he'd probably be severely retarded. They said they didn't care, that they loved their baby."

"And the doctor?"

"We reported him, but he resigned before he could be fired. He lost his medical license, but he stated during the hearing that it didn't matter. He said he'd realized he had to change his life and use what had happened to educate others."

"Did you ever find out what happened to the parents and the baby after they left the hospital?"

"No. I prayed that he didn't suffer from too many limitations because of the trauma he'd experienced during birth and afterwards." Hesitating, she asked nervously, "Do you know what happened to him? I've been praying for him and his parents for so long."

"The baby didn't suffer from any physical or mental delays. He's a bright, caring, honest man who is a very successful high school principal. He and his new wife just found out they're expecting their first child."

"Oh, thank God!"

For a moment, Sean couldn't make out what was being recorded. Then he realized Miss Jackie was crying.

"I've thought about that miracle baby every single day and how he changed all of our lives. Thank you. Thank you so much for listening and for telling me what you did. It makes the miracle even greater."

"You have no idea," Caleb had said. "That baby has done more good for his own family, for mine, and for total strangers than you can imagine. I'm very blessed to know him."

The recording ended there. Caleb ejected the CD and handed it to Remy, who put it back in the paper sheath. For a long time, none of them spoke. Sean had no idea what to say or think and felt confused and conflicted.

Finally, Caleb said, "Back at the hospital, you asked me to tell you that all of your efforts to do right by everyone hadn't been in vain and that your life had meant something. I hope what you just heard will convince you of that. I also hope you don't dwell on it. Your parents were very wise not to tell you about what happened. They wanted to give you the opportunity to become the man you were destined to be without putting any unreasonable expectations or limitations on you. Take a lesson from them: Don't overanalyze this. Trust that you are exactly who you were meant to be, but don't attempt to second-guess your destiny. Just keep living your life as a good man and allow yourself to rest a little easier. You've already done quite a lot, Sean. Rest."

Sean slept.

Chapter Twenty-four

Prim stared down at her unconscious husband. Her father and Remy had brought him directly to the apartment and carried him up the stairs when they'd gotten him back from Nashville. They'd laid him on the master bed and covered him with a throw from the couch. He was still wearing the scrubs he'd been given by the nurses.

"Prim?"

She turned towards her father, who was standing in the doorway of the bedroom. He looked totally exhausted and understandably so. He also looked worried.

"Prim, how are you holding up?"

"My emotions are all over the place. I'm concerned, shocked, anxious, sad, and angry. How about you?"

"Pretty much the same. We all need rest, especially you."

"I'll rest soon. The baby and I can be up a little longer."

"I need to go home and figure out what I'm going to say at the services today. It's almost dawn. I need time to think, so I can decide how to approach what's happened to Sean, his parents, and his sister when I address the congregation. I'm sure most of the town will know the main points of the story by mid-morning, and I have to work on the best way to handle this so that Sean and Tiffany will have the least amount of distress possible. No matter what I say, it's going to be terribly difficult for them. I'll try to formulate a sermon that will be inclusive regarding boundaries and grief."

"You'll do a wonderful job," she said reassuringly. "But you're not going to tell anyone about the miracle that happened after Sean was born, are you?"

Looking chagrined, he said, "No. I apologize for breaking my promise to you about keeping quiet. I felt it was necessary to tell him. He was very despondent at the hospital and was filled with guilt about both his father and Debra. I'm praying that what he knows now will help him to be somewhat at peace." Sighing, he asked, "Are you mad at me?"

"Not mad. Maybe a little unhappy."

"Prim, it's perfectly acceptable for you to be angry."

"I know, but I can't really be angry with you. You approach everything with good intentions. If you felt like Sean needed to know, then I accept that. I just wish you'd told me about your visit with that nurse. It hurt me that...I felt like you'd gone behind my back."

He put his bulky arms around her narrow shoulders and apologized again before wondering aloud if Tiffany would be angry or hurt by what he'd done.

"You'll have to ask her." Hugging him, she urged, "Go home and work on your sermon. Try to get some sleep."

"Later. Remy's asleep on the couch, and Dr. Stanford and I are only a phone call away," he reminded her. "Plus, Tony's sleeping in your guest room. You know Maureen and LouAnn will stay with Tiffany as long as they're needed."

"Remy told me his mom offered to move in with Sean's mom. I think it will work out for everyone if Tiffany's interested." Kissing her father on the cheek, she said, "Go home, Daddy."

Once he'd left, Prim shut the bedroom door and went to the bathroom where she showered and put on a white cotton nightgown before brushing her teeth. She carefully removed the throw from Sean and got a lightweight blanket that would cover both of them. Once she'd draped half of it across Sean, she lay beside him and covered herself with the other half.

Prim studied her husband's bruised face. She had asked Caleb how blows from a human fist could cause cuts that warranted stitches. The police had explained to him that Patrick had been wearing a ring. Most likely that had been the cause of the torn flesh.

The stitches under his eye and on his lip weren't the only signs that Sean had been engaged in a fight. His face was badly bruised. Remy had said the hospital staff had warned him not to be alarmed if they saw Sean's chest and belly.

"They assured me there was no internal bleeding but said he'd be pretty stiff and in pain for a while. I told them he liked to work out, but they said no lifting weights until he was cleared by an M.D."

"Did they tell you anything else?"

"That the coroner's people said it looked like Sean did a pretty good job of whooping that bastard's ass before the guy shot Debra and got shot himself. They also said Debra had bruises all over that were in various stages of healing. Why did she stay with men like that? It doesn't make any sense."

And therein lies the problem, thought Prim. *Sean has been trying to make sense out of Debra's victim mentality for years.*

She fell asleep, wondering what the long-lasting effects of the previous day's events might be for Sean. When she woke, he was still unconscious. Worried, she checked the time. It was 6:00 in the evening.

She experienced a few moments of panic. If Sean was still unconscious, then perhaps the doctors had missed something more serious. Maybe he was bleeding in his brain.

Stop it! she told herself. *People are talking in the other room. Surely they've checked on us. They wouldn't let Sean stay unconscious too long.*

After making a quick trip to the bathroom, Prim slipped on her robe and went to the living area. Caleb, Remy, Tony, and LouAnn were seated at the dining table drinking coffee and eating muffins. They all looked terrible.

"Has Sean been unconscious all this time?" Prim asked, as she took a seat beside LouAnn.

"He's on his third dose of pain medicine," Remy admitted. "I was really surprised that he asked for it each time. I think he wants to be knocked out for a while so he doesn't have to think about anything."

"He woke up while I was asleep?"

"Several times," Tony told her. "He asked us not to wake you."

"Did he say anything else?"

"He was pretty uncommunicative. Among the shock, pain, and medication, it's to be expected."

"Dr. Stanford came by to check on him," Caleb offered. "He'll be back later tonight to see how he's doing."

"What about Tiffany?"

"Mom's taking care of her," said Remy. "Tiffany wanted to come to Sean, but everyone told her Sean was unconscious and needed her to get more rest before he was awake enough to need her. She understood that and agreed to do what we thought was best."

Breaking off pieces of a muffin and slowly eating them, Prim asked her father, "How did the sermons go at church?"

"Very well."

"I knew they would. Have you had any sleep?"

"No. I'll hit the sack in a little while."

"Does Byron know?"

"I waited until I knew he and the family would be back in town. It must have been an hour ago. I didn't want to ruin their trip to Six Flags with the kids by telling them this kind of news. He'll be by tomorrow."

"And Tammy Lynn?"

"I let her know," Remy said. "She asked that you call her when you were up and had time to talk."

"I'll call her later, Prim told him. "Right now, my only concern is how Sean and Tiffany will handle all this."

"Especially Sean," Tony Eichstadt said seriously. "He's going to feel like he didn't do enough to save his father and sister. I was in that same boat when Gillian was ill and then after she died. People who have personality types like Sean and me are used to getting things done and being successful at it. When life doesn't cooperate on such a grand scale, you feel like you've failed. I thought I could handle it, but it was rough – even though I had time to prepare. I've come to accept that I couldn't have done any more, but it's taken me months. Maybe Sean will bounce back more quickly, but I'm skeptical. All of this was horribly sudden. His situation is much more dramatic because of what happened at his sister's. The loss of his father like that would have been enough." Rising, he proclaimed dryly, "And on that happy note, I have to go. I have a Board of Directors meeting for Kensington tomorrow. I must be there, especially in light of what happened yesterday. There may be a couple of members who will want Sean removed as principal because of the incident in Nashville. I need to quash any questioning about his character. Those members are still jumpy after the last principal's indiscretions. I have to make them comprehend that this is a totally different circumstance and that none of it reflects poorly on Sean."

Prim thanked him, not only for his future efforts regarding her husband's job security but also for his help during the difficult time they were experiencing. He promised to be in touch the following day after the Board meeting and left wishing everyone a good night's sleep.

Once Eichstadt was gone, Prim asked the others to go to their respective homes and get some rest. They protested, but she insisted. She reminded them they all lived nearby and that she could call them back to the apartment if she and Sean needed help.

"Pixie, Sean's not in the best of shape, plus he's drugged. You can't support his weight."

"Remy's right," LouAnn put in. "You could hurt yourself and the baby."

"The baby is tee-tiny at this point. It's pretty well-protected."

They continued to protest, but Prim held her ground. She needed to be totally alone with Sean when he woke. She had to assess how serious things truly were regarding his frame of mind and what needed to be done by her to help him come safely through this crisis.

When she was alone, Prim heated a pot of water and boiled some noodles. Once they were ready, she drained the pot, added butter, and withdrew a container of grated Romano from the refrigerator. Then she sat at the breakfast bar and ate in the quiet of the apartment. When she was full, she rinsed out her bowl and refrigerated the noodles that were left in the pot.

Sean was stirring in the bed when she returned to their room. She climbed onto the mattress beside him and stroked his forehead. He gradually emerged from unconsciousness and looked blearily up at her.

"Who's with my mother?" he asked fuzzily.

"Maureen."

"How is Mom?"

"Heart-broken about your father and Debra. Worried about you."

Closing his eyes, he turned his head away from Prim and asked, "Where is everyone?"

"I sent them home against their wishes a little while ago. I wanted to be alone with you."

"Are you okay?"

"Very sad and worried about you and your mom. How are you?"

He didn't answer.

"You need to eat something," she told him. "Have you had any food at all since we had cake yesterday?"

"No."

"I made some noodles with butter. Will you eat some if I bring them to you?"

"I guess."

After helping Sean to sit up and placing two pillows behind his back, Prim hastened to reheat the noodles and brought them to him with the cheese and a glass of water on a bed tray. He surprised her by eating everything that was in the bowl and draining the glass of water. Feeling heartened, she took the tray back to the kitchen and then returned to the bedroom. Sean hadn't moved and was staring disconsolately at nothing in particular.

"Do you need another pain pill?"

"I want to shower first. Then I'll take the pill."

"Let me call Remy or Daddy to help you."

"No."

"Sean, if you're unsteady and fall, I won't be able to catch you."

"I won't fall, and I won't have another man help me shower."

"Then I'm coming in with you."

He sighed but nodded. He grunted with pain as he swung his legs over the side of the bed and slowly stood. Prim held her breath as he swayed slightly. She put an arm around his waist in order to give him emotional support more than physical. He put an arm around her shoulders, and they inched their way to the bathroom.

"Will you cut these clothes off me?" he asked once they'd reached the shower. "I don't think I can lift the shirt over my head without it causing me a lot of pain."

She cut away the pants first. He had bruising on one thigh and the opposing hip but nothing too severe. She set to work on the shirt.

"Oh, Sean."

His torso was covered in blue-black marks. They made the tattooed wings on his chest look odd. She could literally see the impression of Patrick's ring in one discolored and swollen area. The sight of it made her want to throw up.

"It'll heal," he told her as he walked into the shower. "It'll hurt, but it'll heal."

"The people in Nashville said you did a thorough job on Patrick before he was shot. You've been in fights before."

"Not in years. I think the last time I was in a fight I was about seventeen."

"Why were you fighting?"

"Which time?"

She shrugged and said, "The last fight."

"Some ignoramus called my parents stupid animals who should've been drowned at birth."

"People actually *say* things like that? How can they even *think* that way?"

"You'd be amazed at how callous some people are. I started fighting against that kind of injustice when I was pretty small. If other kids wouldn't listen to reason, I'd make them listen to my fists. They eventually got the message."

"How often did you get into fights because of your parents?"

"I don't know. Here and there."

"So, you beat up the people who were uncomfortable about your parents being delayed."

"They were cowardly bullies. They'd call my parents' names behind their backs or to their faces or say they were less valuable because they were delayed. I couldn't take it. Mom and Dad have always been such sweet and wonderful people. I couldn't let them be humiliated, even if they weren't aware of it. The whole mentality was just so wrong."

As Prim removed her nightgown and stepped into the shower with Sean, she thought of Debra. Prim was no therapist, but she was formulating a psychological theory about her now-deceased sister-in-law. As she suggested to Sean that he stand still and let her soap his body then rinse, she reviewed and refined her theory.

Debra loved Sean and their parents. She probably idolized her brother, who took care of the whole family. Not only did he virtually run the household, but he also defended their parents against other people who made fun of them or worse.

At some point during her teenaged years, Debra herself became uncomfortable with Tiffany and Kenny and their limitations. She knew it was wrong but couldn't seem to stop herself from feeling the way she did. She couldn't confide in Sean or their parents. She was ashamed and felt that she should pay somehow for feeling the way she did. So, she sought out men who would hit her and put her in her place, because that's what Sean did to people who were mean and wouldn't listen to reason. She felt like she deserved it because she was a bad daughter, a bad sister, and a bad human being.

Prim shampooed Sean's hair and told herself that she was completely overanalyzing things. Still, she couldn't help but wonder....

"Sean, what did Patrick look like?" she asked, as he rinsed out the shampoo.

"He had blonde hair. I don't remember too much else, except that we were about the same size and build. Why?"

"No reason. I was just wondering."

After she'd shut off the water, she dried her husband and asked him if he was ready for his pain pill. He looked as though he was about to collapse. He nodded.

Sean agreed to put on boxers but said he would sleep without a shirt. She gave him a painkiller, and he was soon unconscious. This time, he was lying in the bed underneath the covers.

There was a soft knock on the apartment door. Prim slipped on her robe and went to see who was waiting on the landing. It was Dr. Stanford, wanting to know how she and Sean were doing. She invited him in and explained about Sean's meal, shower, and his recent ingestion of the pain pill.

The internist went to examine Sean, returning not long afterwards and asking Prim various questions about her own health. She assured him she was physically fine.

"I can't stay long," Stanford told her. "Call me if you need anything tonight. I'll be back in the office tomorrow, so I can run across the street if there's a problem. Do you have any idea about funeral services, yet?"

"No. I'm sure Sean and his mother will want to see each other tomorrow, and I know we'll have to talk about it. Debra's body will have to be brought here after the autopsy. Are they doing an autopsy on Kenny?"

"They have to. I'm certain it was a coronary, but you know they have to make sure everything's on the up and up for the record. His will probably be performed tomorrow. I couldn't say about Debra's. I don't know what their time frame is in Nashville. I'd think her body would be released by the middle of the week, but I could be wrong."

"I'd like to see the funeral take place by Friday. It's going to be awful, and it needs to be over as soon as possible."

"Agreed. Maureen is talking about moving in with Tiffany at the house on the Kensington property. I think that would be a very wise move."

"Sean will want his mother closer, but I agree that it would be better for her to stay where she is for now. It would be good for Maureen, too."

"I'm glad that things seem to be going well between her and Remy. There's nothing stronger than the love one has for one's spouse and one's children."

Prim returned to bed at midnight. When she woke the next morning at 10:00, Sean was not beside her under the covers. She rolled onto her back and scanned the room. No Sean.

She padded to the living room and found him dressed in shorts and a casual button-down shirt. He was on the phone talking to someone about moving his little sister's body to Aurora. She overheard him say that he'd already been in contact with the funeral home and that they hoped to have the services for both family members on Friday morning. He thanked the person on the other end and hung up.

"Well?" she asked tentatively.

"She'll be here by Wednesday afternoon. I've got to go back to Nashville today or tomorrow to get her some clothes. The police said a family member can go in now that the scene's been cleared, and the owner of the house wants all of Debra's things out as soon as possible so he can bring in a cleaning crew and get it ready to rent again. None of the furniture was hers, so it shouldn't take much to get it all accomplished. If I leave tomorrow morning to drive there –"

"Absolutely not."

"I have to go. It has to be taken care of."

"You do *not* have to go. Physically, you're not supposed to be lifting things. Emotionally, you don't honestly think you can go back into that house, do you?"

"I have to do it."

"No. *Someone* has to do it. I'll go with Daddy and Remy and a U-Haul. We can bring her stuff back here and put it in storage, so you and your mother can take your time and sort through her things when you can handle it."

Obviously agitated, he snapped, "It's *my* responsibility!"

"It's not. I'm your wife, and Caleb is your father-in-law. Remy's like a brother to you and me. We're family. Families help each other, right?"

"What if you hurt yourself moving things? If I don't go and you lose the baby because I let you go instead –"

"*Let* me?" she interrupted. "I'm a twenty-five-year-old woman! My husband doesn't *let* me do things! I may not know a lot about growing up in a normal household, but I know that that's wrong. You don't *let* me do anything anymore than I *let* you! Plus, we both need to stop worrying about the baby. I'm in good health and shouldn't have any problems. If something happens with the pregnancy, then it wasn't meant to be this time."

"If I don't go to Nashville, then what do I do? I have to be doing something."

"It's one day. Spend it with your mother. She needs you as much as you need her."

Sean didn't argue. Instead, he sulked. It was uncharacteristic, but Prim understood.

Byron came by to offer his condolences and to ask if there was anything he and his family could do to help. Dr. Stanford came over at lunch to examine Sean and pronounced that he was healing appropriately but reminded him it might take some time before he was back to his normal physical strength and appearance. In the afternoon, Prim drove Sean to the Kensington Academy to see his mother.

Tiffany began to cry when she saw him and asked if he was in a lot of pain from all the bruises and stitches. Prim knew that he was, although he'd refused any further painkillers and would only take Advil. However, he assured his mother it wasn't too bad as she gently hugged him.

"When will we go to the cemetery?" she asked him.

"Friday."

"Dad and Debra will be next to each other?"

"Yes, Mom."

"Will you tell me what happened at Debra's house? I have to know, Sean. She was my baby, just like you are."

For an instant, it looked like he was going to break down. He quickly regained control of himself. Maureen asked him if he wanted her to step outside, and he shook his head.

The three women listened as he told what was certainly a watered-down version of the events that had taken place at Debra's house. He explained how he'd gone to tell her about their father, how he and Patrick had fought, how Debra had agreed to get help and come home, and then how Patrick had shot her. He spoke of how he'd held her in his arms as she died and of what she'd said regarding seeing her father. Sean told them about Patrick's plan to shoot him that had been thwarted by the police officers. Somehow, Sean managed to maintain his composure throughout his explanation.

"At least Debra's happy with Dad in Heaven," his mother said. "She was so sad these last few years, and Dad and I hated to know she was unhappy. She'll be happy with Dad and God and everything good that will be around them. Heaven is a happy place."

Maureen excused herself and retreated to the bathroom. Prim wiped at her eyes and told Tiffany that Debra was certainly much happier in Heaven than she'd been on Earth. Tiffany nodded and forced a smile.

"Someday, we'll see her and Dad again. I wish it was soon, but then I don't wish it was soon because I want to stay on Earth with everyone here and the baby that's coming. I want to be here with all of the students when they come back to school."

"Mom, you should move to Aurora where you can be closer to Prim, the baby, and me."

"No, Sean. You're usually right about everything, but you're not right about this. I like it here and like being with all of the children. Maureen says she'll live here with me so neither of us has to be alone. I think that would be good. This is my home, the place your Dad and I wanted to grow old in. I want to grow old in it, because I know he's here with me even if his body isn't here. Now, Debra can be here with me, too. She can be with all of us all the time now that she's in Heaven."

Prim had anticipated a persuasive speech from her husband, but he searched his mother's face and simply nodded. He told her that if she changed her mind to let him know.

"If I bought a house in town, would you stay there sometime?" he asked. Looking towards Maureen as she came back into the room, he proposed, "Maureen could stay there whenever she wanted, too."

"Most people with two houses live in town and have a house in the country on TV shows," Tiffany said. "We'd have a house in the country for our main house and a house in town to visit. I'd like that. We could see you two and Remy and the baby when we weren't working or if you needed help. Could we live in the house you've been renting? That would be a good house."

"I'll see what I can do," Sean told her. "I'm sure it can be arranged."

Tony Eichstadt called that night before they went to bed to see how they were doing and to tell them there were no problems within the Board regarding Sean's continued presence as the principal. He had the support of every member of the Board and their sympathies. Prim offered a silent prayer of thanks for Tony's successful efforts.

The next morning, she, Caleb, and Remy set off in her car for Nashville. They went to a U-Haul store near Debra's house and rented the smallest truck available. Since the furniture was not hers, they decided the truck should adequately hold her other belongings.

A policeman met them at the house and unlocked the front door. Prim became queasy as she stepped into the living room where two people had died the previous Saturday.

"Does everyone else feel like they're going to be sick or is it just me?" Remy asked.

"As a pastor, I've seen a lot of death," Caleb confided. "It still makes me nauseated every time I go into a place where there's been violent death."

"Pixie? You okay?"

She nodded distractedly as she stared at the bloodstains in various places on the carpet. She couldn't imagine what Sean had endured in that house and in the woods at Kensington. It would only be a matter of time before he cracked if he didn't open up about what he was feeling or thinking.

Remy suggested, "Let's get started and get this over with. Caleb, do you have the garbage bags?"

"Yes. How do you want to do this?"

The two men went to empty the contents of the refrigerator and all of the trash in the cans around the house and take it to the curb. Prim went to the bathroom with a garbage bag and began to clean out the medicine cabinet and drawers beneath the sink. She threw out all toiletries and medications, including birth control pills. She found an empty pregnancy test box and stared at it for a moment before tossing it in the bag.

While Remy and her father packed the dishes, glasses, pots, and pans in the kitchen, Prim went to Debra's bedroom to begin taking her clothing out of the closet. The first things she saw when she stepped into the room were the Sock Monkey robe, slippers, and doll Sean had bought for his sister the first day he and Prim had met. Prim began to cry quietly. He had been so desperate to reach her. Evidently he had, but had his efforts made her feel better or worse about herself?

By the time Prim, Caleb, and Remy returned to Aurora with Debra's things, it was 10:00 p.m. Caleb parked the U-Haul truck in one empty corner of the lot behind the Aurora building that faced the Town Square. He and Remy made plans to unload it the next day after work. Neither of them felt that it would be prudent to keep the hardware store or book shop closed for another day.

"Unloading shouldn't take too long," Remy told Prim. "The packing is the most time-consuming part, right?"

Caleb concurred and added, "Byron offered to help tomorrow when he gets off at 6:00. It ought to go quickly with three of us. The storage unit isn't far."

They went up to the apartment and found Sean asleep on the couch. The bottle of pain pills sat on the coffee table. Prim hurried over to count the pills remaining in the bottle.

"He's taken two since this morning," she told the others. "He has four left."

"We probably should have had someone stay with him while we were gone today," Caleb said.

"He insisted he didn't want anyone and needed time alone," Remy reminded him. "But you're right. We probably shouldn't have given him the choice."

"It's too late to cry over spilt milk," Prim remarked. We're back, and he's here. He needed time by himself, I'm sure."

After her father and Remy had gone home, Prim wandered around the apartment. She had an odd feeling Sean had been to Hell and back while they'd been in Nashville but that it had been a necessary trip for him. Nothing was broken or out of place, but she knew that something of importance had happened. She just wasn't sure what.

She found the empty red wine bottle in the recycle bin under the kitchen sink. It had been given to the both of them as a wedding gift by Tony Eichstadt and was supposedly extremely expensive and of an extraordinary vintage. Prim didn't care that Sean had ingested the wine without her. She was pregnant and couldn't drink anyway. What concerned her was that he'd drained the bottle while he was on pain medication.

She hurriedly called Dr. Stanford and explained. He was sitting beside Sean, listening to his chest with a stethoscope twenty minutes later. After checking Sean's pulse and blood pressure, he announced he was going to stay until Sean woke up since they had no idea if he'd taken both pain pills at the same time and whether or not it was before or after he'd had the wine. There was no evidence that he'd eaten either, which worried both Prim and the internist.

Sean gradually came awake at 1:00 a.m. He seemed disoriented and groggy. Philip Stanford asked him a barrage of questions, and it was clear that Sean wasn't able to coherently answer them. Prim's heart ached for her husband, who seemed to be so utterly lost and dazed.

After an hour had passed, Sean's mind appeared to clear somewhat. He was able to tell them he hadn't eaten anything since breakfast and that he'd taken one pain pill later in the morning and then another later in the afternoon. He'd intended to have one glass of wine with dinner but never ate and had quickly found the bottle empty.

"You have to eat something now," the doctor told him. "I'm not leaving until you've had some food."

Once he'd grudgingly consumed a bowl of oatmeal and was able to give appropriate verbal responses to Stanford's questions, the doctor performed another exam before agreeing to leave. Prim profusely thanked him before seeing him out. After she'd shut and locked the door behind him, she went to sit beside Sean on the couch and said, "You scared me."

Without looking in her direction, he said, "I'm sorry. I didn't mean for this to happen."

"I know. Just don't let it happen again."

He nodded and asked her how things had gone in Nashville.

"We got it all packed and loaded. It's in a truck behind the building. I'm glad you didn't go. It was very hard for us, and we didn't really even know Debra."

"Did you find anything interesting?"

"Interesting?"

"Unusual."

Prim instantly thought of the pregnancy test box but refrained from mentioning it. Instead, she said, "There weren't any pictures of the family around, but she had all of the things you and your parents sent her for her birthday and Christmas all over the place. I'm sure a lot of the other things we packed are things you all gave her, too. It was like she treasured you so much, but she…hid you in plain sight."

He shut his eyes and said, "I talked to someone at the Nashville Medical Examiner's office this afternoon after the autopsy. I'd asked them to let me know the results, even though I knew the bullet had killed her."

"And?"

"She lied to me and to Patrick."

"I don't understand."

"When Debra said she was going to leave Patrick and come back with me, he said that she wasn't going to do anything while she was pregnant with his baby. I asked her if she was really pregnant by that loser, and she said no, that she'd made it all up to keep him with her. She apologized to him for lying about it then told me she should've listened to me all along. That was when he shot her, I think."

"Oh, Sean."

"The autopsy revealed that she was about twenty weeks pregnant. It was a girl. I'm not going to tell Mom."

Prim drew in a deep breath and released it. So, there had been four deaths on Saturday, not three. More blood on Sean's hands, at least in his mind.

Chapter Twenty-five

Sean was sitting at the funeral for his father and sister when he realized what Prim must have figured out while they were in the shower almost a week earlier. Instead of listening to Caleb's sermon, he reflected upon his childhood, his need to defend those who couldn't defend themselves, the fights he'd gotten into, and Debra's interpretation of it all.

In her early teen years, she'd dated boys like Remy – friendly but slightly reserved intellectual types who were not big into lifting weights, being aggressive, or playing team sports. Her taste in boyfriends had changed as she'd progressed towards graduation from high school. The boys had become more like Sean – pleasant, assertive, intellectual types who liked to bulk up and were actively involved in football, baseball, wrestling, or track and field. However, these new boyfriends also seemed to have a penchant for being emotionally abusive.

This hadn't gone unnoticed by her parents or Sean, but Sean hadn't been able to be around enough to have any sort of influence on her decisions regarding relationships. He had been busy working almost full-time at Mr. Spiro's restaurant, taking care of all the family business, and attending college then graduate school. He thought of the year their mother had developed the lump in her breast, and he'd had to coordinate required pre-op testing and the scheduling that had accompanied the surgery and figure out how to pay the extra bills resulting from the procedure and treatment.

Was that what had triggered Debra's discomfiture regarding their parents? Had his physical absence from their apartment forced her to see her parents' limitations more clearly? Had she been afraid of the responsibility she might have to assume regarding their care once he had his master's degree? Perhaps she was worried she couldn't perform the necessary duties that came with having delayed parents. Perhaps she was simply afraid she wouldn't have a life of her own.

That thought had never occurred to Sean. He'd always known he'd have his own life but couldn't imagine an existence where he

318

wasn't responsible for overseeing his parents' affairs. He had never looked on it as a burden. It was only right that he take care of them. If not for them, then he wouldn't exist and wouldn't know what real love was.

This line of thinking brought Sean back to a topic he'd been avoiding for the past week, which was the miracle that had taken place after his birth. He didn't want to dwell on it, because he didn't know how to interpret what had happened. He couldn't deny it. All he could do was ask himself why God had given him back his life. Was it to take care of his parents and sister? Was it to make an impression on the heartless doctor or outraged nurses? Was it to help his students? Was it to help Prim? Was it to father the baby she was now carrying? Was it none of those things or something yet to come?

Sean knew that the knowledge of the miracle should have made him feel as though there was a greater purpose to his life. However, it almost felt like an added weight. It seemed as though God was watching him more closely. Was God disappointed?

What if it was his fault that Debra chose to be with men like him who had the added quality of being abusive? After all, Sean would fight until the "cowardly bullies" saw things his way. Was she hoping that one day being beaten would somehow make her view their parents differently and free her of her guilt and shame?

"Sean? Sean, what's wrong?"

He turned to Prim, who was looking worriedly at him. He wanted so badly to talk with her about what he was thinking, what she'd already thought. But he knew he couldn't. They were at the funeral; his mother was sitting beside him; and the church was filled with their friends as well as some of Debra's friends and co-workers.

"Sean?" Prim persisted. "Are you okay?"

He started to speak, but then settled for shaking his head very slightly. She took his hand and asked him quietly if he wanted to step outside. He shook his head again. The sermon was nearly over. They would go to the cemetery afterwards for the graveside service. He couldn't do anything now except what needed to be done. It was only a little while longer….

They stood under a canopy that had been set up by the funeral home staff. Despite the shade it provided, the July heat was oppressive. Everyone was sweating and fanning themselves with paper fans provided by the funeral director.

Sean stared at the two caskets and imagined his father's lying in the one wearing his brown corduroy pants, his tennis shoes, and the 'Granddad' shirt that Prim had insisted he would want to wear. Sean's mother had wholeheartedly agreed, and Sean had accepted this with no hesitation. He thought his father would be thoroughly pleased regarding his funereal attire.

Debra had been dressed in a cream-colored blouse and blue pantsuit. Sean suddenly felt as if he'd made a mistake. He should have requested that she go to her grave in the robe and slippers he'd given her for her birthday. They could have put the doll in with her as well. He fought the urge to run forward and throw open the casket and order that they change her clothing.

He blindly shook hands with the people who passed him as they filed out from under the canopy. He was aware of everyone's talking in hushed tones and didn't pay much attention to what they were saying until he heard his mother speaking seriously to Tony Eichstadt, who had come in for the funeral and was staying on-campus at Kensington for the week. She was telling him that all her daughter had ever wanted was to be loved by a good man and to love him in return.

"It made me and her father real sad. She had so much to give, and there was so much to love. She just couldn't see it."

And people have called my parents stupid, Sean thought wryly.

Soon, he was sitting on the couch at his mother's home. LouAnn had provided all of the food for the post-funeral reception, which was attended by him, his mother, Prim, LouAnn, Remy, Maureen, Caleb, Dr. Stanford, Tony, and Byron and his wife. Sean didn't eat anything or say much to anyone. He couldn't stop thinking about his father, Debra, and his unborn niece.

"Sean, I think we should go home. I'm really tired, and you've needed to be away from everything since the funeral this morning."

He looked at his wife and nodded. He was past ready to go but didn't want to leave his mother. He went in search of her and found her sitting on the bed in the master bedroom.

"Mom?"

"I just needed to be alone for a minute," she told him. "There were so many people today, telling us how sorry they were and how sad everything was. It was nice that they cared so much about Dad and Debra, but it got to be too much for me after a while. I needed some peace and quiet."

As he sat beside his mother, he said, "Prim asked me if we could go. She said she was really tired."

"When you're growing a person inside of you, then you get extra tired sometimes. Her body is working hard at helping her baby be healthy. You take Prim home. You need extra rest yourself. You're still all bruised up."

"I don't want to leave you alone."

"I'm not alone. Maureen is with me now, and we'll be okay together. She's only a little older than I am. I like her, and she likes me. I think living together will be a good thing."

"But everyone's still here and —"

"The others will be going home soon. Everybody's worn out." Gingerly touching one of the bruises on his face, she said, "You should give me a hug. I need one from you, and I think you need one from me."

He awkwardly twisted so that he could hug her. She placed a hand behind his head and pulled him down until his cheek rested against her shoulder. Then she took her other hand and rubbed his upper back and rocked slightly forwards and backwards. It made him feel as though he were a little boy again.

"I'm so confused," he confided.

"I know," his mother said gently. "I wish you hadn't found out about what a miracle baby you were. Dad and I didn't want you to feel funny about it. It's not something we were meant to understand. You have to find a way to accept what happened and not try to figure out why. All you have to know is that we love you and that you are your own man. No one expects you to be perfect. You're the only one who expects that. You ask too much of yourself. Live your life and trust that everything will happen like it should."

He nodded against her shoulder and said, "It was so terrible to be with Dad and Debra when they died."

"I know, but you were there to make them feel safe when they had to leave this world. It must be so hard on you, but you helped them so much. I'm glad you were there to take care of them like you did."

"But what if my showing up at Debra's is what made Patrick kill her?"

"Sean, Debra needed help. If Patrick hadn't killed her that night, then he would've done it another night. Or it would've been another man. Remember what she told you before she died. She said you'd been right about everything."

"I wanted to save her."

"You did. She understood before she went to Heaven to be with Dad."

"That's not what I meant."

"I know. Sometimes we don't get what we want. At least she's not being hurt by anyone anymore. That makes me feel better about her going to Heaven so early."

His mother kissed him and told him things would get better in time. She reminded him it would get easier every day and that the coming arrival of the new baby would make for a happy diversion.

"My first grandbaby," she declared proudly. "Somehow, I always figured it would be Debra who would give us our first grandchild."

Sean hugged his mother tightly as he squeezed his eyelids closed and clenched his jaw. He was *not* going to break down or tell her that Debra was the one who would have given her parents their first grandchild had she not been killed by her baby's father. He couldn't do that to his mother and sadden her more.

"Mom, I have to go."

"You go then. I love you, Sean."

"And I love you."

He stood and made to leave the room. When he neared the door, his mother said his name. He stopped and turned back towards her.

"You're trying to protect me from something, just like Dad and I tried to protect you from finding out about being born dead. I don't know what it is you don't want me to know, but I trust that it's something you think will be bad for me to find out. I think Dad and I were right to not tell you about the miracle, but you were obviously meant to find out. Don't feel bad about not telling me whatever it is. I'm upset enough and don't want to be confused or more sad. If I'm meant to know, then someday I will. You don't have to tell me."

"Thank you for understanding."

She smiled tiredly at him and said, "That's what parents are supposed to do. Just promise me that you'll talk to Prim about whatever is bothering you so much. She's your wife. You're partners. You're there to help each other with things that no one else can share."

He and Prim said goodbye to everyone and left for their apartment. Prim insisted on driving, saying that Sean had been too distracted and looked too exhausted to drive. He didn't argue because he was well aware she was right.

Sean wanted to talk to Prim about everything he'd been mulling over since the funeral but didn't know where to begin. So, instead he decided to ask her something that was completely unrelated and give his mind a diversion.

"Does Dr. Stanford's wife really exist?"

"She does. She's very nice."

"When is the last time you saw her?"

"Around the time I moved back to Aurora almost two years ago."

"Why don't we ever see her?"

"She has Multiple Sclerosis, and it's gotten worse over the last couple of years. She was always very involved in community events. Once the MS began to take its toll, she decided to retire from public life. I think she and Dr. Stanford go out sometimes, but not around here. She doesn't want people to remember her like she is now. I call her on the phone once a month to chat."

"You do?"

"Yes. It's only right. I wish she'd let me come visit her, but she always declines. I feel depressed after we talk because I think it's so terrible she's chosen to withdraw from the world. I have to remind myself it's her life and her choice and that at least I can maybe brighten it up for a little while each time we talk. I'd call her more often, but she says not to, that I have my own life to lead. She was very excited when I told her I'd fallen in love with you, when we got engaged, when we got married, and now that we're having a baby. I really wish she could've come to everything and participated. Her family's been in Aurora since not long after it was founded."

"How come you never told me about any of this before?"

"You never asked. You don't know everything about me, Sean Proper. Do I know everything about you?"

He didn't answer, and Prim didn't press him to respond. When they went into the apartment, Prim reminded him that he hadn't eaten much all day and encouraged him to have a peanut butter-and-jelly sandwich, which he did. Once he'd drained the glass of milk she'd given him, he stared at the counter of the breakfast bar while she rinsed off the plate and glass.

Prim walked over to stand behind him and slipped her arms around his waist, being mindful of his healing belly. She rested her head against his back and suggested they take a long, hot bath together.

"We can't. Remember in the parenting classes the teacher said pregnant women weren't supposed to take really hot baths?"

Her hold on him tightened, but Prim said nothing.

"Prim?"

"I forgot. How could I forget that?"

He could hear the fear in her voice and hastened to place his hands over hers and lift them away from him. Turning the barstool around, he looked at his wife's face. She was crying.

"Prim, what is it?"

"I'm so stupid," she said bitterly. "What am I thinking? I can't have a baby. I'm going to hurt it by accident before it's even born. I probably already have. You and I took a really hot bath together every day of our honeymoon, and I was already pregnant. Then I got overheated and kind of dehydrated that day I realized I might be pregnant. Our baby's probably already been damaged by my stupidity! I shouldn't be a mother. I shouldn't have a baby, but I want it so much!"

Taking her face in his hands, Sean kissed her wet cheeks and said with conviction, "You are not stupid. You're very smart, very beautiful, and very loving. We're going to have this baby, and you're going to be a great mother. That doesn't mean that both of us aren't going to make some innocent mistakes. All we can do is try our best. Don't feel guilt for something you didn't do on purpose."

"Are you going to take your own advice?"

"What do you mean?"

"You've spent your entire life trying your best and doing more than most people would've ever done for their families and total strangers. But you're blaming yourself for Debra's situation and her death and for not being able to save her or your father. Are you going to be like this with our baby? If something doesn't go perfectly for it, are you going to go off on a major guilt trip?"

"That's different," he said stiffly.

"Is it? You do so much good in the world, but you take on blame for things that aren't your fault."

"I don't want to talk about this right now."

"Of course you don't!" she said furiously, surprising him with her vehemence. "If you can't have control, you can't deal with anything! That's why my fears frighten you, and that's why you had such a hard time trying to deal with Debra and her irrational choices when it came to men. What would you have done if she'd lived and had her baby?"

"I don't know! I couldn't have let an innocent child suffer because of its mother's refusal to get help! If I could have, I would've taken Debra away from her own life a long time ago! I *knew* she was letting herself be abused, but I couldn't see how to do anything about it! I couldn't stop it! How do you think that made me feel? It was my responsibility to take care of my parents and my sister! I'm the one who got her killed! I failed completely, and now she and her baby are dead! They're dead because of me, and so is my dad! I should've insisted he go to the doctor right away and not wait, but I didn't! Now he's gone and our baby will never know what a wonderful person he was! I'll never get to hug him again or call him when I'm feeling down and have him make me feel better or listen to him laugh or tell me some corny joke over and over! I'll never hear him tell me he loves me ever again!"

Sean got off the stool and headed for the master bathroom. He slammed the door and locked it behind him. He was so shaken that he didn't quite know what to do with himself. Finally, he filled the tub with hot water and soaked in it for a long time. Unfortunately, it didn't help him relax.

He emerged from the bathroom nude and clean. Prim, who had evidently showered in the guest bathroom, was sleeping in their bed. He carefully folded back the covers and found that she was also naked. Her strawberry blonde hair was still damp.

He sat on the mattress and studied her bare flesh, admiring as he always did her beautiful body, the delicate features, and the lovely hair. The blue eyes were suddenly open and staring up at him.

"I'm sorry," he said quietly. "I'm just so sad, and I don't know what to do! I can't fix this! I want to fix it!"

Prim sat up and wrapped her arms around his shoulders then guided him until he was lying prone on the bed. Slipping one arm under his neck, she offered him one nipple, much as a mother might offer her hungry baby a breast. Sean took the nipple in his mouth and felt instantly comforted. He drew on it and put his arms around his wife's waist, pulling her closer to him. It wasn't long before Prim had taken him inside of her.

They hadn't made love since they'd found out they were going to have a child. There had been too many problems and traumatic events that had left them physically and emotionally drained. But Sean was in Prim now, and it felt so good. As he took her other nipple in his mouth, he forgot about everything except how much he loved this woman, his partner.

Afterwards, Prim lay on her back and held him in her arms, his head resting against her chest and one of his palms on her flat stomach. He was still sad, lost, and confused, but he was with Prim and their baby. Things would get better, clearer.

When he woke that Saturday morning, Prim was gone. He found a note on the dining room table that read, *I realized something important last night. There's someone I have to see. I'll be back as soon as I can. I love you. Prim.*

The note was innocuous enough, but something about it made Sean's heart pound with dread. He called Prim on her iPhone, but the call went straight to voicemail. That was when he called Caleb, Remy, LouAnn, Byron, and his mother. None of them had heard from Prim.

When he tried Dr. Stanford's number, Sean got a voicemail. The same thing happened when he tried Tony Eichstadt. He left messages for each, stating that Prim was in trouble and to call him back right away.

Inexplicably filled with terror, he phoned Caleb and Remy again and asked them to meet him at the apartment. He had a feeling he was going to need their help in order to save Prim, although he wasn't quite certain what he was saving her from. He hoped his mind was playing tricks on him because of the stress he'd been subjected to over the course of the past week. He didn't believe it. Something was terribly wrong, and if he didn't find Prim quickly, then she and their baby were going to die.

Chapter Twenty-six

Prim stood on Dr. and Mrs. Stanford's back porch and knocked again on the door. She hadn't been surprised when no one came to the front. Knowing about Mrs. Stanford's medical condition and her current reclusive nature, Prim hadn't really expected her to welcome those who attempted to visit. So, she'd strolled around the two-story brick home to see if the lady of the house would come to the back door. She hadn't. Mrs. Stanford's car was the only one in the driveway behind the house, and Prim began to worry. What if she was in need of help?

She took a chance and tried the door handle. It was locked. She decided to try a trick she'd seen Remy use once when she and his little brother had followed him without his knowledge.

The two of them had been seven and he'd been sixteen. They had wondered where he went sometimes when he would disappear for several hours. So, they'd followed him and watched him break into a house. He'd emerged with a couple of cloth bags filled with what they later discovered was food. Neither of them had ever followed him again or told anyone what they'd witnessed. They knew what he'd done was a necessity if anyone in the Artigue household was going to eat regularly.

Prim removed a decorative floral throw that had been draped over one arm of a nearby rocking chair. She wrapped it around her right hand and broke a square pane of glass near the door handle. She unwrapped her hand and reached through to unlock the door.

"Ow!" she hissed, as a shard of glass cut a long, thin line across the top of her hand. She grimaced but didn't stop until she'd turned the lock from the inside. Once she'd withdrawn her bleeding hand, she lifted the hem of her dress and applied pressure to the wound.

She wondered how many times Remy had cut himself in his first attempts at stealing food. She supposed he had learned very quickly how best to accomplish his goal without getting hurt or caught. He'd always been skilled at learning whatever he needed to know in order to survive.

"Mrs. Stanford?" she called out. "It's Prim Proper." When there was no response, she tried, "It's Prim Aurora! Are you here? Are you okay?"

There was no answer. Prim hastily washed her injured flesh and located a tea towel, which she wrapped around her still-bleeding hand. She winced. How could such a little line of cut skin be so tender?

Mrs. Stanford was obviously not in the kitchen. As Prim wandered the first floor, she found the rooms empty. She climbed the stairs, noting the chair lift that allowed the woman to go to and from the second floor.

Mrs. Stanford was lying in her bed. She looked as though she was taking a nap, but Prim sensed she was actually dead. She swallowed hard, said a prayer for the woman, and reached in her pocket with her left hand for her iPhone.

"Don't, Prim."

She whirled around and saw Dr. Stanford standing in the doorway. He appeared horribly sad, and she could certainly understand why. She gave him her apologies for breaking into his home and explained her reasoning then offered him her sympathies.

"I can call Byron," she told him. "You don't have to do it."

"Neither of us is going to call Byron."

Bewildered, she asked, "But why not? Your wife has passed away. Byron will come and take care of things so she can be examined then brought to the funeral home."

"She can't be examined."

"Why not?"

"Because if they examine her, they'll know she didn't die a natural death."

Prim glanced back at the bed and speculated, "She killed herself?"

"No."

"I don't understand."

"No, I imagine you don't. This is a very ironic situation, although the humor involved is quite dark."

"Ironic?"

"I saved your life when you were a baby."

Prim knitted her brows and remarked, "But I thought I was okay. It was my mama who was sick."

"I didn't save your life when you were born. It was later. You were in danger."

"Danger? What kind of danger?"

"Have a seat, and I'll tell you."

She instantly felt as though she should run, but the internist was blocking the doorway. This was a man she'd trusted her entire life, so why did she feel so much fear now? Could she rush past him and get safely out of the house?

"I have a gun," he told her. "I'd really rather not use it. An injection would be so much less painful. It was easier for my wife to go that way."

Stunned, she stammered, "You…you killed her? Why? Because she was sick? Did she ask you to help her die?"

"No."

"No?" As chills ran up and down her spine, Prim asked, "Why did you kill her then?"

"Because she was going to tell the truth, and nothing good could come of that. I was trying to protect you and your family plus me and mine. My wife was already dying a slow, terrible death. It was better for everyone this way."

Shaking, she asked, "What were you protecting us from?"

"Sit down, Prim." Pointing to a chair, he ordered, "*Now.*"

"You're planning to kill me and my baby," she said as comprehension dawned.

"I'm afraid I have no choice. That's what's so ironic. I saved you, and now I have to kill you." Sighing, he said, "If only you'd come here a little later. I would have moved my wife by then, and no one would have ever known."

"That's where you went, to find a place to bury her?" When he nodded, she asked, "What were you going to tell your sons?"

"I hadn't gotten that far in my plans, yet. I could tell anyone anything indefinitely. My wife has been a recluse for years now. Even our sons haven't seen their mother in quite a while. They can't handle her declining health. As her husband, I considered it my duty to help her as best I could."

330

"Whatever caused you to do this must have been necessary," Prim lied. "I won't tell anyone. Just let my baby and me live, and I'll keep your secret."

"I can't take the chance."

As he reached into his pocket, Prim frantically attempted to think of a way to escape. She needed time and opportunity.

"Will you at least tell me the story before you kill me? I think I deserve that much."

"You deserve more than that, but that's all I can do for you."

"So tell me," she prompted. "What danger did you save me from?"

"The Auroras were a strange bunch. Mr. and Mrs. Aurora were religious fanatics. Myrtle was emotionally unstable. Sandra wanted a normal life and couldn't have one. She was known around town for being a loose girl, so I wasn't surprised when it came out that she was pregnant with you. Then she got sick and died, leaving you with that group. Your Uncle Buddy was the only sane one of the lot, but I knew from other men around Aurora that he'd turned to prostitutes for sex not long after he and your aunt were married. The whole family situation saddened me, and I didn't know the half of it." Looking across the room at her, he said, "I was praying you'd have a better chance at a happier life than your mother had been given. What did I know?"

"Was that the danger you were talking about? I still don't understand what you meant about protecting everyone."

"When you were a year old, Buddy called me one night after dinner and said you were real sick. You'd been running a high fever all day while he'd been at work, but no one from the house had brought you in to see me at my office. He asked if I could come by to examine you since Myrtle and her parents wouldn't hear of doing anything except using home remedies that weren't working. I went right over.

"You were a very sick baby. I suggested you be taken to a hospital, but Mr. and Mrs. Aurora said they were going to pray over you and that your fever would break soon. I was incensed and told them that if they didn't let me take you to a hospital I'd report them to the child welfare agency. Buddy was on my side, but the older Auroras wouldn't budge. We were arguing about it in the living room when we heard Myrtle scream from upstairs."

Dropping his head, he admitted, "Everything happened so fast after that. Buddy and Mr. and Mrs. Aurora were ahead of me on the stairs, and I could hear you bawling. We all rushed into Sandra's room and found this stranger holding you not very securely. You were already sick and were crying piteously. Myrtle was screaming that *this* was the man who'd raped her, that *this* was Sandra's father. Talk about a shock for me."

"What did you do?"

"Nothing at first. Buddy yelled for the man to put you down, but he refused. He said Myrtle had just told him she'd had his daughter, and he'd been denied ever knowing her. He said he was going to take you away and love you like he would've loved his little girl if he'd raised her. The way he said it was revolting. We all sensed what he meant and were sickened and scared. We knew we couldn't let him leave with you, but he was holding you. We outnumbered the man, but he had you. We couldn't touch him."

"So…?"

"Buddy lunged forward and yanked you out of the man's arms. He practically tossed you to Myrtle, who ran from the room. Mr. and Mrs. Aurora followed. We heard the attic door slam shut and lock." Sighing heavily, he continued, "The man was crazed. Buddy and I struggled to restrain him, but he was wild and extraordinarily strong because of his fury. Despite the fact that there were two of us against him, it seemed like we were losing. He was saying obscene things about what he'd done to Myrtle and what he was going to do to you. He hit Buddy hard enough to temporarily stun him. He lifted one of Sandra's trophies and was about to bash Buddy's head in with it."

"You stopped him," Prim murmured. "How?"

"Buddy had been doing some repair work in Sandra's empty room. There was a claw hammer lying on the desk near the window. I grabbed it and brought it down on the back of the man's skull. He staggered for a few moments then toppled and fell onto the rug. He was dead.

"Buddy came to and thanked me for saving his life. After telling him that he was welcome, I went to the bathroom and threw up. Then I told him we had to call the police. I'd just killed a man."

"And he asked you not to," Prim said quietly. "He knew you'd be found not guilty because the murder was justified but that everything about Aunt Myrtle and the rape and my mama would come out."

"Yes. I told him it didn't matter, that we had to call the authorities. He pleaded with me not to. He pointed out that my career as a doctor might be over even if I wasn't convicted. Everyone's good name would be ruined, and you would grow up with the stigma of being a bastard child of a child of rape. He reminded me that your grandfather had said he wanted to take you away so he could do despicable things to you like he'd done to Myrtle, and it was no one's loss that this evil man was dead. I argued that I'd killed a human being, which was a crime and against moral law. We went back and forth for a long time."

"What finally made you decide to hide the truth?"

"You. Myrtle and her parents came out of the attic and saw what had happened. Your condition had worsened, and they promised me that if I would keep what had happened between us, then they'd make sure you were always brought to me for proper medical care. I made up my mind right then and there that Buddy was right, and you would suffer more than anyone else if all of it came out. So, I told them to do what they must but to let me take you to the hospital."

"You didn't help them put the man in the trunk."

"No. I never knew what they'd done with the stranger's body."

"What had been wrong with me?"

"Double pneumonia. You were in the Pediatrics Ward for six days. You would have died if they'd kept you at home any longer."

Darting a glance at the bed, Prim asked, "When did Mrs. Stanford find out?"

"Last night. I'd never told a soul, and everyone else who was involved was dead."

"What made you tell her after all these years?"

"Kenny Proper. I couldn't stop thinking about what a nice man he was and how he was gone so suddenly. I knew my wife didn't have long. The truth about that night twenty-four years ago was the only thing I'd ever kept from her. So, I decided to tell her everything about the incident."

"And she told you to call the police and explain."

He nodded and said, "I suppose I should have expected that from her. She was such a good woman but always very black and white about things. She said if I didn't go to Byron today, then she'd phone him."

"You could still go to Byron," Prim pointed out desperately.

"And tell him that I killed my dying wife to protect you and to keep my sons from knowing that their father had committed murder?"

"You have to!"

"I can't. It's gone too far now. Nothing matters except my sons and their futures. I've been a good son, husband, father, and doctor. I've always tried to do what I thought was best for my family and my patients. If what happened comes out, then it will all be for nothing. My life's work and my sons' futures will be destroyed."

Livid, Prim said furiously, "You killed your wife! You're going to kill me and my unborn baby! You *were* a good man, but now you're nothing but a monster! You deserve to be called a murderer!"

"You're absolutely right," he agreed. "Perhaps living with the knowledge of what I did finally broke me. No matter what happens now, I'm damned." Slowly advancing towards her, he remarked, "All I wanted for you was happiness."

"So, let me be happy with Sean and our child! Don't take my happiness away now that I've finally found it!"

Prim scrambled to get around Philip Stanford, but he was ready for her. He hastily withdrew his gun and used the butt of it to hit Prim on the side of the head. She saw stars and stumbled. She was soon lying on her back on the floor.

Please, God, she prayed. *Please don't let me and my baby die. Sean will give up if he loses us, too. He needs me as much as I need him.*

She felt Dr. Stanford lift her left arm and wrap something above the crook of her elbow. Barely conscious, she knew he must be preparing to inject her with a lethal dose of some medication. She was virtually defenseless.

"Back away from Prim!" ordered a familiar voice. "Do it *now*!"

Prim felt the prick of a needle on her arm then heard a loud, popping noise. She cried out as the tip of the needle was wrenched from her flesh, and Dr. Stanford collapsed. Blood began to pool under his head as his lifeless eyes stared at nothing.

"Prim, look at me," Tony Eichstadt directed, as he knelt beside her. "Prim!"

She forced herself to focus on his face and reached up with her injured hand to touch the lump on the side of her head. When she tried to sit up, Eichstadt stopped her.

"Lie still. Help is on the way."

"Help?"

"Byron and the cavalry will be here shortly. I called them when I arrived and saw your car in the driveway and Dr. Stanford's parked out front."

"I don't...I'm so...how did you know I was here and that I was in danger?"

He pushed some loose strands of hair away from her face and said, "Sean left me a voicemail that said he thought you were in trouble. In that voicemail, he also said he reached everyone else except Dr. Stanford. I'd suspected Stanford for years and decided to take a chance and drive over to his house just to see if my hunch was right. Obviously it was. I'm glad I brought my gun."

"Suspected him for years? What did you suspect him of?"

"Of killing my brother and saving you from a fate worse than death."

"Your...brother?" she echoed.

He nodded and said, "My brother. Your grandfather, the rapist. Remember when I told you I had very cruel parents and a brother who was brilliant but liked to be abusive to women and children?"

They heard the sirens in the distance, and Prim grabbed the man by the wrist and said, "Don't leave!"

"I'm not leaving. I want to tell you everything. I have a lot to explain." Looking around the bedroom, he said, "There'll be a lot to explain about the scene here in this room. Don't worry. Just lie still until they take you to the hospital."

"Hospital?"

"Dr. Stanford just tried to kill you by lethal injection. I don't think he got anything in you, because I shot him pretty quickly once I saw what he was going to do. They'll still want to make sure. Plus, you've been hit on the head. You're also pregnant. There are lots of things to check out." When they heard the sound of people entering the house, he called out, "Up here!"

"But you killed Dr. Stanford! They'll take you to jail!"

"I'll be out by the time you get back to your apartment. I'll meet you there as soon as I can."

The room was suddenly filled with policemen and paramedics. There was temporary chaos. Once Prim and Eichstadt had given quick explanations, the police began their work while the paramedics attended to Prim. She was whisked away to the hospital where she was subjected to a thorough exam, an ultrasound, and blood work. She kept expecting Sean to show up, but he didn't come. No one came. She began to worry.

She was dressed and sipping a cup of orange juice when Caleb arrived. After taking the cup from her hands, he put his arms around her and apologized for not getting to the hospital earlier.

"What happened? Where's Sean? Where's everyone else?"

"Sean is talking with the doctors. He wanted to come directly to you once we found out where you were, but the hospital staff insisted we wait until they were done with you."

"They're done. I want to see him."

Her father lifted her injured hand and asked her if it hurt. She told him that it did, as did the side of her head and the area on her arm where the needle had been wrenched out.

"Something's not right," she remarked. "What aren't you telling me? Am I really all right? Is the baby okay?"

"They say you'll make a full recovery and that there shouldn't be a problem with the pregnancy as a result of this. However, Sean was very emotional when he heard what Dr. Stanford had done to you and what he tried to do. It took me, Remy, and Byron quite some time to calm him down. His soul is bruised at the moment because of the deaths of his father and sister, and I believe he thought you and the baby were dead and that we just didn't want to tell him."

"Is he better now?"

"Yes. He'll be in shortly."

"Tony saved my life."

"And I'm eternally indebted to him for that."

"Where is he?"

"With his lawyer. He promised he'd be out of jail and at your apartment by the time you got home from the hospital. He did kill a man but has no prior record. There was no doubt that if he hadn't shot Dr. Stanford, you would have died. I'm sure he'll get released quickly, although there will be some sort of legal proceedings. I wouldn't worry about it too much."

"Dr. Stanford killed Tony's brother."

"Your grandfather. Tony is your great-uncle."

"He told you?"

"The bare essentials. He said the both of you would explain once we got home. That shouldn't be long. If you're not up to it though –"

"No, I want to know now. I want this last mystery cleared up. Then I just want a return to normalcy and to be happy with my family."

"Will that include Tony?"

"I guess it'll depend on what he has to say once we get to the apartment."

Sean appeared in the doorway. He looked fine, but his distress was almost palpable to Prim. He walked over and embraced and kissed her then asked her how she was feeling.

"Exhausted and confused. Betrayed by Dr. Stanford. Horrified by what he did to his wife and what he tried to do to me and our baby."

"But not by what he did to your grandfather?" Caleb asked.

"Not if what he told me was true."

"I think we should talk about this at home," Sean interrupted. "The doctors say you're okay and can leave anytime."

When they arrived at the apartment over Prim's Corner and Aurora Hardware, Tony, Remy, Byron, and two strangers were waiting at the door. Prim hugged first Remy and then Byron. She went over to hug her great uncle and thanked him again for saving her life. He told her it was the least he could do and was grateful he'd arrived in time. He then accepted heartfelt thanks from Sean before the entourage moved inside.

Once Eichstadt's lawyer had been introduced, he took a seat in a far corner. The county legal representative explained he was going to document the statements that were to follow both in written and recorded formats. Everyone agreed to this, and Prim and Tony signed papers, stating they understood that whatever they said would be admissible in a court of law as sworn testimony. After turning on the digital recorder, the man had both of them swear to tell the truth. Then he left the machine on the coffee table and went to sit across the room from Eichstadt's lawyer.

Prim went first, explaining she'd realized during the night that perhaps Mrs. Stanford might have some knowledge of the Auroras' past she'd never shared with anyone. Prim had decided to pay the woman a visit to see if any new information might be gleaned. Once she'd set the stage for her part of the story, Prim proceeded to give the others an account of everything that had happened after she'd arrived at the Stanford home. She omitted the fact that her efforts to break into the house had been learned by watching Remy, although she knew he would intuit this and would ask her about it later.

No one asked her any questions or made any comments during her recitation of the facts. She was acutely aware of how each of them felt. It was evident in their expressions what emotions were passing through their minds.

Once she'd finished by describing her visit to the hospital, Byron thanked her for her candor and told Tony that he hoped he'd be as forthcoming. He asked him to tell whatever story he needed to in order to explain how he'd ended up at the Stanford home and saved Prim's life.

The Head of the Board of Directors for the Kensington Academy stared at his hands and began, "My father was a superb businessman who made millions and didn't have an ounce of love in his heart for anyone, not even himself. He married my mother, the daughter of an oil tycoon, to advance his fortunes. She didn't care about anything except appearances and possessions. They had my brother because convention dictated it and because my father expected his son would take over his company someday when he died." Looking towards Prim, he said, "Devon was routinely beaten by our father and demeaned by both him and my mother. He exhibited extraordinary intelligence and atypical social

338

behaviors from an early age. The abusive home life combined with his personality and genius made him warped. He was a brilliant student at school but liked to hurt other people and animals. My parents quickly realized he wouldn't be able to run my father's company."

"So, that's why they had you," Sean suggested. "If at first you don't succeed…."

"Exactly, except it took years for my mother to get pregnant with me. My brother was a grown man when I was born. I was given the same treatment by my parents that he'd received, but they were much older and allowed the nannies to deal with me more than they had with Devon. I guess it was my saving grace. I was afraid of my own shadow and had a speech impediment, but I didn't turn out to be a sociopath like my brother. The fact that our parents tired of me early and sent me to Kensington probably saved my sanity. The principal got me help, and I moved on to college. I fell in love and married my beautiful Gillian, although I vowed I'd never have children. She managed to convince me I could be a good parent despite my own severely dysfunctional upbringing. I was so blessed to have her and eventually our two daughters."

"What about your brother?" asked Prim.

"He and I were never close, but we did see each other at holidays over the years. He'd become a psychiatrist, and this worried me. I knew about his abnormal behavior and didn't think it was a good idea for him to be working with vulnerable people. However, I had no proof that he was causing harm to anyone."

"Did you take over your father's company?" Remy asked.

Tony smiled broadly and admitted, "My father left me in charge. I sold his empire to the highest bidder as soon as I could after he died. I was in my early twenties and my mother had already passed away. It gave me great satisfaction to get rid of my father's business so hastily. I gave Devon his half of the money and told him I never wanted to see him again. For a while, we had no contact."

"What changed that?" queried Byron.

"One night, he showed up at our apartment in New York, demanding to know why I'd told the police about him and what he'd done. Thank God, Gillian and the girls were visiting her family in Atlanta. I asked him what he was talking about, and he said someone had reported him for molesting young girls and he'd had his license revoked even though the investigation hadn't resulted in his arrest. I asked him if he'd molested young girls. He said he'd never molested anyone, that every young girl he'd had sex with had wanted it. I was sickened and told him to leave or I would call the authorities. His parting words to me were that he was going to track down all of the girls to tell them how much he'd loved each and every one of them. He said he had their records and addresses."

"What did you do?" Caleb inquired.

"I started having him followed by private detectives. I decided that would be a good way to find out who his victims were, even though I was disgusted to learn they'd been teenaged girls at their time of treatment by him. Two of the girls had been younger. I vowed I'd turn over all the information my detectives were uncovering to the police once Devon had finished going through his list. I hoped the evidence would allow the authorities to lock him away forever."

"But...?" Caleb persisted.

"Number fourteen was Myrtle Brown. The P.I. following Devon that night said he went into the Aurora house but never came out. The detective determined the identities of the others who'd been inside that evening. After all, he'd been investigating and had the house under surveillance." Studying his hands again, Eichstadt said, "I dismissed the detectives the following week."

"So, you didn't call the police?" Sean asked. "Why not?"

"Because I deduced that someone in that house had killed Devon, and I was certain he deserved it. I knew what sort of creature my brother was. The others inside included an older couple, a younger couple, a physician, and a parentless baby. Knowing what I did about my brother and his victims, I speculated that Devon had tried to do harm to someone, perhaps even the baby. Somebody had struggled with him and killed him. What good would leading police to the scene do for those innocent people? Not only would someone be prosecuted for killing a child molester, but also the truth about whomever he had raped would come out in the little town where these people lived. Everyone would know about the assault and about the psychiatric treatment itself. It could ruin multiple lives.

"So, I hired a different detective agency to investigate the family. They pieced together what had happened, including Myrtle's treatment and rape by my brother, her secret pregnancy, the birth, life, and death of Sandra, and the birth of Sandra's daughter, the baby who'd been in the house the night my brother visited. I set up a trust fund for my great-niece, Prim, and went back through the list of names of those Devon tracked down before he ended up at the Aurora household. Then I sent each victim an anonymous note including a sizable amount of money in order to offer some sort of compensation for her suffering. I didn't want them to have to relive their abuse by being forced to tell the authorities and others what had happened to them when they'd been under my brother's care. It was the best thing I could think of to do."

"What made you suspect Philip Stanford of killing your brother?" Remy asked.

"Because I didn't know which one of the adults present had killed him. They were all suspects. It could have been a concerted effort. I didn't blame any of them and assumed it was completely justified."

"Did you have people spy on me while I was growing up?" asked Prim.

"No. I purposefully stayed away. I'd learned through my investigators that the Auroras were a well-known and respected family and figured you'd be happy and loved and could grow up in blissful ignorance of the dark parts of your past. I had never been to Aurora myself until last fall." Smiling, he said, "I'd connected with Sean from the moment we met during his interview process at Kensington. How fortunate it was that he and my great-niece would fall in love and get married. I was so thrilled to meet Prim and find out what a beautiful, intelligent, successful woman she was and to know that she was marrying a young man I admired so much. I treasured every moment I had with her, even though she didn't have a clue as to our familial relationship. I felt terrible when I learned that she hadn't had the idyllic childhood I'd envisioned and did my best to offer her support and guidance."

"Did your wife know?" Prim asked. "Do your daughters know?"

"No one knew, not even my Gillian. She knew that my brother was deranged, but I couldn't bring myself to tell her what he'd done or what had happened. I suppose I feared rejection."

Caleb said quietly, "Guilt by association."

"Yes."

Sean put an arm around Prim's shoulders and asked, "What made you go to Dr. Stanford's house with a gun today?"

"You. When you said you had a feeling Prim was in trouble and that you hadn't been able to reach the doctor, I was immediately concerned. Stanford was the only adult still living who'd been in that house the night my brother went in and never emerged. If he was the killer and Prim had somehow figured it out, then her life would be in danger. I couldn't let anything happen to her and her unborn child."

"Why not just call 911?"

"And say what? That I thought Dr. Stanford might have killed my sociopathic brother twenty-four years ago and might try to kill Prim because she'd uncovered the truth? I was worried that if the police did take me seriously, they'd show up with their sirens blazing and Stanford would kill whoever was in the house out of panic. Better for me to investigate first, then call 911. I'm glad I did and have no regret about shooting the man who killed his wife and tried to kill Prim. It's a terrible thing. What he was forced to do years ago obviously pushed him over the edge, so to speak."

Once the digital recorder had been switched off and Tony's lawyer and the county legal representative were dismissed, Prim glanced anxiously at Byron and asked, "Will Tony go to prison?"

"It's very doubtful. He shot Dr. Stanford in order to save you. I'm pretty confident Mr. Eichstadt will be fully cleared very quickly."

Prim turned back to her great-uncle and asked, "How can I trust you? I know you saved my life, but you kept what happened years ago a secret and admitted that your brother was mentally deranged. How do we know you're not crazy, too?" Shutting her eyes, she muttered, "What am I saying? The Auroras themselves were all crazy."

"They weren't crazy," Remy said. "Mr. and Mrs. Aurora were zealots, and Myrtle was emotionally unstable as a result. Your mother wasn't crazy, just sad and lonely. None of them were sociopaths like Tony's brother."

"But I'm Devon's granddaughter. What if I'm carrying some genetic trait that makes my baby turn out to be a sociopath?"

"That's not going to happen," Tony said firmly. "My parents were horribly cruel to my brother and me. I think for Devon his psychosis was the result of his nature plus living with my parents in an emotionally destructive environment. I was fortunate to escape earlier, if you will. You and Sean are truly good human beings who will give your baby love and kindness. He or she will be blessed and nurtured and will grow up to be as wonderful as the two of you."

"No one should have to go through life feeling inadequate because of what she was denied by birth or circumstance," Prim said, repeating the words Gillian Eichstadt had uttered that had changed her life. She impulsively leaned across to kiss Sean before adding, "I am a pretty pixie. Nobody is going to break my wings."

Sean placed his hand over his chest where the tattooed wings were covered by his shirt and assured her, "I won't let anyone break mine, either."

Prim felt a surge of love and desire blended with protectiveness towards Sean. She blinked in surprise then smirked as she realized exactly what this meant. He frowned and asked her if she was feeling all right.

"I feel fine," she assured him. "I'll explain after everyone leaves."

Later when they were alone in the apartment, Prim led Sean to the master bedroom and urged him towards the bed. When he asked her what she was doing, she said, "I get it now."

"Get what?"

"What you and Remy were talking about."

"What? When?"

"Protect and…well, you know. You said that's how men felt when they were around me. I realized earlier that it's how I feel about you." Blushing, she said, "Protect and fuck."

Sean threw back his head, laughed, and exclaimed, "I can't believe you said that!"

"Just because I'm Prim doesn't mean I always have to be proper."

"But because I'm Proper, I always need you to be Prim."

"Prim and Proper. That sounds like a great title for a book."

"As long as there's a happily-ever-after ending."

"Oh, there will be," Prim declared, as she pulled him towards the bed. "Let's get on with the rest of our story. I can't wait to find out what happens next."

ABOUT THE AUTHOR

Lauren Cutrera, who also writes under the name Barbara Cutrera, has published over 20 contemporary romance, romantic suspense, paranormal romance, mystery, and fiction novels. Diverse people and plots highlight her works, drawing readers into the characters' unique journeys as they navigate their way through their struggles and triumphs. Lauren and her husband, Budge, are the proud parents of a grown son. They live in southwest Florida and have a cute and naughty Yorkie, Hadrian, who sleeps next to Lauren as she writes each day.

Explore other published works by the author at amazon.com and goodreads.com

Check out all things Lauren (and Barbara) at www.laurencutrera.com

And connect with her there or on

Facebook: https://www.facebook.com/profile.php?id=100063631654302

Instagram: https://www.instagram.com/laurencutrera/

Pinterest: https://www.pinterest.com/laurencutrera/_saved/

OTHER BOOKS BY THE AUTHOR:

The Essential Elements Series

Kindred Spirits
Scorched Creek
Spirits Corner
Memory Lane
Homeward Bound

The Limitless Series

Sight Unseen
Better Left Unsaid
Unheard Of
Under Her Skin
Brain Storm
Out On A Limb

The Seneca & Michael Duet

A Lovely Dream
A Lovely Reality

The Gift Series

The Healer's Gift
Jordan's Way
Bound by Grace
The Nameless

The Real World Series

Over, Under, Across & Through
A Good Man's Life
Mercy
Unfinished Business (Final Chapter)

<u>Standalone Novels/Short Stories</u>

In A Manner of Speaking
Prim & Proper
Lucky
Compromising Positions
True: 3 Short Stories

www.ingramcontent.com/pod-product-compliance
Lightning Source LLC
Chambersburg PA
CBHW061320170626
46817CB00001B/248

9 780099 364220